WINDS
OF
BLAME

Books by Jane Gilmore Rushing

WALNUT GROVE

AGAINST THE MOON

TAMZEN

MARY DOVE

THE RAINCROW

COVENANT OF GRACE

WINDS OF BLAME

WINDS OF BLAME

BY
JANE GILMORE RUSHING

DOUBLEDAY & COMPANY, INC.

GARDEN CITY, NEW YORK

1983

Library of Congress Cataloging in Publication Data

Rushing, Jane Gilmore.
  Winds of blame.

  I. Title.
PS3568.U73W56 1983   813'.54
ISBN: 0-385-17701-1
Library of Congress Catalog Card Number: 82–45268

To
J.A.R., Jr., and the Summer of Eighty-Two

And for his death no wind of blame shall breathe,
But even his mother shall uncharge the practice,
And call it accident.

Hamlet, *IV, vii.*

The truth is not always the same as majority opinion.

Pope John Paul II

PROLOGUE

I may as well say at the outset that this is a story of guns and trouble. It is not exactly a story of the Old West, although in the teen years of the century (when these events occurred) the part of Texas where I live had not outgrown its frontier ways.

I used to think this lingering wildness had something to do with what happened in the Doane family, but I am not so sure now. The Doane story is part of our folklore and therefore once seemed to me peculiar to the community of Greenfields; but I have found out it involves a kind of violence not much limited by time or space. In recent years, I have come to believe it is a tale worth telling carefully, with attention to the truth. The truth is a hard thing to know, as this story shows, but I am convinced I can come close to it, for I have heard the events narrated many times, and during the last years of my grandmother's life I questioned her closely about them. I have also had access to diaries and letters that speak to me directly from the past.

I first began trying to tell the story when I was in college, taking a course in folklore as part of my English requirement. Dr. Rider asked the class to record stories passed down by word of mouth in our families or communities, and I chose to tell about the troubles of the Doanes, changing names and concealing my own connection with the family. When I began the project I thought of the affair simply as a curious tale to be collected—nor do I think I was entirely lacking in perception then. My attitude had come from the way the events were talked about—really told as a tale—

and no doubt also from the fact that I first heard it when we had only recently moved to Greenfields and I didn't even realize the characters were relations of mine. But when I asked my grandmother for help, and she began talking freely about what had been to me community lore, I was touched by the reality, the profound and far-reaching tragedy of it. My eyes and heart opened to the full sense of the story, as though I had finally seen *Oedipus the King* performed, after reading only the prose summary of it in some book of myths for children.

Also, I might have understood better because I had fallen in love with a Greenfields boy and was trying to decide whether to go to graduate school or marry him and take a job teaching in the high school at home. This decision required some soul-searching, which brought me into a feeling of kinship with my grandmother and her girlhood chum that I had never experienced before.

Because of this kinship, and because of the way I learned so much more about what happened to the Doanes than I had ever known, I am inclined to see the whole pattern of events through the eyes of Isabel and Joanna. It is for their sake that I have determined to tell the story fleshed-out with human relationships and fully clothed with conversations and descriptions, which (though of necessity partly imaginary) are based very closely on my talks with Grandmother, the diaries and the letters, and my intimate acquaintance with the landscape and the people of Greenfields.

This seems to me the clearest way to arrive at a full understanding of the matter—if truth can somehow be kept alight under the cumbersome structure of the novel. Unfortunately, there has to be a structure. An author has to start somewhere, and although one could darkly seek the beginning far back in the infancy or early childhood of Harvey Doane, I see it as a sunny day in May, with Isabel and Joanna on their way to a wedding. I remember my grandmother always started the story this way.

CHAPTER ONE

The name of the place is Greenfields, but the color of the world there is gray and drab brown. Even in summer, when rows of cotton stretch across the flat land, the strong white light of the sun leaches the freshness of green from the flourishing leaves. The fields are not green and the sky is more often weak copper or silvery gray than true blue. God has given nothing for protection against the pounding sun or shelter from the sky; nothing by nature stands along the pale horizon, nor have human hands placed any tree or structure there arresting to the eye.

This is an empty, undramatic land, or so it must appear to the traveler passing through, who may scarcely notice the hamlets and farmsteads that lie scattered across the countryside, all but lost in the vastness. Yet the people who dwell there do not feel themselves lost or deprived. They are protected, perhaps, by their own moral character, and see what they wish to see: that leaves are green, and sky is blue, and men for the most part lead righteous lives, ruling their wives and children as the Bible says a man must do. So it has always been in that place, since the first settlements were gathered at the beginning of the century and the names of them solemnly agreed upon. For surely it must have been some such vision that led to a kind of naming often met with in that region. How else account for Pleasant Valley, where the visitor sees only a slight depression in the earth, for Walnut Grove, where even the memory of trees is dead, for Flower Hill, for Meadow View, for Mountain Home . . .

For Greenfields? There is no record to show who suggested

that name, but tradition says it was Joanna Waters's mother, wife
of Tom Waters, who built the first store. In those days, when so
much of the land still remained to be broken, she might have imagined that one day cultivated crops would spread in all directions,
lovely and green as the fields of her childhood. Or perhaps she did
not imagine anything; Martha Waters was one of those who, seeing
how things ought to be, assume that they are so, or will be. A farming settlement must always be surrounded by green fields.

But never mind the meaning of the name. By 1916 the place
simply was Greenfields, as a family might be called Black, Brown,
or White, and any connection it ever had with color long forgotten.
"Greenfields" referred to the sprawling community, and also to the
center of it, where in those days stood the depot, the school, the
store, the gin, and a scattering of houses. Most residents lived along
graded roads laid out north and south, east and west, following
section lines, except near the eastern edge where the land slopes
down and the Fontine Breaks begin.

Out of a house on this eastern border, there came, rather early
in the morning of May 10, while the landscape still lay bathed in
lemon light, a slender, dark-haired young woman (or as
Greenfields would say, a grown girl), somewhat taller than the av-
erage of the time, dressed all in white except for a wide pink satin
sash tied to one side and fastened with a wine red rosette. And her
shoes, somewhat cracked, were black patent. They were not very
suitable for walking three miles on dirt roads, but it would not
have occurred to her to put on anything less than black patent for
Miss Lona Miller's wedding.

Although she had more than enough time to reach her destination at the appointed hour, she walked somewhat briskly for a girl
dressed in her Sunday best, and from time to time looked hastily
back, as though fearful that she might be followed.

About twenty minutes later, from a neat, white-painted house
a few hundred yards down the road from the Greenfields store,
there emerged a second girl dressed in white—white eyelet batiste,
with a pale blue sash that was really more of a cummerbund,
fashioned more skillfully than the first girl's, with stays to keep it in
place. As she walked out the gate in the white picket fence around
the yard, and turned to fasten it, someone called to her and she put
on the white starched bonnet that she carried in her hand.

She walked somewhat slowly along the road north; after she
had gone a little distance, putting a clump of mesquite bushes be-

tween herself and the house, she took off the bonnet. The sun gilded her thick, very light brown hair, which she had put up in three buns, one in back and one on each side. She reached up and loosened her front hair, patting it into soft waves.

Presently, across a plowed field cornered by the roads they followed, the two girls caught sight of each other. They waved excitedly, and began to walk as fast as their long skirts and underskirts would allow. At last they came together, at a gnarled old mesquite tree that grew near the crossroads. Very few mesquites around Greenfields had grown big enough to be called trees, but this one had. Since the first settlers came it had looked just this way—with its spreading, twisting black branches and (on sunshiny mornings in early May) its drooping lace leaves of soft gold. It had always been a landmark at Greenfields, and since their early childhood had been a meeting place for these two.

Still some little way from the tree, they called to each other.

"Why howdy, Isabel," said the light-haired girl, feigning surprise.

"Oh, Joanna," said the other, laughing. "I was sure I'd get here ages before you did. I just couldn't wait to get out of the house."

"Neither could I," said Joanna. "Mama said I was putting on my dress before the bride would even have her face washed."

"I like your new dress," said Isabel.

"Mama didn't get done with it till yesterday evening," said Joanna.

"I washed mine and hung it in the sun all day," said Isabel. "I was afraid it was looking dingy."

"Oh, it's white as snow," said Joanna. "And your new sash is just right—that red rose effect is the thing that looks like you." (The rosette had come off an old hat belonging to Mrs. Waters, who had given it to Isabel and showed her how to freshen it and fasten it to her sash. The girls thought it looked almost stylish.)

They began walking along the road north, toward Jedidiah Goolsby's house, where Miss Lona Miller, their favorite teacher of all time, had boarded during her career at Greenfields, and now through marriage was ending that career.

"Well, it's a pretty day for the wedding," Joanna said. Her mother had greeted her with that observation this morning ("Ain't it a pretty day!" she had exclaimed), and undoubtedly women all over Greenfields had said very much the same thing.

"Happy the bride the sun shines on," said Isabel. Certainly the

sun was shining, and it was a wonderful, beautiful day, just because it was Miss Lona's wedding day; but the weather was a little
less than ideal. It was cool for the time of the year, almost too cool
for being outdoors in summer dresses; and little ragged strips of
wind blew every which way, as though thrown toward earth at
random from the sky.

"I knew Ray wouldn't come," said Joanna in a minute or two,
answering something Isabel kept unspoken.

"He wanted to," Isabel said, "but he had to plant today. Papa
needed the other boys to fix fence."

"And Sophie couldn't come."

"Mama didn't feel very good. Sophie said she'd stay with her."

"I don't suppose she cared much."

Isabel sighed. "No, I don't suppose she did. She never wants to
go anywhere, seems like. I don't think it seems right for a twelve-
year-old girl."

"We always wanted to go everywhere, didn't we?" said Joanna,
with an air of looking back on a long-vanished youth.

"Yes, I guess we did," said Isabel thoughtfully. "I don't think I
do so much anymore, but I don't believe anything could keep me
away from Miss Lona's wedding."

"Me neither," said Joanna happily.

They walked again in silence for some little space. There were
no houses on this stretch of road, as the land had not yet been put
into cultivation on either side; it was a comparatively low spot—
lakey, they called it around Greenfields—and every spring, if wild
flowers bloomed anywhere, the girls would find them there.

"Look, the primroses are blooming," Joanna said. They looked
like torn tissue paper blowing in the wind. There were daisies, too,
of several kinds, both yellow and white, and various little flowers
of different colors, that bloomed almost in secret, except for little
children and those who saw sometimes with little children's eyes.
(Oh yes, there is beauty in Greenfields, if you know where to look
for it.)

"How long has it been since we picked a bouquet of wild
flowers?" Isabel asked idly.

"Oh, a long time, I don't know. But I remember we took bou-
quets to Miss Lona, the first spring she was here."

"I guess we thought we'd got too big, after that."

"How old would we have been that spring?" mused Joanna.

"Well, it's been four years."

"Then I was thirteen and you fourteen," Joanna said. "And we thought Miss Lona was about the prettiest and nicest thing that ever stood behind a teacher's desk."

"I think so still," said Isabel.

"And so do I," Joanna said. They had paused to look across a long slope thickly spread with butter yellow, then turned and looked down somewhat pensively at the flowers by the roadside.

Joanna stooped and broke off a slender stem with tiny, pale blue blossoms as delicate as sheer silk. "Look," she said, "a forget-me-not."

Really, they did not know what most of the flowers were. For some, they knew common names used by people in the community; for others, they had made up their own names. They had never seen a real forget-me-not.

"Joanna," said Isabel suddenly, excitement shining in her soft dark eyes. "Let's fix Miss Lona a bouquet and take it to her."

"Oh, let's," said Joanna. "And we can put forget-me-nots right in the middle of it."

"She may not know what they are."

"Well, we can tell her."

Suddenly childhood seemed to them not so very far away; they reached back for it, gave themselves up to it. Joanna took her ruffled bonnet, which she had been carrying under her arm, and tied the strings together.

"Look," she said, "a flower basket."

"We always did pretend we had a basket," Isabel said, "and yet you know we never really did."

They laughed together happily. They had lots of time. They walked slowly, remembering little flower jewels to look for, finding them sometimes.

"Look, Joanna," said Isabel, "do you remember what we used to call this one?"

She had plucked up a flat, spreading plant with a purplish red blossom like a bell, or perhaps if one preferred to see it so, a slightly flattened heart.

"Love-lies-bleeding," said Joanna. "I had read the name in a book somewhere—but to this day I don't know what that flower actually looks like."

"It hasn't got a stem," said Isabel. "We couldn't put it in the bouquet."

"We wouldn't want to," Joanna said. "Don't you remember when we named it?"

"When the oldest Shropshire girl was jilted on her wedding day."

"I said that flower was like a broken heart, flung down on the ground and stepped on."

The girls laughed at how romantic they had been. They stood close together, their heads slightly bending toward the plant in Isabel's hand. Suddenly, in the same instant, both heads jerked up.

"Listen," said Isabel.

They heard a steady, thudding sound, moving quickly toward them.

"It's nobody going to the wedding," Joanna said, "for there's no use in riding that fast."

While she spoke they were turning, looking back down the road; and they saw a horse and rider coming, a big dark horse and a rider with a broad-brimmed dark hat. Both the horse and the hat of the rider looked black at that distance, but both girls knew they were really dark brown. They recognized the solid, untilted set of the uncreased hat on the head and the solid, heavy appearance of the man settled into the saddle.

"Papa!" gasped Isabel. "What can be wrong?"

"Why should anything be wrong?" Joanna said, not convincingly. Both girls knew that Harvey Doane was riding after Isabel, for nothing else would bring him this way. It was not likely he was going to the wedding.

Isabel did not answer, but stood clutching the trailing vine in her hand. The girls did not speak anymore while they watched the horseman draw steadily nearer. Neither did he speak, even when he came close enough to have called out a greeting. At last he came even with them, stopped his horse, and for a long moment sat looking down at them. He was dark of hair and eyes, yet pale of skin. Isabel had got her coloring from him, though few ever said she resembled him. She had a slender face with high cheekbones and delicate, arched brows; his face was broad and square-jawed, with a straight and heavy brow. When he smiled, he was not an ill-favored man—he was not smiling now.

"I'd like to know what you think you're doing here," he said to Isabel at last, in an even, conversational tone.

Isabel spoke low, and did not look up at him. "It's Miss Lona Miller's wedding day, Papa," she said. "You know that."

"I might have heard something like that, but I don't recollect giving anybody permission to deck theirself out like a dance-hall girl and go traipsing down the road picking flowers."

He jerked the red rose from her waist, let it fall with her sash in the dirt.

"Come on," he said. "Your mama's sick, you're needed at home."

"Is she worse, Papa?"

"I don't know whether she's worse or not. When I left home you was still there, and I thought you'd stay and see about her."

"Sophie stayed." Isabel spoke so low that Joanna doubted the man up on the big horse knew she uttered a sound.

"Get on up here," he said.

"Papa, I can't get up there and ride that horse, wearing this skirt." She spoke up a little; he heard that.

He looked hard at her for a while, but finally only said, "Well, then, turn around and start home. I've got to go by the store and get some steeples. I'll expect to catch up with you on the road somewhere."

He turned his horse and started back the way he had come from. Isabel did not speak anymore, or look into Joanna's face.

"Oh, Isabel," Joanna cried. But still her friend did not turn to her, and after a long moment she began to walk away.

Joanna stood looking after her. Her gait seemed neither fast nor slow. She held her head high and her shoulders straight. Joanna had to take the handkerchief tucked up her ruffled sleeve and wipe the tears away, but she saw no sign that Isabel was crying. She watched a long time, then finally bent and picked up the sash and the rose. She left the love-lies-bleeding in the dust.

It seemed to Joanna at first that she could not go to the wedding without Isabel. She thought of running after her, and did at last walk a few steps toward home, yet with no design of catching up with her friend. Then she saw her father's Maxwell, pulling out from the store and heading north, toward the crossroads. This would be her mother coming. Her father had said he would like to see Miss Lona married, but he never closed the store on week days except for a funeral.

Joanna stopped for a while and watched the automobile creep along—it seemed as slow as Mr. Doane on horseback. Martha Waters had not much wanted to learn to drive the new car. She never liked to drive a horse or team, for fear it would run away, and she felt much the same about the Maxwell; she never would give it its head. Today she had wanted Joanna to drive her and some of her closest neighbors to the wedding, but was willing to excuse her daughter when she understood what plans had been made.

For Joanna and Isabel had decided many months before, when Miss Lona first announced her wedding date and invited the whole community to the wedding, that they would walk together—and although Joanna would have been glad if Ray had come, and felt she must inquire politely about Sophie, it was the walk alone together both girls had looked forward to. Their times together had grown fewer, especially since Isabel had been out of school the past year. This walk they planned would in some little way make up for that lost time, they had said to each other. It would do more than that, Joanna had secretly thought, and she remembered as she stood in the roadway how she had vaguely envisioned it as a walk back in time, reclaiming their childhood (and they had come some way toward that vision, gathering flowers for Miss Lona's bouquet), but also perhaps relinquishing it. Joanna had wanted them to talk of their future—of Isabel's brother Ray, of his ambition; of her own plans for becoming a teacher; of what Isabel now hoped for in her life.

And now all they looked forward to had been snatched away by Harvey Doane—a hateful man, a spoiler, her friend's father and her own future father-in-law. She stood and looked down the road, hating him. She could see him, past the crossroads now, keeping south on the way to the store; he rode as slowly and deliberately as though nothing had happened at all. It was nothing to him, she supposed, but thought he might at least have shown some sign of triumph: he must enjoy hurting people and ruining their good times. She turned her eyes on Isabel, a sad white figure dwindling gradually away, and saw when she met the women in the automobile. She could not tell whether any words were exchanged. At the rate her mother drove, they easily might have been, but neither the girl walking nor the approaching vehicle seemed to change course or move more slowly.

Joanna stepped to the roadside and stood waiting. As the open car drew near, she recognized Mrs. Lane—the section foreman's wife—in the front seat with her mother, and Mrs. Akers—who lived on a farm across the railroad—sitting in the back. All three of the women wore ruffled bonnets that shadowed their faces, but even so, Joanna fancied she could read on them expressions of shock and avid curiosity.

"Well, get in, Joanna," said her mother, bringing the car to a halt.

Dreading their questions, Joanna was tempted to say she still preferred to walk, yet felt, too, that if they left her alone she might sink by the roadside. She clambered into the backseat beside Mrs. Akers, Isabel's sash still clutched in one hand and her bonnet, full of forgotten flowers, crushed under one arm.

"What have you got in your bonnet?" Mrs. Akers asked.

"Oh, nothing," said Joanna, and emptied the flowers out onto the road.

"I expect you've got a ruined bonnet anyway," said her mother, not scolding. Joanna knew they could guess what the flowers had been meant for.

"Now don't start bawling," her mother went on. "Sometimes these things can't be helped. What was wrong with Isabel?"

Her mother's voice, stern but with an underlying hint of understanding, pulled Joanna back from the brink of tears. She took a long breath and swallowed before she felt able to speak. "Her mother didn't feel well. I don't think it was anything much. Sophie stayed with her."

"I wonder if it was her leg," said Mrs. Green.

Joanna did not answer. Her mother said, "Well, I don't think she ever got over that acci*dint* plumb good."

"*Accidint*," repeated Mrs. Akers with ironic stress. (Both women pronounced the word as Greenfields did then and still mostly does: accent on the last syllable and the short *e* changed to short *i*.) "I was there at the store when she had that acci*dint*."

Joanna hoped her mother would change the subject. Up to now, no one had heard Martha Waters suggest in public that Mr. Doane deliberately whipped up his horse that day just as Mrs. Doane was trying without help to climb into the buggy.

"Well, it was a bad fall, whatever the cause of it was," Mrs. Waters said now. "That must have been six months ago or more, and I don't believe she's been back to the store since."

"I heard she's been kind of sickly for years," said Mrs. Lane, whose husband had only recently been transferred to the railroad job at Greenfields.

"That may be," said Mrs. Waters. "That well may be." She was concentrating on turning the car around a corner onto the road that led past Mr. Goolsby's place, and that was all she said.

The Goolsbys had a good house for that community—an old-fashioned box-and-strip house such as the first settlers built, without weatherboarding, but painted white with a broad brown trim. Mr. Goolsby had been the first to settle in what was now Greenfields, so that the chinaberry trees he had planted were mature and provided good shade. Beneath them, a large crowd milled.

"Looks like half the county's here," said Martha Waters, as she drove into the open space between the road and the yard fence.

It was not half the county, but it was most of Greenfields: only men and boys who had to work and women who were sick or stayed to tend the sick were missing that day. Miss Lona had wanted everyone. Some thought it would have been more appropriate, and certainly more convenient for the bridegroom, if she had gone back to East Texas to marry, to her old home and her fiancé's—the place where they now would live. But she wanted to marry at Greenfields. She had come here newly orphaned, to board with the Goolsbys, and they had treated her like their own daughter; now she had no thought but to be married in their house, with Mr. Goolsby, who was a justice of the peace, performing the ceremony. She had been well liked in the community, and even admired (except for a few queer notions, such as thinking women ought to have the right to vote); and Greenfields felt flattered at her decision. In those days, in country places, schoolteachers were often looked up to.

Mrs. Goolsby herself came out to greet the Waters party. She was a plump little pigeon of a woman; her tongue and her snapping black eyes were seldom still. "Just put your dishes out on them tables," she said. "Lawsy, Joanna, that dress looks like a picture, your ma done a good job. My lands, where's Isabel?"

There was no time to answer her; she had gone to meet a wagonload of wedding guests even before the last word was off her tongue. The women got down from their seats in the Waters car and took out baskets and boxes filled with food.

Joanna knew bringing food to the gathering was her mother's idea. Martha had told Miss Lona, when she was fitting the wedding dress (and Joanna standing by with a paper of pins): "If you really want your wedding to be a community affair like you say,

with everybody feeling like part of it, you've got to let us bring victuals and have a regular dinner on the ground."

Joanna felt Miss Lona hadn't really been prepared for that
much community participation, but she saw at once it was what
Greenfields would expect, and therefore had attended to the setting
up of boards on sawhorses under the chinaberry trees, where
Joanna and the older women now put out the various contributions
they had brought. Joanna could smell her mama's salmon salad as
she took a covered dish with a flower-sprig pattern out of a Fault-
less starch carton from her father's store. That bowl had held
salmon salad at so many picnics, funerals, rabbit drives, and hog
killings that Joanna thought it smelled like salmon even when it
was sitting empty in the kitchen safe.

"You-all go ahead with your visiting," Joanna said to her
mother and Mrs. Akers and Mrs. Green. "I'll arrange all these
dishes on the table."

The ladies moved away among the crowd, and Joanna made
her job last as long as she could. She dreaded the mingling, the
meeting with girls and women who would all be asking her one
question: "Where is Isabel?"

No one expected to see Joanna without Isabel—certainly not
as Miss Lona's wedding. For these two were the teacher's special
pets: everyone knew that and no one resented it, because they
were pretty girls, and well liked, and they made the best grades in
school. Perhaps if there had been only one such girl, the other pupils and members of the community would have envied and
disliked her; or if they had disliked and competed with each other,
people might have taken sides; or if they had been standoffish, the
two of them keeping themselves to themselves (as close chums
would sometimes do), then of course their status would have been
different. Joanna understood all this, and knew, too, that people
considered her more friendly and outgoing than Isabel. "Popular"
was a word they were beginning to find useful in those days: if
there had been a contest for most popular girl at Greenfields,
Joanna would have won it. Joanna explained this attitude to herself
by the fact that she really lived at the center of the community.
She often worked in her father's store; and as people said, she always had a smile for everyone and time for a chat with the women.
Isabel lived off in the breaks, and for the past year (since her father made her leave school) had seldom been allowed to come to

Greenfields except for Sunday school and church. Everyone understood her position, and felt sorry for her (felt sorry for all the Doane children). Joanna had heard women say they might not have a bright smile on their faces all the time either if they had to put up with what Isabel did.

Joanna felt, though, that even in happier circumstances, Isabel might have been the same. She was a thoughtful, inward-looking girl (Joanna didn't know the word "introvert"), and although she was quietly pleasant to anyone she met, had never had what you could call a sunny disposition.

Well, they liked Isabel. It made Joanna a little angry to know they had to feel sorry for her, too, and probably enjoyed it, but they liked her—their questions about her would come from real concern. So Joanna would answer cheerfully, but with sufficient seriousness, that Isabel's mother wasn't feeling well and so she had to stay at home. The women would all know what to make of that, but they wouldn't press Joanna any further.

There were not, after all, so very many questions; for shortly after the Waters party arrived, came a surprise that drew everyone's attention: music from a portable Victrola set up on a table on the front porch, where soon the marriage ceremony would take place, before the guests seated out in the yard. Dr. Venable, who lived on the southern edge of the community, had brought the machine and put one of the Goolsbys' young grandsons to playing records. Joanna joined a little group of girls sitting on a bench facing the porch, and soon it seemed the music had drawn everyone to the front yard. Only the bride and groom were not visible. Justice Goolsby stood up against a trellis twined with roses and honeysuckle, and then finally, as the last strains of "Oh, Promise Me" died out, the bridegroom came out of the living room and took his place facing Mr. Goolsby.

Few had seen Professor Endicott; he had never come out to Greenfields to visit, for Miss Lona had always gone home to an aunt's house for Christmas and summer vacation. Now occurred a hissing of whispered comments and a craning of necks. Perhaps there were also disappointments: no one could really have been good enough for Miss Lona, and this man was old (at least forty) and bald and wore a pince-nez. But Joanna decided in her own mind that he looked both kind and distinguished. She would like him. Of course she would like Miss Lona's husband.

Now young Freddie Goolsby was winding the Victrola again,

and putting on another record. It started with a drum roll. People hushed and listened. The second door onto the porch, the door to the front bedroom, was seen to open. The music took shape as the piece they all knew as "Here Comes the Bride." Miss Lona stepped out, and every girl and woman sighed, "Ahhhhh!"

She was a vision. It was not the custom in that time, or at least in that place, for brides to wear white. White was the commonplace of dress for girls and young unmarried women on any summer occasion. A bride chose some pretty color suited to herself and the season, in as fine and soft a material as she could afford. Joanna had seen Miss Lona's dress when her mother was making it; it was yellow voile, draped in a style thought of as Grecian, with a two-tiered skirt and the new V neck. But she had not quite known how lovely Miss Lona would appear in it, with her rich deep chestnut hair and her skin like ivory. Not one girl in the front yard (not Joanna, for in this she was like all the rest) failed to see herself as a bride in golden yellow, standing up against an arch of yellow roses.

When the ceremony was over, the bridal couple stepped down onto the front steps and stood to shake hands with every guest who wished to come to them. Joanna deliberately waited till the last.

"And here," said Mrs. Endicott to her husband, one arm around her former pupil, "is our Joanna."

He put out his hand, and Joanna gave him hers to shake. He had, she thought, a firm and manly handshake.

"I am delighted to see you at last, Joanna," he said. "I have met your charming mother already, and we had a good talk about you."

What a strange man this was, who could call her mother charming, a stout middle-aged woman in her home-made crepe dress, with all sincerity and without airs, as though "charming" were a word he might use of a woman any day, and would if she deserved it. Or probably he was not strange at all, but in the city, at the normal college, this was the way men were. Even she and Ray might be like this couple someday, as dignified, as—yes, charming. (But Ray would never use that word, she guessed; at the thought of it on his tongue, a little secret smile betrayed itself.)

Professor Endicott smiled back and said, "Yes, we shall get along—we shall get along."

"Now Albert," said Miss Lona (but of course she wasn't Miss Lona anymore), "You go and get your dinner, because you know I couldn't eat a bite—and I will take Joanna to help me change to my going-away suit."

This was something Joanna had not thought to hope for; yet presently she found herself alone with Miss Lona—with Mrs. Endicott—in her bedroom with the window shades pulled down and the scent of violet talcum powder thick in the air. She unfastened the yellow voile dress (on which she herself had sewed the hooks and eyes), and—feeling embarrassed and excited—watched her former teacher remove the dress and draw a silk kimono over her lace-trimmed petticoat and vest.

"And now we can talk a little bit," said Mrs. Endicott, sinking onto a cushioned stool and gesturing toward a chair for Joanna.

Joanna sat down. "Isabel—" she said.

"No, we won't talk about her, not yet," said Mrs. Endicott. "I know she would be here if she could, and I can guess why she isn't. I don't want you upsetting yourself."

Joanna nodded. Thinking of Isabel, she was close to tears again.

"We'll talk about you," Miss Lona said. "You are coming in September, aren't you—Ray won't change your mind?"

"Ray wouldn't want me to change my mind," Joanna said. "We don't aim to rush into anything, because we know it will take time to be what we want to be."

"Does he still think he can go to Kansas City?"

"Yes, he does. When he's of age no one can stop him, and he's found a way to save a little money."

"He'll be twenty-one next fall?"

"Yes, ma'am. And when this crop is out we think he can go. By the time I get my teaching certificate, he'll be a skilled automobile mechanic. He'll be the best, you know, and I think I can be a good teacher."

"Of course you can. I've already seen you teaching the younger children—and you'll do well in college. But you do understand—you might not be admitted to college at once?"

"Oh yes, I've always understood that. My brothers have had to take college prep at Canyon. I guess it would be unusual for anyone from a one-room country school to go right straight into college."

"But then you might. Your brothers are bright, but they never worked as hard as you have."

Joanna shook her head. "Oh no," she said, "I'm sure I couldn't

pass the entrance examination. But at least I'm really going off to
school—I can't believe that all we've talked about so long is really
going to happen."

"Well, it is," said Miss Lona. "Now is there anything we still
need to talk about? We'll write, of course, all summer."

Joanna thought there was nothing. Everything had been arranged long before, and nothing they said today was really new. It
had been agreed, almost from the time Miss Lona knew she would
marry a professor at the East Texas Normal College and go to live
at Commerce, that Joanna would come to her, to help with the
housework in exchange for room and board while she attended college. Joanna's father had agreed to let her have what she would
need for fees and books and a little pocket money, for whatever
time it took for her to earn a first-class teaching certificate.

Miss Lona had wanted Isabel to come too. She said she knew
of another professor's wife who would be glad to have Isabel live
with her on the same terms. But there were a dozen reasons Isabel
couldn't go—or really just one: her father.

"Now tell me about Isabel," Miss Lona said at last, and for the
first time Joanna related the story of all that had happened on the
way to the wedding. Even as she told it she could hardly believe it.
This was not the first time Isabel's father had treated Isabel harshly
—it was not by far the worst thing he had done, and both Joanna
and Miss Lona knew it—but all three (the pupils and the teacher)
had dreamed so much of this perfect day, this wedding day, that it
was as though Harvey Doane had crushed with his bootheel a frag-
ile vessel containing the essence of hope and love. At the end of the
story, when Joanna told of dumping the bonnetful of flowers on the
ground, the tears she had held back all morning gushed forth.

Miss Lona let her cry a little while, then poured out some
water from the pitcher on the washstand into the matching china
bowl and wet a cloth.

"Here now," she said, putting the cloth in Joanna's hand.
"You've cried enough, and it's time for me to dress and go."

Gradually, while the bride put on her navy blue coat suit and
packed her dress and kimono, Joanna ceased crying.

"I didn't help you dress after all," she said.

"Never mind, I don't really need a maid. I just wanted you
with me a little while. And Isabel—I wanted her too; you must tell
her that."

"Oh I will," said Joanna, "but she knows it."

"And I will write to her. If I put a letter for her in with yours, can you be sure she gets it?"

"Oh yes." (No need, Joanna thought, for either one to say why a letter for Isabel must not be allowed to reach Harvey Doane.)

"And one thing more I must say," Miss Lona went on. "One thing above all, and then I have to go."

She sounded strangely intense; Joanna looked at her, wondering.

"You must get Isabel away from there," Miss Lona said. "She must not be trapped in that house, with that evil man."

What was wrong was the word—surely it was wrong: Joanna could not remember ever hearing an ordinary person speak the word "evil" before, not in any ordinary way. "Deliver us from evil." That phrase spoken every Sunday at church or Sunday school—did it mean anything? That was not the sort of question Joanna was accustomed to asking herself. She felt confused and, oddly, almost resentful.

"I tried to talk her into going to college with me," she said.

"You tried, of course," Miss Lona said. "But more than that must be done. You and Ray must see to it—she must leave that house. The other children—well, I'm sorry for them. But it's Isabel who will be caught, Isabel who will suffer—and it's she who matters most."

Joanna shook her head. She really did not know what Miss Lona was saying.

"Oh yes, I'm sorry, Joanna, but even more than Ray. There's more to her than she herself has any notion of. Something rare and precious that none of the others could even understand. She *has* to get away."

Miss Lona stood before Joanna, her brown eyes uncommonly dark and wide, her creamy fair face gone white. "Promise," she said. "You must force her out of that house."

By this time shocked out of any tendency to tears, Joanna stood up and faced her, gazing into her set face for some clue to fuller understanding. "I don't really know what to promise," she said.

Miss Lona then suddenly smiled, as though she were herself again. "I'm sorry," she said. "I went too far. But nevertheless, I did mean what I said. You do it if you can."

"Yes, I can promise that," Joanna said.

And then they went out of that dim and violet-scented room

onto the porch, where the sun was bright and Professor Endicott was waiting to take his bride away in the shiny blue Buick that he had driven up to the front gate. There were old shoes attached to the back of the car, and the whole assembly gathered to shout good wishes as Miss Lona waved her last good-bye to Greenfields.

CHAPTER TWO

Isabel trudged slowly back along the way she had come. She was disappointed, but had not felt as shocked and upset as Joanna when their long-cherished plan for the wedding day was disrupted. At first, when she left home without having consulted her father, she had half expected him to come raging after her before she reached Greenfields crossroads, although she knew he had gone with the younger boys to the far side of their big pasture. Then by the time she joined Joanna, she had nearly persuaded herself that he would not come back to the house before the morning was over, or that he hadn't noticed her absence or simply didn't care. Sometimes he didn't. She often thought she was like those beetles in a box that the boys used to play with. One would start across the bottom of the box, from one side to the other; once in a while they would let it go all the way, but usually a boy would poke it with a stick, changing its course. Then the poor insect would struggle, confused, to regain its direction, but in the end forget and go a new, uncontemplated way, as if it didn't know the difference. Isabel knew, but the final result was the same as if she hadn't. In time, she had almost come to believe, she would not know the difference either, or not care.

Her mother had lived the same way so long that she no longer even tried to cross the box. Her sister Sophie had been born passive, as if her mother's weariness had infected her in the womb. When, infrequently, she appeared to want anything for herself, she seemed already to expect it would be denied her and gave no sign of caring when it was. But Sophie's was a peculiar passivity: Isabel sometimes caught a glassy glimmer of light in her usually rather opaque eyes that made her suspect it was not so much that Sophie didn't care as that she took delight in appearing not to.

The boys' lives were somewhat different. Their father worked them like slaves or dumb animals, especially the oldest two, Ray and Travis; but occasionally he gave them money, and he rarely objected to their going to a party or a ball game, if all their work was done. The one he seldom spoke to, or even seemed to see, was his afflicted son, Burnie, who went around the community on a blind horse led by nine-year-old Leonard.

"Was Papa always like this?" Isabel had once asked her mother.

"Oh, I guess so," her mother had said quickly, turning away from Isabel as from the question.

Actually, Isabel thought he was not. At least she knew he had once been happier at home, even sometimes talking and laughing with the family at the table. She thought she knew when the deep change had begun: some six or seven years ago, when having attempted to establish a horse ranch on his property, he had lost part of his land and all of his stock—had miserably failed. As long as Isabel could remember, he had talked about how degrading it was to be what he called a dirt farmer. His grandfather, so he said, had owned a big horse ranch in East Texas, worked by a dozen black slaves. He seemed to want to re-create that establishment for himself, in this new country; and Isabel had sometimes thought that if he had been able to own slaves he might have succeeded. He had refused to hire help, and often blamed the inadequacies of his three older children (then all under fourteen) for his failure.

Yet she knew it was not just the failure of the horse ranch that made him a tyrant. Her mother was right, in a way; all that he had become he had always been, but there was a time when his wife and children did not live with a sense of impending reasonless violence. Not that they had ever been free from his abuse; but in those days they used to forget to expect it.

She was only five when Burnie was born, and she had never really known what happened then. It was a time for her of such terror—such incomprehensible, paralyzing terror—that she had never wanted to know. The labor went on and on—how long she had no idea—with frightening screams that seemed to be tearing her mother apart. There were women in attendance—Mrs. Waters and Mrs. Goolsby, Isabel thought, and others, no doubt. The house seemed full of strangers. But there was no doctor; in those days at Greenfields not many women had doctors when the babies came, and certainly Lizzie never did. That night someone went and brought one, nevertheless; not Dr. Venable, the one who lived there now, but another man, who did not stay at Greenfields very long.

And this part Isabel remembered very well. The doctor came, and her papa met him at the door with a shotgun. It was Mrs. Goolsby who got that baby born. Some way, some strange way. Isabel had heard her hint at it, but such matters were not talked of before unmarried girls.

She didn't know what her father had said to the doctor that night. In later years she had heard him say he didn't want any man laying a hand on his wife; getting babies into the world was women's work.

They thought Lizzie Doane would die. She didn't, but she was sick a long time, and Isabel was the one who tended the baby brother. She thought he was more beautiful than any doll—only, as he grew, it became apparent that the dollmaker hadn't done a very good job on his left arm and leg. They were stiff and queer-look-ing; the arm, bent at the elbow, could never be straightened out. Still Harvey refused to let the doctor see the child, even when Mrs. Waters and Mrs. Goolsby came and begged him. He said there wasn't anything the doctor could do, and in this case the doctor had to admit that Harvey was probably right. He might have helped if he had been there for the delivery, he said, but the dam-age done that night could never be undone.

So perhaps, after all, you couldn't blame Harvey Doane. At least Isabel suspected this was what the men said. She knew the women did not agree, but she heard them say (talking in low voices among themselves) that it was best to forget that wild night.

There were other incidents best forgotten, most of them kept secret in the family, and in recent years it had begun to seem there was little anyone would want to remember. Even so, as Isabel said to herself, you had to go on living. She realized that Harvey Doane did not always have his mind on his children, and so would allow herself sometimes a measure of joyful anticipation, as on the wed-ding day.

But it was a very limited measure; she had certainly known all along what might happen. Neither was she surprised, as she drew nearer and nearer home, that her father did not overtake her. She could picture him at the store, reared back in one of Mr. Waters's cane-bottomed chairs, discussing the war in Europe with whoever happened to be present. He argued cheerfully, with no firm convictions, never growing angry with the men at the store. He seemed at his happiest there; and, consequently, Isabel suspected that if he had found some of his cronies and started talking, he might have forgotten all about her. As he might have forgotten the boys needed staples (or "steeples," as he and all the rest of Greenfields called them) to finish their work on the fence.

But of course he would remember. He would remember, but as there was no way she could tell what he would do when he remembered, she could only go home and take up her life as though this were a day like any other. Still, she did wish she could have seen Miss Lona one more time, to tell her a last good-bye.

As she let herself think of this loss, some tears rolled down her cheeks. But she wiped them away fiercely.

There had been a time when she cried almost every day; that was in her last year of school, during most of which she was only sixteen and as it seemed now quite young for her years. She had thought she was in love. No one else thought it; she felt then that even Miss Lona was against her. But by the time her father had discovered the plans for elopement and put a stop to them, she had herself begun to suspect she did not love Norman Nix, who was a schoolboy from a neighboring community that she never even got to know very well. Miss Lona was right: all she really wanted was escape, and even after she knew she had seen the last of Norman she tried to get away. Her father sent the sheriff after her.

Then he said she couldn't go to school anymore, because he couldn't trust her out of his sight, and she made the mistake of pleading with him, of trying to make him understand what schooling meant to her. By means of a whipping that she still blushed to remember, he had taught her not to plead with him or offer reasons about anything. It was then, too, that she learned not to cry. Her crying gave him so much pleasure that she learned to hate herself for tears.

The sun was almost at the zenith as she came to the top of a little rise, from which the Doane house first became visible to anyone coming from Greenfields. Before proceeding down the slope home, she turned back; she could just see the dark patch that she knew to be the chinaberry trees in the Goolsbys' front yard, where she imagined the guests were gathering at the tables, the marriage ceremony having ended. Really, she seemed to be watching the whole thing from this eminence. She had not seen Miss Lona's yellow dress, but Joanna had described it to her, and she pictured the bride in it now, standing with the bridegroom (she had not seen him either, except in a photograph Miss Lona showed her once) as they cut the wedding cake. The bride handed the first piece to her new husband and then turned and cut another slice and gave it to Joanna. Yet somehow it was not Joanna but herself, herself as she would have looked if she had been there, still wearing the rosetted ribbon sash. She took the piece of cake from Miss Lona, and then standing there in the middle of the road, without her sash, tired and dusty, and, yes, hungry—she began to laugh.

There was not even going to be a wedding cake, Joanna had told her. Miss Lona didn't like that idea—she said the ladies would bring so many delicious cakes that it would be unkind to single out one special wedding cake.

Isabel was used to such imagining—and knew it for what it was, a means of escape that her father could not deny her. It bothered her a little though—as she revealed when she wrote of the experience in her diary that night—that the notion of herself taking Joanna's slice of cake had slipped into the scene. She didn't believe she was jealous of Joanna, but she seemed to be afraid she might be sometime. Joanna had so much, was such a lucky girl— and Isabel was glad, for she truly loved her; but she confessed to herself that she couldn't help a little self-pity now and then.

She laughed it away though, and turned from that scene, back toward her own house, at the foot of the long, gradual slope that led down to a little rocky, dry creek. As always on approaching it, in spite of the sorrows it held, she felt her heart warm to that house. From where she stood, she could not see much of it—only the gray roof and part of a low weathered wall. Her father had built a good enough house, the usual box-and-strip structure of earlier times there, with three main rooms and a long shedroom across the back, partitioned into a big room for the boys to sleep in and a smaller one for the girls. It was the back of the house—of this room—that she saw from the hilltop, for the house faced the other way. There was a considerable amount of thick native growth that partly concealed the house, and Isabel liked that. It made her feel a little like a rabbit going home to its burrow or a bird to its nest.

Her father disliked the house. He had built it soon after they moved to that place, to get them out of the dugout where the first settler on that land had lived. He had meant to put on weather-boarding and paint it white, with green trim, but he had never been able to afford that. Also he often said he wished he had known how the county would lay out the roads. He wouldn't have built down there facing the creek then, but up on the high ground, facing the road that turned and ran south along his land (at this corner where Isabel now stood). As it was, anybody driving from Greenfields had to go nearly a mile south and over a quarter of a mile east, and then drive over the narrow track that led along near the creek bank back north nearly a quarter of a mile before the house was reached. A person coming on foot or horseback usually left the road here where Isabel had paused and cut across the pasture, following something close to the hypotenuse of the right triangle formed by the graded dirt road.

Isabel started down the trail now, somewhat more briskly than she had been walking, to be met halfway down by the shepherd dog, Rouser, barking and capering joyfully at her return.

"Well, let's race," she said to him, and picked up her skirts and ran like a child (though hampered by her tight Sunday shoes), to where the hill trail ended near the barn, then across the barnyard, past the buggy shed and the smokehouse, and on to the side porch that opened into the kitchen.

The boys were all resting there, waiting for their dinner.

Isabel leaned against a porch post, laughing and breathless; the panting dog sat on the ground near her, watching to see if she would start to run again.

"No, that's all, Rouser," she said firmly, and he lay down, still watching her, expecting praise for his obedient response.

She bent and patted him, calling him a good dog, and he moved to sit on the edge of the porch. She sat by him.

"Did you run all the way there and back, Sis?" asked Ray. "Because if you didn't, that must have been a awful short wedding."

She thought he guessed what had happened. There was warmth in his voice, what she took to be a note of sympathy. Ray was almost three years older than Isabel, but she felt closer to him in many ways than to any of the other children—even Travis, who was almost seventeen and nearer in age.

"Ray, I never got to the wedding," she said.

"Oh, Sister, what happened?" asked Burnie anxiously.

She turned to look at him, where he lay (like the others) stretched out on the porch floor, and she moved to sit by his side. His eyes—big dark eyes, like hers and their father's—were swimming with tears, so that she longed to throw her arms around him, give way now herself, let Burnie cry, and let them cry together. She undoubtedly felt closer in understanding and shared interests to Ray, but she had no tighter bond of affection with anyone in the world than with Burnie.

She lightly touched her brother's withered arm. "Oh, it wasn't anything bad," she said.

"It was Papa, wasn't it?" Burnie said.

"Well, I guess it was my fault," she said. "I ought to have asked him. But it's all right. I got to see Joanna, and Miss Lona will understand."

"Don't tell me it's all right, Sister," Burnie said. "I know better than that." His voice grew thin, as if the life were being squeezed out of it—nothing but the thought of Harvey Doane ever made it sound that way. "Papa didn't have any right to keep you away from Miss Lona."

"Say, you mustn't worry, Pal," Ray said. "If Sis says it's okay, it's okay. You don't want to make her feel any worse about it than she does already."

No one else called Burnie "Pal." No one could; neither Ray nor Burnie would allow it. No one could soothe him as Ray did; no one tried so hard to protect him. Or perhaps Isabel did try as hard, but there seemed to be more ways that Ray could help. He was the one, when it appeared doubtful that Burnie could ever go to school, who persuaded their father to let him ride the blinded horse Sancho. Burnie had begged to go to school for two years, but his mother kept saying not yet. He could walk, but so slowly and awkwardly that it hurt her to see him try. It seemed he would never hold out to reach Greenfields on foot; certainly there was no way he could keep up with the other children. Then Ray thought of the plan. Doubtfully, without mentioning it to anyone except Isabel, he went to his father. Isabel wondered even now how he had dared and, still more, how he had succeeded. Ray was at his most vulnerable then in his relationship with his father; the horse-ranch venture was going wrong, and Ray as the oldest son was charged with too many responsibilities and punished for what often were his father's miscalculations. There had been no way, though, for Harvey to blame Ray for the blinding of Sancho. He himself had forced that horse through a thicket, in pursuit of a frightened calf, and then later, seeing the horse would lose an eye to an injury from a thorn, in the fury of his frustration picked up a branding iron and seared the other eye. Night and day, taking all the time his father would allow, Ray stayed with the horse, until the burn was healed and the animal trained to know and respond to the touch of a friend. After he persuaded Harvey not to sell Sancho but to keep him for Burnie's use, Ray would set Burnie in the saddle and lead the horse himself. Later Travis and sometimes Sophie would lead him, but when Leonard started to school he claimed the job and would now relinquish it to no one.

All the children liked to wait on Burnie. Isabel thought perhaps she was the one who taught them that; she had also tried to show Burnie how to be gracefully waited on, how to accept himself as he was and be glad of friends to help him. She was the one who used to go to him in the night when she heard him sobbing because he couldn't play the way the other boys did at school. She had helped him past that bad time; and she was glad, and yet less than glad, because it couldn't have been their mother. Harvey had forbidden Lizzie to go to him when he cried in the night, saying he might be a cripple but he didn't have to be a sissy. But Isabel would hurry to him when she heard him, because if she stopped him soon enough, then often Harvey wouldn't hear the sobs at all, and Burnie wouldn't get a whipping the next morning.

And when Isabel's time came, the time of her foolish, aborted elopement and her shameful punishment, Burnie used to come to her in the night and weep with her and caress her. He would have given anything he owned (if he had owned anything) to protect his sister Isabel.

"It really is all right, Burnie," she said to him.

The screen door to the kitchen opened then, screaking, and there appeared a brown, freckled child with thick reddish hair hanging in long untidy braids.

"Oh, Sister," she said, "do come on in. I know it's time to eat, but I can't tell what to do about getting dinner on the table."

Isabel got up and followed her into the kitchen, saying, "Why, Sophie, I thought you said you could manage without me just fine."

"Well, I can *do* everything, really I can," Sophie said. "But Papa hasn't come home—"

"Now, Sister, don't scold Sophie."

These words came in a low, somewhat muffled voice from a dim corner where Lizzie Doane spent many hours of each day in what they called the popping rocking chair, her shoulders bent to some household task. When she churned, she churned there; she patched and darned and did her hand-sewing there, and when she had time she crocheted. She liked the pine cone pattern and never produced anything else—only a wide strip of crochet intended to trim dresser scarves, tablecloths, or pillowcases, but never put to any use. Isabel thought there must be miles of it packed into the cretonne-covered quilt box in her parents' bedroom. While Lizzie crocheted, she dipped snuff (the reason why she never spoke quite clearly). A tin can with the label not quite removed sat on one side of her chair, and every once in a while she picked it up and spat in it. She looked like an old woman, with her gray-streaked hair pulled into a knot on top of her head, her shapeless faded print dress, and the little trickle of brown juice lodged in a deep fold of flesh just below the left corner of her mouth. No one would have believed she was only thirty-nine years old. Isabel thought she had probably forgotten it herself.

"Well, what's the matter, Mama?" she said, going to the black wood cookstove where a large square pan of unbaked biscuits waited on top of the warming oven and a skillet of salt pork was frying away over the fire. She set the skillet off the fire and put the biscuits in the oven.

"Well now, Sister," said her mother, "I don't know whether we're ready to put them biscuits in or not."

"You see, Sister," Sophie explained, "Papa hasn't come in for dinner, and you know how he is if the bread's cold, so we thought we ought to wait. But then I went ahead and fried the meat, because I thought it had to have time to get done. And the boys are hungry and need to get back to work. You know what Papa will say if they're still here at one o'clock. But we can't eat without him —" She stopped, no doubt realizing that Isabel already knew everything she was saying.

For the Doane women, this was no new predicament. Harvey Doane expected his meals to be ready on time, fresh and hot; he expected his family to wait for him if he was late. Sometimes when he went to the store at Greenfields during the morning, he would be very late getting back for his dinner, and sometimes he wouldn't want it at all. He would buy himself a hunk of cheese, a nickel box of crackers, and a can of tomatoes. Mr. Waters would tear off a big sheet of wrapping paper and spread it on the counter for him and he would eat there in the store. Drummers sometimes liked to eat this way if they happened to be there about dinnertime, and sometimes Harvey would get to talking to some drummer and decide to eat with him.

"Well," said Isabel, "we don't have any way of knowing whether he's coming or not, and we don't want to fool around till the boys have to go back to work without getting anything to eat. I say we go ahead and get dinner on the table, and if Papa comes home griping I'll tell him everything's my fault." She looked around the kitchen, to see what still needed to be done. "Sophie, you haven't even got the table set."

"I'll set the table, Sister," said Lizzie, "if you're sure we ought to go ahead and eat."

"I'm sure, Mama," said Isabel, "but you stay where you are. No need to be on your feet."

"Oh, my leg's not bothering me today," said Lizzie. "I've been doing around a good bit this morning. I reckon I could stand on it all day if I was called on."

"Mama made the biscuits," Sophie said.

"Oh well, then," said Isabel. "You-all go ahead any way you please, and I'll go and change out of my Sunday dress before we eat."

She went through a door that opened from the kitchen into the smaller of the children's rooms, where she and Sophie slept and kept their things. As she changed to a striped cotton flannel dress (outing, they called it—this was her ol' outin' dress) and a pair of nearly worn-out tennis shoes, she wondered about her mother. There was really no way of knowing whether she was all right or not. Isabel and Ray had wanted to have the doctor after that accident with the buggy at the store, but Lizzie said no need and Harvey laughed at them. She still limped when she was tired, but that limp might not mean anything bad. Lizzie had been in poor health for years; she had "female trouble"—a phrase spoken always in a low voice or a whisper—but she never had told Isabel exactly what ailed her. Anyway, it was probably better for her to keep doing as much as she could. Mrs. Waters had told Isabel that, and she believed it.

Back in the kitchen, she looked at the big rectangular table that stood in the middle of the room. It was covered, as always, with a white oilcloth once patterned in blue checks that had now been almost completely wiped away with soapy dishrags, and set with eight places: one for Papa, of course, for they could predict his wrath should he come home and find no place for him at his own table. There were biscuits and meat on the table, a bowl of dried peaches, and one of mushy fried potatoes.

"Where's the beans?" Isabel asked.

"Oh, Sister, I forgot the beans," Sophie said. The dried red beans, cooked yesterday, were enough for two days and should have been warming on the back of the stove while the rest of the dinner cooked.

"Well, they'll just have to eat 'em cold, I guess," said Isabel, and called the boys to dinner.

They all ate heartily, not complaining about overcooked meat or cold beans. Indeed, they did not say much of anything; they were not accustomed to talking at meals and were, besides, hungry. The girls ate well enough, too, but Lizzie swallowed only a few bites before she put down her knife and fork and said, "I'll just go set on the porch and watch. He might come yet."

When the boys had gone back to work and the girls had washed and put away the dishes, their father had still not come home. Lizzie came back in, to sit rocking and crocheting, and from time to time would say, in her soft muffled voice—hesitantly, as though she knew she ought not to speak—"I just don't know what to think about your papa."

Isabel felt tempted to say, "I don't know why you want to think about him, Mama," but at the same time knew very well that thinking of Harvey Doane was never a matter of choice. When he was present you could not ignore him, and when he was absent you could not escape the threat of his return.

What she did say, as soon as she and Sophie had put the kitchen in order, was: "I believe I'll get the hoe and cut some weeds in the front yard." This was never a job she minded; it would at least be better than sitting in that dim kitchen, listening to her mama's little sucking sounds, the popping of the ancient rocking chair, and the apologetic wondering about Papa.

"Oh, why don't you let Sophie do that?" Mama protested. "You can go and get your patching to work on, and you and me can set and talk."

"All right, Mama," Isabel said. She didn't really believe her mama wanted to talk—she seldom did—but she might want Isabel by her when Harvey came home from the store.

Predictably, Sophie had no objection to hoeing the front yard —was probably pleased at the prospect, but who could tell? Isabel went and got her sewing basket, and for several minutes sat in silence at the table, darning a white cotton stocking, waiting to see if her mother had anything to say.

"You got back from the wedding awful soon," Lizzie observed, after she had rocked a little while.

"Oh, Mama," Isabel said, "didn't you hear me say I never even got to the wedding?"

"Well, no, I didn't exactly hear you say, but I kindly thought maybe you didn't."

Isabel wondered if she wanted to tell her mother what had happened. She thought not.

"Was it your papa," Mama finally said, tentatively, with a downward inflection, as though this might not really be a question she was asking.

"Yes, it was Papa," Isabel said, taking it as a question. But still she was not ready to explain what had happened.

Neither said anything for a little while.

Then at last Lizzie said, as though changing the subject, and with somewhat greater force than she had shown before, "Isabel, what happened to your sash?"

Isabel hadn't supposed her mother even knew the sash was gone—would have preferred her not to know. But now that the direct question was asked, she decided she would have to give an answer. She had always, through what she took to be some natural instinct, kept from talking to her mother very much about the way her father treated the family. Ray agreed with her, and together they had guided the younger children into the same policy. It derived from a kind of loyalty—but Isabel now suddenly wondered to whom—and a desire to protect their mother, who had, nevertheless, received so many blows both physical and mental, that it was hard to see how any fuller knowledge could damage her much more.

In this vein Isabel's thoughts ran now, though not fully articulated in her mind, and at the same time came some sense that it was foolish or even dangerous for the children and their mother to go on thus pretending to each other.

"Papa tore it off of me," she said, "and stomped it in the dirt."

Her mama did not appear stunned at that, or even surprised; she did not change expression.

"And you left it there?" she said.

"I left it there."

"Well—" Mama said, as if she would presently offer some suggestion or conclusion; but then she seemed to forget if there had been any such thing in her mind, or else to be unable to express it.

In her unwonted mood of recklessness, Isabel went ahead to describe the whole scene—the pleasure she and Joanna had felt gathering flowers for the bride as they walked along the road like two schoolgirls; then the sudden assault, as it seemed, when her father rode up to them on the big horse, Jupiter, and how at the end she felt bruised, as though the horse had knocked her down and trod upon her.

"I did, Mama, I felt bruised," she said. "I still do."

"Yes, I know," Lizzie said. "I know that there's all kinds of bruises."

Then Isabel thought how silly she had been, after all her mama had been through, to build up such a story out of what happened to her this morning. But she didn't say anything for a while, and neither did her mama, who did, however, seem about to speak when suddenly Sophie came running through the house from the open front door.

"He's coming!" she cried. "He's nearly here. His horse is on the hill."

"Oh my goodness," Lizzie said, "I wonder if he's had any dinner." She jumped up, thrust her crochet under the black sateen cushion on the chair seat, and began shuffling around the kitchen, opening doors of cabinet and safe, as though she couldn't remember where they kept their food.

"If I'as you, Sophie, I'd just go on back outside and hoe," said Isabel to her sister.

Sophie ran back out the way she had come, and Lizzie stood looking out the door, across the open space toward the barn.

"There he is," Lizzie said presently. "He's unsaddling the horse."

"Why don't you just go on with your work, Mama?" Isabel said.

"I'd better see if he wants anything," Lizzie said. She went out onto the porch.

Isabel worked on her stocking; she finished closing up the hole while her mother waited for her father.

Then she heard her mama greeting him, saying anxiously, "Have you had anything to eat, Papa?"

And he walked on past her, through the kitchen door, shouting (with an odd kind of good-humored fury), "Good God, woman, do you think I'm a plumb idiot? When it's dinnertime, I eat."

He walked over to the table and stood looking down at Isabel.

"Well," he said, "so you're back."

"Yes, sir," she said. Although she had finished darning the stocking slipped over her hand, she kept plying her needle, kept looking down at her work.

"It's a good thing," he said, not threateningly though, but somewhat absently, as if he hardly remembered the morning incident and had his mind on matters more momentous than that.

"Oh," he suddenly said, "I nearly forgot. Where's Sophie?"

Isabel looked up at him then, looked into his face, and saw some unaccustomed liveliness in his features, some new light in his smoldering eyes.

"She's in the front yard, hoeing," she said.

"Well, call her in," he said. "I want her to take them steeples over yonder to the boys."

"I'll go and tell her, Papa," said Mama, who had followed him silently into the room.

"You can tell her I left them down there by the lot gate," he said.

Without another word, but glancing back anxiously as though she thought he might call her back—she scurried out through the living room to the front door. He never even turned to look at her, but addressed himself to Isabel.

"All right now," he said. "Put them blame stockings up. I've got some things for you to do."

"Yes, sir," she said.

She did as he said, without giving much thought to what he might order next. She did not feel apprehensive, because he seemed lighthearted, almost gay. His manner reminded her of days long past, when he used sometimes to prepare some happy surprise for her; but she did not expect surprises like that now. If he were sheltering some secret happiness, it was for something he was planning for himself; all the same, it was usually better for the family to have him feeling good than feeling bad. She felt some little stir that was almost like excitement in her breast.

Yet as she returned to him, her face did not reflect this unaccountable mood of his. She felt some sort of superstitious admonition: don't let him see you hopeful. She cast her eyes down, and waited.

"All right now, Sister," he said. (He rarely called her that, or anything else, anymore, scarcely seemed to know that anyone in the family had a name.) "All right, now, what I want you to do is air out my Sunday clothes, press my suit, and pack me some underwear and stuff in a suitcase—put in whatever I'll need for a few days. If you don't know what all a man might need, you can ask your mama."

Lizzie had come back into the room and stood listening to him talk to Isabel. When he finished, she said, "Are you fixing to go somewheres, Papa?"

"Hell no," he roared—not with anger though; there was a sense of sly laughter at his own wit lurking beneath the blustery surface. "I'm fixing to start keeping my things in the suitcase all time, so they'll be handier for me."

He turned and walked heavily (as he always walked, for he was a heavy man) out the back door and down the porch steps. Lizzie and Isabel both followed him to the door and stood watching as he went past the hackberry tree at the corner of the yard and took the path that led down to the dugout, which he had always kept in good repair. They used it for storage mostly, and sometimes would go there for shelter from a storm.

"Now what can he be up to?" Lizzie said.

"Don't even wonder, Mama," Isabel said. "Just thank the Lord he's going somewhere away from here."

"Why, Sister, I'd be ashamed," said Lizzie.

"Mama, you're an everlasting marvel," Isabel said.

Lizzie went back to her rocking chair and took out her crochet, while Isabel set about preparing for her father's mysterious journey.

The younger boys had to come in from fence fixing in time to milk. Ray came a little later, but he quit earlier than usual because it was his night to go to see Joanna. He went two nights a week, Wednesday and Saturday. This was Wednesday.

When Isabel saw him coming from the barn, she went to meet him, as she would often do, especially if there were anything to tell him about Papa. It was easy for trouble to spring up between this father and son, but she knew Ray would avoid it if he could.

"Did Papa get back?" he asked.

"He got back. Then he went off somewhere afoot. Down to the dugout, I think."

"I wonder what for."

"No telling. He's fixing to go on a trip, I reckon."

"A trip. Where to?"

"He didn't say, but he's going all right. And he was sure in a good humor about it."

"Maybe he'll have such a good time he won't never come back."

"Ray, you don't think he might, do you? I mean, just go away and not come back? Some men do, you know—just walk off and leave their families and they're never seen again."

"I doubt it," Ray said.

"But he hates us all so much—looks like he'd want to."

"He needs to be here with us to get the good out of his hating."

On the porch, Ray stopped to wash. He pulled off his shirt, wanting to clean himself up better than usual on account of going to see Joanna, and Isabel saw the scars across his back. She didn't see them very often; sometimes she almost forgot they were there. They were marks of chains, from a whipping he took when he was eighteen, the last one his father ever gave him. Ray told her it was the last one he would ever take. He said he would try to get along with Papa as long as he stayed in that house, but if it ever came to a whipping again, he wouldn't stand still.

They saw Papa coming, up from the creek.

"He won't say anything about you quitting early, if you don't mention it," Isabel hastily said. "He's too worked up."

"Don't worry about me, Sis," Ray said.

She went on into the house, to help her mother and Sophie put supper on the table, and shortly the family were all gathered there. For a little while they ate in their usual silence, but there was something unusual—an awareness like some physical pressure, charging the air. It emanated from everyone at the table, Isabel thought, from Papa himself, and from all the rest, as they became conscious of the queer look Papa had, as though some secret joy were glowing inside him. Isabel wanted to warn all the children: don't let him see you've noticed. But she knew they didn't need warning. They were used to holding their tongues and making masks of their faces.

So nobody spoke except to say something like "Pass the taters," until Harvey, who was crumbling the remains of his corn bread into his milk, turned to Ray and said, "Ray, I want you to take me to Greenfields in the morning, to catch the train."

"Sure, Papa," Ray said.

Everyone knew the morning train came through Greenfields at five o'clock, so that Ray would have to have the buggy hitched up and ready to go by four-thirty. There was no need to discuss further plans, and Harvey didn't.

He didn't say anything else for perhaps a minute. He might have been waiting for Ray to ask him questions; but Ray didn't, nobody did, and finally Harvey said, addressing Ray, "I don't know just how long I'll be gone, but you know what to do here. You'll be in charge."

"Sure, Papa," Ray said. He hardly ever spoke more than two words at once to his father.

No one said anything else. Isabel imagined they were all thinking about how things would be for them with Papa gone, and what they might do in his absence. Even if he were away only a couple of days, and it seemed from the clothes he was taking that it might be longer, they would have a taste of freedom.

As she speculated about what other members of the family might be thinking, Isabel was working out a plan for herself. It had been so long—she didn't even want to think how long—since Papa had let her stay away from home all night, since those old days when she and Joanna used to lie in the darkness whispering and giggling as they played silly girlish games to see whom they would marry. Isabel thought of the good times they had almost recaptured on their way to the wedding, and she determined that at least once more they would be girls together.

Before Harvey left the room, he gave still another order. "Now I don't want you girls fooling around in the kitchen tonight," he said. "I want it cleared out and a bath fixed for me, just as quick as you can get the water hot."

He went into his and Lizzie's bedroom, where they could hear him stirring around—packing some last little things, perhaps, that Isabel hadn't been told about. Mama went to see if she could help him, but he sent her out, and she came back to the kitchen to see about getting his bath ready. Ray came out of the boys' room with his curly hair oiled and dampened down as flat as he could ever get it.

"I've got to talk to Ray," Isabel said, and followed him onto the porch. Her mama might worry for fear Papa's bath would be delayed a minute or two, but Isabel could assuage her concern by bringing in the big washtub from the smokehouse when she came back.

"Ray, do something for me tonight," she said.

"What is it, Sis?" he said.

"Ask Joanna if I could stay all night with her tomorrow night."

"She'll be tickled to death," Ray said. "And I will too."

"Say I'll be there about middle of the evening, if it's all right with her and Mrs. Waters."

Ray said good-bye and walked off toward the barn to saddle his horse, Whitestar. This was his own animal, that he had acquired through a series of trades starting when he was twelve years old and traded a mongrel pup to Jack Waters for a bicycle that had been run over by a wagon. Papa made him pay for the feed for Whitestar, out of what he could make hoeing or picking cotton for the neighbors when the Doanes were caught up with their own work.

It was nearly sundown, and Ray cast a long shadow. Distorted as it was, Isabel seemed to see in it how Ray was growing toward independence and fulfillment of his dreams: a tall man, reaching farther than anyone ever believed he would. She watched it until Ray moved into the larger shadow of the barn. As she walked across the yard to the smokehouse, she asked herself if she had come to the point of preferring shadow to reality. But then she found her answer: No, for tomorrow she would go to Joanna's house, which all her life, in any season, had been for her a place of summer sunshine.

CHAPTER THREE

Joanna stood at the kerosene cookstove in her mother's kitchen, stirring cake filling in a blue saucepan, dreamily stirring and stirring. You had to stir all the time for at least fifteen minutes, till the mixture turned clear and thick. She no longer had to ask her mama if it was thick enough; she had made this lemon jelly cake so often now that she could feel when the filling was ready, by the force exerted against the spoon as she drew it through the smooth tart-smelling mixture. She was not even thinking about her cooking; from where she stood, she could look out the north window and up the road, the way Isabel would come from, and so she was watching for her and thinking of her insofar as she was thinking at all, letting little glimpses of Isabel and the Doane family into her mind.

Isabel had sent word she would try to get there "about middle of the evening." That meant around three o'clock, and it was nearly three. Joanna was both eager to see her coming and hopeful of getting the cake together before she arrived. This was Isabel's favorite cake, and it had been a long time since Joanna had had an occasion to make it for her.

Strange to think how long, for she could remember when the Waters and Doane families would be together almost every Sunday and the girls could spend the night with each other any time they pleased. True though, she had almost always liked it better when Isabel came to her than when she went to the Doanes'. She thought about one time when she was little, six or seven maybe. Mrs. Doane asked how many eggs she could eat for breakfast, and she didn't know but was afraid not to say. The Doane children all said two, and she ate two at home sometimes, especially if the white was crisp and brown and the yellow cooked all through. She said two. "Papa won't like it if you don't eat them," Isabel whispered. But it was too late: Mrs. Doane was already breaking eggs into the big iron skillet, and Joanna didn't know how to take back what she'd said. At the breakfast table, with Mr. Doane frowning so darkly down on them all and the eggs so greasy white and thick, like the very plate she ate from, she tried to hide them under the two halves of a buttered biscuit. Then Mr. Doane talked loud and hard about wasting food, and he threatened to whip Travis if he didn't eat the last bite on his plate. He didn't say anything to Joanna, but she cried.

She learned how to keep out of Mr. Doane's way most of the time, and at meals to escape his notice. Now looking back, she couldn't remember when she stopped going to stay all night with Isabel. After a while, she just didn't want to go, and Isabel didn't ask her.

"I don't like that house," she said to her mother once, after she had been to the Doanes', but she couldn't tell why. Then later she thought she understood. On a summer morning her mother was sweeping the living room, stirring up dust motes that made paths of gold where the sunlight streamed in at the windows, and as always when she worked she was singing—"Annie Laurie" that day, in her strong clear voice that climbed so easily into the high registers.

"I know what's wrong with Isabel's house," she said to her mother then. "It's all so dark inside, and nobody ever sings there."

The realization had surprised Joanna, because nearly all the Doane children liked to sing. When her brothers, Jack and Winnie, were at home, and Ray and Isabel visiting, all four would gather around Joanna at the piano; and they all would sing till their voices gave out. Sometimes Isabel and Joanna sang duets—even as a little girl, Isabel had a sure, sweet alto voice that tinged any song with sadness.

The filling began to thicken, and soon Joanna set it off the burner to cool. She went out into the front yard, where her mother was cutting spent blossoms from the larkspur and poppies.

"Is it done?" her mama asked.

"I left the filling to cool," Joanna said. "I think I got it just right."

"Well, you know Isabel will like it, whether you got it just right or not. I bet she hasn't had any lemon jelly cake since the last time she was here."

"No, they don't make it."

"Lizzie Doane never did fix any kind of dessert but one-egg cake and biscuit pudding."

"Mr. Doane won't let her, that's why. Isabel made our white cake recipe one time, and he fed it to the hogs. Said he didn't want his family to get used to such wasteful ways of cooking."

Mrs. Waters shook her head sadly. She knew all about the Doanes, of course; she had heard the story of Isabel's white cake before. But they would tell things like that over and over, marveling at how mean Harvey Doane could be.

Mrs. Waters straightened and looked up toward the crossroads. "Yonder she comes," she said.

She was just turning south, toward Greenfields. If they hadn't known anyway that Isabel was coming, they would have recognized her by her walk. She took long steps, for a girl, and moved along easily and freely, with a subtle rhythm more felt than seen, as though she might be keeping time to some unheard music that came to her secretly out of the earth or the sky. This was the way Isabel walked when she was happy and in union with herself.

"I'm glad she's feeling good," said Mrs. Waters.

"Oh, Mama, I did want to go and meet her," Joanna said, and her mother said she would go in and finish the cake.

"Oh, will you?" Joanna exclaimed, and started out at once, still wearing her cook apron tied around her waist.

"You'd better come back and get your bonnet," her mama said, but Joanna didn't.

Isabel and Joanna met somewhat shyly, like children who have been apart a long time. They did not now mention the disappointment of the wedding day or the joy of having this unexpected time together. They lived among people who did not ordinarily betray their deepest feelings in speech; words like "love" or "beauty" or "joy" embarrassed the residents of Greenfields.

"I made a cake," Joanna said. "Mama's spreading on the filling for me." (This was really all that needed to be said.)

"Lemon jelly?" Isabel said, understanding.

"Sure enough. What else?"

"I can't hardly wait."

Joanna had entertained a notion that she and her friend would first go by the store and drink a soda pop. But of course Isabel had her "things," done up in a paisley shawl and looped over her arm. And Joanna was still wearing her kitchen apron.

"Let's *don't* wait!" she suddenly said. "Let's go and have a piece right now."

"Let's do," said Isabel, and laughed heartily, deep-throatedly.

Joanna loved Isabel's laugh. It sprang forth in a way that seemed natural and yet controlled as a song; it was like music that was joyful without being either light or gay. She laughed too: her own laughter always seemed to escape in spite of herself. She had been self-conscious about it ever since Jack, her older brother, told her it sounded like a mare nickering. She did not quite know why she laughed now, or really wonder; she laughed because Isabel did, and they were together, and happy.

Isabel's laughter was released by a sudden sense of freedom—of Joanna planning to go ahead and cut the cake instead of waiting till supper, knowing Mrs. Waters would agree, and not only agree but sit down with the girls and have the biggest piece herself. And no one nervously listening for footsteps or glancing over shoulders. Because of course Mr. Waters wouldn't come in, but if by any chance he did, he would not scold about wastefulness. He would eat cake too.

It happened as Isabel foresaw: as soon as she had put her

things in Joanna's bureau drawer, the three women sat down together at the small square pedestal table on the screened-in back
porch. Isabel could remember when this had been the center table
in Mrs. Waters's living room, but that arrangement was no longer
fashionable. There was a library table now, placed in the lace-cur-
tained bay window, and this pleasant new eating place on the
porch. Mrs. Waters was always changing things—she had space in
her house for change.

"Is your mama to'bly well, Isabel?" asked Mrs. Waters; then
receiving a polite assurance that she seemed to be, let that subject
go, and after a thoughtful pause continued: "I hope this visit is the
sign things is fixing to get better around Greenfields. You know
Jack and Winnie will be here Saturday for a visit, and in another
two weeks they'll be home from college for the summer. I want you
young folks to get together and have some fun." Not one word
about Harvey Doane's trip, which was the only thing that made
this event possible.

Anyway, Isabel thought, it was nice to pretend. "Sure, we'll
have some fun, Mrs. Waters," she said.

"Oh, I expect Jack and Winnie will be too smart now to have
anything to do with us," said Joanna.

"Well, they'll have to have somebody to show off to," said Mrs.
Waters, and all three laughed.

"Really, we could do something," said Joanna, "—something
like old times. Let's go on a picnic to Paint Rock."

"Let's do," said Isabel.

They talked for a while as though they really believed she
could go on a picnic. Then—the girls having finished their cake—
Mrs. Waters wanted them to catch a chicken and kill it for supper.

The chickens ran free in the open land that stretched from the
barnyard to the railroad, but they came when Joanna called them,
scattering feed on the ground. They clustered around her feet, a
mixture of breeds, sexes, and ages. She picked out one, a strutting
young Dominecker rooster, and caught it easily, using a long stiff
wire bent into a hook at one end.

"He makes life miserable for the pullets," Joanna said. "He's
just been asking to be fried for supper."

The flock seemed alarmed momentarily, but resumed eating
before Joanna had carried their squawking companion more than a
few steps away.

"Why don't you go back to the house if you'd rather?" said Joanna to Isabel then.

She had remembered Isabel's weakness. Isabel suspected Mrs. Waters had not forgotten it either, and wanted to see if she hadn't outgrown it. Well, she might have, Isabel told herself. She hadn't seen a chicken killed in years.

"I'll go with you," she said.

"Well, if you want to," said Joanna doubtfully.

They went around north of the house, outside the yard fence, to a space kept clear of weeds and grass. The boys had always played ball there, and Mrs. Waters had always gone there to kill her chickens, as it provided a clean open stretch of ground with plenty of room for the chicken to flop, and yet was outside the fence, so the mess she made could be left there. Mrs. Waters kept a clean, well-scraped yard.

The chicken stopped squawking and stayed still in Joanna's arms, as a not quite tame cat might have done, compliant but not altogether trusting. Joanna stopped near the yard fence, with Isabel at her side; then stepped out a little way and almost before Isabel knew it had with one quick jerk of her wrist wrung the young rooster's head off. She flung the head away from her out into the weeds, where a dog or some wild animal would find it, and stood waiting for the body to stop flopping. It tumbled in the dust, first one way and then another, a round bundle of desperate, reasonless life, leaving great drops of blood in its aimless trail. Suddenly it moved several feet straight in the direction of its castaway head.

Isabel gave a little cry and ran away toward the yard gate.

"Wait for me by the well," Joanna said.

Isabel fumbled with the gate latch, not consciously seeing it, and slowly walked across the yard to the windmill, which stood at the edge of Mrs. Waters's vegetable garden, some twenty feet away from the door to the screened porch. She sat on a bench and waited for Joanna, who she knew would presently come and finish dressing the chicken there. She sat very still and in the end did not either throw up or faint, as she had feared she might.

What had happened was less Joanna killing the chicken than the rousing of an old, old memory. Her mother wringing the chicken's neck, standing on a grassy open space along the creek bank, not far from the old dugout, where they must still have been living then. How it flopped and tumbled, then moved, as if pur-

posely, in a straight line. "Oh, Mama, will it find its head?" she had
cried then. And her mama answered, "No, silly, it's dead." Still moving, still tumbling, still bleeding—but dead. It reached the edge of
the bank, rolled down into the dry creek bed—and her mother sent
her to get it. Weeping bitterly, she brought it back, the lump of
feathers warm in her bloody hands. Then her mother, who noticed
more in those days, saw what she had done to the child. After that
she practiced a leniency scarcely permitted in the Doane family.
Isabel did every other kind of work a farmwife had to do, but she
had never killed a chicken.

But this was an early childhood experience that Isabel had almost forgotten. She chose not to think of it now, or of anything else
around her: she had a way of retreating into herself. She thought
of the place she escaped to as a grassy, sunlit glade hidden in the
depth of a dark forest. (She had never seen a forest.)

Soon Joanna came, bringing the naked rooster. She had
stripped off most of the feathers to blow away in the wind; now
she filled with water a pan kept hanging on the wooden windmill
tower, took an old butcher knife stuck between two boards, and set
about completing her task.

"Isabel, you're a sissy," Joanna said, but her voice showed concern.

Mrs. Waters came out then. "I saw you setting here," she said
to Isabel, "and I watched to see if you was all right—but I thought
you'd be better off left alone a little bit."

"Yes, ma'am, I guess I was," said Isabel. "I'm all right now."

"What are you going to do," Joanna asked teasingly, "when
you get married and have to cook for a family?"

"I don't know," Isabel said. "I used to worry about that."

Mrs. Waters looked at her closely, as though understanding
the use of past tense. "Oh, you'll just have to make your old man
kill the chickens," she said cheerfully. "I had a friend back in East
Texas that done that. She would faint at the sight of blood, so he
found out he had to kill the chickens. He used to chop their heads
off with the axe."

Isabel laughed shakily. She didn't try to explain that it wasn't
the sight of blood she couldn't bear, but the terrible, mindless
dying.

Joanna looked at her and realized she was pale. She wished
she hadn't let her watch the killing of the chicken.

"As soon as I get through we'll go up to the store and get a sody pop," she said. "If you'd like to."

Isabel said she would like to, and Mrs. Waters said what a good idea (she pronounced it "idy") she thought it was, and would they bring her a can of English peas when they came back.

The Waters house was set back some two or three hundred yards from the main county road, where Mr. Waters had built his store, an unpainted, step-fronted structure gone gray with the passing of time. Isabel and Joanna could remember when it was yellow and new, and even when it wasn't there at all; but now it seemed to them as ancient as rocks and trees.

Mr. Waters, having evidently seen them coming, stepped out onto the front porch and called howdy. Like the store, he seemed always to have been there, and always to have looked just as he did at that moment. He looked exactly like a storekeeper; you could not imagine him as anything else, nor could anyone who had grown up at Greenfields imagine a storekeeper who did not resemble Mr. Waters. He was rather short of stature, and slight but plumply rounded, with thin, gray-streaked hair receding from his forehead, hair that had originally been the color of Joanna's, though it was hard to associate it with her luxuriant, well-brushed, gleaming locks. He wore round steel-rimmed spectacles falling down onto his nose, a neat little mustache, and distinguishing him most completely from the farmers at Greenfields, black bow tie, suspenders, and sleeve holders.

Isabel answered his greeting. "Good evening, Mr. Waters."

"You know what it seems like to me this would be a good time for?" he said as they stepped up on the porch. "Seems like it's just about the right time for you girls to drink you a sody pop."

Isabel could not remember ever going to the store with Joanna when Mr. Waters didn't offer them soda pop or candy. Her father always spoke rather contemptuously of this generosity of Mr. Waters toward his children and their playmates: "Them kids is always eating and drinking up his profits." The point was, Harvey did speak of it—he enjoyed making allusions to the friendship that existed between the Doane and Waters families.

Joanna selected orange and Isabel grape, from among the bottles in the homemade ice chest. While they were drinking, Mr. Waters said to Isabel, "I don't think anybody from your house has been after the mail today. Your papa's got some kind of a paper." He always knew just what mail everybody had in his box.

"Thank you, Mr. Waters," Isabel said, "but if that's all there is, I believe I'll just leave it." It would be the farm magazine Harvey Doane subscribed to. No one in the family would glance at it before he had opened it, anyway.

Mr. Waters gave Isabel a slightly frowning look over the tops of his spectacles, but he didn't say anything.

"Mama wants some English peas," Joanna said. She went behind the counter and took down a can from the shelf. "And we're having fried chicken for supper, and I made a lemon jelly cake."

"Well, I may close up a little early," her father said. "I feel like I'm just about to get as hungry as a bear." He turned to Isabel. "And if we eat early, we can have a game or two of dominoes before bedtime," he said. "You and me ain't had a chance to beat Joanna and her mama in a long time now."

Isabel laughed and said, "That's so, Mr. Waters." Both Joanna and her mother were better players than either Isabel or Mr. Waters; it would have been more sensible to arrange different partnerships, but somehow this was the way the four of them had always played dominoes. The reason might simply have been that Joanna and Mrs. Waters cared more about winning.

Walking back to the house, neither girl spoke for a minute or two. Then Joanna said, "I believe Papa thinks you're still mad at him about that letter."

"No," Isabel said, "I don't think he does. He knows there's no use in me taking that magazine."

"I didn't mean that. Something about the way you said what you did, when he mentioned the mail."

"Well, I don't forget it," Isabel said. "But I know it was something he had to do."

"Yes, it was," Joanna said. "It really was."

Isabel did not doubt what she said, what Joanna echoed. But just at first, when it happened, when her father faced her with her letter addressed to Norman Nix, she had hated them both: both fathers, all fathers. Until then she had thought Mr. Waters was different—the whole Waters family seemed different, so happy, so free. But then when her father had guessed she had written to this boy he had forbidden her to see, and he went and demanded to know of Mr. Waters if such a letter had been mailed, no one at Greenfields would have expected Mr. Waters to do anything but what he did: place in Harvey Doane's hand this letter that his daughter had entrusted to the U.S. mail. Fathers must protect their daughters. It was Mrs. Waters who had tried to make her understand that law—not either of the men, of course: there was no law that said a father had to offer explanations.

At this time Isabel got her first inkling of a power that ruled outside the law. Greenfields gave considerable thought to what they called the law of the land; next to God, it was what they believed in. Consequently, all the Waterses had been drilled from the first moment Mr. Waters got his appointment as postmaster in the sacred inviolability of the mail. And as Joanna's friend, Isabel heard it all too. Probably none of the children ever knew what would happen to anyone who interfered with the mail. Federal prison was in all their minds. Sometimes Mr. Waters allowed one of the children to go behind the partition that divided the post office from the store; but never without the warning that if the postal inspector ever came and caught one of them there something terrible would happen. Prison? Perhaps they no longer quite believed that, but it was the dark fate they had always imagined.

Isabel was therefore incredulous—stunned speechless, a state which probably saved her some lashes when faced with that letter. She simply could not believe Mr. Waters would have done such a thing; she half thought her father must have followed her to Greenfields and snatched it from the post office himself; only he said so plainly, "Tom Waters give me this today; now I'll have your explanation, Missy."

When that first phase was over—when Harvey Doane had been restrained from going to horsewhip Norman Nix and Isabel had been suitably punished—Joanna begged her to talk to Mrs. Waters. Joanna could not understand, either, how her father could be right in tampering with the mail; but she knew there was a reason. It was something he had to do, something her mother could explain. But this one time, Mrs. Waters—always so reasonable, so sympathetic, so sure whatever was was right—did not give Isabel much satisfaction.

She went then to her teacher, to Miss Lona, who turned white with rage when she heard the story. "We'll take it to court," she cried. There was no justification, she told Isabel. Absolutely none. Even if this act had not been a violation of federal law, it was an invasion of privacy for which there was no excuse. She wanted to go straight to Mr. Waters, and Isabel had to beg her not to. She did not want Mr. Waters to go to prison, and could foresee nothing but trouble for both herself and Miss Lona if the teacher tried to interfere with this power beyond the law.

"I see I can't help you now," Miss Lona said. "But there will be a time—there'll come a time—"

Isabel scarcely knew what she meant. Miss Lona often talked about rights for women, but whether these nebulous rights would also belong to a sixteen-year-old girl, Isabel had no idea.

In the end Miss Lona didn't really help her any more than Mrs. Waters had. She said she could offer no advice, that she saw nothing to be done as long as Isabel had to live under her father's roof. Isabel never did believe Miss Lona was suggesting that she run away from home, but the idea came to her then. She was thankful to be saved from Norman Nix—none of her angry resentment stemmed from the loss of Norman Nix—but it came to her then that elopement wasn't the only way to flee from tyranny. It wasn't Miss Lona's idea—she never told anyone it was—but Harvey Doane blamed Miss Lona's influence and put an end to Isabel's schooling.

"I wish you would talk to me," Joanna said. "I said, we don't have to play dominoes tonight."

"No, I want to," said Isabel. "I really do."

Mr. Waters came in at six and they ate supper. It was good. Everything always tasted good at the Waterses', and not solely because Mrs. Waters was such a good cook and was teaching Joanna to be. Part of the reason was eating in a dining room, away from the kitchen stove and cooking odors, with dishes set out in neat patterns on a real cloth table cover. And another part was enjoying conversation along with the food, free of any threat of unexpected condemnation.

After supper, the three women hurried to wash dishes; then Joanna set up the card table in the living room and they played three games of dominoes. Isabel and Mr. Waters won a game, and then it was eight-thirty. Mr. and Mrs. Waters went to bed at eight-thirty every night of the world, and got up at five the next morning. Breakfast was at six, and everybody in the house was expected to be at the table when Mrs. Waters took the biscuits out of the oven.

Isabel did not see anything paradoxical in the strictness with which Mrs. Waters regulated the life of her family as compared with her own sense of freedom when she came into that open, sun-lit house. For one thing, there were from time to time the mildly surprising little exceptions, as when Mrs. Waters sat down to eat cake in the middle of the afternoon. More important, such regular-ity was simply the basis of society in Greenfields, as in every com-munity and rural town across a wide expanse of western plain and prairie. It underlay every category of their lives, and no one ques-tioned the rules. There might from time to time be found someone to darkly circumvent them; but no one questioned them. They con-cerned order in families, the ethics of horsebreaking, the opening and closing of wire gates (leave a gate the way you found it), the music permitted at parties (group singing—no fiddles)—a hundred matters big and small, but nothing more serious and fundamental (nothing more surely common to every place) than the rules of sex, mainly as it pertained to the behavior of courting couples, but also (rare in the sense that it was mostly concealed) the straying of a married man or woman.

No—Greenfields lived by rules, as any community surely must; and neither Isabel nor Joanna would have dreamed of protesting when, the domino games at an end, Mrs. Waters said: "Now you girls talk awhile if you want to, and name the corners like you used to do; but don't forget there's gonna be a hereafter." She laughed, as though she knew the admonition was not necessary. What she meant was getting up in the morning, and coming to breakfast washed and fully dressed by six o'clock.

Joanna's room was an afterthought—such as almost every house in the country round about sooner or later had built onto it, even this well-planned and comparatively spacious abode of the Waterses. It was located at the end of the back porch, next to the kitchen, and its only door opened off the porch. Isabel had always loved it. It was cozy in winter, cool and open in summer, and sepa-rated by the length of the house from the parents' bedroom, so that young girls sleeping together there could talk and squeal and gig-gle without ever evoking an angry shout or a bang on the wall.

"Let's do name the corners, Joanna," she said, after they had "stepped outside," put on their gowns, and brushed their long, thick tresses.

"Well, you'll have to name all mine *Ray*," said Joanna. "It's not like it used to be when we were girls."

They referred to a method, one of many they had learned as

children, for discovering the name of the man a girl will marry. It is intended to be used by two girls sleeping together. On going to bed, each one gives to each corner of the room the name of a boy who might make a suitable husband for the other girl. Then next morning, the other must notice which corner she looks into first when she wakes up and opens her eyes. The name of that corner is the name of her future husband.

"Oh, silly," said Isabel. "It always was just for fun. If we took it seriously and remembered all the different husbands we've found out through the years, no telling how many times we'd have to get married."

"Well," said Joanna, "all right. I can tease Ray about it and make him jealous."

"No, you'll look at Ray's corner," Isabel said. "Because now you're engaged, and you've announced your engagement, and so you couldn't possibly look any other way. This will be the proof."

They let themselves giggle at that. Lying in the dark, with the slick-starched sheet pulled up to their chins and their muslin gowns tucked around their ankles, they half believed they could giggle themselves back to childhood.

But alas, childhood was past. "I don't think there's anybody left for us to name," said Joanna after a little while.

"Oh, I can think of several," Isabel said. "What about Isaiah Birdsong?"

Joanna laughed her long high laugh (like a mare nickering). "Good Lord, Isabel, I'd nearly forgot you really used to name a corner for him."

"Well, you know Jack and Winnie always said I ought to. They said he'd tried so hard he ought to have his chance."

"As long as you put him in the corner behind the bed," Joanna said.

They laughed. Joanna knew Isabel always did, and she never had looked in that direction.

"I guess he won't come to see your papa this year, anyway," Isabel said.

He had come right after Joanna's birthday every year since she was fourteen to ask permission to court her. He was an old bachelor, past thirty, who lived alone on his farm west of Greenfields and served the community as Sunday school superintendent. He was tall, narrow, and angular, with a face always brick red, either from embarrassment or the sun. Jack and Winnie called him Ichabod Crane.

"I'll be in Commerce on my birthday," Joanna said.

They were quiet awhile again, thinking of that change and others. Then Joanna said, "But who is there for you?"

"Oh, Joanna, what a question! There is no one for me."

"Don't be that way," Joanna said. "How can we have any fun?"

"Oh well, of course there's Jack," said Isabel.

Jack was a kind of joke, too, but not like Isaiah. There had always been a corner named for Jack, Joanna's older brother, probably because when they were very little Jack and Isabel had "claimed" each other. But for years they had been good friends and nothing more. Brother and sister marrying brother and sister might have been a pleasant arrangement—and was not an uncommon one around Greenfields—but in this case no one expected it, least of all Isabel and Jack.

"There's somebody new," Isabel said at last. She had thought awhile before she spoke, but she said to herself, Why not? This was all just "playlike" anyway.

"Oh, Isabel," Joanna exclaimed. "Really?"

"Of course not really. How could it be? It's just somebody I saw at the rabbit drive."

"What's his name?"

"I don't know."

"Then how can we name his corner?"

"We can't—I was just being silly."

"I bet I know who it is—the man from the newspaper."

"Yes, that's who it is."

"Then I'll name his corner *newspaperman*. And if it turns out you're liable to marry him, you'll just have to find out what his name is."

They made jokes about that situation, and laughed some more, and were quiet a little while again, and at last each announced that she had finished naming the corners. It seemed almost as though they had made some vow against seriousness, but finally, as they were growing sleepy and the quiet times got longer, Joanna said, "Isabel, I'm glad you're here. Whatever it is about your papa, I'm glad you're here."

Something about the way she said that made Isabel ask, "Do you know anything about where he's gone to?"

"No," said Joanna, "I don't know anything."

"Well, I'm glad I'm here, too," said Isabel. "We'd better go to sleep though."

And Joanna did, but Isabel lay awake a long time. Joanna may not know anything, she thought, but she may know that Mr. Waters knows. But then she told herself, No, I don't care—I can't afford to care what Papa does. I'll think about something else.

It was easier, it was natural, it was almost inevitable, to think about the rabbit drive and the young man who came there a stranger, asking questions of every man and writing down words in a book. She had no expectation of ever seeing him again—hoped she never would see him again, because there had been a moment as they looked at each other when something moved her heart in her bosom.

That part was not playlike, not fancy. Something moved, as they stood facing each other. But it would most certainly be playlike—it would be foolish—to imagine the same thing happened to him. He was too far above her. In those days people assumed a difference between country and town, and often it was real, but in this man Isabel thought she sensed a superiority even to any town dweller she had ever seen. He was educated: somehow from his speech and manner she was sure he had a college education. He was well dressed. Although his clothes were entirely appropriate for the country, there was no man at Greenfields who owned boots or a leather jacket like his. Yet there was nothing in his manner to suggest he thought he was better than anybody else. Isabel recalled everything she had ever read about the characteristics of a gentleman: here was one, she knew for sure.

And yet—or rather, *therefore*—he could not love her. And she feared if she ever saw him again she might by some glance betray her secret feeling—if she had not, shamefully, already done so in their meeting at the rabbit drive. But of course there was no need to fear she would see him again. He had never been to Greenfields before, and she could imagine no reason why he ever would return. Nor was she herself—even supposing she should ever go to town again—very likely to walk into the newspaper office asking for a man of whom she knew neither name nor position, but only that he once attended a Greenfields rabbit drive.

It was easy to persuade herself she would never see him again, and it was this conviction that made it possible for her to dream that someday she might. Here was the only kind of man she dared dream of—the man she dared not love. For suppose she really loved a man and he loved her. A real man, not a pimply-faced, snuffy-nosed, not quite clean boy (Norman Nix). Suppose they loved each other and wanted to marry—there could be nothing but grief for them both. For at that time of her life Isabel had become convinced that she could never marry. She was still at heart a young dreaming girl who longed for romance, but when she let herself think beyond the marriage vows she always found she was visualizing Norman Nix—or her father. Marriage could be wonderful, of that she had no doubt, but there was an excellent chance it wouldn't turn out that way. This was what she meant when she said to Joanna, "There is no one for me."

And it was just as well that Isabel felt that way, because she couldn't marry anyway—or at least not for many years. So she believed, and so Mrs. Waters had encouraged her to believe. "I don't know how your mama would manage without you," Mrs. Waters had said, "not till the young ones get grown, anyway." Isabel didn't know either. Life seemed hard for her; but without her, life for the whole Doane family might be even harder.

For all these reasons—and having enumerated them, to protect herself against disappointment in dreams that could never come true—she could take herself back to that well-remembered day, that early April day in a pasture west of Greenfields, when the filaree in its brief bloom spread a delicate lavender lace on the ground and filled the air with that faint sweetness so elusive it was easy not to smell it at all unless you stopped, stood still, and gave the soft air time to caress you.

It was a beautiful, horrible day. Afterwards, she realized she hadn't understood how the rabbit drive would be.

Her father had been deeply involved in the planning of the drive, admittedly "real worked up about it." The whole community was worked up, for jackrabbits were uncommonly thick that spring, a serious threat to field crops and gardens. Something needed to be done. Talking around the pot-bellied stove in Mr. Waters's store, the men had determined to stage an old-fashioned rabbit drive. For years rabbit drives had really been rabbit shoots; but the men decided this time to go back to the ways of the earliest settlers. No one quite knew why—it seemed to be Harvey Doane's idea—but everyone supported it. They would save on ammunition that way—an economy that they also assured themselves would assist the Allies in Europe. "Send the bullets over there and let 'em use 'em on the Kaiser."

Harvey had wanted his whole family to go, even suggested that Lizzie could go if she wanted to, but at this time it was still almost impossible for her to get around on her bad leg and she said she didn't see how she could. Isabel felt her father wanted his family there to see what he had done: at home, at least, he seemed to take credit for the whole affair. It was so uncommon and heartwarming to have him talking with the children and even letting them talk, too, that Isabel to her amazement found herself making a suggestion. Since her father had said they were sending out word to neighboring communities, and hoped men from all over the county would come, why not send an announcement to the county paper?

The climax of the event was to be a barbecue at noon, with meat donated by several prominent farmers and ranchers and old Mr. Goolsby in charge of the cooking. Smoke rose from the barbecue pit as the Doane children arrived in their wagon. (Their father had ridden ahead on his horse Jupiter, for he was to be one of the three men who supervised the drive.) Women and younger children carried dishes of food to the improvised tables set up near the barbecue pit, which was located some little distance from a large, nearly circular pen.

"We'll see you back here in a little while," Ray said, and he and Travis went on to join the men at the other end of the pasture, some two miles away. Leonard ran off to play with some other children, while Sophie and Isabel began to take out the dishes they had brought. Isabel watched Burnie somewhat anxiously, for no one had found a part for him to play. But he, seeing that if there was any work at all for him it was not among the men, went over among the women, smiling his wide happy smile (that Mrs. Waters used to say just broke her heart), asking for any chore he could do. It was Mrs. Waters who put him to tending the fire where the big coffeepots were set to boil.

After a while those waiting near the rabbit pen heard shooting, but Isabel had been told few rabbits would be shot. These shotgun blasts were intended to scare the rabbits and start them on the run. Before long they began coming. Lengths of wire slanted out two hundred yards from the small opening in the pen, and several men and boys were stationed at each extremity to keep the animals from escaping and drive them toward the entrance. Isabel stood watching as the enclosure filled with rabbits hopping aimlessly, fearfully, stirring themselves together till they were like the contents of some gigantic pot kept furiously boiling.

At last all the men closed in upon the pen, and about half a dozen of them, bearing thick clubs, walked in among the rabbits. Harvey Doane was at the head of that force; Isabel watched him strike the first blow. Although theoretically she had known how the rabbits were to be disposed of, she had in no way tried to visualize the scene. She stood for perhaps a full minute as though mesmerized, while the men methodically swung their clubs and dying rabbits piteously cried. She glimpsed her father's face, and he had never looked so full of glory.

It was then she turned away, stumbling a little, and walked toward a clump of chaparral, with perhaps some notion of putting it between her and the slaughter pen. Either she was not noticing where she was going then, or the man put himself deliberately in front of her. She looked up into a pair of large gray eyes that spoke to her of shared anguish, at the scene those eyes and hers had just observed.

"You don't care for that?" was what the man really said, gesturing toward the pen.

She shook her head. "Do you?" she said.

He smiled gravely. He had a broad expressive mouth, a wide brow, a nose somewhat overlarge, long and straight, like the noses of Greeks in the ancient history books. The noblest-, kindest-looking man she'd ever seen.

"This is my first rabbit drive," he said. "I think it may also be my last."

She knew he didn't come from anywhere around there. His speech, his whole bearing, were like nothing she had ever encountered. It almost seemed he might have sprung up just like that from the ground, an enchanted prince brought magically from the other side of the earth.

She did not know how long she had been looking at him—but surely not long, or he would have spoken again himself—when she realized they could be seen by the women at one of the tables. She knew the women would be talking already.

"Excuse me," she said. "I have to help get the dinner ready."

Afterwards, she saw him talking to some of the men, including her father, and evidently taking notes. Later she heard someone say

he was from the paper, and it pleased her to think he had come because of the announcement she had sent.

She did not talk with him again. Once she thought he was
approaching her, but at the same time she saw her father's eyes
upon her, and so she turned her back and began a conversation
with a friend she had known at school.

She had no expectation of seeing him again. But she dreamed
herself to sleep now with the vision of his oddly gentle face before
her.

Shortly after five o'clock every morning, Mrs. Waters began
banging pans in the kitchen. For anyone sleeping in the adjoining
room (except Joanna, who had grown immune to it), this clatter
was better than an alarm clock. Isabel came awake smiling, thinking of the Waters brothers' jokes upon this subject. It was good to
be here, even if the kitchen alarm did go off so early. She thought
of what a good time the four of them had had the night before
(parents and children laughing and playing), and she thought of
herself and Joanna talking late in the dark and giggling like girls.
But there was something that pricked at her mind, a recollection of
some uncomfortable impression, made just before she had begun to
fall asleep. She lay trying to recall the explanation for it, and presently it came to her.

"The Waterses know about Papa."

Mrs. Waters might tell her, when they had a chance to talk
alone. At least she had a feeling, looking back, that there was
something Mrs. Waters meant to talk to her about. She got out of
bed, dressed quickly, washed her face at the bench on the porch,
where a blue-rimmed white porcelain wash pan stood under a
dripping faucet, and made the necessary morning trip to the
outhouse by the yard fence.

Then she presented herself to Mrs. Waters. "Can I help do
anything?" she asked.

"You can set the table," Mrs. Waters said.

Unless there were a good many guests in the house, breakfast
was served at a small square table in the kitchen by a window
looking out over the prettiest part of the backyard, where pink
roses climbed on the picket fence and pale petunias filled the
flower beds.

Isabel worked quietly, waiting to see if there was anything
Mrs. Waters would say.

Soon she spoke. "When are you-all looking for your daddy

back?" she asked. (She knew the answer to that, for Ray had told them; this was a prelude to something else.)

"We just don't have any way of knowing, Mrs. Waters," Isabel said.

"Ray said he didn't tell you where he was going."

"No, ma'am, he didn't."

"What would you do if he never did come back?"

"Oh, he'll be back. Ray says he will."

"Yes, I reckon he will. But what would you do?"

Isabel had thought about this possibility; it would have been difficult not to. "In a way," she said, "I don't think it would make so much difference. The boys can farm the place. Even if Ray goes off like he wants to do, Travis could do almost as well."

"And your mama," said Mrs. Waters, adopting the faintly challenging tone that meant she knew she was saying something delicacy would forbid, "might get along better than she has in a long time."

Isabel didn't mind hearing Mrs. Waters say that, because they both knew it was true. They had talked freely before this about her mother's condition; Isabel had gone to her friend's mother more than once for advice and support. The best advice had been: "You can't help her, where he's concerned. You'll just have to watch and when she can't keep going, take her place. Take care of the younger children. Keep the house clean. Do what you can."

Soon after Isabel had tried to run away, they had talked like this, and she had asked, "But how long, Mrs. Waters, how long?"

There was no answer. Now, for a brief glimmering moment, she visualized her mother well and capable again, like Mrs. Waters, and herself free. As she turned away from the safe (where Mrs. Waters kept her everyday dishes), she felt almost dizzy at the prospect, and stood still with a stack of cups in her hands, for fear she might fall and break them.

Having placed the cups in their saucers, she had finished her task, and she went to stand by Mrs. Waters at the stove, stirring the pan of oats from time to time while Mrs. Waters attended a skillet of sausage and eggs.

Isabel was thinking of something she wanted badly to ask someone. Mrs. Waters seemed the only one, and in this warm morning intimacy, linked to this older friend by the communion of shared women's work, she spoke.

"Is it a sin," she asked, "to wish he would never come back?"

"No," said Mrs. Waters firmly, "it is not a sin."

She offered no rationalization, and Isabel asked for none. She wanted to believe it, and she did. At last she asked, "He might not, you think?"

"Come back? Oh, I reckon he will. I just thought—sometimes you hear of a man that just disappears, wants a new life, as you might say."

But Isabel could not believe she would say even that much, without grounds for it. "You do know something, though, don't you, Mrs. Waters?"

Mrs. Waters did not answer at once. "I believe them oats is done," she said.

Isabel set the pan off the burner. She didn't ask again, but stood waiting.

"You might hand me that platter," Mrs. Waters said.

Isabel brought it, and the older woman began taking up the sausage and fried eggs.

"You do, don't you?" Isabel insisted.

"No, I don't," Mrs. Waters said finally. "I don't know anything. Only I guess you may know that he eat dinner with a drummer at the store that day. Mr. Waters come on home and left them eating cheese and crackers on the counter."

"But what would a drummer have to do with Papa going off?"

"Mr. Waters heard him mention some woman's name."

"Who, Mrs. Waters?"

"No one we know." After that Mrs. Waters held her mouth tightly closed, and pursed just a little, as though she had to concentrate to remember how to put the victuals on the table.

Isabel guessed it was a name Mrs. Waters had heard before, but she asked no more questions.

"I'll go and see if Joanna is up," she said.

Joanna was out of bed, and hurrying to dress.

"Oh, Isabel," she cried, "which corner did you look in?"

"Oh gosh, Joanna," Isabel said. "I forgot to look at all."

"Well, I didn't forget," Joanna said. "I thought about it first thing, and I looked in that one."

She pointed diagonally across the room from the corner she slept in.

"Oh, that was Ray," said Isabel. (They had all been named Ray, and she knew Joanna knew it.)

As soon as she had helped Joanna wash the breakfast dishes, Isabel said she must go home. "They may need me," she said. "They're used to depending on me."

"Well, that's the way it should be," said Mrs. Waters, nodding with satisfaction.

Joanna walked a piece with Isabel, as she always did, and they stood awhile under the old mesquite tree, where they always parted.

"It's too bad you don't know which corner you looked in," Joanna said at last. "But you must have looked in one of them somehow—and so it's all right, because I named them all for the newspaperman."

Her high-reaching, cascading laughter followed Isabel as she walked on down the road home.

CHAPTER FOUR

"All happy families are alike, but each unhappy family is unhappy in its own way." Isabel had read that statement in a book once, or something closely resembling it. It was, in fact, the opening sentence, and consequently might be understood to be the true subject, of a very strange book lent to her in her last year of school by Miss Lona Miller. The school owned no books at all—textbooks were purchased by the pupils' families—but Miss Lona had a few books of her own that she would lend to anyone she thought capable of appreciating them. She knew Isabel dared read nothing at home but a textbook or the Bible (Harvey Doane being suspicious of any reading matter not clearly sanctioned by some institution he approved of), and so used to give her hours of free time at school to read as she pleased.

Isabel knew her father would have been shocked and, probably, infuriated by this book—as would almost any resident of Greenfields, for it treated with some sympathy a condition least tolerable to Greenfields of all sinful conditions, the adultery of a woman. Miss Lona said she would not recommend the book to Joanna, who in any case showed little curiosity about it. Joanna generally preferred books that enabled her to better herself, as she

put it—taught her something that would help her reach her goal of
getting a college education and becoming a grammar school
teacher. Novels she considered mostly a waste of time, though
sometimes in the summer she would read, just for fun, some romantic and virtuous book like *St. Elmo*.

Isabel liked romances, too, but she could lose herself in a book
like this queer Russian novel. As she read, many questions occurred
to her that she would like to discuss with Miss Lona, but as it happened the edict against further schooling came before she had the
opportunity. Although she did occasionally see Miss Lona of course
—at the store, at church, and even on short, forbidden visits in
company with Joanna, there never was a time for the kind of talks
the teacher and pupil had once enjoyed. And yet Miss Lona might
not have seen in the book what Isabel did, anyway. When Miss
Lona brought the book to school for Isabel she had told her to notice especially how unfairly women were treated in that time and
place and to ask herself if they were better off in modern America.

But Isabel, from her viewpoint, was more inclined to dwell on
other themes. That opening sentence had gripped her, and she
thought of it all through the book. She had often wondered if it really could be true, and if so what exactly the author had meant by
it. She had no way of testing it, as there was only a handful of
families she could be said to know at all well, and they all lived in
Greenfields, Texas. She knew nothing about that author except that
he was a Russian and evidently belonged to a high class of society
accustomed to servants, great houses, extravagant balls, and intel-
lectual conversation; she could not tell whether he would have ex-
tended his observation to include the families of plain country people.

As far as she knew, most Greenfields families considered themselves happy; her acquaintances at school all seemed to feel comfortable at home. But the Waterses were different. She knew of no
other house where father and mother and children, while all living
according to the rules that prescribed their places in the family hi-
erarchy, were able to find so much pleasure both in each other and
in themselves. But perhaps by "happy" Tolstoy simply meant living
together without distrust and fear. If so, there might be some fundamental principle underlying happiness: that all lived according
to some sense of proportion and order, under some sort of law
based on reason and love. Was not the unhappiness in this terrible
book brought about by the breaking of law: even the Command-

ments themselves? Unhappy families, then, like her own, were made miserable when one person (and wouldn't it usually be the father, as most powerful?) ruled without order by his own whim, moved more by hatred than by love? So then unhappy families were alike, too, if not in the kind of misery they experienced, then in what lay at the root of it?

But no—she was not sure. The story was too complicated to be explained that way. The beautiful, pitiful adulteress was not the sole cause of the misery in *Anna Karenina*. Neither was her hateful husband. There was such wickedness in this book, it was hard to tell who was most wicked or who most deserved punishment.

As Isabel walked homeward after parting from Joanna, she struggled with these attempts at understanding the condition of her family; but at last she let them go, and concluded as she had often done before that she could find no useful answer. The games and songs, the laughing and talking together were not the reason the Waters family was a happy one; these were the blossoms, not the root. But they were pleasant while they lasted, and she made up her mind to offer them to her family while she could.

Mrs. Waters had given her advice to this effect one time, when Isabel had asked her in despair if she saw any way out of misery for herself and her brothers and sisters. "Just try to have a little fun," Mrs. Waters had said. "It makes the burden a little lighter, and at least you-all will have that to remember."

That night when the rest of the family were in bed, Isabel took her diary from its hiding place and, taking advantage of her father's absence, lit the china-shaded lamp in the front room and sat by the pedestal table in there, writing page after page. She made no attempt to write every day; there was no way she could have, for her father was likely to open any closed door without warning, any time of the day or night. She kept the book in a place where he would never think of looking—under the cup towels in a drawer in the kitchen cabinet. If her mother had taken the interest in housekeeping she once did, she might have found the diary there (not that Isabel would have minded so very much if she had), but as things were, Isabel was the only one in the household who had occasion to know what was in the bottom of the cup-towel drawer.

She tried to write down the thoughts she had experienced walking home that morning—twisted, fragmentary, puzzled sentences, groping for some meaning in that book or in her life. She wrote of Mrs. Waters's advice: Don't think you can change things. (That had been part of the answer Mrs. Waters gave—"accept your papa as he is, don't think you can change things; and once in a while, when you see there's a chance, you younguns ought to have a little fun.")

She wrote of a layer cake she made—not lemon jelly, because she had no lemons or even lemon flavoring, but dressed up with a vanilla icing that never got quite hard enough and kept slipping down the sides of the cake. Of how the kids liked it anyway, and ate it all, and bragged on her cooking, and after supper, how she encouraged Burnie to get out his French harp and they sat on the porch with the music, till old Rouser came up howling, telling them that racket hurt his ears. Burnie refused to play anymore then.

"A wonderful, free day," she wrote, "for which I thank God, for only He can know when there will ever be another one."

Next morning when breakfast was over, Ray said to her, "Come with me, Sis, while I hitch up the team."

"The dishes—" she said.

"If Mama or Sophie don't wash 'em," he said, "they can wait. There ain't nobody here that cares much."

She went with him to the barn, and they sat on an old wagon seat behind the buggy shed and talked awhile before he got the planter ready to go to work.

"I aimed to talk to you yesterday," he said, "but I never could get a chance to get you by yourself."

"I guess you think I might have heard something at the Waterses'."

"I thought from the way Joanna talked Wednesday night, Mrs. Waters might know something."

"About Papa?"

"Yes."

"I thought so too. But she didn't say much. Only I believe they think he's gone to see a woman."

"What woman?"

"She couldn't say, or wouldn't. But I felt like she thought he might not come back."

"I know who it is—who it has to be."

"I think I do too. She used to catch a ride to town with a drummer sometimes."

"Do you think he really didn't know where she went when she left here?"

"I don't know. Do you know why they left—her and her brother?"

"To get work, I thought. Why, Ray? What do you know?"

"Well, Joanna don't know this, and I don't want her to."

"I wouldn't tell her."

"In the first place, that wasn't her brother."

"But Ray—not her husband, surely?"

"They was living like he was, is all I know."

"But—I thought—*Papa?*"

"I'm not aiming to try to tell you about that. Papa went over there a lot, and when he did the brother would go off somewheres and stay awhile."

Isabel felt her cheeks grow warm and covered them with her hands, even though she supposed she didn't care if Ray saw how ashamed she was. "I didn't know it was that bad," she said.

"There's more you don't know. Mr. Waters and Mr. Goolsby went over there to that shack where they'as living and told them to get out of the country. Or what I think they said was there wasn't any place for a woman like her in this community. And the feller said if his wife had to go he'd go too—yeah, I'm pretty sure they said he called her his wife. And they said that was fine with them, but just make sure she wasn't seen or heard of at Greenfields anymore."

"And as far as I know she hasn't been."

"I'm pretty sure Papa never heard from her. It's nearly always me or Travis gets the mail—we'd know it if he had."

"So you reckon that drummer might have found out where she was somehow, and told him?"

"I reckon he might. She might have sent him some word— something that would make him decide to go and see her."

"But he'll come back."

"Of course he'll come back. What else could he do?"

"Mrs. Waters said what I thought of once. Sometimes men don't. Sometimes they want a new life."

"It makes a nice dream, don't it?"

"Oh, Ray, I don't know. I feel ashamed to say that about my own papa."

"Well, don't worry, he'll be coming in just any evening on the five o'clock train. At least I reckon we can figure on that much."

"Yes, I guess so." She sighed, and rested her head in her hands a moment, then sat up and smiled. "Well, I'll make us a custard pie this morning, then, and we'll have one more good day."

"That's fine, Sis," he said, and got up to go.

Then she laughed—her full, free, head-thrown-back laughter. "Ray, that reminds me of something Mrs. Waters told us once about her and her sister in their childhood. They used to worry and feel scared to death all morning, and then as soon as dinner was over they'd laugh and sing and feel so good, till morning came again."

"Why was that?" Ray asked.

"Because they'd always heard about the resurrection *morning*, and they knew if judgment day didn't come before dinner it wouldn't come that day at all. Now whenever we hear the five o'clock train go through without stopping, we'll know the world's not coming to an end that day."

Ray shook his head as though he failed to understand her. But he said, "Keep laughing, Sis," and went to get his horses.

She kept sitting on the wagon seat awhile, sunk not in amusement but in recollection and perplexity. For there was a picture in her mind of Alma Greeping, as she had seen her once, rising out of a cotton patch before her eyes.

She was walking home from school by herself, later than the others because she had stayed to talk to Miss Lona about catching up with lessons she had missed during the past two weeks while her father kept his children out of school to pick cotton. The road that led east from the Greenfields crossroads ran for about a quarter of a mile alongside a cotton field that belonged to Mr. Goolsby, whose house was at the other edge of his land, a mile north, on another road. Isabel was vaguely aware, as she came alongside this field, that several persons were picking cotton there, scattered up and down the rows, but she had not noticed that anyone was working near the road until, just as she came even with a stunted hackberry tree in the fence row, a figure rose up in the shade of it, from behind some tall weeds that grew there.

It was the figure of a tall, slender woman, wearing a dress of some dark-colored, rough-textured material, with the broad strap of a cotton sack over her left shoulder and across her chest. She did not stand quite erect; that might have been because of the heavy burden she had been dragging down the row, but she gave the impression of never rising to her full height. She untied her split bonnet and removed it, then drew her fingers across her forehead, pushing back her dull hair (the color known as dishwater blonde) that had escaped from the bun at the back of her head.

"Hello," she said to Isabel. Her voice was high-pitched and weak; the last syllable she spoke bent in the middle like a tallow candle in the sun and drooped uncertainly.

"Hello," answered Isabel firmly.

The woman moved closer to the fence. "I just wonder," she said, "if you might be Harvey Doane's girl."

"That's my father," Isabel said. She walked close to the fence too; her skirt brushed against the weeds with a dry, dead whisper.

"Well, I just want to say," said the woman, "—maybe I oughtn't to, but I just want to say—you don't know how lucky you are to have him for a daddy."

Good Lord, thought Isabel. It's *her*. She might not have heard all the talk, but she had heard enough to guess that this was Alma Greeping. She did not answer, but stood looking at the woman who now leaned closer and peered nearsightedly into Isabel's face. Seeing her at that range, Isabel was surprised to find she did not consider the woman old. She might have been thirty, or less, although there were lines in her face, and her mouth seemed to express all the weariness of her body.

"You're just lucky he lets you go to school," the woman went on. "My daddy took me out of school when I was ten years old, and made me go to work."

Isabel had not considered herself lucky when she had to stay out of school and pick cotton for two weeks, but this practice was fairly common at Greenfields. Teachers understood and helped pupils catch up with what they missed, if they were willing to work. She supposed things could be worse.

"Yes, ma'am," she said. Then furious with herself for having said "ma'am" to such a person, she turned away and walked briskly on down the road.

Alma Greeping! Isabel had never seen her again and, in spite of having studied her so closely, wondered now if she would know her should they meet. Though she could recall certain characteristics of her face or body, it was hard to visualize her now because as a whole person she had really looked like nothing. Isabel had thought of her as a wicked woman, but she did not look wicked. Neither did she look as though she would be good or kind.

That was the nearest Isabel could come to a summing-up of her: she looked like nothing.

It was hard to see why a man would ride three miles on horseback to visit such a woman, and impossible to imagine him taking an expensive journey on a train. During the next day or so, however, the apparition in the cotton patch kept returning, until Isabel began to wonder if there might have been something in the woman she herself could not see—something that would call a man to her and even (Isabel conjectured in her diary) some mysterious magnet that would keep him there.

But Isabel did not believe Alma Greeping or any other woman would keep her father very long. Property, position, and power meant too much to him; and while he had no great amount of any one of those, what he had was all in Greenfields. She couldn't guess how far he had gone or how much money he had with him, but somehow she felt he would return by the end of the week. Saturday was the day fixed in her mind. He would be back in time for Sunday school on Sunday, because he had a position there. He was on the board that governed the union Sunday school and had been responsible for securing a minister for one of the regular preaching days. He always sat in the same place, among a small group of men that constituted what Greenfields called the amen corner.

He would surely be there. Ray agreed with Isabel about that. They looked for him on Saturday.

Isabel made a butter roll for dinner, and flavored it with nutmeg. "Yes," said Lizzie, when Isabel consulted her about it, "let's fix something extra for the kids one more time."

So she knew her mother, too, thought this would be their last day.

Ray had to work all day because he was determined to get the planting done. The younger boys finished their fence job before dinner, and Ray said he didn't aim to hunt up any more work for them, they could do as they pleased for the rest of the day.

What they pleased to do was, it seemed, just what would have pleased their father if he had been there, and this choice might seem strange, as Isabel observed to Ray, but wasn't really. Target practice was one of the few amusements approved by Harvey Doane for his sons' idle times, and consequently about the only thing they could think of to do. Anyway, they liked it. The Doane boys were all good shots, down to nine-year-old Leonard. Harvey had given them all .22 rifles and taught them to shoot—all except

Burnie. He wouldn't fool with Burnie, who couldn't even hold up a gun. But Ray did. He showed Burnie how he could rest the rifle barrel on some stationary object and take aim. Burnie never tried to join the boys when they went hunting, but he could hit a target as well as any of them. Ray had given him permission to take his gun anytime he wanted to practice; then Leonard and Travis agreed that he could take theirs, too, whenever they weren't using them.

Lizzie, Sophie, and Isabel spent most of the afternoon cleaning house. Harvey could be highly critical of a dirty house if it suited him to be.

Probably none of them forgot for very long to think about the hours they had left before five o'clock. Before that time they had gathered together, on the shady front porch, to listen for the whistle of the train. Ray had finished early. He had barely taken time to eat his dinner before hurrying back to the field so he could get through. He lay stretched along the porch floor still sweaty and caked with dirt; he would go to the kitchen presently, when they had learned what they were waiting to know, and take his bath in the big washtub.

The railroad came up out of the breaks about a mile south of the Doanes' house. They could not see it because it ran through deep cuts, but they could hear the roar of a train on the track if the wind was right, and always heard the locomotive whistle for the Greenfields crossing.

Today the train was so nearly on time that they heard the distant-sounding roar as the kitchen clock began striking five. They waited in utter silence. The whistle blew two longs, a short, and another long blast.

"That's just for the crossing," Leonard said, showing off his knowledge of the signals. Really, all the children knew them, and most of the adults too. The railroad was just new enough at Greenfields to make such knowledge desirable and elite.

"It's not slowing down," said Sophie.

"You can't be sure," said Travis. "Listen for the signal." If the train was going to stop at the station, the engineer would blow one short blast. It didn't stop unless it had a passenger for Greenfields, or someone was flagging it down.

What they heard was one long, moaning wail, as it rushed past the Greenfields station.

"Well," said Ray finally, "I guess that's it."

For the children Ray's pronouncement was like an official ruling intended to set off a minor celebration.

"Hurray!" shouted Burnie. "Another of day of freedom!"

Leonard jumped up and—crying "Freedom, freedom!"—began
to run around the house, with Rouser, barking wildly, tearing after
him.

Isabel and Lizzie sighed and looked at each other.

"Mama, we can all get ready in the morning and go to Sunday
school," Isabel said.

But Lizzie frowned nervously, and looked away. "Oh, I don't
know about that, Sister," she said. "Your papa—" Her voice
drooped, or was muffled in snuff juice. It really didn't matter what
she said.

CHAPTER FIVE

At the Waters house the next morning, there was no question of
who would go to Sunday school, because (for one reason or another) everyone always willingly did. Jack, the older of the
brothers home from college, was amusing himself and mildly upsetting his sister Joanna by examining these reasons as he sat on a
stool in the kitchen and watched her wash the breakfast dishes. She
suspected he was teasing her, and was trying not to mind what he
said. Her mother had never scolded him for teasing but rather had
taught Joanna how to smile and see the fun, or pretend to. So they
had rarely quarreled, but for the most part tacitly congratulated
each other on sharing what they considered a somewhat superior
sense of humor.

But at college this year, Jack had encountered some unsettling
new ways of thinking—not, apparently, in his classes, but in infor-
mal sessions with older students and professors. On earlier visits,
when he hinted at these different ideas, Joanna hadn't supposed he
took them very seriously; but now she suddenly wondered whether
his humorous attempts to deflate pomposity or expose hypocrisy
always had been more serious than his bantering manner
suggested. He had in early adolescence developed a way of tearing

apart commonly accepted convictions, much as the younger brother, Winnie, had pulled apart bugs and butterflies. No one thought of accusing either boy of cruelty. In Winnie's case, people soon realized he was satisfying a scientific curiosity and, as he was invariably at the head of his class in school, predicted he would be a big doctor or professor someday. No one had ever expected anything to come of Jack's wild ideas; but now, this morning, Joanna felt somewhat uneasily that in spite of the comic mask he wore he might mean what he said.

He had always laughingly insisted he knew he was descended from a monkey because he liked bananas so well. Now he told Joanna there was more to Darwin than most people realized. He had once (after discovering Ingersoll when he went to hear a debate at the county seat) announced that he would rather be an Ingersoll agnostic than a Campbellite; now he told Joanna about a professor that said, "Ingersoll's dead but Huxley lives." She had no idea what he meant.

This morning he had said, "Seriously, Jo, there can't anybody have a rational belief in God."

"Then why is practically everybody in the community getting ready to go to Sunday school this morning?"

It was then he began to explain what he offered as the reasons in his own family. "Papa wants to keep his customers. Mama wants to get the latest gossip from the other women."

"Now, Jack, you know that's not true. They helped organize the Sunday school. Papa works harder than anybody to make sure there's a preacher every preaching Sunday, and puts more than most in the pot for his pay."

"And you—you know why you go. You like to play the organ for the singing."

"Jack, I know you're just teasing. But you—why do you go? Why go this morning, after all this talking you've been doing?"

"Well, for one thing, I want to see Mary Varton. And for another, I want to see if Isaiah Birdsong can explain to the class why there's two contradictory orders of creation given in Genesis."

"I wish you wouldn't."

"Oh well, I may forget that when I see Mary."

Joanna laughed, relieved. Jack really hadn't changed, she saw, or hoped she saw.

"And then the Doanes," Jack went on. "Our old friends the Doanes. Now why do you reckon they go?"

"Oh, let's don't talk about this anymore. And let's don't talk about the Doanes."

"Surely after all these years you haven't quarreled with Isabel —or Ray?"

"I never would, with either one, and you know it."

"Does Mama really think Mrs. Doane might come to Sunday school and eat dinner with us today?"

"Well, I guess she might. She sent her a special invitation by Ray."

"Of course she won't."

"Well, you know so much—why do the rest of them always come to Sunday school, and why won't she, today?"

"Ray comes to see you. Isabel—well, she's deep, she's different, she may be really religious, for all I know. But the other kids come for the same reason other Greenfields kids come—it's a place for them all to get together."

"And Mr. Doane seems to want them to go, and even goes with them. Now why is that?"

"Aw shoot, Jo, you know. He likes to be seen at preaching, with his children all around him—like some kind of a Bible patriarch or something."

"You mean—because he cares what people think of him?"

"Sure he cares. More than anything."

"Then how can he be so mean?"

"Well, I don't know. But I've thought about it. I reckon he just plain can't help being mean to his family—especially his wife and the girls, but mean to anybody that he's got control of. There's a name for that—at least I think this is what it is. Sadism. I read about it in a book at college, and there's a lot more to it than I could tell a woman. But I reckon it's something he can't help, kind of like a disease. And he don't want other people to know about it —he wants everybody in the community to like him. It's just a separate thing—how he is about his family, and how he is about other folks."

"What are you younguns fussing about now?" said their mother, coming in with an armload of flowers she had cut for Sunday school. "Joanna, if you're through at the sink, I'll just put these in it till I find me a jar."

"Yes, ma'am, I'm through at the sink," Joanna said. "I'm just putting up the last of the dishes. And what we've been fussing about was Harvey Doane."

"What about Mr. Doane?" said Martha sharply, thrusting the poppies and larkspur into the sink.

"Jack says he can't keep from being mean."

"Oh, I expect he could if he wanted to," said Martha, "but the question is, whether he could want to."

"You just about hit it there, Mama," Jack said.

"But still, in his own way he's a good man, you know. Your papa says he's a asset to the community."

"Then why," asked Joanna, "won't he take Mrs. Doane to church and Sunday school? Jack says he likes to be seen at church with his children around him—but what about his wife?"

"Oh well, you know she hasn't been feeling very good for a long time now," said Martha.

"Yes, I guess that's the best way to explain it," Jack said.

"You better go get yourself ready," his mother said.

When he was gone, she said, "There ain't no use in talking about all that, you know."

"No," Joanna said. She and her mother had done a lot of talking about Harvey Doane before the engagement between Ray and Joanna was announced. It never got them anywhere, except agreement that it was a good thing the couple planned never to live at Greenfields. Joanna suspected her father wouldn't have consented to the marriage under any other terms. And yet it was true what her mother said: out in the community, among the other men, Mr. Doane made a good appearance and might even be considered outstanding.

What a contrast he made to Mrs. Doane, who looked pitiful anywhere. "You don't really think she'll come today, do you, Mama?" she asked.

"No," said her mother. "I sent her word by Ray because I wanted her to know she was welcome, but she won't come to Sunday school. He's kept her down too long."

If Lizzie Doane came to Sunday school now, her shrunken body lost in her ten-year-old Sunday dress and her sad little knot of a face (probably bruised) staring anxiously around her, she would appear as a stranger. No one would know what to say to her. Joanna pictured to herself how that would be, and though she did feel ashamed of herself, knew she hoped her future mother-in-law would stay at home.

The Waters family always walked to Sunday school, which was held in the schoolhouse a little to the north of the store on the main road. They took a diagonal path leading across an area that served as common pastureland for the residents of the village. It was a pleasant walk this Sunday. The weather had improved since the wedding day: it was warmer, less windy, a little more humid, so that the air came caressingly against their faces and the sky (softened by a few feathery clouds) looked a true baby blue. There were blades of green among the browning grass, and a sprinkling of small white daisies. The world looked lovely to Joanna, and she thought the Waters family looked nice, too, as they walked in it.

She liked the way she looked, herself—dressed in pink and carrying a big jar of predominantly pink poppies and larkspur. Her brothers and her father all wore their serge Sunday suits and bow ties—which were handsome but somehow made the younger boy, Winnie, look the least bit sissy. Or maybe it was only his name that made everyone feel there was something slightly girlish about Winnie Waters. Couldn't her parents have known, Joanna had often wondered, what would happen when they named him Winfield Scott?

Jack was handsomer, that was sure, with his dark hair and eyes, his finely modeled features, with straight brows jutting out just enough that they might have been called brooding had it not been for the twinkle in his eyes. He resembled their mother, although she had grown so complacently plump that it was hard to imagine she might have been beautiful in her girlhood. Winnie looked like his father, even to the round spectacles slipping down his nose. No doubt he would have a neatly clipped mustache someday.

The Doanes were approaching the schoolhouse, coming along from the crossroads, at the same time as the Waterses were arriving from the opposite direction. There were only four of the Doanes. Lizzie had remained adamant, offering no excuses, only occasionally murmuring something that began, "Your papa . . ." Both Sophie and Travis had simply said they didn't want to go to Sunday school, and Isabel had not argued with them, except to remind them they would miss a good dinner. Mrs. Waters had sent an invitation for them all to come to her house after Sunday school. It was disappointing not to have all the family together, as in old times when they used to go home with the Waterses; but still, no matter what she let herself hope for, Isabel knew very well that those old times were gone. She felt no one could blame her brother and sister for wanting to keep to themselves. Sometimes she was tempted that way herself, knowing the questions that must always be asked and the speculations indulged in. It would have been easy for her today to say she had better stay home with her mama; but at the same time she did look forward to this gathering of friends, and she remembered that Mrs. Waters had urged her not to let the family withdraw from community life. "At least you can set an example for the younger children," Mrs. Waters had said.

In any case, since Lizzie insisted on staying at home today, it seemed as well that someone would stay with her. Travis promised Isabel he and Sophie would see that the three of them there had something to eat for dinner. Sophie had already run off to the creek when the group left the house, but Isabel guessed she'd come back when she got hungry.

Ray had meant to hitch up the wagon if his mother was willing to go with them, but when it turned out only the four of them were going he said they had just as well walk. That meant, of course, that Burnie would ride Sancho, and so they made pretty much the same picture arriving as the Doane kids did getting there every day during the school term. Only Ray and Isabel, walking ahead, no longer looked like schoolchildren; they were man and woman now, and from a little distance might have been taken as the father and mother of the stately little boy leading the big dun horse and the strange child with the large handsome head and skinny crippled body who sat up high in the saddle. Isabel knew how they looked. She thought there was something ancient, even biblical, in the scene.

But it was commonplace at Greenfields. She knew no one there would take a second look at them. They looked as ordinary as the Waterses, whom they now hurried up to meet. Ray helped Burnie down and hitched Sancho to a fence post.

"Oh," said Mrs. Waters, "I sure did hope your mama could come today."

Isabel said, "We tried to persuade her but she just didn't think she could come. Sophie and Travis decided to stay with her."

"But the rest of you are coming home with us?"

"Oh yes, ma'am."

The two family groups stood talking together a few minutes, until the young ones began scattering to find their friends and Joanna said, "I'd better go in now."

Ray walked her to the door and said, "You don't want me to come in with you, do you?"

She shook her head. She knew he'd rather stay outside. In good weather, almost everyone stayed on the schoolground visiting till time for Sunday school to start.

Rows of desks bolted to the floor and a smell of chalk and something else nameless and damp and schoolroomy made it hard to think of yourself as being in a church here. But there was the pulpit, already moved onto the stage, where the Sunday school superintendent stood with his big family Bible open before him, finding the text he would read in his opening remarks.

"Good morning, Miss Joanna," he said.

(There were also three old ladies, sitting at the back of the room, who always came in early to hear Joanna play the organ. They didn't say anything.)

Isaiah was a plain dirt farmer all week, and a Sunday school superintendent every Sunday; but on the Sundays when there wasn't any church service, he became, at least in his own view, a preacher. There was no church organized at Greenfields: this was a union Sunday school, and the men of the community had arranged with churches in other communities—who couldn't afford the luxury of a preacher every Sunday—to let their preachers come to Greenfields once a month. On preacherless Sundays, Isaiah came as close as he dared to filling the pulpit.

"Howdy, Mr. Birdsong," Joanna said. "Mama sent these flowers."

"The Lord bless her," Isaiah said mellifluously.

"I'll find another jar and separate these, and get some water for them," Joanna said.

"I'll open the organ box for you," said Isaiah.

Some of the men had built a box to lock the organ into, during the week, to keep the kids from tearing it up; and although school was out for the summer, the precaution was still taken, with the assumption that some tramp might come up from the railroad and break in.

Joanna took a fruit jar from a shelf in a back corner and filled it from the water bucket that stood on a bench nearby. Superintendent Birdsong, having opened the organ box, turned to her to take the jar from her hands.

"Thank you, Miss Joanna," he said, smiling. (He had such large, square teeth.)

"Thank you, Mr. Birdsong, for opening the box." She smiled broadly, too, because what she honestly wanted to do was burst into laughter both at herself and him. She felt as if they were part of a scene in a comic play she once had a part in, on this same stage.

At her smile he turned quite red, and she thought, Oh my, he thinks I'm really smiling at him. She turned quickly away and sitting down on the round stool (already adjusted to her height) began to pump the organ. She always liked to be playing by the time people started coming in, choosing songs like "Jesus, Lover of My Soul" and "Nearer My God to Thee." At the end of the service she played "God Be with You till We Meet Again."

Now as she played she couldn't help thinking of what Jack said about why she went to Sunday school. It made her a little mad at him. Of course she liked to play the organ, and was pleased when people said they enjoyed her music (as they often did, especially old women). But this wasn't the reason she was there. She went because going to preaching and Sunday school on Sunday morning was the thing to do. And there were reasons why it was—good reasons. Jack was just up to his old tricks, really; she determined not to think about his questions anymore.

After the people came in, Mr. Birdsong made some opening remarks and then prayed. He might well have asked some pillar of the community to lead the congregation in prayer, the way the preachers always did, but no one was ever surprised when the superintendent undertook the exercise himself. And many felt deeply gratified. Joanna had often heard some middle-aged or elderly woman declare, sighing with mournful passion, that Isaiah Birdsong prayed the prettiest prayer she had ever heard in her life.

Mr. Birdsong knew he did. Sunday school, and in particular the beautiful prayers he prayed, might have been what he lived through the week for. Without this one day, this one chance, he would have been nothing but a ridiculous, Ichabod Cranish sort of figure, nervous among the girls, and not quite certain he was the equal of other men. So Joanna mused, as he prayed for God to bless the service on this wonderful sunny day—to fill all their minds and hearts with knowledge of His works and glory in His grace—to bless the beautiful music rendered in His name—and the beautiful floral offering given by Mrs. Martha Waters—to sustain those who were kept at home this glorious Lord's Day, through sickness or other misfortune.

Aw shoot, Joanna said to herself in the middle of the prayer. Jack was right about Mr. Birdsong too. But God must be in it somewhere—God was good, and made up to Isaiah Birdsong for the absurdity of his daily life by giving him Sunday school. She hoped Jack wouldn't try to spoil it for him by talking about contradictions in the Scriptures.

Before the various classes went to their separate parts of the schoolroom, Mr. Birdsong read a biblical text and commented on it, offering the congregation his substitute for a sermon. Then some hymns were sung, and the classes formed.

Joanna saw that Mary Varton had not come today, and she whispered a quick question to Mary's sister Emma, as the members of the young folks' class moved toward the row of benches set up on the stage behind the pulpit. "She's got cramps," Emma whispered back to her.

Joanna made up her mind then about what she would do, and she said in a low voice to Isabel, "Jack's fixing to guy Mr. Birdsong today, and I aim to stop him. Talk all you can."

The lesson, presented through an essay in the Sunday school book, took as its text the parable of the house built on rock. The author of the lesson, which was intended for young men and women who were (as the lesson said) just stepping over the threshold into the house of adulthood, somehow at the same time seemed to believe they were still constructing the foundation of this house. The stones of which this foundation was built (or perhaps the stones upon which it was built, as in the parable—it was difficult to tell about this distinction too) had been given names of various Christian virtues, and each one was susceptible of being discussed at great length by an enthusiastic class.

They had gone about halfway through the list, with Joanna subtly guiding the discussion, when Mr. Birdsong looked at his watch and announced that fifteen minutes remained of the period allotted for their lesson. The next stone to be turned was labeled "Devotion to Truth."

Several members of the class were able to give examples proving that it pays to tell the truth. Most admitted they had stretched the truth once or twice in their lives, but all declared they had repented.

Then Jack, who had not said a word throughout the discussion, sat up a little straighter, cast a quick glance at Joanna, and raised his hand.

Mr. Birdsong looked at Jack and nodded apprehensively.

"Well, let's put a question to the girls," Jack said. "What if you was married, or fixing to be, and some kind of a bandit, some outlaw, was trying to kill your man? What if he come looking for your man, and he asked you a question, and you knew he would believe you when you answered? What if your man was in a room, with a closed door, and the outlaw said to you, 'Is he in there?' And you knew if you said no he would go on by; but if you said yes—if you told the truth—he would go in and shoot the man you loved? Would you say yes or no?"

"Oh, Jack, that's a trick question," cried Joanna. "Nothing like that could ever happen in real life, and if it did the outlaw wouldn't believe the woman anyway."

"Well, say your husband is the outlaw, but you love him and he's the father of your child. Here comes the posse, and you know they'll hang him if they find him. Would you lie?"

"Nobody would answer such questions as you're asking. They don't mean a thing," Joanna said.

But most of the girls, it seemed, did want to answer. They all began talking at once, some passionately saying they would never tell a lie for any man, others vowing they would save the man they loved at any cost.

Mr. Birdsong stood helplessly before them saying, "Girls, girls," and clasping one hand in the other.

Then Jack said, "Let's let Mr. Birdsong say what he thinks the woman should do," and they quietened down a little. "Tell us, Mr. Birdsong," he said, "would it be a sin to tell a lie?"

Joanna looked hopelessly at the teacher. She felt she had failed him, though why she owed him anything she could not have said. She caught his eye, and he blushed and looked away from her. Suddenly she thought what she could do. She was the only girl in the class that wore a wristwatch (her father had bought it at a wholesale price, for her sixteenth birthday), and ordinarily she didn't like to make a show of it. But now she lifted her wrist, looked at the watch with astonishment, and cried, "Oh, Mr. Birdsong, isn't it time to dismiss us and gather the classes together?"

He drew his watch out of his pocket again and looked at it, puzzled. Some of the young men and boys in the class began to reach for pocket watches, but Joanna did not wait for them to compare the time.

"Oh, I'm sure mine is right, because I set it just before I left home," she said.

Mr. Birdsong turned his large, watery blue eyes upon her. There was in them a faint glow of hope.

"I do believe you're right," he said. "I remember now that the clock struck just as I was leaving home, and I noticed then I was slow." He drew himself up tall and looked sternly over his pupils. "You are dismissed," he said, and turning to the pulpit, called the classes to come together and report their attendance and collections for that day.

On the way home, Jack whistled like a mockingbird, an old way he had of poking fun at Isaiah Birdsong or teasing Joanna about him.

"Oh hush, Jack," Joanna said. "I'd think you've had enough fun at poor Mr. Birdsong's expense for one day."

"Well," Jack said, "at least you provided a practical example of how a woman could rescue a man by telling a little old sinless lie— if you'd do that for old Ichabod, no telling what you would do for Ray."

Joanna reached out to Ray, who was walking close beside her, and took his hand. "No," she said rather crossly, "there's no telling."

They were in a group of about a dozen children and "young folks," all walking across the flowery pasture, with Burnie on blind Sancho in the midst of them, rising above the others like a king. Winnie had in fact long ago devised this name for him, which was often used when a group such as this one today set out together. "Here," said Emma Varton merrily, "—here's flowers for Your Majesty."

Mrs. Waters, who had really entertained some hope that Mrs. Doane would come today, had out of consideration for her invited no one outside the Doane family before this morning; but when she saw that her old friend had disappointed her, she told her children to ask anyone they pleased home with them. Mr. and Mrs. Waters had gone on ahead, because Mrs. Waters was anxious to get dinner started.

By the time the young people arrived, she was ready to put

them all to work—the girls in the kitchen and dining room, the boys on the back porch freezing ice cream. Mrs. Waters herself remained constantly at the cookstove frying chicken in a big iron skillet. She fried half a dozen chickens before she was finished, and no one was allowed to touch that job but her, because no one at Greenfields could approach her when it came to frying chicken.

After dinner, the boys waited for the girls to get the dishes washed, and Mrs. Waters said to them, "Now what are y'all fixing to do this evening?"

The answer, after considerable discussion, turned out to be, "Go Kodaking."

"Remember you boys have got to catch the train back to Canyon," Mrs. Waters said to Jack and Winnie.

Jack said he guessed they would go Kodaking down the railroad as usual, and so they could take their suitcase and leave it at the depot, in case they didn't have time to come back by the house. Winnie said he really needed to go on this outing, because he had promised to catch some bugs to take back for biology lab.

"I kind of think I ought to go on home," Isabel said.

"They'll be all right at home, Sis," Ray said. "Let's all stay, and we'll be here to meet the train, because I can't help looking for Papa to come in today."

"I'm the one that ought to go home," said Burnie.

They all knew he meant his papa's homecoming might be happier if Burnie and the blind horse were not there waiting for him at the station.

"I don't want to go home," Leonard said.

"Oh, you can stay," Burnie said. "Me and Sancho can get along just fine."

It was true, they could. Although Leonard always led the horse when they went to school or church, out of established custom and his own pride in his position, Burnie had long ago taken to riding alone around the Doane place. Sancho had learned to respond so well to the slightest pressure from Burnie that Isabel sometimes felt the boy and horse could read each other's minds. But Burnie wouldn't be able to open a tight-stretched wire gate, something he would have to do at either entrance to the Doane place.

No one mentioned that disability though. Isabel said, "Oh, Burnie, let's stay. You know you always like to ride down the railroad."

In the end the Doanes all stayed, and, as on many another sunny Sunday afternoon, the Greenfields young folks went Kodaking. Most of them had snapshot cameras of some sort (though the Doanes did not), and no matter what company had made them, they were all referred to as Kodaks. Thus Kodaking—long, companionable strolls, and afterwards happy hours of pasting photographs in albums. (Joanna always carefully wrote down names and dates in her album, making a record for her descendants as revealing in its way as Isabel's diaries—but of course she never thought of that in those days.)

They might go Kodaking anywhere, but the favorite way to go was down the railroad, to a high bridge over a canyon that, like other watercourses in the area, was usually dry, but was part of what they called Buffalo Creek. The young people had been drawn to the railroad since the first news came to Greenfields of where it would be built. Boys the age of Ray and Jack half believed they had built it. Now it was the focal point of their landscape; at Greenfields it was just about the only place to go.

Two of the young men had to go home and get their cameras; they lived close by and were able to join the group by the time they started through the cuts where the track left the edge of the level land. Winnie, with Emma Varton staying close but not helping very much, was at work with his butterfly net. Leonard would lead Sancho awhile and then wander away to try to catch bugs. Burnie seemed quietly happy, going slowly along near the track and sometimes stopping a little while, sitting quite still. He loved the railroad and was fascinated by locomotives; but Sancho was terrified of trains and inclined to bolt if he was brought too close to one.

Parents, who were very watchful in those days even of their grown sons and daughters, felt it was safe to allow such far wandering in bunches, though it would have been forbidden to any couple alone. Mrs. Waters always said it was a good thing if there were some young children along too; they made the best chaperones, because they didn't know enough to keep their mouths shut about what they saw.

Ray and Joanna walked at the head of the procession, with Jack and Isabel following, not too close. Jack, who was known to be flying at Mary Varton, as they called it (but not very hard), would have walked with her if she had been there, but as it was,

Isabel (with no resentment at being second choice) was happy to walk beside him.

"Hey!" Jack called to the couple ahead of them. "Hey, Ray! Y'all look back." They turned around, and Jack snapped a picture of them standing on a crosstie, with the rails drawing together in the distance. A little later Ray (with Joanna's camera) took a shot of Jack and Isabel sitting on a stack of crossties.

They never took many pictures, though, until they reached their destination. On the way the couples mostly let each other alone. It was a time for private talk.

Ray and Joanna spoke at first about the other couples, conjecturing about their futures. They expressed an old wish, that Jack and Isabel would learn to care for each other in the way they themselves knew so well, but accepted the likelihood they never would.

"He was looking for Mary Varton today," said Joanna. "I believe if she had been there he wouldn't have started asking his smart-aleck questions."

"It was something to think about though, what he said."

"I guess so. But he only wanted to get poor old Mr. Birdsong mixed up and embarrass him."

"And as Jack said, you rescued him. What time was it really by your watch?"

"Oh, I told a story all right."

"And would you do the same for me?"

"Oh, Ray," said Joanna, rather tickled by that. "I honestly think you're jealous—of Isaiah Birdsong."

"Well, would you?"

"I don't ever have to worry about you making a fool of yourself."

"But for any kind of reason. To help me in some way—if something happened, I don't know what, just anything. Would you lie for me?"

"I don't like that kind of talk," said Joanna. If he hadn't used the word "lie," she thought she might have told him yes. It was a very strong word, like a curse word. "I never lie," she said.

He began to talk about something else.

Meanwhile, Jack and Isabel were also talking about the Sunday school lesson.

"You didn't say anything when all the rest of the girls were telling what they would and wouldn't do," Jack said. "Did you think I posed the question just to be silly?"

Isabel looked at him keenly. Sometimes she imagined she was the only one in all Greenfields that knew what lay behind Jack's twinkling eyes. "I didn't say because I didn't know," she said. "I understood that you wanted to make people think."

"Well, even if that was it—do you think you would lie for a man?"

"I might. I don't know." She was quietly thoughtful; had they been counting crossties, they might have counted ten while neither spoke. "I don't think," she said at last, "that devotion to truth means exactly that."

"You don't?" He looked at her eagerly. "What does it mean then?"

"I haven't thought it out, I don't know. Maybe it means the truth of God. But that's kind of faraway and scary. I think it's something people can get at, I think it's maybe just recognizing the truth you know—not hiding it from yourself, not pretending."

"Not being a hypocrite."

"Yes, that." She looked down again, frowning in the shadow of her Sunday bonnet's brim. "Or maybe not. I'm not so sure I mean *deliberately* pretending."

Jack raised his eyebrows but made no response, as Leonard shouted just then that he heard a train coming. He had been laying an ear to the track all along, to be the first with the news when it came.

"It's a long ways off," Jack said.

"Yes, but I'd better go help the boys decide what to do," said Isabel. "Burnie always gets a little worried about how Sancho might act when he knows a train's coming."

Ray turned back and called, "Tell Leonard to lead Sancho off as far as that bunch of chaparral yonder. And tell Pal to get off the horse before the train comes too close."

Isabel and Jack walked back to where the boys were, but they had heard Ray, or else Burnie knew anyway what to do. Isabel suspected he did, but both she and Ray had always tried to protect Burnie against all the different dangers that they felt for him.

When Jack and Isabel had resumed their walk together—at the tail end of the party now; even the bug catchers had passed them—Jack said, "I believe you forget sometimes you're not the mother of them kids."

Isabel shook her head. "No," she said. "It's not a mother I feel like. Or at least I don't suppose it is. I don't think I know much about ordinary families."

"That was your family you'as talking about, wasn't it, when you said that about pretending a while ago," Jack said.

"Maybe so. I guess we've tried to believe we're like everybody else. Or that Papa is."

"I didn't mean you-all so much," Jack said. "I meant the whole community. There don't nobody want to see how things really are for you."

"It may be best," Isabel said. "I don't think I can talk about it myself."

"No," said Jack, "I know you can't. But is there anything anybody could do, if they'd admit the truth?"

She shook her head. "I don't think so."

"Bel," he said then. (He was the only one who had ever called her Bel.) "Bel, if there ever is, if you ever think of any way I could help, will you tell me?"

She nodded. She believed she really would.

They didn't say much else to each other then; it wasn't long before a freight train came in view. Everyone left the track then, and came together on a small knoll where Burnie had dismounted and stood half embracing his horse, talking to him gently. As the train passed, they waved to the engineer and he waved back. Then Ray helped Burnie back onto the horse, and they all went on together to the bridge. They descended the railroad bank into the dry canyon bottom, and then most of the party climbed up onto the beams of the trestle to pose for the pictures. (Here are Isabel and Joanna, wearing light dresses and dark stockings, their bonnets in their hands, having climbed about three or four feet above the ground upon a slanting timber. Here are Ray and Joanna, standing as close as they dare, knowing whose eyes will be studying that picture; here's Burnie on Sancho, with the horse's scarred eye turned away from the camera; here's Jack, with his shirt sleeves rolled up and his cap on the back of his head; here are Leonard and Winnie, with the butterfly net; and all the other boys and girls, whose names may or may not be remembered, who may or may not have been happy that day, who may have been pretending, as Jack thought, or may not as yet have seen any need to deceive themselves about happiness.)

The walk back always seemed faster than the walk to the

bridge. The fun was over, the day was ending; probably, they walked faster.

When they got to the depot, Mr. and Mrs. Waters were waiting, sitting on a bench by the depot door, having driven the short distance from home in the Maxwell.

"I aimed to have a little more visit with you boys before you left," Martha said to her sons. "And we come in the car because we thought we could take Mr. Doane on home if he happened to come in."

"I'd better flag the train down though, in case he don't," said Winnie.

When the train came in, it was soon apparent that the flagging had been necessary. Winnie and Jack ran to board the train, and with little delay it moved on again. No passenger alighted.

"He didn't come!" Leonard shouted excitedly.

The others looked at each other and shook their heads, but no one offered any conjectures about Harvey Doane.

Mrs. Waters said she wished they could take the kids home, but of course they had that horse to see about. Isabel assured her they would just as soon walk, they were used to walking and had plenty of time to get home and do their night work.

There was ice cream left, Mrs. Waters said, packed down in the freezer since dinner, and she persuaded the Doanes to stop and help finish that. The sun was reddening the western sky when they started on home, and they were sorry (all in their different ways, as Isabel observed to herself) to see that day ending. They did not talk much.

Once Leonard spoke—suddenly, out of a comfortable silence. "Papa might not ever come home no more," he announced.

"I pray every night that he won't," Burnie said, quite loudly, from his height.

Ray and Isabel looked at one another. Isabel realized some reprimand ought to be offered, and supposed Ray felt the same way. But neither spoke. Isabel did not quite know whether she had prayed that same prayer, but she was afraid she had. Ray might have too.

They turned east by the gnarled mesquite—they were on their road home, a road dyed red-gold by the sun's rays, a pleasant road, that ran between soft-colored furrowed fields with fencerows grown up in tall weeds that sheltered invisible, murmuring birds. The little group moved slowly, by tacit consent. It seemed to Isabel that it was just this sense of moving along the road home that they wanted. Home would not be what this golden road promised. But they were happy with the promise, going home.

Gradually, invading their soft sporadic talk and the bird calls, came a disturbing sound somewhere on the road behind them. It was not altogether an unfamiliar sound, but certainly an uncommon one. Only a handful of men in the community of Greenfields owned automobiles, and none of them lived in the direction of the Doane place.

It might have been the Waterses coming, but it wasn't. "It's not the Maxwell," Ray said, turning to look back.

They all looked. On the road that led north from Greenfields, clearly slowing to make the turn east toward the Doanes', silhouetted against the pale orange sky, was the shape of an open-topped car with two passengers in it.

"Who can it be?" said Leonard.

"Shhh!" said Isabel, as though she feared the occupants of the car would hear his words above the chig-a-chig of the engine. That seemed a strange thing to fear, and yet they all stood now silent, as though stricken by some dread. For they all knew almost at once who the driver was, in that dark hat high-crowned against the sky.

The car bore quickly down on them but slowed as it drew near. Their father's features became clear. They saw his passenger was a woman. She sat almost as tall as he, a narrow person, with narrow drooping shoulders, wearing a cream-colored summer coat and a length of veiling tied over her hair and partly concealing her face.

As the car came even with them, their father waved and called to them cheerily: "Don't want to stop—I'm afraid I couldn't get this son-of-a-bitch started again."

The woman turned to look at them. Her face was pale yellow in the evening sun, her eyes pale beneath the heavy, drooping lids; her mouth, though it, too, drooped, seemed at the same time to be smiling a faintly mysterious smile.

Harvey Doane drove on.

Ray looked at Isabel. "It's her, ain't it?" he said.

Isabel stood as though stunned. For a moment she felt lifted out of time, with the false sense of repetition that she had learned from some book to call *déjà vu*.

"Ain't it?" Ray said again.

And she knew the sense of repetition was not false. That same face had looked at her once before, once long ago, in almost that same place, only from the other side of the fence, at the end of a cotton row.

"It's Alma Greeping," Isabel said.

CHAPTER SIX

In the afternoons, when the dinner dishes were washed and put away, Joanna and her mother were in the habit of sitting awhile on the back porch, quilting. In warm weather Mrs. Waters nearly always had a quilt up out there, on the opposite end from the little table where they liked to eat their supper. The quilt frame hung from the ceiling, just far enough removed from the end and side screens to allow room for chairs all around it. Often, on summer afternoons, when women and girls dropped in for a visit, they would take up a needle and sit down with Joanna and Mrs. Waters to quilt awhile.

This summer they were quilting Joanna's Lone Star. She had taken more than two years piecing it—one huge eight-pointed star, made not from blocks set together, as most quilts were in Greenfields, but from nearly five hundred diamond-shaped pieces of cotton broadcloth that fit together like a puzzle to form the star. This was no ordinary quilt: it took skill to fit all those pieces together smoothly so they didn't pucker anywhere, and came out straight around the edges as a figure in a geometry book. Also, it was made not with scraps saved from sewing but with pieces of material bought especially for the purpose, in shades of yellow, orange, and gold. It was beautiful (and it still is today). Joanna thought so, and everyone said so. Some said that with the colors Joanna had picked it looked more like a sunburst than a star. And that was like Joanna: she always did like sunshine better than starlight.

Putting up the Lone Star was as near as the Waterses came to a public announcement of Joanna's engagement. The quilt was the visible, tangible symbol of a serious, well-considered promise sealed with parental and, yes, community, approval. As soon as word got around that the quilt was up, everyone who ever visited

Mrs. Waters and Joanna came to contribute their tiniest, best stitches to this cover for the bed of Ray and Joanna. And now—since Sunday—it seemed they all began to come again.

On the Wednesday after Mr. Doane came home, Joanna said to her mother as they sat down at the quilt, "Oh, I do wish we wouldn't have any company today."

"Well," said Mrs. Waters, "maybe we won't. Seems like to me everybody's done been here."

They would arrive saying they had come to the store with their husbands (or fathers) and just thought they'd run by and see Mrs. Waters and Joanna a little bit, maybe put in a stitch or two on the quilt. Then there'd be a word about Mr. Doane's new car—had they seen it?—and didn't he bring somebody home with him for a visit? It didn't seem possible that so many had seen him driving by, but everyone had talked to someone who had.

"All we know is what we've heard," Martha would say. "Tom saw the car when Mr. Doane come after his mail on Monday, but he hasn't been back since then and we haven't seen any visitor."

But they all thought Joanna would know.

"Ray comes to see her Wednesdays and Saturdays," Martha would explain. "She hasn't seen any of the family since Mr. Doane come home."

Now Joanna sighed and said, "I reckon they'll all descend on us tomorrow."

"Some will," said her mother. "But most will have another thought and realize they've been a little bit crude. There ain't nobody wants to hurt your feelings."

"Oh, I know," said Joanna. "They're just naturally curious about what's going on at the Doanes' house."

"Well, ain't you?" demanded Martha.

"Maybe. I don't know." Joanna had wondered, like everybody else, when she first heard the report of Mr. Doane's car and the passenger he brought home in it. Then she had been irritated at all the gossip, the suggestions not quite made, the conclusions not quite drawn, and she said to herself how much better she would feel when everything—no matter what—was known. Now without reason she felt more apprehensive than she had done before and wished she'd never have to know the truth.

"Mama," she said with sudden alarm.

Martha looked up from her quilting, waiting to hear.

"I dread seeing Ray tonight," she said. "I wish he wouldn't come."

"I thought you was wanting him to come Monday night," her mother said.

"I did just think he might come and tell me what was happening. But now I've thought about it—I don't know—I almost wish he wouldn't tell me anything."

"What do you think you'll hear?"

"Oh, Mama, what do you think?"

"Joanna, I haven't got any idy, not the least in the world."

"That woman?"

"There was something going on between them when she was here before, living with her husband or whatever he was. You did know that?"

"Not exactly."

"Well, there was. Something that hadn't ought to have been. I just can't imagine him bringing her into Lizzie's house after that."

"But, Mama, surely he hasn't?"

"Where do you think she is, then?" demanded Martha angrily.

Joanna knew it wasn't actually anger in her mother's voice. Or certainly not anger directed at her. But this was a tone of voice Joanna was well acquainted with: there was a challenge in it, as though whoever she was speaking to was responsible for all the immorality in the community. And there was fire in it, which burned in her righteous indignation that such a scandal could take place at Greenfields. It made Joanna feel accused, denounced; and half believing that through her association with the Doanes she really bore some blame, she began to cry and fled to her room. She knew her mother would not follow her. Let her have her cry out, was always Mama's way.

She flung herself across the bed and wept, but not very long. Someone still might come. To be caught with swollen eyes and tear-streaked face would be the same as saying to the neighbors that the worst they suspected was true. She did not know what they suspected; she really did not know for sure what Mama meant her to think. Of course Mr. Doane wouldn't—; at that, she put a mental hand before her mind's eye. She might have been able to imagine what all the women of the community were imagining if she had tried, but she refused to try.

She was a sensible girl. Everybody said Joanna was a sensible girl. She would simply have to wait and see. She wiped her eyes

and bathed her face with witch hazel. Looking at herself in the bureau mirror, she decided to comb out her hair and put it up again,
taking more pains than she had done when she dressed this morning. She liked to arrange her hair and dress especially for Ray's
visits, but she didn't always have time to. Although she had to
admit that when he first started coming to see her and she realized
he really was courting her, she was so thrilled at every visit, and
took so much time getting dressed and ready, that the boys used to
ask her if she was getting ready for a party at the Astors' or the
Vanderbilts'.

Now she didn't spend so much time getting fixed up for Ray,
because she knew he loved her and wanted to marry her for her ordinary, everyday self. She had known for sure about his feelings for
more than a year now; she had felt certain of her own for much
longer. She had known Ray nearly all her life, and it seemed now
had been planning to marry him almost as long. There would be no
awkward surprises, only natural fulfillment, when they came together as man and wife. They had experienced nothing more intimate than a gentle hug and tender kiss between them, but this
seemed as predictable and certain as her friendship with Isabel,
who (another wonderful thing about this engagement) would now
be her sister as well as her friend.

"You had better think a long time about whether he might
turn out like his daddy," her mother had said. But Joanna said of
course he wouldn't, she knew him better than that. And really, her
mother had not seemed worried either, though she did her duty by
bringing up the question.

Things might be different now. As Joanna recovered from her
crying spell, she realized it was that threat as much as her mother's
rancor that set her tears flowing. Deep down, secret almost from
herself, there had always been the awareness of a problem she
would never have to solve, the promise of escape from any need to
solve it. She knew Ray: she was absolutely certain that he had no
meanness in him, and that was not the thing. But if Ray's father
continued to treat his family worse with every passing year, might
the time not come when being a member of that family could seem
a shameful thing? Her mother would speak sometimes of persons
who had done something so bad that they "couldn't hold up their
head in the community." Could a connection with Ray's family
ever place her in such a predicament?

The question had lurked. Now, standing before the mirror

with her hair falling long and straight about her face, she let the
doubt come honestly out of hiding. If this terrible thing that people
suspected should prove to be true, there would be no avoiding it.
But the escape would still be provided. If she and Ray had not already made their plans to live their married lives away from
Greenfields, she did not know—looking herself straight in her
green-gray eyes, she could not honestly say—whether she could go
on with the engagement.

She had known this secret before, yet without letting herself
see the full meaning of it. She had dreamed of a nice house in
town, with modern conveniences, perhaps even a woman to come
and help with the housework so that she could devote herself to
teaching school. Ray would work hard and soon have his own ga-
rage, with a staff of mechanics to do the greasy work. They would
visit Greenfields, of course, but Ray's family didn't figure much in
her pictures of these visits. Except, to be sure, for Isabel—and she,
although unwilling to make plans now for ever leaving home,
might change her mind. In Joanna's dreams, she lived just down
the street and the two friends taught in the same school.

Thank God, she now said to herself in her new honesty, she
and Ray would never have to live in Greenfields. With this prayer
in her mind, she thought she could accept whatever Ray might
have to tell her tonight. She went back to her mother, who still sat
alone, quilting.

"Well, do you feel better now?" Martha asked.

"Mama, whatever it is, it won't make any difference to me and
Ray," Joanna said.

Mr. and Mrs. Waters would always sit and talk awhile when
Ray came in. Sometimes the two couples would play dominoes, but
there was no game tonight.

"How's your daddy liking his car?" Tom Waters asked Ray.

"Oh, it's just like it used to be when he'd go off somewhere and
trade horses. He's really worked up about it."

Not much more than that was said about the Doane family.
Mrs. Waters didn't even ask Ray how his mother was.

"Why don't we go sit in the porch swing?" Joanna asked. "It's
such a pretty night."

"Yes, why not?" said her mother, thus giving her permission.

The porch swing was on the back porch just outside the dining
room windows. Dusk was deepening now, but when there was

company Martha kept a lamp lit in the dining room, so the porch was never quite dark. The outlines of a couple sitting on the swing would be easily visible to anyone passing through the room, but if they talked softly they would not ordinarily expect to be overheard. Martha considered that Ray and Joanna had as much privacy there on the porch swing as any courting boy and girl could properly be allowed.

Ray never talked much. He would hold Joanna's hand as they sat in the semidarkness, knowing that Mrs. Waters could not observe that small sign of his affection and would find no fault with it if she did. Ordinarily, he seemed content to let Joanna do most of the talking. Sometimes she would exclaim, "Oh, I'm not letting you say a word," but he would answer in his low murmuring voice, "I just like to listen to you."

Tonight she did not begin to talk, except to say, "Look how pretty the moonlight is on the flowers." The moon, a few nights short of full, shone brightly, turning Martha Waters's many-colored beds of phlox, larkspur, and poppies into a garden of white. There was a light breeze, faintly moist, that wrapped them in sweet intermingled scents. It was just a May night. It could not be anything else. Joanna thought, as often she had done, that if she were taken out of the world so that she lost all sense of time, and then suddenly set down here, in this spot, she would know immediately what season it was, what month, even what part of the month. Another time, she might have talked to Ray about that notion. Perhaps she had at one time done so. But he was preoccupied tonight, rigid with a deep concern that she would have to try to understand. It would not do to chatter; he would not hear her if she did.

She waited until at last, his voice so tight it seemed close to breaking, he said, "You need to know what's happening at our house."

"Yes," she said simply.

It was a long breath of time before he spoke again. Then he said quickly, "Papa brought Alma Greeping home with him."

"I knew that, Ray," she said softly. "I think everybody knows that."

"And they're all talking, and wondering what it means."

"You know they are."

"Well, it looks like he's brought her to stay."

"Oh, Ray," she said, "your poor mama." Really, she scarcely knew what he meant. She felt instinctively that this must be a hard thing for Mrs. Doane, but could not picture what might be happening in the household.

As he did not respond at once, she began the question that precipitated itself: "But where does the woman—" She broke off, suddenly realizing the implication of what she had been about to say.

He said it for her, grimly. "Where does she sleep."

"Maybe we oughtn't to talk about it," she said.

"We have to," he said. "If you're going to marry me."

"Tell me then," she said.

"He's moved her into the dugout. He made Mama and the girls clean it up. He's moved a good chair and dresser down there, and Mama's best feather bed."

"But Ray—"

She did not know what she had been about to say. He seemed to. Although they could not see each other's faces clearly, he turned away from her as if to conceal his shame. "Most nights," he said, "he stays with her."

So she knew. Until then, she had not really understood—because she hadn't really wanted to, or because, like many girls of her generation, reared by mothers born at the full tide of the Victorian era, she was more innocent and ignorant than girls of generations both before and after hers. Full knowledge might have come at any other moment, but somehow, for her, it came just then. In an instant she seemed to learn the whole vocabulary of the older women's language of frowns, grimaces, raised eyebrows, and mysterious little smiles.

"Ray, what can you do?" she cried.

"I don't know," he said. The words came in a low moan, as of physical pain. She longed to put her arms around him, but she never forgot that someone's eyes might be upon her.

At last, he spoke again. "What I want you to do," he said, and his manner was formal and almost cold, "is tell your mama what I've told you, so she can tell your papa. They may want you to break our engagement."

"I never will," she said.

"Folks will pretty well guess the truth anyway," he said, "but I want Mr. and Mrs. Waters to know just how it is. Then we'll see what they say."

"It won't make any difference," she said.

"It may to them."

"Then not to me."

He quickly leaned toward her, and (though always aware that any movement they made might be seen) kissed her on the cheek. They didn't talk anymore, but sat a long time hand in hand before he said good-night.

Isabel sat on the side porch waiting for Ray to come home. The rest of the household, including her father and Alma Greeping, had gone to bed. This was the fourth night of the radically changed pattern of life Harvey Doane had imposed upon his family, and yet Isabel was still visited over and over again by the shock. The intrusion of Alma Greeping was like sudden death—it was an alteration no one could have prepared for. It even seemed to Isabel that night, as she sat alone in the moonlight, that the Doanes' predicament was worse than death, for there was nothing to be done and no help to be looked for. No preacher called, nor did neighbors come bearing cakes and fried chicken and asking what they could do. No neighbor would ever come to that house again. There was nothing anyone could ever do. It would have been a relief if there had been someone to bury.

As she sat on the edge of the porch thinking these death thoughts, the old dog Rouser, who had been hunting in the moonlight, came up to her whining pitifully, as if some sense of deprivation struck him too.

"Oh, Rouser," she said, "what can we ever do?" He put his head in her lap, and she hugged it against her breast. Then, for the first time since her father's return, she wept.

The screen door to the kitchen opened, with its screak like a hurt cat's cry. Isabel looked up, wiping her eyes on her hand.

"Sister." It was Burnie limping out to her. He looked ghostly in the whitish shirt he had thrown over the underwear he slept in.

"Burnie," she said. They spoke as people do who can only repeat each other's names for comfort in time of great trouble.

He sat down on the edge of the porch beside her and reached out a hand to rub Rouser's head.

"Rouser knows," he said, after a little while.

"He knows something's wrong," Isabel said.

"I couldn't sleep," Burnie said. "I heard Rouser whining, and I knew you was out here."

"I'm waiting for Ray," she said. "I want to hear how Joanna takes the news."

"She wouldn't break the engagement."

"No." Isabel wasn't sure how much Burnie could understand of the effect their father's strange action might have on the position of the family. "She wouldn't, but Ray might."

"I see," Burnie said.

"Do you?"

"Of course I do. In a way things are not so much worse for us. Maybe they're even better, in a way. Papa may not be as mean to us, you know." He paused. "I know what it all means, and we all know it. I think even Leonard knows it. At least he's like Rouser; he can tell something's wrong."

"What is it, Burnie? What is it you think we all know?" She really could not tell what he would say.

"Well, it's shame, ain't it? That's what it is—it's shame."

It was strange to hear the word that had lurked unformed in her mind's depths, coming so clear and separate that the thing itself seemed visible and containable. "Shame." It seemed to shimmer in the moonlight, hard and real, yet touched with the ghostliness Isabel had felt earlier.

"Yes," she said, "it's shame."

"Can't we do anything? Have you tried to think what?"

"I don't think there is anything, Burnie. I think we'll have to wait a little, and see."

"Wait for what?"

"I don't know. Somehow it may turn out that things are not as bad as we think."

"I don't see how they could be worse, for Mama."

"No."

"Couldn't we just all leave—slip away in the night, and take Mama?"

"You know what happens when you try to run away from Papa."

"Mama could go. Ain't there some place she could go? He wouldn't send the sheriff after Mama."

"I can't imagine where. She's got no folks anywhere."

He didn't say anything else. They both sat with their heads in their hands, looking off across the frost white pasture. The dog had gone to sleep at their feet. In the weeds at the edge of the yard, a cricket chirped.

Then a new sound reached them—a sudden, far-off cry. They stiffened, alertly listening, and the dog raised his head. Not a bird;

certainly not a fox or a coyote. There were more cries, reaching a crescendo, then fading away. Far-off. Or muffled, as though they came from underground.

"That was from the dugout," Burnie said.

"Yes," said Isabel.

She didn't say what she thought. She supposed Burnie knew what the sounds meant, but it was not a thing she would mention to him. Attitudes toward sex were somewhat franker with the Doanes than in the Waters family, perhaps because the Doane children had grown up familiar with the mating of animals and also because their father did not always exhibit a Victorian niceness about such matters. Even so, with the Doanes as with any decent family in that place and time, there were subjects not to be discussed in mixed company—a term that included brother and sister and very often husband and wife. Probably, even Harvey and Alma had nothing articulate to say to each other on their bed in the dugout.

"It's all right, ain't it?" Burnie whispered.

"Of course," said Isabel.

"She might not like it here as much as she thought she would."

"I don't know. She might not."

"We'll figure out something, won't we, Sister?"

"Sure," she said. "You go to bed."

They sat again without speaking—close together now, touching. They noticed the crickets again. An howl hooted down the creek.

"I guess I will go to bed," Burnie said at last.

When he left, the dog took his place. Isabel leaned against him. In a little while, hearing hoofbeats, they both straightened eagerly.

Rouser got up hesitantly, looking toward the barn. "All right, Rouser, you go meet him," she said. She might have gone herself, for the path was clear in the moonlight, but she stayed in the shelter of the porch. The path ran so close by the dugout.

"I thought you'd be waiting," Ray said when he came. He sat down near her on the porch edge, Rouser lying at her feet.

"I wanted to hear from Joanna," Isabel said.

"She's all right."

"I knew she would be."

"I made her promise to tell her mama."

"Yes, you would have to do that."

"She said it wouldn't make any difference what her papa and mama said."

"Of course not. She made you a promise."

He lay back along the porch edge, looking up at the high riding moon. "That's not like you, Sis," he said. "You don't believe it—it's not like you to say it."

"I've never known Joanna to break a promise."

"And you never heard of her doing anything her mama didn't approve of."

"It won't come to that," said Isabel. "Mr. and Mrs. Waters know it's not your fault. And anyway, there may be something we can do to change things."

"Name something."

"You know I can't. But still there might be. Burnie stayed out here with me awhile, talking about it. Maybe if all of us got together—sometime when Papa's gone—and talk to her."

"No, I don't think so."

Isabel didn't protest anymore; she really didn't think so either. "We heard them down there tonight," she said.

"What?" he said, and then quickly, "Oh. Oh my Lord."

"It's pretty bad," she said.

"I know that," he said.

"Burnie thought we might help Mama get away."

"I wish we could, Sis. But she wouldn't leave, you know—even if there was anyplace she could go."

"That's what I told him."

"Maybe you could talk to her."

Isabel knew he didn't mean Mama. "What would I say?"

"You said we might talk to her. What did you have in mind?"

"Nothing. I don't know. I didn't think."

"I guess you could try to find out what she really aims to do. Surely she hasn't just moved in to stay always."

"Well, it looks like it. But it may be she hasn't really thought. It's hard to see how any woman could want to do to another woman what she's doing to Mama."

"Maybe she really don't know what she's doing. Maybe she's just weak-minded. You might make her see how much better it would be if she would leave."

"I doubt if anybody could make Alma see anything. She reminds me of one of Mrs. Waters's old sayings—she's like a sick kitten next to a hot brick. She's not much more apt to move than the kitten, and hasn't got a lick more sense."

"You talk to her, though."

"All right, Ray. I will. Tomorrow, if I can."

CHAPTER SEVEN

Alma Greeping had her meals with the family, as there was no cookstove in the dugout. There was an old stove that could have been used down there, but Harvey said he didn't see any reason why Alma should have to cook and wash dishes when meals were being prepared three times a day anyhow.

Not ever accustomed to conversation at meals, the Doanes found themselves dumb in the presence of Alma Greeping. Alma herself was no chatterbox, but she evidently saw nothing inhibiting in her situation and spoke when she had anything to say.

Thursday at breakfast, she made an announcement. "Me and Mr. Doane's going to town this morning," she said. "I've got to get me some new clothes."

No one answered, or even looked up, except Isabel. She was surprised at the childish excitement in Alma's ordinarily expressionless face.

"I imagine we'll eat dinner in some nice restaurant," Alma went on. "No need to fix anything for us."

It would have been hard to thank Alma for that. None of the Doane children, except possibly Ray (who might have gone with the Waterses) had been to town for almost a year; and Isabel couldn't begin to guess when her mother had last gone. It might have been one of those annual shopping trips she used to make with Mrs. Waters, to buy the family's fall and winter clothes. All the same, this trip to town would bring a measure of relief. It was more than anyone ever expected.

Ray and Travis were assigned to work on the buggy shed that day. Harvey had moved the buggy out of the shed and around behind the barn; he might sell it some day, but there wasn't much market for buggies, and it might just sit there till it rotted and rusted. Harvey didn't seem to care much as long as he had a good place for his car. He wanted the shed roof repaired, the open front of it closed in, with wide double doors. That would be a considerable job, but Ray was a good carpenter and with Travis's help could complete it in a few days.

The younger children were being sent to cut weeds in the fencerows around the cultivated fields. Actually, Harvey never mentioned Burnie's name, but he must have known Burnie would go with the rest. Although he couldn't handle a hoe, he could pull up some weeds.

"Now I expect you women will be sweeping and mopping and all that stuff today," Harvey said to Isabel and Lizzie as he rose from the breakfast table, "so I want you to get down there in the dugout and give it a good going-over while you're at it." He had been in such a good humor since he got Alma, that the way he spoke to them seemed to suggest he really didn't want to cause any trouble and was trying to find them the easiest way to do a job that wasn't really much of a task anyway.

An hour or so later, the shiny black Ford, still with its top folded back, backed out of the buggy shed and moved slowly past the kitchen window and along the lane to the main road. Harvey had shaved and put on his serge suit. Alma wore her cream-colored silk coat, which the bright morning sunlight now revealed as frayed and badly soiled. Her straw hat had a hole in it that she had tried to cover with a broad grosgrain ribbon.

Well, I guess she needs clothes all right, thought Isabel, as she watched from the kitchen window.

Then she turned back to her mother, who had not gone to the window when she heard the car leaving, though she must have glanced out and seen it pass by. She stood in the middle of the floor staring out at nothing, a dripping dishrag dangling from her hand. Her felt house shoes had holes worn by the bunions on the sides of her feet, and her faded brown print dress was fastened in the front with safety pins.

Isabel took the rag from her mother's hand, squeezed it out in the dishpan, and dashed the pan of water outside.

"Mama, let's go out on the porch awhile," she said then, coming back in to put the dishpan up.

"Why I've got too much to do—haven't I?" said Lizzie.

"No, Mama, I don't think you've got anything to do at all,"

Isabel said. "I'll fix dinner for Sophie and the boys after while, and I don't see what else there is to bother about."

"I ought to go down yonder and clean up some," said Lizzie vaguely, looking toward the dugout.

"No, Mama, we are not going to clean up the dugout. We may not clean house at all today, if we don't want to."

She spoke to her mother as to someone who had been ill and was wanting to get up too soon.

"Well—" Lizzie said.

Isabel took up a cane-bottomed chair and carried it out to the side porch. It was sunny there and almost too warm, but when her mother sat in the chair she leaned to the sun as though she welcomed its heat.

"I ought to get my crochet," she said after a few minutes.

"Let's just don't do anything," said Isabel.

What she achingly longed to do, was trying ineptly to do, was protect her mother from this new assault, which, renewed continually, now kept her dazed, like one wandering without direction through a landscape suddenly transformed. There must be a way to restore some certainty and meaning in her mama's life—only she realized she didn't know much about what meaning it had ever had. Talking to Alma—confronting Alma, as she had promised Ray to do (and after all probably wouldn't be able to do today)— might reveal some way to help Lizzie; but it occurred to Isabel now that it would not be far wrong to say she understood her mother as little as she did Alma Greeping.

If they could talk— But it was always her mother's way to flee from any word that touched too close to her reality: to literally shuffle off in her felt shoes, or turn her head, perhaps murmuring, "I don't know," "Maybe so," or just, "Your papa . . ."

"Mama, if you want your crochet I'll get it," Isabel said. "But let's do stay out here and talk awhile."

"Well—" Mama said.

Isabel thought she meant get her crochet. She probably felt lost or incomplete, sitting down anywhere without it.

"You might get me my snuff, too, and the spit can," Lizzie said as Isabel started in the house.

These were the stays of Lizzie's life: this endless, objectiveless crochet and this good solid brown jar of snuff. Isabel brought them.

"And, Sister," Lizzie said. "If you could just cut me a toothbrush."

Isabel went back to the kitchen and got a knife.

"From the hackberry, if it's not too much trouble," Lizzie said.

Isabel followed the path that led from the scraped, bare yard to the stunted little hackberry tree and then forked, one branch leading on to the barn and other outbuildings, and a narrower, less used trail turning down the slope toward the dugout. Isabel stood a moment looking down that way—then turned back to the tree, cut off a good thick twig about four or five inches long, made some gashes in the end of it, and took it back to her mother.

Lizzie chewed the end of the twig till it was soft and bristly, then dipped it into her jar of snuff, placed it in her mouth, and settled in her chair with a long sigh.

"Does it help, Mama?" Isabel asked, sitting on the edge of the porch.

"What?"

"The snuff. Does it make you feel better?"

"Oh, I reckon so," said Lizzie uncertainly.

"Do you remember when you started dipping?"

"Why no, I don't reckon I do," said Lizzie thoughtfully.

"Well, you didn't dip snuff when I was a little girl, did you?"

Lizzie took her toothbrush out of her mouth and seemed to study it. "Mrs. Goolsby said it was a comfort. I remember that."

"I guess comfort was something you needed," Isabel said, "if anybody ever did."

The sun and the snuff now perhaps had started a flow of something resembling comfort through the woman who sat, spreading her thighs a little, smiling with a satisfaction that lent her brown freckled face a light not of the sun. At last she spat, turned to Isabel, and unexpectedly said, "You don't really know much about me, do you, Sister?"

"Don't you think you've lived a kind of secret life?" asked Isabel.

"I didn't use to, you know. I used to talk to you, but you may not remember much that I ever told you about myself, when I was a girl. It finally got to where I couldn't even think of anything to tell that you wouldn't be better off not hearing."

"Don't you think it's time I knew though? I don't believe anything you'd tell me could be worse than what I can guess."

"You want to know how it's been with me, don't you? I mean what led up at last to—this?" She gestured toward the dugout.

"Would it hurt you to tell me?"

"I don't think I can tell you, exactly. There's things I couldn't speak, you know. I guess I'd bite my tongue out first."

"Tell me about when you first knew Papa. What was he like then?"

Lizzie had begun to take another dip of snuff, but stopped, holding out her toothbrush with a sudden sort of grace, as in another time and place she might have held a cigarette. She looked at Isabel and smiled a rare smile. Her teeth were brown and broken.

"Lord, he was handsome. Of course he still is, but it's different when you're young. Sister, I don't even know what he *was* like—only I wanted him. And when he picked me up and set me on his horse I thought I'd die."

"Was that when you eloped?"

"Uh-huh. We had to run off to get married—Papa wouldn't even talk to him, or let him in the house."

"And after you married Papa—what was he like then?"

"A hard man, always a hard man. But we had good times, Sister. I want you to know we had good times."

"But then he changed."

"No—for he was always—that way."

"That way," breathed Isabel, but did not ask for an explanation. "Yes, always," her mother said, as though she hadn't heard, or had heard wrong. "You don't know a man till you're married, Sister —always remember that. He was that way from the beginning, but I think at first he tried not to be. And then it got bad. When Ray was a baby it got so bad I went home and I thought I would stay. My papa was dead by then, just Mama and Brother living at home. But when your papa come round, Brother got a gun and run him off. And then I felt like I'd done wrong. If Harvey wanted me and wanted to be a father to his son, I got to thinking that I had no right to leave him. And I loved him, you know. There always has been that."

Did she mean she loved him still? Isabel dared not ask it.

"And you went back?"

"My brother said if I went back to him he didn't ever want to see me again. And Mama took his side. I cried all day long. At last I slipped off and met him down by the river. He begged me to come back, and promised he would treat me right."

"And you went, and he didn't."

"It was all right for a while, till I knowed you was on the way. He never could stand it for me to be—get big, you know. I tried to go back home again, and Brother shut the door in my face. And Mama sick then too. They needed my help." She began to cry, silently, a way she'd had to learn. Tears slipped slowly and separately down her cheeks.

"And did she die then?"

Lizzie nodded. "I never saw her again—nor Brother either."

Isabel took a handkerchief from her apron pocket and went to wipe her mother's face. She sat down then on the porch floor, at her feet.

Presently, Lizzie went on. "I thought I couldn't go back to him. I caught a ride to town and tried to find a job. Cleaning house, or washing dishes in some little old sorry diner. I'd have done anything, but of course the shape I was in, there wouldn't nobody even talk to me."

"So it was back to Papa again."

"What else could I do? What else could I ever do?"

"But didn't things get better after you moved out here?"

"A lot better. He sunk so low. He was carrying on with another woman, and got into it with her folks. Things was bad every way you can think of. Then he said we'd move to West Texas and start over. He said all he needed was to find him a place where nobody didn't know nothing about him. He said we'd be all right then." She sighed, and sat a moment looking off across the pasture beyond the creek, as though back through the years.

"We nearly was," she continued. "The first two years we rented that place down close to Brownwood, and he worked hard. Then he decided to buy a place and we come here. You can remember that."

"Yes, I remember," Isabel said. "And I've thought and thought, the last few years, and it has always seemed to me like he was all right then. But a child can't always know."

"Oh he was. And so proud of you. You remember that little speech you used to say, and how he'd set back just a-beaming when you stood up and recited."

Oh yes, she did remember. The Waterses would be there, and Mama and Papa and Ray (and Travis, too, but a baby then, not noticing her). Joanna, with her fat ringlets (tow color then) and a pink dress with a blue velvet collar and sash, would be asked first to say her speech. She had one the teacher had found for her—that was Miss Ellie, who boarded with the Waterses before Joanna started to school, and she let Joanna say that speech at a school program. Mrs. Waters made that dress especially for that little piece, which ended:

> My mama made this dress for me to say my
> speech in.
>
> Don't you think I'm awful sweet?—I know
> you do!

Miss Ellie had taught Joanna exactly how to deliver that last line, with a simpering little smile and a playful shake of a finger, and everybody thought the performance was the smartest thing they had ever seen a little girl do.

Isabel used to feel a little envious, but not very, because as soon as Joanna had finished she would get to say her speech:

> Roses on my shoulder,
> Slippers on my feet—
> I'm Papa's little darling,
> Don't you think I'm awful sweet?

Isabel couldn't remember who had taught her that verse, but she still knew it as well as she had thirteen or fourteen years ago. Half under her breath she recited it, surprised that it could take her without bitterness back to those times when love seemed to flow all around her—when her papa would rise and pick her up and toss her in his arms, because (surely, she still couldn't help believing) the little verse was true.

But she said, "How silly that was."

"No, it wasn't. It was good. And I had friends. Him and me had friends together. Sometimes it seems like the hardest thing about everything that's happened was losing Martha Waters."

"But you haven't lost her, Mama. She asks about you every time I see her, and it hasn't been very many months since she was here."

Lizzie shook her head. "It never can be the same."

"What happened then, Mama? What really did happen?"

"You mean why Papa changed?"

"I guess I do mean that."

"He just went too far. Bought all them horses, and that extra section of land. Called hisself a rancher. Kind of like he was the biggest man in the community. Then when he lost it all he changed. His old ways was all that satisfied him."

"Away from home, he was still the same though—I mean like on the Sunday school board, or talking to the men at the store."

"He tried to be. And that made it harder at home, you see."

"Harder and harder. Worse and worse."

"Well, you know that as well as I do."

"No, I don't think I do, Mama. I don't know what he's done to you."

"You can see as well as anybody when she sets down to eat at my table." Her voice held a hard strength in it, rarely heard.

"And is that the worst?"

"If you was a married woman, you would know that's the worst. Oh Lord, he's battered and bruised me, in the privacy of our bedroom and on the public road. But yes, this shame is the worst. I reckon you'll feel nothing but scorn for me, Sister, but I say this to you now. The worst is when I think about him driving her through Greenfields this morning, setting up so proud beside him in her fancy hat and coat. And Martha Waters watching, like as not. It's then I know I'm nothing, and will never be nothing no more. I've got no place. It's like I've got no name. And that's worse than being hit by a stick or stomped on the floor."

Neither that day nor the next did Isabel get a chance to talk to Alma. She began to think that her father was so besotted he would never leave the woman's side; but on Saturday at breakfast he announced that he had to go to the blacksmith shop and might be gone most of the morning. Alma was welcome to go with him if she wanted to, he said, but she said no, she needed to wash her hair.

Isabel was alone on the side porch about midmorning, shortening the left leg of a pair of trousers being handed down from Travis to Burnie, when Alma came up from the dugout.

"Where's Mrs. Doane?" she asked.

"Gone to hoe the garden," Isabel said, "and do some watering."

"Well, I hope I didn't run her off," said Alma, "talking about coming back to the house to wash my hair."

"She likes to work in the garden," Isabel said. And that was true, or at least once had been.

"Well now, that's nice," said Alma.

She went on into the kitchen, and Isabel heard her finding a towel, dipping water out of the reservoir on the cookstove, then splashing and humming some tuneless song. Finally, with the towel around her shoulders, she came back out on the porch and said, "I'll just set out here with you and dry my hair."

"Get you that cane-bottom chair out of the kitchen if you want to," Isabel said. That was an invitation, meant to encourage Alma to talk. Isabel waited to see if she would.

Alma brought the chair out without answering Isabel and sat down to comb her pale hair. When she bent her head forward, combing it up over her head from the back of her neck, it almost swept the floor. Ordinarily, pinned up loosely in a roll at the back of her head, it appeared unattractive and drab, but gleaming in the sun it could be described without exaggerating much as silver. The back of her neck looked very white and slender, rising from the ruffled collar of her new rosebud print housedress.

After a few minutes, Alma turned so that she sat with her back to the sun, her hair draping over the ladder back of the chair.

"You didn't say how you like my new dress," she said then.

"It's nice," said Isabel. "I was just noticing it."

"I got several nice things. You could come and look at them sometime."

"Yes," said Isabel. She meant she could. She could not believe that she would.

"It's not bad, down there in the dugout, you know. I kind of like it."

"I know," said Isabel. "We used to live in it."

"Sure. Your papa told me that. Course there's not room for a family, but it's just right for us."

"Papa hasn't moved his things down there," Isabel said. "I didn't know he aimed to live there too."

"Well, he may not exactly. But he says your mama don't care. He says she'd be real well satisfied if he never did come in their bedroom."

It was hard to know whether Alma knew what she was talking about. She must really be weak-minded—she must be worse than that.

"I don't believe any woman could ever be very well satisfied," Isabel said, "to see another woman take her place in her own home."

"But I don't take her place. She's still the lady of the house, ain't she?"

Isabel thought of several ways to answer that, but doubted that Alma could understand any of them.

"I guess y'all hate me, don't you?" Alma said.

"We don't even know you," Isabel said. "But we sure don't like you being here, you must know that."

"Well, I hate it you feel that way. I thought we might be friends."

"Surely you couldn't have."

"Well, maybe not really. But I guess I sort of hoped. I've sure been lonesome—I ain't had no woman friends. There wasn't nobody but my old man, and then he died. When I seen that drummer that used to come to Greenfields, it come to me I might send word to Mr. Doane. And when he told me he still come out this way, and saw Mr. Doane pretty often at the store, it seemed to me it was a sign from heaven."

Isabel was still trying to think whether anything could be said to that when Sophie appeared, followed by Rouser, who—on seeing Alma—stopped, sat down, and uttered a low growl.

"Y'all sure have got a ugly dog," Alma said.

"Looks like he thinks the same about you," Sophie said, sitting on the ground by the dog and putting her arms around him.

"Hush, Sophie," Isabel said, and considered whether to send the child on in the house. But she had already realized nothing helpful was likely to be said. Sophie's presence wouldn't change anything.

"And so you like it here and aim to stay?" she finally asked.

Alma turned around again and let her hair fall forward, veiling her face. "A while," she said. "A good while."

"Until you get another sign?" asked Sophie.

"Yes, that's right," said Alma, smiling her weak, fleeting smile. "Until I do." She flung her hair back then and faced Isabel. "He told me you might be against me," she said. "You always seemed so nice, I didn't want to believe that—I told you I thought we might be friends. But he said if you wasn't good to me, or tried to make me leave, I was to tell him. He said you've got a way of going past your rightful place."

"Maybe I have," said Isabel, "but I won't try to make you go." She would tell Ray that—they would just have to wait out the time, if it should be forever.

Alma didn't answer. Isabel stood up. "I've finished these trousers," she said. "I'm going in now."

Sophie followed Isabel into the kitchen, where Alma's pan of water still sat on the table.

"I'll pour it out," said Sophie.

Isabel watched her through the screen door as she carried out the gray granite pan and tossed the water so close to Alma that it splashed up dirt onto her hair.

Alma got up and walked lazily to the dugout, without a word or gesture to suggest she noticed anything at all.

"I hate her," said Sophie, coming back into the room with the pan, "but I don't care if she stays."

"You must hate Mama, too, to say that."

"She's better off. We're all better off."

"You ought to be ashamed. You don't know what you're saying."

"*You* don't know what *you're* saying, Sister. I've been down there with him in the dugout."

The sisters stood facing each other in the patch of light that reached inside the kitchen door. Sophie's eyes, the color of weak coffee, flashed and darkened. Isabel turned away from her, pulled a chair out from the table, and sat heavily down. Sophie sat down facing her.

"Do you want to tell me what you mean?" Isabel said.

"You know."

"I don't think you know what that sounds like."

"I know."

Suddenly Isabel realized her sister did know. If this were true —if Sophie was saying what Isabel thought she was—it might explain some things about Sophie's manner—her lack of friends, her strange, uncaring ways. And it could be true. There were times— opportunities. And there was that dark force in her father—Isabel had felt it herself, without ever trying to define it.

"But, Sophie, why didn't you ever say anything before?" she asked.

"Because he said he'd kill me if I did," she said calmly.

"You could have told me—I'd have kept it a secret."

"What if I had?"

Isabel could not honestly say that she knew.

"Who could help me? What could anybody do?"

"I don't know," said Isabel. "And yet—I guess you're right—no one must know. Except—I don't know—Mama?"

"No!" said Sophie fiercely.

"She might help you—some way I don't even know about."

"I don't need help now. You mustn't tell. I wish I hadn't told you."

"Somebody needs to know—because what if she leaves?"

"I'd run away, you see. If it ever starts again, I'd run away."

"I tried that."

"But I'd know how."

And Sophie might. She knew much more than Isabel now—about some things. But she was such a child—she might not know if she did need help. (And what Isabel meant by that she refused to think.)

"Sophie, I won't tell," she said. "Unless things get real bad. I can't think—there might be something—some reason I'd need to tell Ray."

"Promise you won't ever tell anyone but him, then."

"I can promise that."

"Then tell him. Because maybe he needs to know."

"And you promise me you won't try to run away without talking to either him or me."

"Yes. All right."

"And so you won't be sorry you told me?"

"Maybe not—I guess not. But you see why I don't care if she stays."

"I do see that. But maybe there's some better way. Something that will be better for you, and Mama, and all of us."

Sophie stared past Isabel, her eyes expressionless, her face blank. There was no use in trying to talk to her when she got like that.

"Will you run to the garden now, and see if Mama needs help?" Isabel said.

"You mean see if she's still there—and hasn't heard us?"

"I guess so."

"Sure, Sis."

Now after these morning talks, Isabel badly wanted some time alone with Ray, but all day long she found no chance of that. Their father came in at noon somehow transformed to his old uncommunicative, hard-faced self—even Alma could get no response from him—and after dinner announced it was time Ray and Travis quit fooling around about that car shed. He said he would work with them that evening and see that the job was done before they quit for supper.

Supper was so late that Ray scarcely had time to change his clothes and damp down his hair before leaving for Joanna's.

"She aims to stay," Isabel told him hurriedly, in a low voice, as he started toward the barn. "I'll wait up for you, and we can talk."

Alone and restless after the family had gone to bed, Isabel walked for a while with the dog on the hillside in the moonlight, trying to keep her thoughts away from the happenings of the day; but at last came back to the house, took out her diary, and (knowing her father could not see the front room windows from the dugout) lit the big lamp and sat down to record such changes as the day had brought about.

She felt unsettled by them. Now she no longer knew whether it would be a good thing for the family if they could persuade Alma to leave. What both Sophie and Burnie had said to her was doubtless true: the children were better off in some ways now than they had been in a long time. Even her mother might be better off, if there were any way she could learn to consider Alma as simply the means for her to freedom from abuse. But even as Isabel thought about that proposition—wrote it down—she knew no woman could accept deliverance on such terms. "In the eyes of the community, she might as well be dead." Isabel wrote that down, wondered about it, wrote something else, scratched it out. "Anyway Mama seems to feel that way," she went on. "The shame for her is worse than blows and bruises."

And then of course this change in Papa might not last. If he grew tired of Alma and began to mistreat her, she wouldn't have Mama's reasons for enduring misery. He might even be going back to his old ways already, for his manner was certainly different today.

Rouser howled. He wasn't used to howling. There were those sounds from the dugout again. She guessed they bothered him.

The clock struck eleven. Ray should have been home. Mrs. Waters would never let him stay past ten-thirty.

She decided to put the diary away, she had said all she wanted to say about that day, had thought all she wanted to think. But then she was restless again—there was nothing else to do while she waited for Ray—and she was lonely. She looked out on the moonlit night and gathered to herself again a dream she had carried with her when she walked on the hill.

She wrote of a man who had walked with her there. "He is

only a shadow," she wrote, "and a shadow is all he can ever be for me. He comes to me when I am loneliest, and soundlessly speaks of little things no one else ever mentions—the whisper of leaves, grass moving as some unseen creature of the night moves silently away, a thin little song, sung by some waking bird or insect.

"Such a man as would never come to Greenfields, or never more than once, and never would walk anywhere with me." She refused even as she wrote in secret to her secret self to admit her thoughts dwelled on a flesh-and-blood man who had spoken ordinary words to her and looked into her eyes. "He is not real," she said, "or if he is, he is not real to me."

She skipped a little space, and then wrote hastily, "I hear a horse now. That's the reality. I'll go meet Ray, and have my talk with him."

But she did not, after all, talk to Ray. She was waiting by the lot gate when he came down the trail, and she saw he had been riding hard. He dismounted and began to unsaddle his horse before he spoke to her. "Go to bed, Sis," he said to her. "I can't talk tonight."

CHAPTER EIGHT

Alma came to breakfast Sunday morning wearing a white crepe dress with a girdle of purple taffeta and a purple straw hat decorated with pink roses.

"Me and Mr. Doane's going to church," she said. "I went ahead and got ready, because I just couldn't wait for y'all to see my new clothes."

As usual, nobody answered Alma, but Harvey turned to her with a relaxed, soft expression that was almost a smile. It made Isabel think of the way he used to look at her when she was little and would stand up to say her speech. Papa will wear his suit today, she thought.

At the same time she thought, what she hadn't realized before, We can't go! It hadn't occurred to her that her father would want Alma Greeping to go with him to church. But now suddenly she saw that he would, of course he would, she should have known.

She couldn't imagine what view he expected the community to take of their relationship, but she understood that he intended no hole-in-the-corner affair and did not mean to appear ashamed of what he was doing.

"I don't guess us kids will go today, Papa," Isabel said, offering no explanation.

"No," said Ray, "I don't aim to go."

"Suit yourself," said their father.

It seemed clear that his children did not figure in whatever picture it was he intended to present Greenfields with this morning.

"But I know my memory verse," Leonard protested.

"Be quiet!" Sophie whispered to him fiercely.

Alma and Harvey didn't seem to notice. They went on back to the dugout, and in a little while Harvey came back to the house, took a pan of water into his and Lizzie's bedroom, shaved, and dressed in his Sunday suit.

No one watched them leave. Lizzie had sat the whole morning in her dark corner, crocheting or fumbling with her crochet. Isabel didn't know where all the children were. Neither did she know where Ray was—she was looking for him. She walked down toward the barn, half thinking he might be planning to ride off somewhere on his horse, determined to stop him before he did. She guessed he didn't want to talk this morning any more than he had last night, but she wanted to talk to him. Something had happened at Joanna's last night, and she couldn't help it, she wanted to know what; and whether he wanted to hear it or not, she had information for him.

She caught a glimpse of him going around the corner of the barn, following the path that the Doanes always took when they walked down into the pasture.

"Ray!" she called, and ran after him.

He stopped and looked back. He was carrying his gun, but probably not for any particular reason—only that if he happened to see a rabbit he would shoot at it. No man or boy at Greenfields would walk off aimlessly without taking a gun. A woman might conceivably walk for the pleasure of walking or to get some fresh air, if any woman ever had that much leisure. But a male, from the time he was twelve years old, unless he was walking to his place of work, would want a gun as proof that he was going about a man's business.

She caught up with him. "Let me walk with you," she said.

"Not now," he said, starting away from her.

"Ray, I've got to tell you something," she said. "Things are worse than you think."

"Things are worse than *you* think, Sister," he said, turning back to her.

"But haven't I got to know? Whatever it is, Ray, haven't I really got to know?"

"Come on then," he said.

They went on the short distance beyond the barn to where the path led through the barbed wire fence. Ray laid his gun on the ground, then put a foot on the bottom wire and held it down, while he stretched up the next strand of wire as far as it would go. Isabel bent over, lifted her skirt, and stepped through. Ray pushed down the top wire and, lifting his long legs high, stepped over the fence. Then he picked up his gun, and they walked on.

"I wonder why Papa never did put in a gate or a stile here," Isabel said. They were following a trail that took the shortest way across the pasture where the creek ran. Whenever any of them walked to the field on the other side, or as little children ran down to play by the creek, they would follow this path that made it necessary to climb the fence or wriggle through it. Many shirts and dresses had been torn there.

"Don't wonder nothing about Papa," Ray said shortly.

The path was too narrow to accommodate two, and so they left it and walked side by side in the dewy grass and flowers. In this pasture, up above the creek where the path led over open, rolling land, there was only a scattering of small mesquites, and they walked along under the soft sky in full sun. The day would be hot later on, but now was warmed just to the point of setting insects humming and field larks singing.

"It's like the world was in disguise, isn't it?" Isabel said.

"I don't know what you mean," said Ray.

"It looks so beautiful," she said, "and everything's so bad."

"Yes," he said, "it's bad."

They went on. She waited for him to start telling her.

A cottontail sprang up from a clump of grass down toward the creek. He lifted his rifle and fired; the rabbit fell.

"Where's Rouser?" Ray asked.

"Off with the boys, I guess."

"He'd like that rabbit."

Isabel didn't say anything. She kept waiting. They went on past the place where the rabbit lay dead. She looked away from it.

"Well," Ray finally said, "I guess me and Joanna's quit."

"Ray, I can't believe that."

"I don't know why not. You couldn't expect a girl from a decent family to marry into a mess like we've got here."

"Is that what you told her? Because I can't believe Joanna said that to you."

"She did though, just about. She said her mama thought maybe her and me oughtn't to see much of each other till I get things straightened out at home."

"What does she think you can do?"

"I don't know. I guess they think I'm the one to do something —and something's got to be done."

"But Ray, that's not the same as breaking your engagement."

"It sounds a lot like it to me. Wednesday night she said it was me she wanted to marry, and what the rest of my family might do wouldn't make no difference to her."

"And then you think Mrs. Waters changed her mind for her?"

"I know she did. I know dad-gum good and well she did."

Isabel couldn't think of any further argument. She believed Joanna truly loved Ray, but how far she would go against her parents' wishes she had no idea. And she wasn't even sure she could blame Mrs. Waters for feeling the way she did about Ray's family. For what family now would want to be allied to the Doanes? "Trash"—wouldn't people have to call them that now? They couldn't hold up their heads in the community.

"But Ray, surely you and Joanna didn't actually break up?" Isabel finally said.

"I reckon we did, I don't even know."

They had come to a place on the creek bank where some large squares of sandstone lay exposed. He sat down on one, and she beside him.

"See," he said, "I tried to get her to marry me last night."

"You mean *marry* last night?"

"Well, I was feeling that way then."

"But you're neither one of age."

"I figured once it was done, her folks might not care."

"And Papa?"

"Shoot, I doubt if he'd even notice."

"But Joanna said no."

"She said we've got our plan, and she wouldn't give it up. I said she might have to, if she loved me. Heck, I don't know what all we said. I guess we got to talking loud, and Mrs. Waters come out on the porch and said maybe I'd better go. I said I reckoned I had. I told Joanna she could send for me if she ever wanted to see me."

"Oh, Ray."

"The truth is, I guess everything would be all right tomorrow if Alma was gone."

"And you'd go back to Joanna."

"Oh Lord, Sis, you know I would. It don't seem to me like she's doing me right, but I just can't even imagine how my life would be if I couldn't think about having Joanna."

They sat on the rock in silence for a little while. There was no shade on the rock, and they began to feel the heat of the sun. Without discussion, they got up and started walking back toward the house.

"Sis," Ray asked then, "is there any chance she'll leave?"

Isabel told Ray all Alma had said. "But of course there's a chance she'll go sometime. Things may not work out like she thinks they will. Either one of them might change their mind."

"But you don't think she'll go."

"I don't think she's got the least idea of ever doing anything but staying right here. She's got it pretty good here—and Ray, I think she may be smarter than we've been giving her credit for."

They walked back along the pasture trail, Isabel wondering— as she had done all along—how to tell Ray the rest of her news, or whether she should even try.

"You said things is worse than I thought," he said. "But I didn't expect nothing else than that, really."

"There's something else, though," she said. "Sophie . . ." She didn't see how to go on.

"What's the matter with Sophie?" he said.

"Well, I don't know," she said. "I'm not sure. But—well—she says Papa's been bothering her."

"I don't know what you mean."

"That's what I said to her. She said I knew all right. And I guess you do too."

At the tone of her voice he seemed to understand. He gripped his gun in both hands. "I'll kill him," he muttered.

"But I guess that's over now," she said. "She says she wishes Alma would stay."

"Looks like we're ruined, whether she goes or stays."

"But there's no use trying to do anything to Papa," said Isabel.

"No. Not that. Course I didn't mean that."

"Looks like there's really just one thing we could do."

"What's that?"

"What Burnie said—get away."

"Look what happened when you tried."

"But like you said—he might not hardly notice now, might not care. He could have the whole house just for him and Alma."

"Who'd do the work?"

She shook her head. "Well, there's that. But still I think we ought to try."

He dropped his gun to his side, relaxed a little. "If I could get away, then maybe—"

"Joanna could go ahead and go to college, just like she's planned, and by the time she could get her certificate we might have things so you could marry. You wouldn't have to support us, Ray, or not for long. I know I could do something—and Travis could."

"Would Mama go?"

"Lord knows. We'd just have to get her to, somehow."

"It wouldn't work. Papa wouldn't let it work, you know he wouldn't."

"I don't know—I think the thing to do is tell him that we want to leave. You could tell him that, Ray. Just say we see how things are here now, and we'd rather not stay. You don't have to act mad at him, or show any disrespect."

"I'm about ready to try anything," Ray said.

"Then don't wait. Tell him now, today, and we'll go."

"Just like that?"

"Just like that. What other way is there? You've got a little money, and I don't know about you, but I'm not too proud to ask for help."

"Well—"

"Today."

"I'll think about it. I'll see."

As they came through the fence behind the barn, they heard a car approaching.

"Papa?" Isabel said.

"It's sure a Model T," Ray said.

It was Harvey and Alma, back far too soon from church. As Isabel and Ray came from behind the barn, Harvey was stopping to let Alma out of the car, before driving it on into the shed.

She walked up to Ray and Isabel, saying, "Well, we didn't stay."

"How come?" asked Ray.

"We wasn't welcome," said Harvey, coming out of the shed.

"Old man Goolsby told us we didn't belong there," Alma said.

"Looks like you'd a known how they'd feel, Papa," Ray said, "after what happened at the store yesterday."

"Go to hell," said Harvey, and went stalking on toward the dugout, with Alma hanging onto his arm.

"What was it, Ray?" Isabel asked, as they stood looking after the couple.

"Aw, I guess not anything much. There was some men there, and they wouldn't talk to him. Got up and left when he set down—or so Joanna said that Mr. Waters said."

"Papa may have to make a choice between Alma and that place in the community he's always talking about," Isabel said.

"He won't. He's done made his choice, when he brought her here. He's too stubborn to change in a hundred years."

They walked on toward the house.

"I guess this won't be a very good day to talk to him," Isabel said.

"Do you think things is fixing to get any better?" Ray asked her.

This was the worst day since Alma's arrival. Dinner was a miserable meal, with Harvey dark-faced and glum. The children withdrew inside themselves, and as soon as possible when they were allowed to get up from the table, all slipped silently away to secret places. Nothing really happened during the afternoon, but Isabel kept wondering where Ray had gone.

He didn't come in till after supper. His right eye was swollen shut, his cheek bruised and cut, his shirt torn. Isabel brought rags and hot water to the kitchen table and ministered to him, then gave him corn bread and sweet milk. Lizzie silently rocked and watched, from her corner.

Ray didn't explain his appearance; but when everyone except Isabel had gone to bed he found her where she was sitting on the front porch with Rouser and, stretching out slowly and with evident pain along the floor, he said to her, "Well, Sis, I can't whip him yet."

"What did he say?" Isabel asked.

"What you see," he told her.

Afterwards, Isabel learned that Harvey had been fairly specific about his threats to Ray. He said he knew how to set the law on any runaway kid; he said there was a law against a wife deserting her husband, too, as far as he knew. Isabel wondered if he remembered Ray would soon be of age, or if he thought that mattered. Probably he knew very well that neither she nor Ray would go away and leave their mother and the younger children. She kept telling herself there had to be a better way.

But weeks went by, and no better way appeared; instead, life became daily less bearable. "In some ways, we may be better off," they had said when Alma first came; but they couldn't have been more wrong.

On June 11, a Sunday four weeks from the day her father brought home Alma Greeping, Isabel sat by an open window in her bedroom with her diary on her lap. Almost every entry in those four weeks concerned either her father or Alma or both. There was nothing else to write about but make-believe. A few times she had returned to that uncertain comfort. Once she carefully copied some verses about a gray-eyed man with a profile like a Greek hero's, a man gentle enough to weep at an injured rabbit's cry. (They must have been her own; they were not very good, but they held a poignant line or two. She may have worked on them a long time before transcribing them on the page of the diary, for nothing was changed or scratched out.)

Following that was a terse account of an incident that must have been fairly typical of those days. "Papa whipped Travis today, with that chain he used on Ray one time. She got him to go down in the dugout with her, and Papa said if he ever saw Travis there again he'd kill him. Travis said she asked him to go down there and kill a snake for her, but Travis couldn't find any snake. She just smiled that sickly smile."

A page or two past that: "Papa and Alma went to the store today, and the women that were there turned their backs on Alma and walked out. Mr. Waters asked Papa not to bring her back there."

And after that, on a Sunday: "I don't guess any of us will go to church again. Papa says he won't allow it as long as Alma is not welcome there. Surely God knows, and forgives us."

Then an entry tears had dropped on: "Papa killed Rouser today. We were all sitting on the porch, and he came panting up, started to sit down by my feet, and then saw Alma and backed away. She said, 'I hate that dog.' Papa got up, went down to the woodpile and picked up the axe, and then came about halfway back toward the house before he called Rouser. Rouser didn't know anything was wrong, and he went running. Papa said 'Lay down, boy,' and Rouser flopped down on the ground, the way he would do. Papa rubbed his foot around on his head, and then, all of a sudden, put his foot down on Rouser's neck and raised the axe. I didn't look, but when I turned back the head had rolled away."

Isabel elaborated less and less, but almost every day noted down some new incident, as though determined to keep a full record of this unhappy time.

On Thursday, June 8, she had written: "Papa knocked Burnie up against the wall tonight and hurt his head."

The next day (or night) she wrote: "Today I went to Greenfields and talked to Mrs. Waters and Joanna."

Joanna and Mrs. Waters were on the porch that afternoon, quilting, as usual. Joanna hardly knew why they quilted anymore, but the quilt was begun and must be finished. Every prick of the needle seemed to pierce her heart as she remembered the joy with which she had begun the work that now stretched so tediously before them. She and her mother worked together now without saying very much. They considered they had said everything there was to be said. Nor did they have very much company now. People had not quite figured out what to say to Joanna.

This hot afternoon, after a long session of unbroken needlework, Martha raised her head and wiped some beads of sweat from her brow. She looked around over the landscape, not in search of anything, just resting her eyes.

She said, "Yonder comes Isabel."

"Oh, Mama," Joanna cried. She looked up and saw her friend's plodding figure coming along the path that led by the schoolhouse. "Poor Isabel," she said, with a kind of distant sympathy.

"I've wondered why she didn't come," Martha said.

Joanna knew she had wondered. She had said so before. But

Joanna had not looked for her. Since she had given up expecting Ray to come back, she had felt she never would see any of the Doanes again. Now something strange was come upon her, something that held her still as though cold hands pressed her down in the chair. Isabel was coming across the schoolground, and Joanna did not go to meet her and did not know what she would say when they met.

Finally, as Isabel approached the yard gate, Martha stepped out on the back walkway and called out, "Howdy, Isabel!" Then Joanna went out to stand uncertainly beside her; but when Isabel came close enough for Joanna to see her pinched face and sad eyes, the cold hands drew back and a warm wave rose in her breast. She ran and threw her arms around Isabel, but even so could not think of anything to say.

Martha led them into the house. "I'll make a pitcher of lemonade," she said. "Y'all set and talk. After while you might want to quilt a little."

Isabel stood a moment looking down at the Lone Star, wondering, as Joanna had done many times, what was ever to become of it. She couldn't believe Joanna would ever use it if she didn't marry Ray; it might lie folded in the bottom of her cedar chest forever.

"I don't guess I'll try to quilt," Isabel said. "I can't stay long. I didn't really know whether I ought to come here at all."

"Well, I never thought I'd hear Isabel Doane say a thing like that in my house," Martha said. "Of course you ought to come."

"I—I don't know," Isabel said. She couldn't make herself say what she felt: that if the Doanes had got to be such a sorry family that Ray couldn't come to see Joanna, then surely his sister couldn't expect a welcome in the Waters house either.

Martha went on to the kitchen to make the lemonade. Isabel and Joanna waited dumbly; they didn't know how to talk without mentioning Ray's name, and yet each felt that to mention it would be to open doors perhaps better left closed.

When the three were sitting at the table on the porch, with lemonade and a plate of spice-flavored tea cakes, Martha said briskly, "Well, y'all don't come to preaching no more, and Mr. Doane's took to going to Walnut Grove to the store, so we don't have any way of knowing how the Doanes is getting along. So now I want you to tell me, because I need to know."

"I guess that's what I'm here for—to tell you," Isabel said. "And how we are is bad—you just couldn't believe how bad."

"What way bad?"

"The same old way, I guess you'd say. But things happen—bad, scary things—worse than ever I think, and more often." She hardly knew what to tell first, but Burnie was uppermost in her mind. "Well—just the last thing," she said, "—last night after supper Papa hit Burnie, and he fell against the wall and hurt his head. I was scared, and I know Mama was too. But I guess he's all right today—he's bruised, but he says he hasn't got a headache."

"How does he treat your mama?"

"He talks ugly to her, but mostly he leaves her alone."

"Well, he's got Alma Greeping to take out his meanness on." Mrs. Waters (it seemed to Isabel) spoke with conscious, deliberate emphasis, in a tone almost defiant, as though to say "There: I've spoke her name."

"I guess so, Mrs. Waters, but he treats her all right, as far as I can tell. And of course that's one trouble—that he does, and she's there, wearing her new clothes, acting like she thinks she's one of the family. And Papa treating her like a spoiled child." Again Isabel paused, as though doubting how far to go, then went on: "She didn't like Rouser, so Papa killed Rouser."

"Oh, Isabel," gasped Joanna.

"And now Burnie is afraid he might kill Sancho, or sell him for scrap, because she says she can't bear to look at that scarred face."

"He wouldn't do that to Burnie," Martha said.

Isabel only shook her head. There was no explaining how she felt now about what her papa might do, how far he might go.

"I heard Ray fought him," Joanna said.

"Ray was hurt pretty bad," Isabel said. "I think he's just now getting over it completely."

Joanna covered her face in her hands. "It nearly killed me," she said, "when I heard."

"Mr. Goolsby came by and saw Ray a day or two after the fight," Isabel said.

"Yes, that's who told us," Martha said. "I believe him and Mr. Waters tried to figure out if there was anything to do. By the law, you know."

"You mean about Ray?"

"I mean the whole family—your mama. Mr. Goolsby said if your mama would go to court and tell everything Mr. Doane ever done to her, it might do some good. But I told 'em Lizzie would never do that. What woman would do that?"

"Mama wouldn't," said Isabel. "Ray and I wondered if something like that might be a thing to do, and I mentioned it to her once. She just said, 'No, I wouldn't want to talk about your papa that way.'"

"No," Martha said. "She wouldn't, of course."

"So you see, there we are."

"Couldn't you just all go off somewhere?" asked Joanna.

"I guess not," said Isabel. "That's what Ray and Papa fought about."

"Don't any of you ever leave the place?" Martha asked.

"Papa won't let us go to church—and I don't know whether we'd be very welcome if we did. I guess we don't think we'd be very welcome anywhere in Greenfields."

"I wish you'd tell Ray to come and talk to me," Martha said. "I think he misunderstood some things that last time he was here."

"I hoped he might have," Isabel said.

"And you tell Burnie and Leonard to come. I want to make Burnie some ice cream—it don't have to be Sunday. I don't want you kids to quit coming to see us."

"I don't know, Mrs. Waters, I don't guess we'll go anywhere. I was a little afraid to come today, but Papa was gone, and I just hoped he wouldn't catch me."

"Well, whatever your reason was," Martha said, "I'm glad you decided to come."

"I guess I just needed to see you all," Isabel said. "I told myself you might know some way to help—or Mr. Waters would. But that's all been thrashed out, I guess."

"I'm afraid it has, Isabel," Martha said. "You know, we even talked to the preacher about it—Brother Crenshaw, the one your papa got to come and preach—but he just says he can't interfere no more than the law can. He says Mr. Doane appears to be living in sin, but that don't alter the commandment."

"What commandment, Mrs. Waters?"

"You know—honor thy father and mother, that thy days may be long."

"Oh," said Isabel, "I hadn't thought of that."

Martha Waters laughed shortly.

Soon afterwards, Isabel got up to go.

"I'll walk a piece with you," Joanna said. "I didn't even get a chance to tell you any news."

The girls followed the path that cut across the pasture and the schoolground. Joanna suggested going by the store to drink a soda pop, but Isabel said she had better take the short way.

"You might want to go on back," Isabel said as they reached the margin of the schoolyard. "You may not want to be seen on a public road with anyone named Doane."

"I wish you wouldn't talk like that," Joanna said. "I know what Ray must have told you, but he didn't understand."

"You sure hurt him though."

"He hurt me."

"Well, I'm sorry, Jo. I've cried over it."

"And so have I—night after night."

"Do you want me to tell Ray that?"

"Yes—no—I don't know. Oh, Isabel, will things ever get better? Is there anything at all to do?"

"Are you saying you can't marry Ray because of Alma Greeping?"

"No. I still think we can marry—can go on with all our plans. But not now, not yet."

"Because of her?" Isabel insisted.

"All right. Because of her. Mama and Papa say they just can't think about linking our two families by marriage, the way things are now. You see, we can all still be friends, just like always. And they like Ray, they'll always like Ray. They say we can be secretly engaged, but we can't go on the way we have been—in kind of a public way."

"So it really was true, that you told him all he said. I couldn't hardly believe it. I really thought he had misunderstood."

"You won't forgive me, will you? And he won't?"

"Oh yes, Jo, I will. I do. I do understand how your mama and papa feel. But it might be too much to expect of Ray."

"If only she would go—if only there could be some way to make things better."

"They weren't always so good for us before she came, you know."

"Oh, I do know, Isabel, but there was hope. There always used to be hope."

"Hope takes a long time dying. Like I said, I guess I had some hope today that I'd find help at Greenfields."

"Well, they've talked about it, just like Mama told you. And the only thing they ever seem to decide is that Ray's the only one that can do anything. That's what Papa and Mr. Goolsby say. Ray's the one."

"I can't think what they mean."

"I don't know either. But they say he'll have to take things in his hands. You tell him that."

"Well, he's tried, Jo. But I'll tell him."

They were nearing the crossroads; they walked on and stood a few minutes in the shade of the old mesquite.

"I didn't tell you the news," Joanna said. "But there wasn't any news you'd care about—just who went with who to the party last week."

"Well, I'd like to hear," Isabel said. "Maybe I'd feel more like I still live in the world. But I've got to go, you see; I've got to hurry home."

They said good-bye. Isabel started on.

Joanna stood under the tree a little longer, and then called her. "Isabel."

Isabel turned back.

"You tell him I've cried."

In her diary that Sunday afternoon, Isabel completed an entry. "I told Ray last night what Joanna said," she wrote. "He didn't seem to be mad at me for going. He said he thought he saw now what she meant before, and he was going to think about it."

It must have been while she was still sitting there with the diary in her lap that Ray came in asking, "Where is everybody, Sis?" (She was to write again in her diary that night, describing incredulously the event to which that question was the prelude.)

"Why, Papa and Alma went off in the car. She said they were going to visit somebody she used to know at Walnut Grove."

"I know that—but where's the kids? Where's Mama?"

"Well, they're all around the place somewhere, I think. It's too hot to be anywhere else."

"Let's round them all up. I've got something to talk about to everybody." He sounded excited, almost jubilant.

Isabel looked at him questioningly, but he said, "Don't ask me anything yet. Help me find everybody, and tell 'em to come to the kitchen. I think it's cooler in there than anywhere else."

Isabel knew already that her mama and Sophie were on the front porch. Mama was sitting with her crochet on her lap, and Sophie was lying on her back staring up at the rafters. Isabel told them what Ray wanted, and then went to the barn loft to see if any of the boys were there. It was fairly cool up there, with both ends of the barn open to the breeze. Burnie especially liked the loft, and though it was a struggle for him to climb the ladder, he could often be found there alone, reading one of the dime novels from his secret cache under some old tow sacks in one corner.

She found him there. "Ray has something to tell us," she called to him from the top of the ladder. "He wants us all to come to the kitchen as soon as we can."

"What's he up to, Sis?"

"I don't know. I believe he thinks he's got some idea that will help us about Papa."

"Is he all right?"

"Why do you ask that?"

"I don't know, I just thought he was acting kind of funny today."

Isabel thought so, too, now that she considered what Burnie said. He had been full of that strange excitement since morning, she realized now. It showed in his glittering eyes and his quick, restless movements.

"Well come on," she said. "We'll see."

Ray had them all there. Mama in the popping rocker, her crochet untouched in her lap. Sophie in a straight chair, pulled up for coolness close to the screen door, Travis, Burnie, and Leonard sitting around the table, where Isabel joined them, coming in last. Nobody smiled or spoke. They waited for Ray, who kept standing in the middle of the room, his hands in his pockets, clenched. A breeze stirred the white curtains at the window, but it was not a very cool breeze. Since both door and window were sheltered by the porch roof, it was always dim in that kitchen and so perhaps seemed cooler than it was. Ray looked pale in the dimness, and his voice, when he spoke, was stretched thin.

"I have made up my mind what to do," he finally said, "but I don't aim to do it unless you all agree." He paused, as if for some response, but no one made it. "Listen then," he continued, "and listen to me good. This is something not very many people are ever going to hear in all their lives, but I have made up my mind to say it."

Then Isabel knew she was afraid.

And Ray went on. "There's no use telling you how bad this is—this mess we're living in. Now what I want to ask you all is—how long can you stand it?"

No one answered.

"Mama," he said, "how long can you go on?"

"Oh, Ray," she said. "I don't know."

"You boys," he said. "What about you?"

"Could we run off, Ray?" asked Leonard.

"Ask Mama about that," said Ray.

"No," Lizzie said. "You boys might go some time—and surely there'll be a time when you can. But there ain't no place but here for me."

"You know we can't leave," Burnie said. "Ray knows that—he found that out. I wouldn't want to either, not without Mama—not without every one of us together. What I think is—we may not do much good here, but still, sometime, we might keep him from killing somebody, if we all stick together."

"He's not gonna kill nobody," Travis said. "Is he, Ray?"

"I don't know," Ray said. "I don't think he aims to, I think he'd rather have us here alive, and enjoy the things he does to us. But I don't say he mightn't sometime, in one of his mad fits. What I do say is it's not right for us to have to live this way. Wondering if we will be killed—or our dog or our horse will. Watching Mama put down, farther down every day. Giving up every chance to live decent lives like other people do."

"What else is there then?" said Travis. "What is it you're trying to say?"

"Just this," Ray answered. "And I ain't gonna beat around the bush no more. What I got you here to say is that if you-all haven't got any objections, I aim to go ahead and kill him before things gets any worse."

It seemed to Isabel that she had known he would say that word. "Kill." It rang in her head like a bell, or the echo of a bell. For a moment she almost believed it rang out joy and freedom. "If only he wouldn't come back," they had said, when Papa had gone to get Alma. And then he did return, bringing troubles worse than they had ever known. And what could be done to release them?

Only kill. It was the eternal answer. But Ray? Ray the appointed assassin? We ought to be like the Romans in that play about Caesar, she thought. Each one of us should stab him, and watch his blood run. Stab Father? Kill? Let Ray kill?

She became aware that Ray was asking each one, and they were all saying yes, kill. Even Mama, who seemed unable to bring forth a sound, responded with a faint nod.

"Isabel?" Ray spoke sharply. "I asked you before. Can't you answer?"

"No, I can't, Ray." She had not been quite sure till she spoke. "We can't do it. We can't let you. If the law can't protect us, we must pray that God will."

"I have prayed for twenty years," said Mama. She did not say it as though she were answering Isabel, but rather as though she had, independently of the rest, suddenly made this discovery. She spoke out so much more loudly and clearly than ordinarily she ever did that they all turned to stare at her.

"We have all prayed," said Ray. "We have all begged and argued, and pleaded with Papa. You've even gone and begged help in the community. Now, Sister, you tell us: what more can we do?"

There was nothing. They had been through it all. There was nothing.

"Answer me, Isabel. Everyone but you has spoke. Now will you go against us all?"

Against the family—their well-being, their hope for the future, perhaps even their chance to survive. Against this simple act that would set Mama free. Deny them their only chance of living normal lives, and enjoying the respect of the community they lived in. Oh God, she silently prayed, with no feeling that in that atmosphere of hatred and despair (and she hated, too, and despaired), there was any possible way to reach God.

"Well, Sister?" said Ray, and they all looked at her with a dull expectancy.

She stood up facing Ray across the kitchen table. With some feeling that she might faint when she tried to speak, she clutched at the table's edge for support. She looked into his eyes, which had changed to a stranger's eyes, steely and cold.

"Thou shalt not kill," she said, and sat weakly down.

There was a long silence. Ray finally spoke. "Well, you've give your answer," he said. "And you are one among seven. I hoped you'd all agree with me, but I will do what the majority has said."

"Have you thought what may happen to you?" Isabel asked.

"I have thought," he said, speaking almost conversationally now, "and of course I don't know what may happen. I might go to the pen for life, and they might hang me. But I've had a lot of provocation—that's the word, ain't it, Sis? And it's been put to me that the protection of this family is up to me. The way I figure it, it's like Papa ain't responsible no more, and I'm the one that's got to act. Well, there may be some other action I could take, but there ain't nobody told me what it is."

"What you're asking"—Isabel suddenly saw the matter in this light—"is for us to agree to Papa's execution. But I don't agree. And I always heard that just one person could hang a jury."

"This is not a jury," Ray said, "and you don't have to agree. Everybody but you is with me, and I have decided what has to be done."

"They haven't thought about it, Ray," she said. "We ought to think about it."

"Anybody want to change their mind?" Ray asked.

No one answered. Burnie shifted in his chair and raised his head, but did not at first speak.

"Burnie's got something to say," Isabel said.

"You changed your mind, Pal?" Ray asked.

Burnie shook his head. "Uh-uh," he said. "Or not exactly. But I just don't see why it's up to you to do this, more than any of the rest of us. What I say is, we all ought to have our chance. Or all of us boys. We ought to draw straws, or something."

"He's right, Ray," Travis said.

But Ray said, "No. I'm the one. It's my job to do, and I'm not giving it up to nobody."

"Let me just say one more thing, Ray," Isabel said. "I'm afraid you're headed for bad trouble. And yet—I can't tell what will happen—I guess you might go free. But even if you do, you'll be known for the rest of your life, and you'll know yourself, as the man that killed his father."

"So be it," said Ray, and walked out of the house.

CHAPTER NINE

The crack of rifle fire had never been uncommon around the Doane place. Few days ever went by when the boys or their father wouldn't be shooting some varmint, doing a little hunting, or firing at a tin can on a fence post. Isabel had never noticed gunshots very much as long as she could remember, but now she often would jump with terror at the sound.

Ray usually took his rifle when he went anywhere around the place—if more than ever now, no one would be likely to notice, unless it was one who had been present at that Sunday afternoon meeting in the kitchen. It seemed to Isabel that the other boys were carrying guns more often, too, and that even their father was shooting more than he usually did. Frequently that summer, he would walk in the pasture before breakfast (and naturally, carrying his gun)—Isabel wondered if he woke up needing to get away from the dugout.

All the boys would be out early on those long, late-June days; they got the milking and feeding done before breakfast. And every morning Isabel, in the kitchen, waited tensely for the next shot. She knew her mother was the same way. One day she dropped a pan of biscuits when somebody shot a gun off close to the house.

Isabel had made up her mind that it was at this time of day Ray would do it. Once he had left for the field in the morning, she could feel almost relaxed for the rest of the day. Then as day after day passed, she began to hope he might not do it at all. She suspected he was finding it harder to kill than he had expected. And when the time came—when he had his father in the sight and his finger on the trigger—he might at last see clearly what he was about to do and put his rifle down, unable to act at all.

Burnie, too, wondered about the delay—no doubt they all did, but Burnie was the one who spoke of it to Isabel. "Sis," he said to her—she had gone to the windmill for a bucket of water and found him bathing his feet in the little dirt tank they had there—"Sis, he won't do it, will he? He can't."

"I don't know, Burnie. I pray he won't."

"Because of what you said—that it would always brand him?"

"Did I say that?"

"That no one would ever forget what he'd done. Do you think it would ruin his life?"

"I do, Burnie. I do think so."

"Do you think Joanna would marry him?"

"I just don't know. If Mr. and Mrs. Waters don't want them to marry because Papa's got a woman in the dugout—"

"I see. You don't think they'd want her to marry a killer."

She sighed. "Oh, I just don't know, Burnie. I'm just so tired. Sometimes I can't even think about anything."

"Life won't be any good to us this way, will it?"

"Oh, it will. Some way it will. Burnie, we just have to pray."

"I do, Sister."

Isabel wondered if the other boys prayed. If Sophie prayed. None of them, even Sophie, had ever talked to her freely, as Burnie always did—as Ray had used to do. Ray didn't talk now, and Sophie hardly ever spoke to her at all. But no one in the family (no member of that jury in the kitchen) talked very much these days. Everyone was waiting.

Isabel began to suspect Ray was waiting for Papa to do something that would make him so mad he wouldn't think what he was doing when he raised his gun. The night Papa hit Burnie—Ray could have killed him then. But for several days after the meeting, nothing quite like that happened. The misery was with them always, but passions were not inflamed.

Then one night—it was a Monday, just over a week since the meeting—Harvey called Lizzie a whore. This was by no means the first time, but the word applied to his mother was a hateful thing to Ray, as well as his brothers. (The mother and sisters may actually have cared less than the brothers, through an instinctive valuing of reality above the word; for men, there were always fighting words, and "whore" was one of them.)

Lizzie had stumbled, going to the table from the stove with a big bowl of gravy. Isabel thought her worn-out house shoe had caught in a splinter in the pine floor—at any rate she fell, against Alma's chair, spilling a little gravy on the floor.

"Watch where you're going, you decrepit old whore," Harvey said, more with annoyance than anger.

Ray jerked his chin up, but he didn't say anything. Nobody

said anything. Isabel thought, This might be it. He's angry enough to do it now, tonight. But nothing happened.

Next morning, while Isabel and Lizzie were in the kitchen cooking breakfast, a rifle cracked again, somewhere close to the barn. The women looked at each other, then turned back to their work: Isabel frying meat, Lizzie cutting out biscuits. It might be— it might not. They could only wait and see.

Breakfast was ready; Leonard had already come in; Isabel was wondering if she ought to go outside and holler at the rest, when she heard steps on the porch and then the painful screak of the screen door. She looked up, and Ray stood there.

"Sister, come here," he said.

Isabel set the skillet of meat off the fire. From the porch, Ray silently gave her a sign to follow him. He led her past the barn, along the path that ran to the place where they climbed through the fence to go into the pasture. Neither spoke, or looked at the other.

The weeds had grown tall along the fence, so that Isabel did not see the body at first. It lay with its feet just under the wire and its length parallel to the narrow, beaten path. A rifle lay beside it. She turned away from the sight, quickly, before she quite saw it; but then it came up clear and large, and it seemed to her the bloodstain on the shirtfront was still spreading.

She walked a few steps away without looking back or saying a word. She had a sense that she ought to kneel by the body and feel for a pulse, but she could not have touched it. She did not know what she would have done if she had loved her father. This minute she could not remember any warmth of love.

She paused; Ray stood at her side. At last she looked at him, and saw his face pale and rigid, his eyes unspeaking and old.

"Ray, is he dead?"

He nodded grimly. "I made sure of that," he said, "before I come to the house."

Her love was for her brother. Clearly, in a moment, the pain of that certainty reached her. "Oh, Ray," she moaned, and turned and embraced him.

They stood in embrace a long moment, then drew apart and regarded each other.

"Ray," she said, "I don't like this—I never wanted this—but whatever may happen, and I can't think what will, you know that I still love you."

"Do you, Sis?" he said softly.

She knew he meant he loved her, too, and needed her, but they were not used to putting such concepts into words. It was perhaps the first time she had ever spoken of love to Ray—indeed to any brother or her sister—unless to Burnie, when he was very young. You take it for granted that you love your brother, don't you? And your father? No, she thought, love is not a law of nature, after all. Or if it is, it's a law that can be broken. She believed she would always love Ray, but she could not predict what might happen now. Whether she would lie to save him—as it seemed possible she might have a chance to do in court—she could not tell. But she ached to comfort him.

They looked at each other, and she saw that he was comforted. At least some color had come back to his face, and softness to his eyes.

"What do we do now?" she asked him.

"We'll tell the folks, and then I'll go get Mr. Goolsby."

"And what will you tell him, Ray?"

"The truth."

"Yes," she said.

They walked a few steps, till she said, "Ought we to leave him? Could we carry him to the house?"

"Seems like I've heard you're supposed to leave a body alone till the officers come."

"I'll stay with him," she said. "Somebody ought to bring a sheet or something."

"I'll see that somebody brings one. I think I'd better go on and find Mr. Goolsby."

"Yes, go," she said.

"I'm sorry, Sis," he said. "Can you bear it?"

"I won't look," she said.

Presently, she heard the Ford engine turn over. It started easily, and the car was soon moving toward the main road. Ray was a natural driver and a fine mechanic. Yet this was the first time he had driven the new car—his father would never offer him the wheel, and Ray would never ask.

As the car was pulling away, she saw the family coming—with Alma Greeping at their head. They would all have been in the kitchen, for it was breakfast time and past, by now.

As they came closer, Alma began to run. "Where is he?" she cried.

Isabel dumbly gestured, and Alma flung herself against the fence. Perhaps she had not even seen it in her rush toward her dead lover.

"Oh!" she screamed shrilly, and stood back as though dazed, holding out a hand that was bleeding from the puncture of a barb.

While she stood there, Travis lifted his mother in his arms and set her over the fence. Then she sank into the grass and weeds and laid her face on the bloody breast.

And Alma was scrambling, trying to get through the wires, her skirt catching on the barbs. "He's mine," she shouted. "Let me to him."

Isabel stood marveling at the sight of these two women who loved this cruel man. But one was his wedded wife and the mother of his children.

"I'm sorry," she said to Alma, and at the moment really felt compassion for this bewildered, grieving soul. "But your rights to him passed when he died. It's my mother that will follow him to his grave and when her time comes be buried at his side."

She helped Alma free her skirts from the fence, and gave her a hand as she stood up facing Isabel.

"Who killed him?" Alma asked.

"Wait," said Isabel. "Ray has gone to get the justice of the peace. We will see what he says."

"It don't matter," Alma said. "It's all over."

"Yes," said Isabel. "It's all over. You had better go now and pack your clothes."

Alma glanced back once, but she walked on alone toward the dugout.

"Get Mama now and we'll take her back to the house," Isabel told Travis. "You and Burnie might stay here till Ray comes back."

"To keep the dogs away," said Burnie, glancing toward the dugout.

"Yes," said Isabel.

When Ray returned, he brought Mr. Goolsby, and Mr. Waters in his Maxwell came along behind. Mr. Goolsby had been at the store; Ray had seen his paint horse at the hitching post and stopped there. Jack and Winnie, home from college, were working in the store, so Mr. Waters was able to come along and see what he could do to help.

When the men came, Isabel gathered all the family together in the front room, to wait for what Mr. Goolsby had to say. She went to the door of the dugout and called Alma to join them one more time.

In about ten minutes Ray and Mr. Goolsby came in, Mr. Waters having stayed with the corpse.

Mr. Goolsby, a stubby little man dressed in blue ducking overalls, stood in the middle of the room and addressed them in a formal manner, which—though at odds with his appearance—struck no one as strange. He was not quite Mr. Goolsby anymore, but stood there as an embodiment of justice.

"I wish to extend my sympathy to you all," he began, then looking around, letting his eyes fall momentarily on Alma, amended his statement—"to all the family." He straightened and cleared his throat. "I understand there wasn't no witnesses of this—er—what happened," he said.

No one spoke. Alma raised her head and looked as though she might, but meeting Justice Goolsby's eyes, she held her peace.

"I understand," he went on, "that all you boys was busy with morning chores—that Mrs. Doane and the girls was in the house—and Mrs.—uh—Greeping was in the dugout."

Again, there was silence, as he looked around the room.

"Then I've just got to use the evidence of my own eyes," he said, "and my ruling in this case is accidintal death. It's plumb clear what happened. He was crawling over the fence with a loaded gun in his hand. I am sure he knew better, but the wisest of us can be careless sometimes." He shook his head slowly. "It was a sad accidint," he said. "And that's my ruling: that no blame can be attached to anyone alive."

Mr. Waters and Mr. Goolsby then carried the corpse to the house and laid it on the bed that stood always clean and ready for guests in the front room. Harvey Doane was the first guest to lie there in many, many years.

Isabel realized that breakfast had all been ruined long before. She put on fresh coffee, and invited the men to sit with the Doane children at the table, for refreshment before they left. Lizzie had retired to her bedroom. Alma had gone to the dugout, perhaps to pack.

"I'll go back now and make some arrangements for you—call the undertaker," Mr. Waters said. "Mr. Goolsby will stay with you

awhile, and I'll send some women to help you. Now is there anything else I can do before I leave?"

"Yes sir," said Isabel. "Take Alma Greeping with you."

For the first time then, Isabel went down the dugout steps to
visit Alma Greeping. It was a dank, dim place, as it always had
been, but Alma was leaving it clean. If there had ever been any
signs of Alma's individual presence, they were already gone. She
expressed her willingness to leave with Mr. Waters, who had said
he would pay her way on the train to wherever she wanted to go.

"Could I just go in and see—" she seemed to stumble trying to
say a name—"see him one more time?" she asked, and was permitted some time with him alone.

When she came out, tears marked her face but her expression
had not changed. She and Isabel looked at each other, and Isabel
seemed to see the same face, with its inscrutable set of mourning,
that had once looked at her from Mr. Goolsby's cotton patch. She
thought at first Alma would speak, but she did not. Isabel had an
impulse to offer some kind word, but in the end could not manage
to utter it. Where Alma had come from, what she had hoped for,
Isabel never was to know.

She and Ray stood together on the front porch as they
watched her depart. "I don't blame her for anything," Isabel said.

Ray shook his head, whether in agreement she did not know or
ask.

"I've got to go and see about Mama," Isabel said. "But first—
would you just tell me one thing?"

He looked at her, waiting.

"Just this," she said, as though he had questioned her. "I
thought you said you would tell Mr. Goolsby the truth."

"The truth—" said Ray, and paused, as though wondering
what the word meant. Then he turned more directly to Isabel and
said, "This is exactly the way it was, Sister, and I want you to know
and remember. I told Mr. Goolsby and Mr. Waters straight out
that I done it. Then when they got here—when they saw how it
was—Mr. Goolsby said he understood that I was mixed up and
scared and maybe felt to blame for something that wasn't my fault.
But he said anyone could look at Papa and tell that it had been a
accidint. And Mr. Waters said the same thing."

"Did you plan it that way?" Isabel asked.

"No," said Ray, "it just happened. I kept thinking of different

ways I might do it. I thought I'd call him out sometime, stand up
to him and tell him why I was doing it. I guess it was like some
idea of revenge. But I never could decide what to do—it just happened."

"Do you mean he didn't ever know it was his oldest son that
killed him?"

"No," said Ray, "he didn't know that."

By midmorning, people began to come, bearing food and offering help and condolences. Mrs. Goolsby and another old woman,
who with her attended every death and birth, went in to wash and
dress the corpse. Mrs. Waters came, accompanied by Joanna, and
took charge of the kitchen. She said she had come to stay as long as
she was needed.

She sent Isabel out of the room: "You get some rest," she said.

At that time the kitchen clock struck the half hour, and Isabel
looked and saw that the hands stood at ten-thirty. She was as-
tounded to see that time was still passing.

"At six-fifteen I was standing there at the cook table slicing
meat," she said.

There were two or three women in the kitchen then, besides
Mrs. Waters, and they all sighed and threw up their hands.

"Come on," said Joanna, and led Isabel to her bedroom.

Sophie was in there, kneeling on the floor, looking through her
trunk. "I was wondering what I would wear to the funeral," she
said.

"Would you mind," Joanna asked her, "if we stayed here by
ourselves a little while? Isabel and I haven't had a chance to talk."

Sophie got up and gave them a small, neat smile. "No, I
wouldn't mind," she said. "I don't mind anything anymore."

She walked out of the room and left Isabel and Joanna to lie
across the bed, propped on their elbows, as they had done so many
times in the years of their friendship.

"Sophie may get along better now," Joanna said.

"I guess she will," said Isabel.

"And your mama?"

"I can't tell how she will be. Whatever he was, he was her husband and she's lost him."

Joanna did not answer that. They lay without speaking a little
while, holding words they were not quite ready to say.

"Mama didn't much want me to come," Joanna said. "She said

it might not look right, on account of Ray. You know how she's always been about a girl going to a boy's house."

"But she changed her mind."

"I made her see I had to come."

"And I guess she feels different now."

"Different?"

"About you and Ray. I mean with Alma gone."

Joanna didn't precisely answer that. She was silent a long moment, pursing her lips, a way she took from her mama. "Isabel," she finally said, "is he going to forgive me?"

"Forgive you for what?"

"Well—that. I mean that I let Mama influence me. That I sent him away."

"You couldn't help it. He always knew that."

"It will be all right now, won't it?"

"I imagine it will—if you think so."

"I mean really, Isabel. I mean—can he live with what he's done?"

"So you know what really happened? What kind of accident?"

"Mama had to tell me. I overheard something. She told me the rest—what Mr. Goolsby said."

"And you don't care?"

"Care?" said Joanna. "It's the only way your mama or Ray and I, or any of you, could ever hope for anything again. Care? I love him more than ever. Everything will be all right now, and our lives can go on."

"Then we had better go and find him," Isabel said, "and let you tell him how you feel."

"Yes," Joanna said. "It's what I came for."

The two of them went out then, walking hand in hand, up on the hillside, away from the barn and the pasture path. Ray would see and come to them, Isabel knew, and she would walk away alone and give them the gift of each other.

Joanna squeezed Isabel's hand. "Oh, it's all going to be so wonderful from now on," she said.

CHAPTER TEN

Ray and Joanna had their few words as they walked on the hillside, in view of everyone. No one could hear them but everyone could see, just as on the porch swing at home. They didn't say much. Joanna had not meant to say much. She had made up her mind her presence would be enough.

"People will talk," her mother had said, when she insisted upon coming.

"I want them to," was Joanna's reply.

Her mother had seen what she meant. "I reckon you're determined to stand by him," she said, making it something of a question.

Joanna was. Of course she was. This hard thing he'd had to do wouldn't affect a promise made to last a lifetime.

She stayed on at the Doanes' through dinner and helped the women wash the dishes; then, as she had told her mother she would do, she returned home. Her mother was going to stay as long as she was needed, all day and all night probably. Her father would go to the Doanes' after supper to join a group of men sitting up with the corpse.

At home, Joanna resumed what she had been doing when she heard the news—going over the furniture with a rag soaked in cedar oil. As she had told Isabel, she really overheard it. Her father had not meant her to know so soon, she realized, but she was working by an open window close to the verbena bed where her mother was hoeing.

"What was it, Tom?" Joanna heard her mama say, and looking out saw that Papa had appeared and Mama had straightened up, facing him, gripping the hoe handle. (Winnie had come to the house to tell them Papa had gone with Mr. Goolsby because something was wrong at the Doanes, but they hadn't known what it was.)

"Harvey's dead," Papa said. "Ray shot him."

Rag in hand, Joanna sat back on the floor by the library table she had been polishing. Her first rational thought was, I ought to have known. There wasn't anything else he could do.

But she did not pursue the thought. It was more important to look ahead—ask herself what she ought to do next. She was not yet a married woman, but she considered her duty to Ray to be the same as if they were married. For some reason she recalled something she had heard about court trials: "A wife can't testify against her husband." She didn't know whether Ray's case was ever likely to come to court (not having heard then of Mr. Goolsby's verdict), and she knew she would not be called as any sort of witness. But that principle seemed to suggest everything about a wife's duty. It was as important to be for a man as it was not to be against him. And there were many ways of giving testimony.

Thinking back over the morning, Joanna felt satisfied. Ray had reassured her about his own situation—Mr. Goolsby had the same as told him he had nothing to fear. She knew it would take a while for the Doanes to get over their troubles and begin to live like other people again, and there was no way of knowing when Ray would be able to leave and go to school. But there had never been any certainty about that anyway. There was no denying, and no one at Greenfields would surely wish to deny, that the future looked far brighter now for the Doanes and everyone connected with the Doanes.

As she went on with her work, Joanna caught herself singing happily of "The Unclouded Day." She hushed, but still felt guilty, and was not much surprised later on when thunderstorms appeared in the south and clouds moved in to darken the sky. (The rains missed Greenfields that spell, and everyone was thankful for that.)

For supper she fried salmon patties and opened cans of peas and corn. Her father ate hurriedly and left for the Doanes', saying he would be home around midnight. The boys and Joanna lingered at the table a little while, but found little to say to each other.

As dusk came on, they could see fireflies flashing in the bushes in the yard. Winnie talked of them, still calling them lightning bugs as he had learned to do in childhood. He said there had never been so many as there were this summer; there were thousands of them down toward the railroad, where the water stood the longest after rains.

As they got up from the table, Joanna said, "We could play dominoes when I get through washing dishes."

"I was aiming to catch me some lightning bugs," Winnie said.

"Sure, go ahead, Winnie," Joanna said.

After he was gone, Jack came into the kitchen and picked up a cup towel, but he didn't say anything and Joanna was not talkative either. She washed the dishes in the sink and set them on the drainboard. He was not accustomed to doing women's work, but he could do it very well when he wanted to. He dried and polished each piece, and he knew the kitchen well enough to put everything away where it belonged. By the time Joanna had finished washing the dishes, cleared the sink, and wiped the stove and cabinet, he was through too.

"Let's go out on the porch," she said.

It was still not quite dark, though the sky was mostly cloudy. The air seemed heavy, and there was hardly any breeze. They didn't stop on the porch, after all, but went on outside and sat on the bench under the plum tree. They could see a few stars, but the moon was blotted out that night. Joanna breathed a long sigh.

"Too bad it's not Ray here, instead of me," Jack said.

"I wasn't thinking that way," Joanna said.

"You do, though, don't you? I mean it's still Ray you want by your side in the starlight?"

"You know it is, Jack, and always will be."

"This thing's not gonna bother you too much?" he asked.

"You mean the accident?"

"Whatever you want to call it. I mean you aim to stick by old Ray."

"What else would I do, Jack? I've always meant to marry him. I never wanted anybody else."

"When I got home from school I had an inkling you didn't feel so much that way—maybe because of that woman that was living over there."

"I was mixed up. Mama thought maybe I oughtn't to see so much of him, till they got that straightened out."

"Well, I guess Ray got it straightened out."

In the cooling, thickening dark, the soft, drawled words drifted harmlessly a moment; then suddenly she knew what he meant and they changed, they hardened, assaulting her nerves with an unexpected, shocking force. She got up and walked a few steps away and back again before she spoke.

"Oh, Jack, I never thought of that," she said, dropping to his side, with her head in her hands. "I swear to God I never thought of that."

"Well, I'm sorry, Jo," he finally said. "I guess I took it for granted that you had."

"I never meant that," she said, lifting her head, leaning close to see his face in the near darkness. "I don't see how you could have thought I meant that. I know Ray never thought it."

"Well, you wanted things straightened out," Jack said, "and once they had gone as far as they had, what other way was there?"

"I don't know. It seemed like there had to be some way, but I never once thought of a killing."

"No," he said slowly, "I don't believe you did. All you ever thought about was the looks of the thing—Mama taught you that."

"Jack, that's not fair," she said.

"It's true," he said.

She supposed it was true, in a way. It didn't mean what he said, though—nobody would condone a killing for the sake of appearance. "It's not just Mama, Jack," she said. "It's the way we all live. And maybe it's not as bad as you make it sound either. What if nobody ever cared what anybody thought?"

"Are you saying that's the only thing that makes anybody behave theirselves?"

"No, I don't think I am. But it might be one thing. And wouldn't everything be better now if Harvey Doane had cared?"

"Well, I don't know, Jo. Because you see, I think he did always care. He might have fooled hisself about Alma—he might not have seen just how far he could go. But up to then he got along all right. I'd even say people liked him—at least the men did."

"Even when they couldn't keep from knowing how he was at home. How cruel."

"That's what I mean. You see, they did keep from it. And not so much because they liked him, maybe. Papa did once, of course, but I think he backed off. But Harvey Doane was a man in the community, I've heard Papa say that. It was just so much easier for everybody to say he was the head of his family, and what he did at home was not really anybody else's business. And now you see what it's come to."

"So I suppose now you're fixing to say it's bad if everybody in the community wants to talk like Mr. Doane's death was an accident."

"Jo, you know I wouldn't wish any more trouble on Ray, not

for the whole world, but I just can't help thinking everything might be better in the long run if folks didn't always try to cover up the truth."

"Well, Ray didn't mean to cover up anything. You can't blame him for that."

Jack put an arm around her. "I know that, Jo," he said, "don't be mad. I'm sorry I said all I did to you—but you know how I am when I start trying to think out something."

"Devotion to truth," she said shakily, holding back tears.

"Say, that was some Sunday school lesson, wasn't it?" he said, laughing. She tried to laugh with him, but her laugh sounded more like a sob.

They sat on the bench a while longer, till they saw Winnie coming—or saw his lantern bobbing along in the dark.

"Here comes Diogenes," Jack said.

"I guess you think he's come to the wrong place," Joanna said.

Jack had got up, about to go and meet Winnie. He turned back. "You're all right, Jo," he said. "And who am I to say the looks of the thing is not the same as the truth?"

Joanna lay awake a long time, going over the whole day in her mind, coming back always to the talk with Jack. She thought of his accusation: that she had known the only way out of the Doanes' misery was the killing of Harvey Doane. She had really never thought so far, had not anticipated death. But now that she tried to think of any other way out Ray could have taken, she realized she should have known long ago what he would have to do. There was no other way: killing had to be done, and Ray had done it. She was sorry, and she could see (now that she lay alone and slowed the procession of her thoughts) what Isabel had seen from the beginning. Life would never be easy for Ray—he would never be without that memory. Then a lurking fear pricked her, derived from something Jack had said. What if truth couldn't be covered up? What if Greenfields couldn't contain the truth of what had happened at the Doanes'? What if her duty to Ray became more than keeping loyally at his side, and comforting him when painful memories woke him in the night? As her brother suspected, Joanna really was an honest girl, despite her life-long training in the self-deceiving ways of Greenfields. She realized she didn't know much about love, and she couldn't honestly say whether she could love

Ray through a long prison sentence and marry him then. How could Joanna possibly know that?

Next morning Tom Waters took his boys and went to the cemetery, where men were gathering to dig the grave. He said he hated to ask Joanna to stay at the store on the day of the funeral; but she said she didn't mind, she had to keep doing something. He said he would go about middle of the morning and bring her mama home, so she could get ready for the funeral service, which would take place in the Doane house at two o'clock. He would close the store at noon; it was his long-standing custom to close half a day for a funeral in the community.

Joanna printed an announcement of these plans, in black ink on a sheet of good white stationery that she carefully edged in black, and tacked it up in the store by the post office window, as she had sometimes seen funeral notices displayed in town. She knew all that came in would be inquiring, even if they had already heard when and where the funeral would be, and foreseeing how one question might lead to another, hoped to save herself from giving answers that would of necessity be painful today.

About midmorning, when Joanna had seated herself on a stool behind the counter to read the new *Comfort* magazine, she heard a car drive up in front. She raised her eyes and through the screen door could see an open yellow Chevrolet that did not belong in the Greenfields community. Nor did it appear familiar to her, as the car any drummer calling at Greenfields ever drove.

She laid the magazine down and stood up. A man got out and stepped up onto the porch, but she could not see him clearly through the screen and assumed at first he was no one she had ever seen before. Then he pulled open one of the doors and stepped inside. She recognized him immediately.

"Good morning," she said, in a flat tone not altogether concealing a challenge, the way Greenfields spoke to strangers who had not yet offered credentials.

He was not quite a stranger. She had never heard his name, but she knew where she had seen him before. He was a tall, slender, dark-haired man, maybe handsome, if you could admire so slight a frame. She had seen him at the rabbit drive.

"Good morning," he answered, removing his wide-banded Panama hat. "I was hoping to find Mr. Waters here."

Her inner reaction to that was that he talked funny, and wore a funny hat. But she answered, with wide serious eyes, "I'm sorry, but Mr. Waters is not here today."

The stranger walked up closer to the counter, his hat in his hands. All she could think about was wishing Isabel were there.

"My name is Archie Hastings," he said. "I work for the *Western Message*—the county paper, you know."

Joanna nodded. "Yes," she said.

"I met Mr. Waters when I came to the rabbit drive here at Greenfields last April, and I was hoping for a few words with him this morning." He was looking around the store as he talked; his eyes had come to rest on the announcement she had posted, on the wall just opposite the counter where they stood.

"He's at the cemetery," she said, "helping dig a grave."

He looked at her oddly. "Oh, do they do that?" he said.

In spite of herself, her eyes twinkled. "Well, they're aiming to bury a man," she said.

She saw him compress his lips to prevent a smile.

"You see," he said, "I am new in this part of the country. I suppose it's the custom here for the men to help dig the grave for a burial."

"It is out here," she said. "It may not be in town."

"I did know there had been a death at Greenfields," he said, his eyes straying again to Joanna's announcement. "I heard it from Mr. Aylmer, the undertaker, and I was hoping I might find out more from Mr. Waters. I felt when I was here before that he was the usual spokesman for the community."

"Well, I suppose he is," Joanna said, "but I don't think he could tell you anything about this. I guess the undertaker knows all there is to know."

"Look, Miss Waters—you are his daughter, aren't you?"

"Yes," she said. "My name is Joanna Waters."

"Well—what I mean to say is, of course I don't know this community at all. You may have been a close friend of the man—" he glanced again at the paper on the wall—"of Mr. Doane."

"I'm engaged to marry his son," Joanna said. It was none of this man's business, but she meant never to deny Ray.

He looked at her closely. "Then maybe I shouldn't ask you," he said.

"You can ask," she said. "Mr. Doane was climbing over a barbed wire fence near his barn. He had been in the pasture shooting rabbits before breakfast, as he was in the habit of doing. For some reason, he didn't lay his gun down when he climbed over the fence, and it went off and killed him. Mr. Goolsby, the justice of the peace, ruled that it was accidental death. And that's all there is to it."

Archie Hastings took a notebook from the breast pocket of his seersucker suit and scribbled in it.

"Could you tell me who found him?" he asked.

"Ray, his oldest son."

"Your fiancé."

"Yes."

"I don't suppose I could talk to him?"

"I don't think he would feel very happy about it. And he couldn't tell you anything either. He just found him, there on the ground with the gun by his side."

"And they didn't think Mr. Doane was disturbed about anything?"

"He didn't commit suicide, if that's what you mean."

"Well, I suppose this really is all," he said. "I had thought I might attend the funeral, but I see they're having the service at the home, so I wouldn't want to intrude."

"I guess you could go to the cemetery," she said doubtfully. "People do that sometimes if they don't know the family very well."

"But you don't think it would be quite the thing to do?"

"Well, I don't think it would help anybody—and I can't imagine what you would get out of it to write about."

He put his notebook back in his pocket. "I believe you're right," he said. "I thought when Mr. Aylmer told me about the accident that it might be my duty to inquire further, but I see it isn't a case where a stranger ought to intrude."

"Well, I'm sorry I couldn't help you," she said.

"Oh, you helped, Miss Waters," he said. "I understand much better now what must have happened."

"And will you put it in your article?"

"Yes," he said, "I think I will."

"All right," she said. "I'm glad if I helped." She gave him a formal little smile. "Good-bye."

"Good-bye," he said, and walked toward the door. Then, his hand already on the metal handle of the screen door, he suddenly turned back.

"Miss Waters," he said. "There's something else."

"I can't tell you anything else," she said.

"Oh, not about this—not Mr. Doane."

"Then what?" She had not at all known whether she would like this young man, with his strange accent and pompous hat and impertinent questions. She had even intended not to like him, because she half believed he had falsely led Isabel on. But like him she did. He might have asked too many questions, but she supposed he had a boss that expected him to do his job. "Well, ask," she said.

"It's awkward," he said, "but you look like an understanding sort of girl, and I think you'll sympathize with me." He ran his hand through his waving brown hair. She guessed he was nervous. Of a sudden, he looked very young.

"You can try me," she said.

"You see," he said, coming close to the counter, leaning on it, looking into her face. "When I was here before, I saw a girl."

He seemed to wait for her response, but she made none.

"At the rabbit drive," he said, "I turned away from the slaughter—this might sound silly to you, but I had never seen anything like that before, and it made me a little sick."

"I can understand that," she said.

"And there was this girl. She was just standing there—she seemed to have stepped around a bush, as I had, to put it between me and the rabbit pen, and we were face to face. I saw she felt the way I did about the rabbits—that was the first thing I saw." Again, he seemed to wait for her to speak.

"And the next thing?" she said.

"She was beautiful," he said simply. "Can you help me find her?"

"But Mr. Hastings," she said with deliberate facetiousness. "There are so many beautiful girls at Greenfields." She was giving herself time, trying to think. She must not lose this man for Isabel, but somehow she did not want to give Archie Hastings the advantage of knowing who Isabel was before she knew who he was.

He did not even smile at her remark. "She is dark," he said. "Or her hair is—soft around her face. Her eyes are dark, too, I don't know what color. Violet, maybe, if eyes can really be that color, or some kind of gray. I don't think they're brown."

"You don't seem to be too sure what she looks like, Mr. Hastings," Joanna said.

"Oh but I am. I'd know her in a minute. And surely you must know her."

"I'm sure I do. But there are several dark-haired girls—I just don't know."

"There couldn't be another like this one."

"If you've thought about her so much," Joanna decided to say, "I wonder why you didn't look for her before now."

"Because—oh, I can't really tell you. She scarcely seemed real to me—more like a dream. And I'm new at my job, you know, busy there—and meeting other people."

"Courting other girls."

"No, not courting. But everybody's got someone they want me to meet. And my uncle—he's the editor, my boss—says I ought to go to all the socials. And yet I didn't forget this dark girl, you see. And when I saw the name Greenfields on Mr. Aylmer's sheet today, I thought of her."

"Your uncle didn't tell you to come?"

"No. I don't think he even really wanted me to, but he agreed."

Joanna looked at him thoughtfully. She believed him; she liked him. "I might have an idea," she said.

"Of who she is?"

"No, I don't mean that. You say your uncle wants you to go around to gatherings in town. Well, we take the paper out here too, you know. Maybe you ought to get acquainted in the country."

"What is it you have in mind?"

"Why don't you come out here and go to church Sunday morning? Nearly everybody at Greenfields goes to church."

"And you would introduce me?"

"Sure I would." Really, she was thinking of something more than seeing Isabel and Archie meet at church. She didn't see why he shouldn't be invited, along with all the Doanes, to dinner with the Waterses Sunday. In another family, the death of the father might cause her mother to hesitate about issuing such an invitation; but in this case Joanna didn't think the looks of the thing would matter. She thought her mother would invite the Doanes, and she thought they would come.

She went on then and told her plan to Archie Hastings. "Lots of young folks come to our house for dinner on Sunday," she said. "I'll get Mama to ask you, if you say you'll come."

"Are you sure your mother would ask a stranger home from church?"

"Of course she would. She wouldn't think it was proper for me to ask her to invite you, but I'll introduce you to my brothers and they'll see to everything."

"And that would make it proper, would it?"

"Sure it would."

"And you think my girl will be there?"

Joanna wished Isabel could hear him say "my girl."

"I don't know," she said, "but I think there's a real good chance of it."

"I'll come," he said. "Where's the church?"

"I'll show you," she said. She came around from behind the counter and followed him out onto the porch, where she pointed across the open ground to the school. "We have church and Sunday school there," she said. "It's really the schoolhouse."

"Well, thank you, Miss Waters," he said. "Could we shake hands?"

She offered her hand and he took it, pressing it gently in his own smooth hand (so unlike Ray's), that might never have handled any implement heavier than a pencil or a pen.

"I like you, Miss Waters," he said, "and I think you know who my girl is. But if this is the proper way for me to meet her, then I'll be all the more grateful to you."

"I like you, Mr. Hastings," Joanna said. "I hope you will come back to Greenfields, and I hope you find your girl."

She stood on the porch and watched him drive away, watched till the last of his dust disappeared. She sighed, and went back into the store. For a little while, fancying she glimpsed a happy ending for Isabel, she had almost forgotten the worries she had waked with in the night.

The funeral was like any other, nearly. It was a community occasion and almost everyone would go—would be expected to go. At the Doanes', many had to stand on the porch and even in the front yard. Ray and Isabel had asked Joanna to sit with the family, but something held her back—some troubling thought left over from the night. She went to stand with her mother, who had chosen not to claim the seat she was offered in the front room (where the bed had been taken down to make a place for Harvey Doane to lie in state).

"That's wise of you," her mother said. "No use pushing yourself in among the family now."

The funeral was different because it was so silent. There were no sounds of mourning, and when the burial was finished people didn't linger, as they usually did, standing around and visiting among the graves.

Before Ray got in the car to drive his family home, he came to Joanna where she was standing alone, away from the departing crowd.

"I may not be over tomorrow night, Jo," he said.

"I guess they'll need you at home," she said, finding words to use instead of "the looks of the thing." "But come to church Sunday."

"Yes," said Ray, "I think we'll try to come to church. I think we ought to do that."

"And, Ray," she said, "do be sure Isabel comes."

CHAPTER ELEVEN

Lizzie didn't want to go to church Sunday. Isabel talked to her while the two of them were cooking breakfast and tried to persuade her to go, but she only shook her head and mumbled that she guessed not today.

Isabel hadn't believed she would go. She had told Ray she thought their mother would need more time before she felt able to face Greenfields again, but he insisted the whole family ought to go to church.

"It would be better for us all," he said. "Start as you aim to go on—ain't that one of Mrs. Waters's mottoes?"

"I don't think we can rush Mama into anything," Isabel had said.

"Well, it would be better," he had said stubbornly. "Better for me—if that means anything to you."

Isabel and Ray had not talked much since the killing. She had never said a word to him against it, but she felt he blamed her for something.

"I'll try, Ray," she promised.

But as she looked at her mother that morning—standing at the hot stove, strands of hair falling down along her sweaty brow—she said to herself, Mama can't even realize what's happened yet. To look at her you wouldn't guess anything had happened. There was the same uncertain expression on her face, the streak of snuff on her chin; she had on the same shapeless, faded dress she had worn for a week, except when she put on the black skirt and waist Mrs. Waters loaned her for the funeral.

"You could wear those things of Mrs. Waters's," Isabel said, "if you don't think you've got anything else. It might be just as well to wear black."

Lizzie looked up at her, brushing back a wisp of hair. "Oh no," she said, "I'll wait. I won't wear black no more."

At breakfast Ray said cheerfully, "Well, I guess everybody's fixing to go to preaching this morning." He looked at his mother, who shook her head, smiling vaguely.

"I'll stay with Mama," Isabel said. "I want the rest to go."

"Why can't Mama go?" Ray asked. They had long been unaccustomed to asking any questions directly of Lizzie.

"Well, son," she said then, surprisingly, "when the time comes, I'll go. But I'm not ready yet."

And Isabel inwardly observed, "She will be all right. Mama really will be all right." But clearly the time had not come.

"It doesn't matter," Isabel said. "I have some things I need to do anyway. I'd just as soon stay at home."

Ray said brusquely, "If anybody's got to stay I'll stay."

"Oh no, you've got to drive the car," Sophie protested. "I want to go to Sunday school in the car."

"It's best if you go, Ray," Isabel said. "We'll work things out better as we go along."

"You ought to go," Ray said. "Joanna said especially for me to bring you. She wanted us all to stay for dinner."

"You don't have to stay with me, Sister," Lizzie said.

"I'll go next week," Isabel said. "I'm not going off and leave you today."

Later, when Isabel was alone in the kitchen, cleaning up the last signs of breakfast, Burnie came stumping in.

"I wish you'd go, Sis," he said, "and let me stay here. It's not right for you to be the one that gives up everything."

"Burnie," she told him, "it was true what I said. I'd really just as soon stay here. I guess I feel like Mama—it's too soon."

He stood leaning on the dining table, watching her scrub the oilcloth cover, which was so worn that patches of the underlying fabric showed through.

"Maybe we can get us a new tablecloth now, Sister," he said, looking up at her in the slow, careful way of his that suggested his handsome head was too heavy for his stem of a neck and his frail body.

She looked into his face; she thought his widened eyes were seeking some sort of reassurance but couldn't guess quite what he wanted.

"I guess we can," she said. "I don't know anything about how much money we have."

"Papa must have had more than he wanted us to think he did," Burnie said, "or how did he get the car?"

"I don't know," she said. "Ray will have to find out about all that."

She went to put the dishrag in the pan of dishwater keeping warm on the stove. He followed her.

"Sister," he said urgently, "things will be better, won't they? Don't you think it really was the thing to do?"

She turned to face him, shaking her head. "I don't see how we can know about that right now," she said. "I hope it was—I pray God it was—and yet I can't see how."

"Will you ever forgive Ray?"

"Oh, Burnie, it's not for me to forgive him."

"But do, Sister, do anyway. You and Ray have always got along so well. And now—if you don't anymore—" He broke off. She feared he would cry.

"Don't worry, Burnie. Everything will be all right somehow. And anyway it's not your fault."

"It is, though—or I'm afraid it is."

"I don't see why," she said.

He stood looking down at the floor awhile; then finally he raised his heavy head. "I ought to have voted on your side," he said.

"You seemed so sure," she said.

"On account of Ray," he said. "It was wrong on account of him. I didn't think how bad such a thing might be."

"Well, you mustn't worry," Isabel said. "It's done, and maybe for the best. You'd better go and get ready."

He suddenly smiled—his sweet transforming smile. "Yes, I had, hadn't I?" he said. "But first I guess I'd better go tell Sancho that he won't be going to Sunday school anymore."

The talk with Burnie puzzled and depressed Isabel. She

wished she could have told him unequivocally what he wanted to hear. She was not quite sure why she couldn't.

Because of course things really were better. Sophie called her now to come and help her fasten her dress, and Isabel found her standing before the bureau, her hair out of its braids and combed out in a crimped, spreading fan falling nearly to her waist. Isabel was tempted to offer to arrange it for her in a more controlled style, but seeing how pleased the child was at her reflection in the glass, realized Sophie needed a chance to think of herself as a pretty little girl. She said nothing at all until she had fastened the dress, which was an old summer dress of her own that she had re-modeled in the last two days so that Sophie could have something new to wear.

"Now look at me," said Isabel, and Sophie turned around.

"Do I look nice, Sister?" she asked.

"You look beautiful," Isabel said.

Sophie laughed. "With all these freckles?" she said.

"You'll have to start wearing your bonnet more," Isabel said.

Sophie turned back around and looked at herself keenly in the glass. "I might," she said.

Certainly there was a change in Sophie, and how could Isabel not be glad of that?

And Travis—he had come to Isabel the evening before, asking to borrow her Sunday school book so he could study the lesson. "I've decided I ought to have something to say in class," he said, "like some of the rest of them."

When it was time to go, Ray drove the car up in front of the house. Isabel and her mother stood on the porch to watch the de-parture.

"Don't they look nice?" Lizzie said as the car pulled away and out of sight behind the lilac hedge.

"They sure do," Isabel agreed.

"You know," Lizzie said, "I may get Ray to take me to town sometime—I want to hunt me some material for a dress."

The Waters family, as was their custom, walked to the school-house together that morning.

"Who in the world's come to preaching in a yellow automo-bile?" Martha exclaimed.

"Oh, I think I know," Jack said. "That's a friend of mine that works for the *Western Message*. He said he might come to Greenfields today."

"Young feller, is he?" Tom asked.

"Yessir. Older than me, though," Jack said.

"I think I talked to him at the rabbit drive," Tom said. "Seemed like a fine young feller."

"Yessir, he was there," Jack said. "He said the other day he would like to come back and get better acquainted in the Greenfields community. I thought maybe I'd get him to come home with us for dinner today."

"Why sure," Martha said. "You do that, that'll be just fine."

So that part of Joanna's plan seemed assured of success. But then they saw Ray Doane driving up.

"She didn't come," cried Joanna. "Isabel's not with them."

"Lizzie wouldn't come, and Isabel thought she had better stay with her mama," said Martha, as though she had known all along.

"I ought to have guessed she would do that," Joanna said.

Now family members scattered to join their various social groups. Watching Sophie Doane, with something like an older sister's concern, Joanna saw that a group of girls quickly gathered around her. Her father's death might give her a sort of romantic appeal for girls of that age, Joanna surmised, and thought, After all, why not? It's about all he ever did give her.

"Come on, Jo, I want you and Ray to meet my friend Archie Hastings," said Jack then, for his mother's benefit, and the three walked toward the yellow car.

Joanna explained to Ray about Archie and her plan to arrange a meeting between him and Isabel.

"But what do you know about him, Jo?" Ray asked. "How do you know it would be a good thing for him and Sis to get together?"

"Papa knows him. He thinks he's all right."

"Oh well. I guess it can't hurt anything if they meet sometime."

"But don't anybody mention her name," Joanna warned, "because I want it to be a surprise when they do."

Archie got out of the car and Joanna introduced the three young men, then quickly excused herself, saying she had to go in and start playing the organ.

The old women who were usually seated and waiting for her when she came in were not in their places. (She knew where they were: gossiping by the doorstep. She had heard the word "Doane" as she approached them and they all then looked quickly around and greeted her too brightly.) There was no one in the house but Isaiah Birdsong, who came down from his rostrum in great unfolding strides to open the organ box for her. He flung open the doors and stood back with a gesture that held the quality of a bow.

"Thank you, Mr. Birdsong," she said, and he stepped nearer, until it seemed to her he was pressing her against the organ box, although in fact she might have stretched her arm its full length and not touched him.

"Miss Joanna," he said, with a careful sad smile, "I don't hardly know how to say it, but I just want you to know how sorry I am about what's happened."

She looked at him blankly.

"About Ray," he said.

"I'm sure all the Doanes feel pretty bad," she said, "but I don't understand what you're telling me."

"Well, about you and Ray—I know how much you must hate to break your engagement—"

Joanna straightened with a movement so sudden he stepped backward.

"I would hate to very much, Mr. Birdsong," she said coldly, "but there's no question of such a thing and it wouldn't be any of your business if there was."

A deep red stained his neck above his stiff white collar and rose slowly up to the roots of his oat-straw hair. Yet in spite of this apparent embarrassment he moved an inch nearer and leaned toward her face. "I do beg your pardon," he said, "but I felt that under the circumstances—that is, I have long wished to speak to you—"

"Oh please, Mr. Birdsong, don't speak to me," she begged, and the three old ladies, who were just then entering the door, stopped and stared at them.

"Do forgive me if it was too soon," he said softly. "And now we must pray—I shall ask the Lord to be by his side, and with all our brothers and sisters in the Doane family."

"Mr. Birdsong, I have to play!" she muttered fiercely.

But she did not begin at once. As he finally turned to go back to the lectern, she took a hymn book from the shelf above the organ and a pencil that she carried in her little drawstring purse, ripped out a blank fly sheet, and scribbled on it hastily. Then as

she played she kept turning her head to see who came in. When
Winnie appeared, she beckoned to him, and he came to her with a
puzzled expression on his face.

She gave him the folded sheet from the songbook and whispered, "Give this to Ray just as soon as you can—try not to let anyone notice, but give it to him any way you have to."

She had written: "I.B. is fixing to pray for you-all today, if you
don't get to him and shut him up first."

In a few minutes she saw Ray walk forward. She couldn't see
the encounter without turning around, but she imagined the red
wave rising from Mr. Birdsong's collar. Very well, if he was embarrassed. It was better than letting him embarrass God by telling
Him all He already knew about Ray and Harvey Doane.

Mr. Birdsong's prayer disappointed the old women; you could
tell by the way they looked at each other with the slightest movement of their heads from side to side. He prayed "for those among
us who have been touched by sorrow," but he failed to reach his
usual peak of emotional intensity. His Sunday school class was dull.
In a way Joanna felt sorry that Jack didn't enliven it with some of
his unsettling questions, for Archie Hastings's entertainment, but
Jack evidently realized there were times when it was better not to
rock the boat. Travis Doane cleared his throat once or twice, as
though he might have something to say, but Mr. Birdsong didn't
seem to notice and never called on him.

The preacher, a relative stranger to Greenfields, had come
from across the county to fill the pulpit in place of Brother
Crenshaw, who was ailing. He was too old to preach, really;
Joanna didn't suppose anybody heard a word he said. She didn't, at
least. She hoped he was going home with somebody else for dinner.
Since he was a Methodist and her own family inclined toward the
Baptists, she thought surely someone else would ask him, and so it
turned out.

During the sermon she was thinking about who would be at
the Waters house, and who wouldn't. No wonder (and she realized
this herself) she didn't know what this preacher was talking about.
While he was trying to save her soul, she was making up her mind
that Ray would just have to go after Isabel as soon as preaching
was over. Mrs. Doane could come back with them or not, but
Isabel must not miss this day.

Joanna had to play while the worshipers were leaving, but as
soon as the last one was out of the door she hurried to Ray, where

he was standing near the Doane car with his brothers, his sister, and two other little girls who were begging Sophie to go home with them. (She wouldn't; she was set on eating Mrs. Waters's fried chicken and ice cream.)

"Ray, I want Isabel," Joanna said.

"Well, I could go after her," Ray said, "but I don't think she'd be willing to leave Mama by herself. If she could drive the car, I'd just go and send her back over here."

"No," Joanna said. "I want you too." She looked up into his face, in a way she had seldom allowed herself in public. (But Mama had already gone home, to start dinner.) "We've already missed Saturday night," she added softly.

Burnie, who had evidently overheard all she said, limped a few steps toward them from where he had been leaning on the car. "I'll go with you, Ray," he said, "and stay with Mama."

"Oh no, Burnie," Joanna said, "you'd miss your dinner."

Burnie gave her that intimate smile of his that seemed to speak privately even in a crowd to the one he smiled upon. "But you see, I'm not in love," he said, "so it don't make no difference about me."

Joanna laughed. "Burnie, you're an angel," she said. "Let's go by and get a big pan of fried chicken for you to take home. Mama will have a pile of it ready by now, and you can take home enough for you and your mama's dinner and supper tonight too."

"And maybe tater salad?" Burnie said.

"Yes," she asserted happily. "Tater salad and everything. Come on, let's hurry!"

Thus another part of the plan fell into place.

Both Isabel and Lizzie had urged Ray to stay for dinner at Mrs. Waters's, and the younger children had insisted on it till Ray agreed. After they were gone Isabel thought about fixing something like a Sunday dinner herself—she could at least catch a chicken and fry it, if Mama would wring its neck. But when she asked her mama what she wanted to eat, she said, "Oh nothing. I don't care."

Isabel didn't care either. She put off deciding what to cook. She left her mama in the kitchen rocking chair, saying she thought she'd just walk down in the pasture a little piece. It seemed if she could get clear away from the house she could think: about what, she wasn't sure. She kept putting off something in her mind, not a decision exactly, but perhaps a consideration of whether there was anything to decide.

She followed the old path that led by the barn, forgetting till she came to the fence the scene that would form itself before her eyes and stop her as though it had been a physical barrier. She stopped just short of the fence and stood staring at the spot where her father had lain. You couldn't really see any sign of it now, unless—yes, that little dark spot on a clump of bleached, dry grass. She turned away, she could not go on. She would find another place to go through the fence. People didn't always have to keep following the same path.

She walked around to the other end of the barn, but mesquite brush along the fence there made the way into the pasture somewhat difficult. Perhaps there really wasn't any other path. Rather liking this notion that had come to her, she allowed herself to dwell upon it. She didn't much care where she went anyhow. She went on around to the north side of the barn, where the old wagon seat was, and sat down there awhile.

All paths might be closed to her now. The sense of freedom that from time to time washed over her, so that she felt immersed —felt baptized—in it, receded again. Sometimes, as now, she feared the consequences of this act in which all the family had acquiesced, and thus in truth participated (she too, for though she had argued with Ray she had lifted no hand to stop him)—feared their lives would all be blighted from now on. But if not—if the promise of freedom should prove true—she had no inkling of which way she must choose to find fulfillment.

Once, long ago, desperate with longing to escape her father's tyranny, she had imagined love—and tried to impose the structure of her imaginings upon the first boy (and up to now still the only one) that took her behind a bush and kissed her. She thanked the Lord now, and often had, that she had been stopped in that absurd attempt to elope with him. Sometimes she even half believed real love would come to her.

Then, in the first exciting time of knowing Miss Lona, she had dreamed of being on a college campus, in a great library (which she envisioned as an enormous marble hall, one long, high-ceilinged, columned room, all lined with books), where day after day she would read and grow wise. If any single book held the key to a door leading out of that room, into a life more satisfying than

Greenfields life could be, she never grasped or even sought it in her dreams.

Joanna, also inspired by Miss Lona, had far more practical plans, all directed toward normal school and teaching. Ray, from the first time he cranked Mr. Waters's Maxwell, fell in love with the idea of the automobile. Joanna saw in a magazine an advertisement of a school in Kansas City where he could become a trained mechanic able to make a good living at working with cars, and he began to plan and save toward going there. Together they had such practical dreams, such clear-cut goals. They would reach them, Isabel had no doubt. Ray might have to wait a little while to get away to school, but he had not known when he could go anyway. Travis could easily take over the farming in a year or two; there would be nothing to prevent Ray's leaving Greenfields. When Isabel examined the realities of their situation, she could see no reason why Ray would ever have to change the way he planned to go. It was silly of her to conjure up black fears of Nemesis, but perhaps she had simply lived with fear so long it would take her a while to learn to do without it. When she did she, too, would find a path to travel.

At this thought she got up from her seat, but did not after all go on into the pasture. With her mind still reaching ahead into the dim paths her life might follow, she returned along the way she had come and presently found herself back at the place where the path led through the fence.

It was then she heard Ray calling her. "Sister! Isabel!" he shouted.

She turned back toward the house in an anxiety that for a moment approached panic. Ray should not be here: something must be wrong. But there was nothing in his voice to suggest anything of the sort. She calmed herself and went on more slowly, calling out to let him know where she was.

He met her halfway between the barn and the hackberry tree; he could see where she had been.

"What are you doing down here?" he demanded accusingly.

"Ray, I can't keep away from the barn and the path from now on," she said.

"Sure, I know it," he said. "It's all right, forget it."

"What have you come back for though?"

"Yes," he said. "Joanna wants you to come back for dinner."

Burnie came limping along from the house, calling, "Hey, Sis, I've brought home a big dinner for me and Mama to eat here and you're going back to Greenfields with Ray."

She let them persuade her. Burnie would have been disappointed if his sacrifice for her had been rejected.

Above all, thought Joanna several times as she helped her mother in the kitchen and dining room, she wanted to witness the meeting between Isabel and Archie Hastings. She kept to the dining room as much as she could, because from there she could hear Ray's car sooner and hurry to the front porch before Isabel could get out and start in.

Two other women were in the kitchen with her mother: Mrs. Goolsby and Mrs. Akers, who with their husbands had been invited home with the Waterses from church. The three women kept talking in low tones, and with averted heads, about the Doanes. Joanna wished they would change the subject or else go ahead and say what they had to say out loud. Every time she went back into the kitchen from the dining room, one of them would look around and suddenly stop talking.

Joanna thought she would take as long as she reasonably could about arranging the napkins and iced tea goblets on the table. The women would be glad, anyway, for her not to go in and disturb the gossip. So she mused, and without ironic intent; she really did not feel angry with them. Whatever happened in the community was their affair: Lizzie Doane's loss was their loss, the children's welfare their concern. At least Joanna was willing to look at their interest in this light, for they were all good women without malice in their hearts toward anyone who belonged to Greenfields. Joanna was not precisely thinking about the women in the kitchen, but this comfortable unthinking acceptance of their motives kept her awareness of their muffled talk from dampening her excited expectations.

"Oh, Miss Waters," said someone, from the door that led out of the dining room onto the porch.

She looked up. It was Archie Hastings, standing in the doorway. "I beg your pardon," he said.

For what, she wondered, but did not ask.

"Oh, are you lost?" she said. "I told my brothers to take care of you."

"They did very well," he said. "I left them in the backyard, one pursuing an insect and the other a young lady. I wanted to speak to you."

She laughed. "You've got acquainted with Winnie and Jack, I see."

Really, her work in the dining room was finished. "Let me just find out if Mama needs me anymore," she said, "and if not you and I can go sit on the front porch." And watch for Ray and Isabel, she almost said.

She stepped into the kitchen, exchanged the necessary words with her mother, and then went with Archie out onto the front porch. It had a more formal air than the back porch; it was furnished with a wicker chair and settee and shaded with honeysuckle vines.

"It's a good fifteen minutes till dinner," she said. "Let's sit down." She sat in the chair, so that he would not suspect an invitation. He sat on the settee.

"Look," he said, "what I wanted to ask you—she didn't come to church, did she?"

"No," she said. "Or at least I don't suppose so. You said you'd recognize her. But it's still possible she might show up. Sometimes people don't come to church, but they'll come to our house anyway." She had tried to prevent him from suspecting Ray had gone after Isabel; her brothers were supposed to have kept him too busy to notice Ray was gone. She went on talking, seeking a subject to keep his mind off the girl that might or might not come. She didn't want him guessing she was Ray Doane's sister; she didn't want him expecting her at all.

"Well, at least you'll be getting acquainted with Greenfields," she said. "I guess you want to find out what rural communities in West Texas are like, since you say you came from—no, I don't think you did say where you came from."

"I'm from Missouri," he said. "Most people make jokes."

"I'm sure we can show you some things in West Texas," she said, "if that's the kind of joke you mean."

"Yes," he said. "Most people say that."

"Why did you come here?" she asked.

"My uncle wanted me to come," he said. "He's been running the paper here for nearly forty years. He's getting on in years—my father's oldest brother. He thinks he might want me to take it over in a year or two."

"That will be good for you," she said, "if you like it here. Do you think you will?"

"I think so," he said. "Sometimes I don't understand people though. It's true in town, and it's true out here."

"What is it you don't understand?" she said.

"Well, for instance," he said, "a few minutes ago I blundered into the kitchen, looking for you. There were some ladies talking. One said something like 'I feel so sorry for Ray,' and I thought, that's the young man I met with you and your brothers at church—Ray Doane."

"Yes," she said. "It was his father who died. I told you his name."

"And then another one said she did too—felt sorry for him, I mean—and went on to say it seemed to her that if it had to be done Lizzie ought to have done it. I thought she might have referred to some custom I'm not familiar with."

Joanna looked at him straight; he must know, really, she thought at first, but then she did not believe he did. He knew nothing of the family, and so the truth might not occur to him as easily as it would to one who knew the long, miserable history. She groped for a plausible explanation, and without a noticeable delay (she hoped) said, "I don't know what they could have been talking about—unless it was Ray having to drop the first handful of dirt on the casket. We don't always do that anymore here, but our old custom is that someone in the family should do it. I don't think it was very easy for Ray, but I hadn't heard anyone say they thought his mother should have done it."

"No, it certainly wouldn't be easy for her either."

"Nor for anyone," Joanna said. "I wouldn't do it. There's no reason why it has to be done—no purpose it serves."

He looked at her curiously. "You're a rather practical girl, aren't you, Miss Waters?" he said. "Pragmatic, I think might be the word."

"That's a word Jack uses," she said. "I'm not so sure I know what it means—but if it's knowing what I want, and working for it, I think I am."

"And what do you want?"

"I want to be a teacher," she said, "and marry Ray. I intend to do both."

By the time she finished speaking, the attention of both of them had been diverted to an automobile driving up in front of the house, stopping near the front gate. "Isn't that Ray now?" he said. "Just getting here from church?"

"He had to take his brother home," Joanna said.

"Someone's with him," Archie said.

Joanna didn't answer. She was only waiting now. Isabel got out of the car and came on ahead of Ray, looking just as Joanna had hoped she would.

The monthly rose that climbed the arched trellis over the gate was in bloom. Isabel pressed the latch and then paused to look back for Ray. Thus she stood a moment framed by red roses, her profile—wide brow, straight nose, full lips, and ever so faintly receding chin—clear against the sky of powdery blue. Her glossy deep brown hair, piled high in back, was soft around her face. Her dress of lilac sprigged muslin, which she had made herself with Mrs. Waters's help, fell with a loosely fitted simplicity to just above her delicate ankles and was drawn in around her slender waist with a wide silk ribbon sash.

Like a picture on a calendar, Joanna thought. She heard Mr. Hastings mutter, "My God!" and it never entered her head to accuse him of cursing.

Joanna rose and started down the brick walk, with Archie Hastings following her. She knew he had recognized Isabel; she was watching Isabel's face for the first sign she knew who Archie was. She fell back beside him, and they took a few steps together along the walk.

Isabel greeted Joanna before she looked at the man by her side. You could see she hadn't paid enough attention to him to wonder who he might be, until she shifted her head slightly, to give him a casual glance. She stood still then, and Joanna, who was studying her, knew she turned pale—only a shade paler, and she hadn't a lot of color in her face at ordinary times, so that Joanna thought Archie Hastings might not have noticed. Nor would he have noticed—Joanna hoped—a fleeting expression that came like a glint of fear into the soft dark eyes.

Immediately, Joanna was making them acquainted with each other, saying their names, and Isabel gained control of herself, smiled, said, "Pleased to meet you, Mr. Hastings," and went on along the walk. Joanna noticed how she moved then, different from the way she had walked when she got out of the car, slowly, rhythmically, the way she had when things were right for her. It seemed that although she might have felt startled and uncertain upon meeting this man, something inside her was responding as if finding him were a natural culmination of some cycle of her life.

Joanna dropped back beside Ray, and the two couples stepped onto the porch just as Mrs. Waters came through the house calling out cheerily: "Everybody right this way, to see the white mice eat out of the yellow saucepan."

"What is she saying?" asked Archie, and Isabel explained that this was Mrs. Waters's way of saying "Dinner's ready." She had done it always; no one had ever thought to ask why.

Archie laughed happily, as though this were the jolliest custom he had ever heard of, and the young people went in to dinner.

After dinner there was discussion, as always, about what to do with the afternoon. It was too hot to go Kodaking, wasn't it? They could just drive around. Mary Varton had brought a new piece of music; she hadn't learned it, but Joanna could play it at sight and they could all sing.

"No," Joanna said, "it's not too hot to go Kodaking. We can take bottles of cold tea or pop. And Mr. Hastings wants to learn our customs, he's studying us. Let's walk down the railroad."

"That sounds interesting to me," said Mr. Hastings, "although I assure you I'm not studying anyone."

In the end they went Kodaking, though the younger children chose to stay in the shady backyard, and Winnie, Travis, Sophie, and Emma Varton started a domino game.

There were four couples that walked down the railroad. The first two—Jack Waters and Mary Varton, Sam Akers and Pearlie Thaxton—walked on ahead, leaving the others to come as slowly as they pleased, together or separately.

These two lagging couples stayed close together at first, with Archie and Ray making most of the conversation. Archie was curious about the community, the crops raised there, what people did who were not farmers—and Ray gave him considered answers that seemed to satisfy him. He talked like a country boy—the contrast with Archie Hastings's speech was strong, but he was not self-conscious about the difference. Joanna, as always, felt proud of Ray; he was a great deal more intelligent than many people gave him credit for. She thought it was intelligent of him not to draw attention to himself in the community by changing the way he spoke (talking proper, as people said). It was all right for girls to talk proper if they could learn and wanted to; she and Isabel helped each other in trying to overcome their language faults, and everyone understood this was because Joanna wanted to be a teacher and Isabel—was just Isabel. She wasn't like anyone else anyway. But Ray could have done as well as they if he had wanted to.

"No, there ain't much in the way of cultivated crops any farther along than this," Ray told Archie. "This is what they call the Fontine Breaks, named for a rancher that had a lot of land here in the early days. It's pert near too rough for farming."

At that point Joanna winked at Isabel, then said with a startled manner: "Oh, Ray, my bracelet has come undone and dropped off somewhere. I know I had it just a few minutes ago—it can't be very far back."

"All right, Jo," he said. "I'll help you look for it."

"You-all go on," Joanna said to the others. "No need to wait on us."

Isabel and Archie walked on alongside the track. Having come through the first cuts, where the steep grade began, they had reached a stretch of track that ran nearly level with the grassy land on either side.

"She didn't lose her bracelet, did she?" Archie said.

Isabel smiled at him. "She wasn't even wearing one," she said.

"She has placed us here together," Archie said. "She started work on her scheme the day I first met her, the morning of your father's funeral."

"Joanna has been my best friend," said Isabel, "almost as long as I can remember."

"She'll always be my friend too," said Archie, "because she's the one that brought us together."

"Yes, I suppose she is."

"She sent Ray after you, didn't she?"

"Oh yes. I hadn't thought I should leave my mother alone today."

"I should apologize because it's my fault they brought you away. I know you just lost your father. I mustn't ask you to be as happy as I am."

"It's all right to be happy," she said.

"Do you know we have seen each other before?" he asked.

"Yes," she said simply. "And I had better tell you Joanna knows it too. You mustn't imagine she's always arranging meetings with men for me."

"No," he said, "I didn't think that."

She wondered if this meant he knew that since the day they

stood together in the chaparral and heard the dying rabbits cry, she had not ceased to think of him. As he of her?

"Did you come to Greenfields because of my father's death?" she asked. "I mean to write about it for the paper?"

"Well, yes," he said. "I didn't know who it was, of course. I only knew the name, and you hadn't told me yours. I told my uncle —he's the editor, I work for him—that I thought we should know more about the accident than the undertaker could tell us. But what I really thought about was finding you."

She did not know what to say to that. She didn't feel quite like blushing and giggling, yet she was not ready to confess immodestly how she had dreamed of meeting him again.

They walked a good way down the track before he spoke. "Do you have a destination?" he said.

"No," she said. She was thinking about her life, and the paths that were blocked, and the question of where they might lead if they were open.

"Just walk down the railroad till you get tired, and turn and go back again?"

She laughed at herself. "Oh no," she said, "that was silly of me. I was thinking about something else." She told him about the bridge they always walked to. "It seems high," she said. "I don't suppose it is."

"Have the young people at Greenfields always entertained themselves this way—walking along the railroad?" he asked her.

"Since we've had a railroad," she said. "It hasn't always been here, you know."

"How long then?" he asked.

"It's five years since the first train came through. But of course to me now it does seem almost forever. When I try, I can remember when the workmen first came, and how they cut through the hills, and built up the roadbed through low spots. And how excited we all were when they first began to lay the rails. But usually I don't remember all that. It's just—the railroad."

"Yes," he said, "I see. It's like a river."

She looked up at him, interested. "It is, isn't it?" she said. "I don't remember living near a river, although I think we did when I was a baby. But on a map a railroad looks kind of like a river."

They were entering another cut and had begun to walk on the roadbed. They could see the gleaming rails ahead of them; they seemed to flow down through the rolling, rocky land. He stretched out his open hand, as though to follow the rails.

"I grew up with a river," he said, "a pretty little river that would gleam when the sunlight struck it, just like those silver rails. We used to play along its banks, and go swimming in deep holes, and row little boats or go fishing."

"Oh, it was like that for our boys," she said, "—the railroad was. Even when they were first building the track, the boys couldn't keep away from it. And now the younger kids are just the same. They walk on the rails or try to catch a ride when a freight train is switching."

"And then when they grow up they walk down the railroad with their sweethearts, just as we used to walk along the river, on Sunday afternoons like this or evenings when the moon shone."

Isabel wanted to ask about the sweetheart he had walked with, but on the other hand, did not really want to know and realized it wasn't ladylike to ask. But she thought of him arm in arm with a golden-haired girl whose long, white skirts trailed in soft green grass along the riverbank, while the rippling stream reflected the path of a great silver moon and birdsong drifted down to them from tall, swaying trees.

"And is the railroad a very good substitute for a river, Mr. Hastings?" she asked him.

"Well, it's an interesting comparison," he said, "and for carrying freight and passengers, a railroad must be considered an improvement, I suppose. At least they can build one almost anywhere. Still, to walk by on a Sunday afternoon, I guess I have to admit that I would rather have a river." He smiled down at her. "But only if I could choose my company," he said.

She smiled too. She liked talking this way with a man—on subjects she had never thought about before. She also liked the way he guided the subject into a personal compliment, but she decided against responding to that. She turned her mind back to the imagining of a river.

"A river would be more alive," she said.

"That's it," he said. "You can look at the moon in the depths of the water but what can you see in a steel rail?"

"Not much," she said. "Or anyway, it's not very beautiful to look at. But rails can be kind of exciting, you know. You think of where they lead to."

"Yes, you could think of that," he said. "I think I do understand what the railroad means at Greenfields."

She felt he did. He understood her railroad, and she understood his river. She felt understanding flow through her, linking her with him, with couples ahead of them and behind them, with people on trains a hundred miles or a thousand miles away along this track. It seemed to her then that, walking by this man, she would never find any road closed to her. She could go everywhere or nowhere, it would all be the same: the world open before them, and they together flowing into it, knowing all of it, reaching out for it with love and understanding.

Meanwhile Joanna spoke to Ray, without indirection, without maidenly modesty, having come long ago past the threshold where Isabel now throbbingly stood, or having gone round it and entered by gradual slow steps into the state of full understanding Isabel still only guessed at and hoped for. There was something Joanna wanted to know, and she had made up her mind to ask it at the first opportunity, which was now at hand. Part of what she lay awake worrying about the night after Harvey Doane was killed she had already put out of her mind. Joanna was usually successful at putting out of her mind whatever interfered with her plans, and she had easily convinced herself that there was no reasonable doubt that she loved Ray Doane and at the proper time would marry him.

But there was another doubt not so easily disposed of, the one her brother Jack had raised that night as they talked beneath the plum tree.

"Ray," she said, when Isabel and Archie had left them well behind, "I have to know whether you think anything has changed between you and me."

"Why?" he said. "Why would you ask that?"

"Because I wonder if you blame me."

"There ain't nothing to blame you for, Jo."

They walked awhile in silence. Soon she said, "Why did you do it, Ray?"

"Because it had to be done."

"Not because of me?"

"Of course not. What do you mean?"

"I said straighten things out. I oughtn't to have said that."

"It wasn't nothing you said, it just had to be done. For Mama's sake, and all the kids—and sure, for me and you. But you didn't have to say nothing. I could see that for myself."

"I didn't want to be to blame," she said.

"Do you think it's awful bad, Jo?"

"Well—it's bad."

"Yeah. Maybe I didn't really think how bad it'as gonna be."

"You'll get over it, Ray."

"Maybe I will. I reckon I will. But what about you?"

"Me? You had to do it, Ray. That's all I think of."

"I don't believe you've thought about it, Jo. You're gonna be living with a man that for the rest of his life folks will point to and say—when he was twenty years old he killed his daddy."

"But we won't be living at Greenfields. Where we'll be nobody will know."

"I don't think you can get away from a thing like this. They'll know, or I'll think they know."

"Well, then, we'll just have to live with it, won't we?"

"And what if something happened—something Mr. Goolsby hasn't thought of—you know what I mean."

"It won't."

"You can't answer that question, can you, Jo?"

"Ray, I love you. I can tell you that."

"I haven't got any right to more of an answer than that."

She didn't offer more; it seemed enough.

"I've got to say one more thing, Jo," he went on after a little while.

"Well," she said.

"I've got to set you free if you want it. Or if your mama and papa wants it."

"Ray, we've been through this once."

"All right, we have. But I've got to say this much—I've got to offer this. Because if Alma Greeping in the dugout was bad, Papa dead of a bullet from my gun don't seem much better."

"Mama and Papa think that was for the best. I've heard them say so."

"That don't mean they want their daughter to marry a man like me."

"Ray." She made up her mind then. She knew.

"What?" he said.

"They won't care. They like you, and they know what had to be done. But I can tell you something right now. I've thought about all this more than you think I have. We're engaged. We haven't ever got unengaged. And we're not fixing to. We know what we want and we'll get it. Nothing or nobody's going to stop us now!"

"You mean that, Jo." It wasn't a question.

"You know I do."

He moved close to her then, and hesitantly put an arm around her waist.

"They're all far ahead," she said, "and not looking back."

He pulled her close and kissed her hard. Nothing like this embrace had ever happened between them before.

"Oh Lord, Jo, I love you," he said, and his voice was thick with love. "I don't think I could bear to give you up."

They drew apart and walked on, hand in hand.

At last the four couples came together at the bridge, and sat in its shade, on the rocks in the bottom of the red-banked dry creek, to drink their tea. Joanna had washed pop bottles to put it in, and wrapped them in several thicknesses of newspaper. It was still pretty cold.

"What a good outing," Archie Hastings said. "But when do we take the pictures?"

Jack laughed. "Photography is not always the primary purpose of going Kodaking," he said. "Put that in your notes about Greenfields."

CHAPTER TWELVE

Monday morning the Doanes began hoeing cotton. Ray said they had put it off too long; they had better get at it. Mr. Goolsby had promised on Sunday to work with them a day and help them catch up, and Mrs. Goolsby came with him that morning to do the washing and help Lizzie around the house.

"I come so's you could go," she told Isabel. "I know Ray needs every hoe hand he can get, and I'as afraid Lizzie wasn't gonna feel very peart today."

But at noon Mrs. Goolsby told Isabel that Lizzie surprised her. "She helped me plumb good with the washing and cooked most of the dinner herself."

Tuesday morning Martha Waters got Joanna to drive her over to the Doanes' in the Maxwell. She brought a peach cobbler and a salmon salad. Lizzie told Isabel she appreciated all the help, but she wondered why the women didn't think she could manage by herself.

Actually, she couldn't, but Isabel didn't say so. It was an improvement to have her even imagining she could.

After Lizzie forgot to have supper ready when they got in after sundown Tuesday, Burnie told Ray he thought he would do more good staying at the house with Mama than trying to make a hand in the field.

"Sure, Pal," Ray said. "I think that's a dandy idea."

"Things are different now," Burnie told Isabel, explaining it to her later. "I used to think Papa would finally believe I was like the other boys, and I just never could make myself believe I wasn't. But I think I see now there might be some things I can do better than they can."

This was something Isabel had told him herself many times, but she didn't mention those old pep talks. "I think you're right," she said, "and Mama will be tickled to death."

If he couldn't do anything else, he could at least keep Lizzie reminded of what there was to do, and be company for her. But on Wednesday night Lizzie said he had helped her cook supper and could be a better cook than the girls if he wanted to. "Me and Burnie," she said, "we can do just about anything."

The hoe hands quit early Wednesday. The children knew they had worked late Tuesday so Ray could take off in time to get ready to go see Joanna, but they hadn't complained. They would do anything Ray said, and help him before he asked if they could think of any way.

"Are you fixing to take a bath, Ray?" Sophie said. "Let me fix your bath for you."

"No, let me," said Leonard.

Ray said he wasn't aiming to take a bath, just wash up, but they could help him Saturday. Later, when he started out for the first time to go to see Joanna in the car, he let Sophie and Leonard ride on the running board up the road to the gate so they could shut it after him. They ran back screaming with delight.

On many summer evenings the Doanes never lit a lamp, and in seasons of hard field work the children were often in bed by sundown. So it was this night; Lizzie and Burnie sat a little while on the front porch with Isabel, but they soon went to bed too. They said they had worked hard that day. Lizzie put her arm around Burnie as they went into the house, and Isabel felt sadness at their lost years well up in her. More, probably, than any other two members of the Doane family, Lizzie and Burnie needed each other; yet for all of Burnie's life, displays of affection between them had brought down on them the wrath of Harvey Doane.

Isabel was tired, too, but dreaded going in to her stuffy, low-ceilinged little room to lie on the narrow bed beside Sophie, who would be tossing and snorting with her summer catarrh. She said to herself she was too tired to move, and she leaned back with a little sigh against the house wall. She heard some little sound at the end of the house—a field mouse in the grass it might have been—and absently reached out her hand. Then she realized with a shock that she had half expected Rouser to come on around the house seeking her, needing to lick her hand and lie stretched out by her side.

We need to find us a new puppy, she thought.

I'm lonesome, she thought. It came to her that the thing that ailed her, the heaviness that held her, was really loneliness.

And then, without thinking what she would do, she got up and climbed the long sloping hillside behind the house. The sky in the west was still flaming when she first stood on the crest, but as she walked, the fire died down, the sky faded and darkened, and the first stars appeared.

And she was still lonely. She was more lonely here than she had ever been, because the imaginary figure she had once allowed at her side here was real now and, being real, must be kept far away from her.

But he had asked to come. She looked back now to the moment when he was saying good-bye—when they stood briefly beneath Mrs. Waters's arch of red roses—when he lightly touched her arm. "May I visit you?" he asked, and she said no. She had thought of the incident over and over, and she still did not know why she had said no. It might have been just the touch of his hand, the feelings aroused by that touch.

She began to know that she was, truly, very tired. She was lonely but she was tired. She turned back to the house, yet dreaded still to go into that hot little room, to try to sleep on that narrow bed so full of her sister Sophie. She lit the lamp in the front room and fetched her diary from its hiding place. It crossed her mind that the place might not be as safe now. In fact, she half suspected Mrs. Goolsby had come across the book the day she put the washed clothes away. Her mother was more likely to look into the drawer of cup towels now, and perhaps even Sophie would be working in the kitchen more. She thought she'd have to find a better place, a private place. She had a feeling there really was such a place somewhere, but she didn't think that night of where it was.

She sat down by the lamp table with the diary in her lap. Her most recent extensive entry was the description of Sunday afternoon—her meeting with Archie Hastings, their walk along the railroad, their parting under the roses. She read it over several times, then took up a pen from a holder kept on that table, dipped it into a bottle of ink, and began to write.

"Wednesday, June 28. I continue to be satisfied with the answer I gave Mr. Hastings. It would be a mistake to let him come here. He is so well educated, speaks so well, knows so much. He liked the way I look, I think, but if he got to know me he would see how ignorant I am. I don't know anything about books, or anything about fine manners. I guess the girls he knows in town would laugh at me. I don't guess either he or they have ever seen anything like this house I live in, or have eaten the things we eat, at the kind of table where we eat them." She paused a little while; there is a space that suggests that she paused. Then "But I am not ashamed!" she wrote, so vigorously that the ink splattered over the page and she almost ruined the point. She didn't write much more with that spoiled pen, but added, "We do the best we can, and I am not ashamed."

She might have known then she would let him come if he ever asked again.

She put in a fresh pen point, for it was a rule not to leave a bad one for someone else to pick up. Then she wrote, "I hear a car on the road. I guess it's Ray. I wish he'd want to talk to me tonight, the way he used to do."

She took the lamp into the kitchen, put her diary away, and sat down at the table to wait for Ray.

His step was light on the porch when he came.

"Hey, Sis, I'm glad you're still up," he said.

He looked glad. The set of his shoulders, his smile, his wide bright eyes—even, somehow, his whole body—seemed sparked with gladness.

"Why, what happened?" she said.

"Something pretty dad-blamed good," he said. "I couldn't tell you."

"Then what makes you so glad I'm up?" she asked.

He seemed to droop a little. He sat down. "I don't know," he said. "I don't know why I said that. You never would believe what's happened. Isaiah Birdsong wants to marry Joanna."

She laughed. "Well, he always has," she said. "But I admit it does sound funny."

He laughed too. "But then it's not really so funny in a way," he said. "I halfway think Mr. and Mrs. Waters would like for her to do it."

"They couldn't, Ray. Why, Mrs. Waters has always laughed at him as much as Joanna and the boys did."

"They could," he said. "They don't feel about me the way they used to. They try to act like they do, but they don't."

"But Joanna would never change."

He smiled again; the gladsome spark returned. "No," he said, "Joanna would never change."

They sat together in silence a minute or two. They had come a little too close to the subject they never spoke about. She wanted to say, "If only you hadn't done it," yet at the same time could not feel in her heart that he had—he was so much his old self tonight. She had felt that way at times ever since the thing happened. She could not believe this gentle brother she had known so well could really lift his gun to kill a man—any man. He had never described to her exactly how it happened. She supposed he never would, she really did not want to know; but sometimes she thought she could accept the reality of it better if she could picture just what Ray had done. Still she did not ask, would never ask.

Finally he yawned and stretched, got up from his chair, and said, "Well, I've got to go to work in the morning. And that's something else that don't seem to change much."

He started toward the door of the boys' room, then suddenly turned back. "Hey," he said. "I remember why I was glad you'as up. I've got a letter for you."

The letter had arrived at the Greenfields post office that morning. Jack told Joanna about it when he came home from the store about midmorning.

"The return says Archibald Hastings," he said. "I saw Papa looking at it pretty close."

"Oh, Jack, he wouldn't—"

"No, I don't think he would. He liked Archie Hastings."

"Just the same," Joanna said, "I'm gonna let Papa know I know about it. I'm gonna ask him to bring it home tonight so Ray can take it to Isabel."

She asked her papa when he came home to dinner, and he said if there didn't any of the Doanes come after their mail that day he'd bring it. He said he liked that Hastings feller.

Martha said she liked him too, but she couldn't tell whether any good could come of Isabel getting mixed up with him. "He's not our kind of folks," she said.

"Isabel's not your ordinary Greenfields girl either," Jack said. "They might get along better than you think."

"Hmph," said Martha.

Presently Tom said, in the formal tone that he had always used to annunciate punishment, "Joanna, I need to talk to you before I go back to the store. You and your mama."

Joanna felt like asking, "What have I done, Papa?" but only answered, "Yes, sir."

They didn't talk much after that, but ate somewhat more hurriedly than usual. When he had finished, Tom got up abruptly, pushing his chair back, as was his custom.

"I'll wait for you on the back porch," he said, and went on out.

Jack got up, saying, "I'll get on back to the store so Winnie can come and eat, although I expect I'd just as well tell him not to be in any hurry." As he passed Joanna's chair, he bent quickly and whispered in her ear, "Isaiah Birdsong!"

She could not imagine what he meant. He did not look back.

The women went out on the porch then, where Tom was sitting in an old rocking chair pulled up close to the porch swing, and sat down in the swing.

"All right now," the father said, and again it was like the pre-amble to punishment.

(It was something to do with Isaiah Birdsong, with what he had said to her Sunday. But Joanna did not try, did not want, to think what.)

"Well, what is it, Papa?" Martha said impatiently.

"Isaiah Birdsong come by the store this morning."

"Isaiah!" Martha exclaimed.

"He said he wondered if Joanna's position had changed."

"Well, it hasn't!" Joanna snapped. "And I told him that at preaching Sunday."

"Don't get so uppity about it," her father said. "He just asked."

"He didn't have any business asking."

"I told him I didn't know of any change. But he said he thought it might be hard for a father to give his young daughter to a man who—no matter how justifiably—"

"It was an accident!" Joanna broke in. "I thought Mr. Goolsby ruled it an accident."

"Joanna," Martha said, "you know very well that the whole Greenfields community knows what happened."

"How? Who told it?"

"Nobody ever knows that," Martha said.

"Well, Isaiah knowed what kind of accid*int* it was," Tom said.

"He oughtn't to say anything about it, even if he did," Joanna said.

"I kindly felt that way," Tom said. "But I could see he had a point." Pushing his steel glasses up on his nose, he gave Joanna a long, searching look. "I just want to ask you one thing, Joanna. Have you thought, and thought good, about what Ray's done? Are you plumb sure he's still the man you want to marry?"

"He's the same man he's always been," Joanna said.

"Well now," said Martha. "You've got to realize, he may not be. Can you look me in the eye and tell me you don't feel the least bit different about him now?"

"Maybe the least bit, Mama," Joanna said. "I believe I think more of him now than ever, because of his trouble."

"Haven't you ever give a thought to how it's gonna be, all the rest of your life, knowing what Ray Doane can do when he gets mad enough?"

"No, because Ray hasn't ever done anything just because he

was mad. He had to think a long time before he did—that. He did it for the sake of his whole family."

"Well, Joanna," Tom said, "I can see how you might feel that way—"

"Yes, you can, Papa, because you know Ray. And I'll tell you more than that. I know what he's done, but I never can feel like he did it, if I live a hundred years. It's just not Ray. He had to do it—he thought so and I do too—but to me it's just the same as if somebody else had fired that gun. I'll never look at Ray and think of killing."

Tom got up from his chair. "Well, that's that, then. Isaiah was asking permission to court you. He wanted my answer this evening, for some reason."

"He knows it's Ray's night to come," Joanna said. "Surely he couldn't be thinking about coming tonight."

"I don't know," Tom said. "I got the feeling he might want to talk to you and Ray."

"Ask *his* permission to court me, I suppose," Joanna said. She could just picture him on his bony knees to both of them, and she laughed shortly, somewhat hysterically. "Papa, I don't see why you couldn't have just told him no," she said.

"Hush that giggling, Joanna," Martha said. "I know we've always thought Isaiah was pretty silly, but I can tell you why your papa didn't say no. Because silly though he may be, he's a good man, and he's got a good farm."

"But even if I never had *seen* Ray," Joanna cried, "I couldn't bear Isaiah Birdsong—not for a *husband*."

"Well," said her father shortly. "I thought it was something you ought to know about. When he comes back by I'll give him his answer, and we don't need to say no more about it."

He went on out and up toward the store, meeting Winnie about halfway.

"I'd better get Winnie's tea," Martha said.

Joanna followed her into the kitchen. "Mama," she said. "You didn't really imagine I could think about Isaiah that way, did you?"

"No," Martha said, "but for a little bit I thought how things might be. Whatever you say, I'll always worry a little about Ray. And besides, it would be so good to have you stay at Greenfields."

"But I don't aim to, Mama. Even if something happened and I lost Ray, I'd still want to go and be a teacher."

"Well, then—like your papa said—let's don't say no more about it."

They would say, however, just a little more about it.

That afternoon, when the shade had reached the phlox bed in the front yard, Joanna went out to pull off the spent blooms. She was humming to herself, bending over the flowers, counting the hours left till Ray would come. She did not hear a sound on the path that ran along in front of their yard fence, until a hoarse voice spoke to her.

"Miss Joanna!" She knew the voice well.

She straightened and looked around. It was Isaiah Birdsong. She stood staring at him incredulously. Surely, she thought, Papa had told him not to come.

Then she realized he had come from the direction of his own house, which was located north and a little west of the school building, a mile and a half away. He often followed the path on his way to the store, although it would have been closer to cut across the schoolground. Jack and Winnie always said he was trying to get a glimpse of Joanna. They said he always came that way when he knew their mother was sewing for Joanna, and Mama said it too. Just as sure as Joanna was standing before the front bedroom mirror in her petticoat, about to try on a dress, Isaiah Birdsong would pass by. That was exaggerated, but they said it and laughed about it.

Remembering this fun at Isaiah's expense, Joanna had a hint of a smile on her face when she looked up. Isaiah seemed to take it for a welcome, and came on through the gate.

"Oh, Miss Joanna," he said, "I do wonder if you could possibly allow me to talk with you a little while."

"Not really, Mr. Birdsong," she said. "As you can see, I'm busy."

"If we could only sit on the porch a few minutes," he said.

"I'm sorry, Mr. Birdsong, but I couldn't."

"I just wanted to say—I mean I talked to your papa—"

"But then didn't he tell you what I said?"

"That was this morning," he said. "I was on my way back to the store, but I saw you here—such a lovely, glorious view of you—among the flowers—"

She suddenly realized how he had seen her, and her face flamed. My behind! she thought.

"I love your modest blushes, Joanna," he said, growing red too.

"Oh, don't speak to me, Mr. Birdsong," she begged. "You must just go and let Papa tell you what I said."

"All I ask of you," he said, "all I want to know, is whether you could possibly look with favor—"

"Oh, Mr. Birdsong," she interrupted him, "please don't ask, because I could never look with favor." At this point she could not tell whether she was amused, embarrassed, or angry. She had no intention of laughing at him, but in her confusion she let laughter escape—high-pitched and uncontrolled, like a mare nickering.

The red faded from his face and he fled from her, back along the way he had come, going home.

"What on earth's been going on out here?" Martha called from the front porch.

Still laughing, Joanna turned and went to join her. "Oh, Mama," she gasped, "he wanted me to look with favor!"

"I never heard anybody say 'look with favor' in my life," Martha said. "He must have got that from some novel."

"And, Mama," Joanna went on, "he said he had such a glorious view of me—and I was stooped over pulling off phlox blooms."

"And your back toward the gate, I reckon."

"You know it was. What he saw—his glorious view—was—"

"Your tail end!"

They fell into the wicker settee laughing helplessly. Joanna couldn't remember when they had laughed so joyously together.

"Mama," she finally said, "you really wouldn't want me to marry him, would you?"

"No," said Martha. "I guess I just forgot for a little while that he don't have good sense."

Such was the story Joanna told Ray that night. Perhaps she shouldn't have told him—she wondered if it was right to tell him—but he laughed at it too. Still, she thought he seemed a little hurt or angry, and so she formed a scheme (not altogether on the spur of the moment, either) that she thought would please him.

It involved a drive to Mary Varton's to return an embroidery pattern, an excursion Martha was brought to approve of, and a little stop on a stretch of isolated road, a delay she didn't know about.

They were on a little hilltop down in the breaks, from which they could see a long way across the empty road and countryside.

He had followed her suggestion that they drive there, and now that she said, "Stop, Ray," he stopped.

He looked at her questioningly. Whatever happened was up to her.

"Maybe I oughtn't to have told you about Isaiah," she said.

"Oh, it was funny," he said.

"But it made you a little mad?"

"I'd be mad," he said, "if he wasn't such a blame fool. And yet, for a little while I thought I'd like to wring his neck." He stopped and beat his fist on the steering wheel. "Oh my God," he said, "I'll never be able to say anything like that again without folks imagining I mean it."

"Don't be that way, Ray. Folks are not fixing to imagine anything."

"I can't get it out of my head—all that."

"Well, I didn't aim to talk about it," she said. "It's not what I wanted us to come here for."

"I didn't much think it was," he said.

"What I want," she said, "is you to kiss me."

"Do you mean really kiss you?" he asked.

"That's what I mean," she said.

He jumped over the side of the car and ran around to open her door. "Then get out," he said, "and I'll show you something."

There in the middle of the road he grabbed her and held her close, so that their bodies made one long shadow reaching down the red road. Then he tipped her head back and brought his lips down hard on hers. She kissed him back, and knew then she had never kissed him before, not even Sunday afternoon on the railroad. Finally he lifted his mouth, only to hold her closer against him. While they clung together there, if they had looked, they could have seen their shadow lengthen.

They got home before the lamps were lit, and sat awhile talking mostly of Mary Varton and embroidery patterns but thinking separate, secret thoughts. Joanna almost forgot to give him the letter for Isabel.

The weather Thursday was hot and muggy. None of the Doanes worked as briskly as usual, except Isabel.

"Boy, Sis, you act like you've really got it in for them weeds today," Travis said to her once.

She laughed and kept on slinging her hoe. She was trying to

keep from thinking, but she didn't, of course, say that. She concentrated on every weed she cut down, but even so never forgot the single sheet of close-written cream-colored stationery thrust into the pocket of the smock she wore for field work. That was all right; being aware of it was all right, was like the touch of the writer's hand on her arm. But she did not wish to think about sending him her answer: could not bear to tell him no, but (like Mrs. Waters, could she have known) feared no good would ever come of saying yes.

In the afternoon thunderheads began rearing up against the southern sky, spreading and darkening as the hours went by. Lightning streaked across the biggest and highest of the clouds, and before much longer the sound of thunder began to seem very close.

"Sis," Ray called to Isabel, "don't you reckon we ought to quit and go to the house?"

They did, and had to run through the rain the last part of the way. Later, while they were eating supper, a second storm came up, with heavy rain and a sprinkling of hail. They went and stood on the side porch watching.

"It's not enough to hurt the cotton, is it, Ray?" asked Burnie anxiously.

"Nah, Pal, it's all right," Ray said. "That's not much hail, and we need the rain."

It was too wet to go to the field the next morning. Ray said at breakfast he was going to the store on Whitestar, because the road would be too muddy for the car. He said he'd get the mail and pick up a few groceries if his mama needed anything. Isabel said she had been wondering if they couldn't go in the car sometime and stock up on some staples and canned goods. "I guess we can still get credit with Mr. Waters," she said.

Ray explained that Mr. Waters had been to the bank and found out about their money. Harvey Doane had had more than he had wanted anyone to believe. It wasn't a lot, but the family could live as well as most people at Greenfields.

"Maybe we can buy some candy," Sophie said.

"Sure, we can buy some candy," Ray said. "We'll all go to Greenfields tomorrow, Mama and everybody, if it don't rain no more. And we'll get what we need."

This turned out to be the day Isabel had been hoping for, a time to carry out a plan she had in mind. She spoke of it to Sophie and her mother, no one else, and neither of them had any objections.

"I don't see what you'd want to go live in the dugout for," Sophie said, "but I sure don't mind if I can have me a room to myself."

"I'm not exactly planning to live in the dugout," Isabel said. "I just thought it might be nicer down there this summer."

"Oh well," said Sophie portentously, "you never can tell."

The dugout was clean, the floor swept hard. Alma had left it that way. Isabel had no feeling at all that it was dirty; but she carried the feather mattress and pillows that her father had put there up into the fresh air and laid them on the front porch in the sun. She took old, mended sheets and pillowcases (not the ones Alma had been using, they were better than these) and a ninepatch quilt she had pieced at the age of eight and was supposed to be saving for her hope chest. Her mother had let her choose all the brightest-colored scraps for it, and it would make a gay spot of color now in the dim earth room she planned to make her own.

She cleaned the furniture left down there—the dresser and chair, and even the rough boards of the homemade bedstead— and rubbed it with beeswax. She would have liked a table or a desk, and she longed for a rug on the floor.

But she liked the place; already she felt at home there. She brought down most of the clothes she expected to be wearing and her few other personal belongings, including her diary, which she found another secret place for. She made up her mind to buy herself a pen and some ink of her own and perhaps some writing paper, when they went to the store. She might answer a certain letter—or she might write to almost anyone.

When Ray came home, late in the morning, he had another letter for Isabel. Her heart stopped a moment when she first saw it, but the envelope was a delicate blue—no man would use that.

By the time she had it open, the whole family had heard there was a letter and had gathered around her on the front porch, where she stood.

"It's from Miss Lona," Ray said. (It said Mrs. Albert Endicott on the return address.) "Joanna said she'd wrote her about Papa. It's probably about that."

It was, partly. Miss Lona expressed her sympathy for all of

them and sent some special message to each one. But mainly it was another chance for Isabel to go to college. Miss Lona knew, she said, that nothing could make up to Isabel for the loss of her father, but she did wonder whether there might be any changes in the family now that would make it easier for her to leave home. If so, the friend she had once told Isabel about, the professor's wife who wanted a college girl to do housekeeping, would like very much to have Isabel come and stay with her—to work for her room and board. And if there was a problem getting money together for tuition, Miss Lona would be glad to help her get a loan that she could pay back when she started teaching.

"Well, what do you think, Sis?" Ray asked.

"Oh, I don't know," Isabel said. "Probably not this year."

"Girls don't leave home," Lizzie said, "except to get married."

"Oh, Mama, they do nowadays," Burnie assured her. "Miss Lona did, herself."

"Well, she's different," Lizzie said.

"I wouldn't want to be a teacher," Sophie said. "But I'd like to go to town and do something."

Travis said she didn't know what she was talking about—the country was the only place to live. Leonard shouted his agreement, jumping in the middle of the feather bed Isabel had placed there to sun.

"What's this thing?" Ray said suddenly.

"It's the feather bed that's been down in the dugout," Isabel said. She went ahead and told him what she had been doing that morning. "Come and see," she said. "Not that there's much change, really."

They went down the steps, which she had swept freshly clean. They could smell the beeswax. Enough light came through the high little window to show the colors in a mountain landscape picture Mrs. Waters had given Isabel years before.

"It looks all right," he said.

"I'll have some privacy," she said.

"You must want to get away from the rest of us pretty bad," he said, "to live down here where they was."

"Ray, it's not like that. You just never have noticed how little and stuffy that room is where Sophie and I sleep. And she thrashes around and snorts all night."

"I know that," he said. "Forget I said anything."

She sighed. The times of mutual understanding for those two came seldom now.

Still, later that afternoon he came and helped her carry the mattress back down into the dugout. She made up the bed with the nine-patch quilt for a spread, and then invited all the family to come and see her place. She doubted that the boys had any interest in seeing, but she didn't want them to think what Ray had said—that she couldn't stand living in the house with them.

Burnie lingered when the others had gone. "Sis, what do you really think about Miss Lona's letter?" he asked.

"It's nice of her to want to help me," Isabel said.

"I bet you can go," he said. "I bet by fall things are so you can go."

"Oh, Burnie," Isabel said, "I don't even know if I want to."

"But you want to go to college. You've always wanted a college education."

"I would like it, I think—but I don't know about teaching. I'm not really so very sure that I could teach."

"I could," Burnie said. "I think I could. It's what I want to do."

"Maybe you can then," Isabel said. "Maybe by the time you're through with school at Greenfields, we'll be able to send you wherever you want to go. You'd be the one, if just one of us could go."

"I wouldn't want it that way," he said.

"Well, anyway," she said, "you're probably the only one that ever would want to go."

"Me and you," he said. "Because you'd like to go, I know you would. And listen, Sis, if you went, and got a education, and had a job teaching, or maybe something else, I don't know what but something, if you did—I guess you could do all that in five or six years, don't you guess?"

"I might, Burnie. If I tried to, I guess that I might."

"Then see, you'd have a job and I could come and stay with you, you'd find me some job to do, and maybe loan me money if I needed it, just like Miss Lona aims to get for you—"

"Oh, Burnie," she said, "I don't know what I'll ever be able to do, but one thing I can promise: if there's any way to help you go to college, then I'll do it. There'll be some way you can go."

After Burnie was gone, Isabel thought about that talk and decided she would mention it to Ray. They ought to begin planning and see that Burnie got to go to college somehow. At least they ought to start thinking of some way he could make a living.

She didn't talk to Ray any more that day, as it happened. It was nearly suppertime, and she went to help her mother fix the meal. Then after supper they all sat on the front porch in the gathering dusk. They hadn't sat together that way since Harvey died—nor had there been many such occasions when he was living. Isabel thought about the pleasant time they'd had when he went after Alma and they half believed he'd stay away and make them free forever. She recalled some thoughts she'd had about happy and unhappy families. But she didn't much want to think about that now.

"Leonard, go get Burnie's French harp," she said.

Leonard brought it and Burnie played awhile. When he played "Darling Nellie Gray," Isabel and Sophie sang it as a soprano and alto duet.

Once Ray said, "I got to find us a new pup."

(Isabel knew he was thinking about Rouser and how he used to howl at that harp.)

When Burnie quit playing, they all kept sitting or sprawling there, talking a little about the stars or the moon, or lightning in the north. (That cloud was moving the other way, Ray said.)

Suddenly out of a silence Lizzie said, in a voice strangely musical and clear, "You know, I believe everything is going to be all right."

CHAPTER THIRTEEN

Martha Waters, with a dustrag in her hand, stood at her bay window looking toward the store.

"Look, Joanna!" she said sharply.

The mother and daughter were giving the house its "Saturday evening" going-over so it would look nice for Sunday. Joanna, holding a feather duster she had been using on the picture frames, came to stand by her mother.

"Now who in the world is that, just drove up in front of the store?" Martha said.

At first, Joanna, like her mother, thought the car was one she had never seen before. Then she said, "Why it's the Doanes! With the top up."

Together they watched as the passengers emerged from the gaunt, high-topped vehicle. Two children tumbled out of the backseat and, as Martha said, "hit the ground a-running." Then Ray (they couldn't recognize his features from there, but it was Ray—tall, broad-shouldered Ray) climbed out on the driver's side and went around to open the door for the passenger on the left. A slight, slow-moving female figure stepped down, as he took her by the arm.

"It's Lizzie!" Martha exclaimed. "That's why Ray's got the top up—so she wouldn't have to set out in the broiling sun."

"Yes, its Mrs. Doane all right. And there's Burnie and Travis. And Isabel getting out now. Looks like they've all come."

"Well, ain't that a sight!" Martha said. "Joanna, you go straight up there and tell them they're not to leave Greenfields without coming to the house for a visit." She turned and gave a glance around the spotless-looking room, with rigid chairs all in their places, ranged around the oriental-patterned room-sized rug. "It'll do," she said. "I'm fixing to go and bake some custard pies. We'll get 'em to stay for supper."

Lizzie agreed easily to come to the house for a visit with her old friend, and after a little coaxing, accepted the invitation to supper. Travis, who had learned in his few free hours during the past ten days how to drive the Doane car, would take Leonard and the two of them would see about the cows and chickens. "Now don't forget them custard pies," Mrs. Waters admonished them as they drove away.

It was a good old-fashioned get-together, such as the Doanes and Waterses had enjoyed so many years ago. Isabel and Joanna were able to say this sort of thing to each other without evident consciousness of recent troubles. No need to pretend sorrow that Harvey Doane was not there, no need to remind themselves that if he had been alive the visit wouldn't be happening.

They sat an hour or so together quilting the Lone Star, while their mothers were in the kitchen. Sophie had been invited to quilt, but she wanted to go across the railroad and play awhile with Bessie Akers. She said she didn't know how to quilt anyway and might not ever learn. Isabel and Joanna smilingly shook their heads at each other but did not discuss Sophie's new willfulness. Joanna had something else she was bent on talking about.

"You haven't answered his letter," she said accusingly.

Isabel smiled. She didn't ask how Joanna knew. Mail didn't go through the Greenfields post office without the Waters family seeing any letter they happened to be interested in.

"Didn't he ask to come to see you?" Joanna asked, then said, "Of course he did, I know he did."

"I just can't decide," Isabel said. "I just don't know whether I ought to let him come."

"You mean you don't know whether you like him or not?"

"Oh—*like* him!"

"That's what I thought."

"But, Jo, he comes from a different world. Look at him—listen to him talk—you know that."

"Well, you don't aim to stay at Greenfields all your life—or do you?"

"I guess not. You know I never have made plans—not like you have. But I've had my dreams."

"Of course you have. Remember you used to say you wanted to find a man that read books—you wanted one room filled with books, and a fireplace where you could sit and read to each other after supper."

Isabel nodded.

"And how come Archie Hastings is not that man?"

Isabel shook her head. "There's no such man. I never even meant him to be real."

"Well, Archie Hastings is real. And he wrote that letter. Now what did he actually say?"

Isabel reached into a side pocket in her skirt and drew out the much-folded sheet of heavy, cream-colored paper. "Read it," she said, holding it out to Joanna.

"Are you sure you want me to?"

Isabel smiled. "There's no secret in it," she said.

Joanna took the paper and unfolded it. "It's pretty stationery," she said. She read a few lines. "The *river?*" she exclaimed then. "What in the world is he talking about?"

"Read it," Isabel said.

It was a short letter and a proper one, except perhaps for the last two sentences: "I know you must have changed your mind by now. Do write and say I can walk with you again by the river in the moonlight."

Joanna handed the letter back to Isabel, giving her a quizzical look. "You never walked in the moonlight," she said. "There never was a river. Maybe you're right, and he really is a dream."

Isabel told a little of what they had talked about: the railroad and the river, her pastimes and his.

"Well, that's strange," Joanna said. "But I guess it goes to prove what I said—that you-all are alike down deep and understand each other. It shows that you're an idiot not to write and tell him to come."

"You really think so?"

"I know so."

"What will I say?"

"Just say he can come," Joanna said. "I wouldn't say anything about a river if I were you."

Isabel laughed. "That sounds just like what your mother would say," she said, "so it must be good advice."

"And what about Miss Lona's letter?" Joanna asked then. "Was she asking you again to come to Commerce?"

"Yes, her friend still wants me. She doesn't have to know before the first of August, but I might as well go ahead and write because of course I can't go."

"No, I'd wait. Things might look better by then."

"I don't know," Isabel said. She meant to talk some more about how things might be, but the boys came in then.

"When's that newspaper feller coming back, Isabel?" Jack asked.

"I don't know, Jack," Isabel said.

"Well, you get him back out here," Jack said. "I'd like to talk to him some more."

Isabel just laughed and shook her head. She didn't intend to talk about Archie Hastings anymore this night.

Yet his name would come up again. After supper, when Isabel and Joanna were in the kitchen with the older women, drying dishes and putting them away, Martha suddenly said, "I declare I've thought three or four times since y'all have been here about something I've got to show you, and it's gone right out of my mind every time. I'm just gonna quit and go get it."

She handed Joanna the dishrag and went out of the room, to return in a moment with a newspaper clipping in her hand. "Here, Isabel," she said, holding out the paper, "you'd better see it first."

It was an article from the *Western Message*. Isabel recognized the type and heavy, inverted-pyramid shape of the headline at once, having read the county paper at the Waters house all her life.

GREENFIELDS MAN IS

VICTIM OF ACCI-

DENT THURS.

Harvey Doane of the Greenfields community died of a gunshot wound at his farm home Thursday morning, June 22. The funeral was Friday afternoon at the home, with burial in the Greenfields cemetery.

Jedidiah Goolsby, justice of the peace, ruled accidental death in the case. He concluded that Mr. Doane's gun discharged as he was climbing over a barbed wire fence on his farm.

Mr. Doane was very active in Greenfields community affairs.

He leaves his widow, Mrs. Lizzie Doane, and six children, Ray, Travis, Burnie, Leonard, Isabel and Sophie.

Isabel stood looking at the clipping in her hand a good while after she had finished reading it. "It sounds nice," she said. "He says things better than his uncle does."

"Don't you want to show it to your mama?" Martha asked.

Lizzie was sitting on a kitchen chair by the end of the cabinet, with her snuff can on the floor beside her. She had not offered help and Martha did not seem to expect it (though it was strange, at Greenfields, for one woman to sit idle in another's kitchen).

"What is it?" she said, looking up at Isabel.

Isabel handed her the clipping. Lizzie read it slowly, whispering each word. "Well, I declare," she said when she had finished.

"Don't you think it sounds nice, Mama?" Isabel asked.

Lizzie kept looking at it. "Seems like I don't hardly know who it's talking about," she said.

"Why it's Papa, Mama."

Lizzie held the paper closer to her eyes, as if to study it more carefully. "Well, I declare," she said. "It does look like his name."

Martha, looking at Isabel, shook her head slightly. "You-all can keep it if you want to," she said.

"Let me put it in my pocket, Mama," Isabel said, and her mother held out the clipping. Isabel put it with the other sample that she had of Archie Hastings's writing.

"Mrs. Doane," Joanna said, "did you know the man that wrote that is a friend of Isabel's?"

Lizzie looked up, frowning slightly. "Oh, did somebody write it?" she said.

Nobody tried to answer that. It was strange, and yet perhaps not so very strange. If Lizzie had not been dazed by encountering the name of Harvey Doane in print, she would probably have understood what Joanna meant. Yet it seems entirely possible (as Joanna explained many years afterward when she narrated the events of that Saturday night) that never in her life had it occurred to Lizzie that some person actually did write the lines that appeared in newspapers.

Before the women went to join the men and children in the living room, Joanna took Isabel for a talk in her room.

"Isabel, is she always like this?" she asked sadly.

"No, she's been better," Isabel said, "or she wouldn't have come to Greenfields today. But sometimes she acts so strange—I don't know—she can't understand what's happening, or forgets the ordinary things she has to do."

"Ray has told me a little about it," Joanna said.

"So you can see one reason I keep putting off asking Archie to come to see me."

"I do," Joanna said. "I've thought of that before now. So why don't we get Mama to cook supper for Ray and me and you and Archie next Saturday night? You write and tell him about it, and I'll send an invitation too."

"Do you think Mrs. Waters would really want to do that?"

"Sure she would. I'll find a chance to ask her in a little bit, and we'll write our letters tonight, so I can get them in the mail before Papa takes it to the train in the morning."

Martha, when Joanna caught her alone in the kitchen later in the evening (cutting some pieces of pie for the menfolks), agreed to the plan without any of the reservations she had mentioned once before. She was nearly always glad to find an occasion to cook a big meal for somebody—Joanna had counted on that.

Isabel had hoped the visit to Greenfields would mean greater improvement in her mother—perhaps even a dramatic change. But

after all, life went on much the same. Lizzie still did not feel like
going to church on Sunday morning. Ray told Isabel he didn't see
why anyone had to stay at home with her, and Isabel agreed, but
said she thought they all ought to come back for dinner. Since they
did not feel they could invite anyone home with them either, they
had a long, quiet Sunday afternoon to pass by themselves. Lizzie
fell asleep over her crochet, and Isabel, sitting with her on the
front porch, read in a book Jack had lent her called *Tess of the
D'Urbervilles*. "It's pretty scandalous," he had told her with a wink.
"You don't want to let Mrs. Goolsby find out what it's about." This
comment had made Isabel wonder if it was anything like *Anna
Karenina,* and she was finding that in some ways it was. It seemed
strange to her, as she commented when she wrote about it in her
diary that night, that men could write about women like that in a
way to make you feel so sorry for them—as though they were not
really to blame for their own actions.

She also wrote about the plan to have Archie Hastings for dinner, but she intended not to think very much about that. She wrote
she knew she could not expect a letter before Wednesday.

But she was to be surprised about that. At noon Tuesday,
when the hoe hands came home to dinner, there were three
surprises. First, a chubby black puppy with floppy ears, yapping at
them from the side porch. Leonard rushed to it and threw his arms
around it without waiting to ask any questions. "Blackie!" he
shouted. "We'll name him Blackie."

"What makes you think it's ours?" Sophie asked. "And anyway,
Blackie's a sorry name. Anybody in the world can name a black
dog Blackie."

Lizzie came out on the porch, telling them Joanna had
brought the pup. The Vartons had puppies to give away, and
Joanna had picked out this one to take the place of Rouser.

Ray was pleased. "Well, Blackie," he said, scratching the pup's
ears. None of them ever did think of anything else to call him.

Then on the dining table, still warm from Mrs. Waters's oven,
was a big, spicy-smelling cobbler, made from the yellow plums
newly ripe in the Waters backyard.

"Let's get these beans and taters out of the way," said Travis,
"so we can have some of that pie."

The children were already sitting down to the table when Lizzie indicated to Isabel the third surprise—a heavy-looking cream-colored envelope by her plate. Isabel stood staring at it.

"Well, open it, Sis," Ray said, "and see if he's coming." (There was no doubt in anybody's mind as to who it was from.)

She picked it up and went out on the porch with it. Her heart pounding, she forced herself to tear it open. It was a formal, courteous acceptance of her suggestion that they meet again at the Waters house. But there was a postscript: "I have consulted an almanac, and there will be a moon."

Throughout the long week, Isabel thought often of Archie Hastings (in spite of herself—wishing she wouldn't) and wondered what she would say to him when they met again. When Saturday night came, and the guests had gathered in the Waters dining room, she felt grateful they were not to be alone. She was glad to sit and listen to him talking to other people, letting him gradually become a real person again. It was easy, when they were apart, to doubt his substance; he had been so long a figure in her dreams.

At supper he conversed mostly with the men, as a man (at least at Greenfields) was always expected to do. He talked with Winnie about insects, saying he had been quite a lepidopterist as a boy in Missouri. (This tickled Winnie, because he was the only one at the table who knew what that was.) Then he asked about problems with insects that damaged the cotton; both Ray and Mr. Waters could enlighten him on that subject.

Then, amazingly, it turned out that he knew something about Sweeney's automobile mechanics school in Kansas City, where Ray hoped to go. Archie said he had seen the place himself, and had heard men in the automobile business praise it highly. Ray asked several questions about how the school was situated, and what kind of place he might be able to find to live. Isabel thought she heard respect and even liking in her brother's voice, and she was pleased.

Jack asked him what he knew about Robert Ingersoll. He said not much, but his uncle claimed to have heard him lecture. Jack said he wished he could talk to the editor about that sometime, and Archie said he was sure his uncle would be glad to tell him all that he remembered.

Jack seemed regretful when, as soon as supper was over, he had to excuse himself. Mary Varton was expecting him, he said; it almost seemed that he would have preferred the company of Archie Hastings.

Later, after the women had washed the dishes and joined the men in the living room, still another topic absorbed them. Isabel did not know whether it was Archie who had begun this new discussion or not. She rather thought it must have been Mr. Waters; certainly she had heard him on the subject before now. But Archie seemed keenly interested.

Mr. Waters asked Archie if he had ever heard his uncle talk about the Block 97 fight between the settlers and the cattlemen. Archie said he had, but he would like very much to have Mr. Waters's account of it.

"Well, sir," said Mr. Waters, "I could tell you a little about it, maybe not as much as your uncle, but we lived right over there in the middle of where it happened when we first come to this country." He told some stories Isabel had heard before, about the Dark Night Riders of Block 97. "Of course the trouble was all over and done with when we come," he admitted, "but folks couldn't hardly talk about anything else even then. Why, we lived neighbors to one of the nicest fellers you'd ever want to know—a young man with a wife and baby—and folks said he'd killed one of them cattle barons in cold blood when he was just a boy. Had to leave the country awhile, but had come back, him and his daddy, in a few years, and settled down there. Didn't seem like nobody held it against him."

"My uncle knows that family and says they're well thought of. It surprised me to hear things like that when I first came here. They sounded like something out of a dime novel."

"Well, we're not so far from dime-novel times, even now," said Winnie (who was known to be well read in that literary genre).

"That's what I wondered about. Not so much that they happen, but that nobody seems to mind very much that they do. I've heard there was a shoot-out on the courthouse square just a year or two ago, and a man killed, but there were no witnesses to it and no charges filed. I've heard of one or two other things like that. Would you say"—he looked around as though putting the question generally—"that people are a little more inclined to settle their differences with a gun in this part of the country than they are in older parts?"

"No, I wouldn't say so," said Martha firmly, breaking uncharacteristically into the menfolks' talk. "We all come here from older parts, and we're all just as civilized as we ever was."

There was a little silence after that. Something about the tone of this speech put a period to the discussion of gunplay in that county.

"Winnie," Joanna said then, as though just noticing he was there. "I thought you aimed to go hunt glowworms tonight."

"I was just thinking," Winnie said, "that it's getting nearly dark enough for them. Why don't you all come out and help me?"

"Fine idea," said Archie at once.

"We might go with you for about half an hour," Ray said, "if Mrs. Waters don't think the night air would be too hard on the girls."

"All right, Ray," Martha said, glancing out the window at the still-luminous sky. "Have you got your watch?"

"Yes, ma'am."

Winnie led them down a path that paralleled the railroad, through scattered mesquite brush and tall weeds.

"We may not find any glowworms," Winnie said. "I never have, at Greenfields."

Archie laughed heartily. "I'll get the hang of Greenfields ways someday," he said.

"We'll sit on the porch when we get back to the house," Joanna said. "That's what Ray and I always do."

They scattered out somewhat. There was time for a little talk.

"Do all the Greenfields ladies watch over their daughters as carefully as Mrs. Waters does?" Archie asked Isabel.

"Well, Mrs. Waters is awfully strict," Isabel said, "but—yes, pretty much so."

"Your mother?"

"My mother's not well." She knew that didn't answer his question; she wasn't really sure what the answer was.

While they walked, the white moon, riding high in the sky, began to glow.

"I told you there'd be a moon," he said. "I guess I pictured us alone together, looking at it."

She didn't answer that.

"If I came to visit you at your own home, could we be alone together?"

"If you did—"

"Would a visitor bother your mother too much?"

"I don't honestly know. You see, she's not really sick."

"She hasn't got over your father's death yet."

"I suppose you might say that. It's partly that." She wondered now why she had made her mother the excuse for not asking Archie to her home. It wouldn't really bother Mama, she thought. She might scarcely notice he was there, but it wouldn't bother her.

"I'd like to see where you live," he said. "I don't like always having to think of you at somebody else's house."

She knew then she had wanted exactly that. Here, closed off by Mrs. Waters's careful rules, she could keep most of herself away from him. She did not know, she was not yet sure, how much she wanted him to have of her. She was not thinking of a touch or a kiss (she knew very well she did want both of these things), for she did not need Mrs. Waters's rules or her watchful eye to keep her from giving her physical self to a man. What mainly inhibited her (thinking back to their first meetings) was the way he looked so easily into her unspoken feelings. How deep that clear gray gaze of his could penetrate she had not learned, might be afraid to know.

"I have never invited a man to my home," she said.

"Couldn't I be the first then?" he asked her. "That would be such a gift for you to give me—I don't deserve it, but couldn't I be the first?"

If he had said the only one—had asked to be the last as well as first—she might not have consented.

"Maybe," she said.

"Next Saturday night?" he said.

She did not answer at once, but thought about the meaning of the gift. It would be a gift she could never take back. Whatever happened, he would have that much of her.

"Well," she said. "I had better tell you how to get there."

"Couldn't I take you home tonight?"

She shook her head. "Mrs. Waters wouldn't like it. And we're guests in her house."

"All right," he said. "I'll wait."

Within the half hour, the two couples had returned to the house and were sitting together on the front porch, commenting on the odor of the honeysuckle and the sound of a mockingbird. There seemed not to be as much to say for two couples as for one, Joanna thought. After a little while, she suggested a game of dominoes, and they played until it was time for the guests to go home.

Ray and Isabel drove home in silence. Absorbed in her own

thoughts, Isabel did not at first wonder why Ray had nothing to say; but then it occurred to her that he might not have been very happy about the arrangement she and Joanna had made for that night.

"I'm sorry," she said, "that I didn't think about how things would work out for you and Joanna. You-all didn't have much time to yourselves tonight."

"Oh, that's all right," Ray said.

"Well, something's wrong."

"Sis, you oughtn't to have ever let that man come here."

"I thought you liked him. You seemed to be having such a good time talking about Sweeney's school and everything. And Mr. Waters and the boys seemed to like him."

"He asked too dad-blame many questions," Ray said.

"He's a newspaper reporter. He wants to know things."

"What do you reckon made him ask all that about shooting?"

"Nothing in particular, Ray. We've heard all that talked over dozens of times, and you never got suspicious of anybody before. And he's already written his piece for the paper about Papa. You saw that, didn't you?"

"Yeah. It was all right. But if he gets to asking many questions, you be careful."

"He's coming again, Ray," she said. "He's coming to our house next Saturday night."

"I don't like that," he said.

"Well, I've told him he can come. I didn't know how you felt."

"Anybody can see he's nosy. You ought to have seen that yourself. You ought to think a long time before you ask anybody like that to our house."

"Am I never to have a friend," Isabel asked, "because of—" She broke off.

"Of what I done?"

She didn't answer.

"You'll hold it against me the rest of your life, won't you?"

"I don't, Ray. I don't. I don't see either what other way there was. But I don't think we know yet how much we'll have to pay."

He lapsed back into his silence, which she found she did not care to break.

Saturday night, Travis went with Ray to Greenfields. Jack had talked him into coming along and going with him to visit the Varton sisters. (Mrs. Waters might have been responsible for that—she had worried for a long time because Travis kept to himself so much.)

As the brothers drove off, Isabel said, "Leave the gate down, Ray. I'll send Leonard to keep the cows from getting out, and he can shut it after Mr. Hastings comes."

"Well, make sure he does," Ray said. "I don't want to lose no cows on account of that sucker."

The younger children, possibly influenced by Ray, did not appear to be pleased with Archie's coming, but they were at least curious. Sophie went with Leonard to keep the cows in and shut the gate—she said she wondered if that Yankee could drive through a gate; she wanted to see.

"I don't think you call people from Missouri Yankees," Isabel said.

"Well, he's from up north, ain't he?" Sophie said. "Ray said he sure talks funny."

Burnie sat with Isabel and Lizzie on the front porch, waiting. "I'll stay and speak to him, Sister, since you want me to," he said. "But I don't see why you want to bring in some stranger to mess up everything just when we're getting along so well."

"I thought you liked Mr. Hastings when you met him at church that day," Isabel said.

"He was all right," said Burnie. "I just don't think we need any strangers."

The children were all polite when Archie came, but they didn't stay to talk. Neither, for long, did Lizzie, but she told Archie she was glad he came. Isabel felt that perhaps she really was.

When they were left to themselves on the porch, Isabel and Archie remained for a little while as polite and shy as any Greenfields couple might have done. Isabel, wearing her lilac-sprigged dress with her collar turned up in a way that made her look prim, sat very straight in the chair vacated by her mother; and Archie, his Panama hat on his seersucker knees, sat near her on a stool from the kitchen.

He said he guessed Ray had gone to call on Joanna. He asked after her, and the rest of her family. He admired the dog, Blackie, whom Isabel scolded because he came too close.

At last he said, "I like this place."

"I'm glad," she said.

They sat looking southward toward the lilac hedge, over the summer-brown grass turned golden by the sinking sun.

"I'd like to see it all," he said.

"Well, you can't tonight," she said. "But come with me to my hilltop and you can look out over it."

He said, "I might have known you'd have a hilltop."

They walked away westward from the house. Blackie started to follow them, but Burnie came out on the porch and called him back.

"This seems like a large farm," said Archie, looking around him as they started up the rise.

"There used to be a section of land," she told him, "but Papa had to sell a quarter section when he nearly went broke trying to have a horse ranch."

"So what do you raise on it now?"

"Cotton, and a few cows. It's not such good cotton land, and the best was what Papa sold."

"But it makes a living?"

"Oh yes. It makes a living. We're fairly poor, but maybe not as poor as the house and everything make us look. Papa got to be a little bit of a miser."

"You like the place, I think."

"Oh yes, I do. Of course I'd be glad if the house was fixed up some, and better furnished. But I've grown up here. I like the land."

"You're not like your brother and your friend—anxious to leave it and make a life in town?"

"No. Not like Ray and Joanna, that way. I like it here, but I don't think *where* I live—the kind of place, or if it's town or country—is as important to me as it is to them."

"I daresay it isn't. You get past that."

She wasn't sure what he meant, and did not ask. They had come to the hilltop.

As they came up, facing west, the sky seemed all consumed with a crimson fire. Set up darkly against it like a child's toys ranged along a tabletop were blocks, towers, and rounded shapes, which were the houses, barns, windmills, and trees of Greenfields.

"Look," she said, pointing west and a little south. "There's the store, and that clump of trees is where Joanna's house stands."

"I'm almost getting to like these open spaces," he said.

She turned, and he with her.

"It's a little different this way," she said.

The land and sky faded to gray in the east. Low hills led the eye as far as it could follow, without the sharply drawn horizon of the west, or any clear-cut silhouettes against the sky.

"Doesn't anyone live in this direction?" he asked.

"A few," she said. "It gets to be ranch country. They like to build their houses in the shelter of hills, close to creeks."

"Almost like part of the natural landscape," he said. "Like yours."

"Yes," she said. "In the beginning," she went on, pointing to a mound of earth just visible beyond the house, "we lived in a hole in the ground. And that really was like being part of the landscape."

"Say, is that a dugout?" he asked. "I've heard of dugouts, but I supposed they were all gone."

"There's still a few around, I think."

"But you don't use it, I guess."

"Well—not really. I've got some things down there. I've been sleeping there this summer."

"You mean it's your own place—no one else goes there?"

"I don't suppose they'd want to."

"Would you let me see it?"

"Maybe—sometime."

"Yes, of course, it's too soon," he said.

"Someday I'll show you all over the place," she said. "We'll walk from one end to another, down along the creek, where the rock bluffs are, and there's a water hole that never dries up, with good-sized hackberry trees around it."

"When?" he said.

"Someday," she said.

They began to descend the hill.

"There's the barn, I suppose," he said.

"And the shed, where we always kept the buggy, and now we keep the car."

"Somewhere near the barn," he said, "is where your father died?"

"Yes," she said. "Where Ray found him."

"You said something once that made me wonder—is your family really not grieving very much?"

"Not very much," she said. "If you're going to be our friend, you'll have to know. My father was a cruel man. We're all of us happier without him."

"I'm sorry," he said.

She did not answer. They walked on slowly to the house. She thought of what Ray had said about answering Archie's questions, but they seemed to spring from normal, friendly interest, so that she felt she would be both foolish and unkind if she refused to answer him.

She sat on the edge of the porch, and he beside her, before she realized what she had done. "Oh, your trousers," she said. "I sat here without thinking, because I always do, but you'll get your trousers dusty."

"If you permit me," he said, "I'd like to sit by you."

She didn't say anything; he seemed to take her silence for permission, and they sat close but not touching. They were facing the moon, which was full or nearly so, but neither spoke of it. It pleased her somehow that he didn't say, "Look at the moon."

Leonard, always the last of the children to disappear for the night, was running around the house, racing the puppy.

"You'd better go in," Isabel said to him.

"In a minute," he called as he raced by.

"It must be fun to have younger brothers and sisters," Archie said.

"Why," she said, "are you the baby of the family?"

"Oh yes," he said. "In a way, it's why I'm here."

"Tell me," she said. "I've wondered about that."

He had come to West Texas on account of his uncle, Will Hastings, who had always been considered a black sheep by the family. He had been a wanderer in his youth, but in the early days of settlement here he had established a newspaper, the *Western Message*. He had never kept in close touch with his family in Missouri, but had written last year to see whether any of his brother's sons would like to come and learn the newspaper business and eventually (if both uncle and nephew were satisfied) take over as publisher. Both of Archie's older brothers were already married and established in the family business. Archie—unknown to his uncle—had gone to work for a newspaper upon graduation from college. The opportunity had come as a complete surprise to him, but he decided at once to give up his job and take a chance in Texas.

"And you didn't mind leaving your family?" Isabel asked.

"Oh yes, I did mind," Archie said. "I miss them. But we all write lots of letters. And my mother and father are coming to visit in the fall."

"Then yours is one of the happy families."

"I never thought of us that way, but I suppose you might say so. We're a pretty ordinary bunch."

"Maybe that's what Tolstoy meant."

"Tolstoy?"

"Yes. The author, you know. I read his book called *Anna Karenina*—however you pronounce it."

"I've read that too."

"And you remember how it starts? All happy families are alike, but unhappy ones are all different. Something like that. I've wondered and wondered what he meant."

"I don't think I really noticed that when I read it. Had my mind on seeing what the story was about, I suppose."

"You wouldn't notice, maybe, unless you'd had reason to think about unhappy families. And if you belong to a happy family, you wouldn't think. You wouldn't notice. Because, like you say, that's ordinary. I do think that's what it's about though—the beginning of that book. Nothing much happens in happy families—nobody writes books about them. But something has to happen to make a family miserable, and in every family what happens is a little different."

"Dear Isabel," he said softly, "have you been so miserable?"

"Yes," she said simply. "We have been miserable."

"But life will be better now?"

"I don't know—I pray it will."

They sat in silence a little while, before he said, "You like to read then?"

"Oh yes," she said. "I don't have much to read though."

"I could let you have some books," he said.

They were interrupted then by Burnie pushing open the screen door. "Where's Leonard?" he asked.

"Oh, chasing Blackie, I guess," said Isabel. "Come sit and talk to us a little bit."

Hesitantly, Burnie came and sat on the edge of the porch beside Isabel.

"Burnie is a reader too," Isabel told Archie. "He and I are the only ones in the family that really like books."

"What do you read, Burnie?" Archie asked.

"Oh—anything," Burnie said.

"How about Kipling?" Archie asked him.

"He's all right," Burnie said.

Actually, Burnie had been excited when he first read *Barrack-Room Ballads* and a book of Kipling's stories that Jack Waters lent him. He wanted that book of poetry for himself, and Isabel hoped she could buy it for him someday. She was sorry he wouldn't talk to Archie about himself, it wasn't like him; but like the other children, he seemed to take his cue from Ray.

They heard Leonard shouting then, and Burnie said, "I got to go. Mama wants me to get Leonard in to go to bed."

Burnie went to the end of the porch calling Leonard, and presently the two went into the house.

"Good night," Archie called to them.

They did not answer.

"Are they shy?" asked Archie.

"Leonard is, with strangers," Isabel said. "Burnie—I don't know about Burnie. He's not like himself lately."

"It's a bad time for you all. I shouldn't have come, maybe."

"No, it's all right. I wanted you to come."

They sat there a little longer, while she wondered how long she should let them stay close together like that. At last she suggested that they might be more comfortable inside, and they went into the living room. The house was dark and quiet—Lizzie and all the children had gone to bed. Isabel lit the lamp on the center table: it illuminated the table and the two rocking chairs drawn up to it. The room didn't look so bad this way, but she wished they didn't have to have the bed in there.

Archie didn't seem to notice. He picked up the book she had left on the table.

"You like Hardy?" he asked.

"Yes, I think so. That's Jack's book, that he let me borrow. I've read it twice now."

"Do you usually read books twice?"

"Well—if there's nothing else and I've liked it. Seems like I always hate to tell the characters good-bye."

"Did you read *Anna Karenina* twice?"

"Oh yes, I did love Anna."

"In spite of her sin?"

"Yes—and still, I couldn't help thinking there must have been some better way. I felt sorry for her, but I did so much want her to find a better way. Like us."

"What do you mean?"

"Oh, nothing. I don't mean to talk about my family anymore."

"Of course not. I understand. Tell me—where did you get a copy of *Anna?*"

"From my teacher. I had to leave school more than a year ago, but she used to lend me books when she could. My father didn't like me bringing them home, you see."

"She must have been a good teacher," he said.

"A wonderful teacher," she said. "She married last spring—a professor at the normal school in East Texas. She wants Joanna and me to come and go to school there, and learn to be teachers."

"Will you go?"

"Joanna means to. I don't think I do. I didn't think I could, but things are different now. I suppose I *could* go. Miss Lona wrote to me the other day and told me about a friend of hers that wants a girl to do housekeeping, in exchange for room and board. I haven't answered the letter yet."

"I wouldn't like to see you go away, just as I've found you—and yet, why wouldn't you want to go?"

"I'm just not sure. I don't really want to be a teacher, but I want to be well educated more than anything in the world. But that's not right for a woman, is it? Because there's not much reason for a college education for a woman, unless she means to teach school."

"Your Miss Lona should have taught you better than that," he said.

"She used to say education is a worthwhile goal in itself, but it's hard to tell what that means."

"It does mean something though—and it means as much for a woman as a man. Even if she does nothing but support him in his work and play her part in bringing up the children. But as far as work goes, a woman can do almost anything a man can, if she really wants to."

"But you see, I'm so ignorant, I can't even imagine what a woman could do. At Greenfields there's only one place for a woman outside the home. And that's the teacher's desk."

"Yes," he said, "I suppose you really ought to take the opportunity to get away. But surely you'd come home fairly often?"

"Not very. It must be about four hundred miles from here to Commerce."

"We could write."

"Well, I haven't gone yet. I don't suppose I could, really."

He grinned. He didn't, very often, but when he did it brought forth little radiating lines from his mouth and eyes. She had already learned to like his grin.

"But just in case," he said, "we'd better see each other as often as possible."

They decided on the following Saturday night. He said he would like to come sooner, but his uncle often wanted him to attend some church or civic affair on weeknights. She was rather glad of this. She suspected she would have let him come on the soonest day he named. (It is not good for a young man and woman to be together too often too soon; that was a lesson she had learned long ago from Mrs. Waters, and she was beginning to understand what it meant.)

It wasn't long after they had settled on the time of their next meeting that Isabel, glancing out the window, saw a glimmer of car light on the main road.

"That will be Ray and Travis," she said.

The lights turned toward the house, stopped briefly (while Travis opened the gate), and then came on.

"I'm going to kiss you," Archie said.

"Yes," she said.

He rose and approached her chair. She turned her cheek to him.

"Very well, the cheek this time," he said.

The kiss went all through her, as his first touch had done, as she had known it would. She turned away from the light, because she knew her face was suffused with unaccustomed color.

"Dear Isabel," he said. (He had said that once before.)

"I suppose Ray will think it's time for me to go," he said, "since he's already home from his visit to Joanna."

Of course he was right. When the brothers came in, they shook hands with Archie; but Ray said at once, "I've left the gate down for you—I'll ride back on your running board and shut it after you."

"I suppose that means I'd better go right on, before a cow gets out," Archie said.

"It does," said Ray.

Archie and Isabel, having said their real good-bye already, took a polite leave of each other and Archie followed Ray out the door.

Travis went on to bed then, but Isabel sat waiting for Ray to come back. He wasn't long about it.

"Did you talk to him?" she asked.

"No," he said. "What was there to say?"

She had been afraid he might tell Archie not to come back, but she did not tell him that.

"Nothing, I guess," she said. "How was Joanna?"

"Fine," he said.

"Well, good night," she said, and went to the dugout.

She wrote in her diary again that night. She almost let herself say she was happier than she had ever been in her life, but (perhaps from superstition) stopped short of that extreme. She described the kiss and her blush; she wrote of the views from the hilltop. Then she considered the possibility of going away to college. "There might be some work I could do, better than hoeing cotton," she wrote, "if I had a college education." And then she added, "If I ever hope to marry an educated man, one I know now or one I may meet in the future, then I had better try to be an educated woman."

It rained again on the weekend, heavy rains that kept the Doanes home from church and, for several days, out of the field. Ray and the younger boys spent most of the time hauling wood from over in the breaks, replenishing the supply for cooking and next winter's heating. Isabel and Sophie worked around the house.

Occasionally some visitor called, "to see how Mrs. Doane was getting along." Lizzie would usually talk for a while with a degree of animation, but then in the midst of a conversation might suddenly fall into silent preoccupation. One morning, after she had failed to answer a direct question put to her by Mrs. Goolsby, the old woman took Isabel aside.

"Let's walk down and look at your garden," she said.

They walked and looked, but Mrs. Goolsby did not mention the squash or tomatoes.

"Now see here, Isabel," she said, looking up through the long cylindrical split bonnet she always wore outdoors, "I don't know what you're up to, but you're not helping your folks a bit."

"I don't know what you mean, Mrs. Goolsby," Isabel said.

"Yes, you do," said Mrs. Goolsby sharply. "I mean you taking up with that stranger, and moving to the dugout."

"Mrs. Goolsby, I've seen Mr. Hastings three times, since I first met him to know his name, and I don't think that's exactly taking up with him. And I haven't moved to the dugout—I've been sleeping down there, because it's cooler."

"Well, I expect you just haven't been very thoughty about all this. You never was one to consider the looks of the thing—not a bit like Joanna that way—but o' course Mrs. Waters taught her."

"I don't know what you think it looks like, Mrs. Goolsby—anything I have or haven't been doing."

"All right, I'll tell you what it looks like." Mrs. Goolsby stood compactly between two bean rows, and folded her arms across her stomach. "In the first place, everybody knows you wasn't in with the rest of the family about what Ray done."

"How do they know that?" Isabel asked.

"Well, you wasn't, was you?"

"We had a talk about it, in the family. I said I was opposed to killing. I still am. But I don't see how the whole community knows that."

"Things gets around."

Isabel didn't answer.

"And now, you've moved out of the house, and you've took up with this stranger. And him a newspaper feller coming around asking questions."

"I don't know what questions you mean, Mrs. Goolsby."

"All kinds of questions. You was there, wasn't you, at the Waterses', when he commenced asking all about shooting, and whether folks around here don't shut their eyes to it. Mrs. Waters told me she put a stop to that talk."

"Mr. Waters had been telling all about Block Ninety-seven. That's why he asked."

"And I've heard he was at Greenfields asking questions on the very day of the funeral."

"Joanna told me about that. I didn't see anything wrong with what he asked."

"And no telling what he's asked you, and what you've told him."

"Mrs. Goolsby, I don't think that's fair. He wouldn't ask anything more than any sympathetic friend would ask."

"Well, I don't know so much about that—because he's not a friend, not a real friend, not like Greenfields folks. But whether he does ask or he don't, there's something amiss around here. And what I think, and what folks is saying, is that your mama ought to be getting along better than she is by this time. We thought we'd be seeing her at Sunday school and preaching by now—how long has your papa been gone, about a month ain't it?"

"About that. But it's been a good many years since Mama was really all right. It's not an ordinary case of a widow getting over her grief."

"I know it's not. That's why I think four weeks is long enough. And if she's grieving, you ought to be at her side, helping her. It may be she's not grieving over Harvey, anyway, but over you, and what you may be doing to the family—to Ray, and after all he sacrificed to help you all."

"If it's going to keep me from ever living my own life, Mrs. Goolsby," Isabel said, "I'm not sure I can appreciate the sacrifice."

Afterwards, she was sorry for what she said. It would give Mrs. Goolsby more to talk about, and Isabel had to consider that she herself might be wrong. Maybe she had been thinking too much about Archie Hastings—too much about college. Certainly, if Mama didn't seem better soon, she would have to write Miss Lona and tell her it would be impossible for her to come to Commerce this year.

Then, thinking of the accusations Mrs. Goolsby had made about her own revelations to Archie Hastings, she remembered regretfully one or two things she had said to him. She made up her mind to be more careful when she saw him on Saturday night. And probably not let him come to see her so soon again. At least she would try not to.

CHAPTER FOURTEEN

On Friday, Ray and the boys went fishing at a tank on a ranch several miles east of them, where they had been going for wood. Isabel helped them get their "grub" together, as the boys said, and they loaded their fishing gear into the wagon. Rain had fallen off and on through the week, but there had been two dry days now, and Ray told Isabel the main roads were passable if she wanted to go to the store in the car. She thanked him (rather formally, the way those two often spoke now) and said she didn't know of anything they'd need. All the brothers and sisters could drive the car now—even Leonard and Sophie, although Ray wouldn't let them go anywhere by themselves in it, and Burnie, who had learned to manage very well with his one good arm and leg.

Fairly early in the morning, between eight-thirty and nine, Isabel went to the garden barefooted, to gather squash for dinner. The garden was so muddy that shoes were a nuisance. Not only did they collect gobs of mud, so that moving around was awkward, but they were a lot harder to clean than feet. Even Lizzie was likely to leave off her shoes if she went to the garden when it was muddy; Isabel and Sophie always did.

Isabel had put on an old print dress, patched and faded and really outgrown. It was a little too tight across the chest, and not altogether comfortable, but the skirt was short enough to keep out of the mud and the dew-drenched vegetation. It was a good garden dress, but she meant to change to something else before dinner. She was bending over, reaching down among the thickly grown leaves for the scalloped white squash, when she heard a car turn in at the gate, which had been left open because Ray had moved the stock to the east pasture and there was no reason to shut it.

Oh gosh, who's that about to catch me here like this? she thought, straightening up quickly to look around her.

There was, of course, no way now to avoid being caught. If the visitor had had to stop, open the gate, drive through, close the gate, as ordinarily the case would be, she might have had a chance; but the car was coming straight on and would have to pass within a few feet of the garden. She could have run for cover, but whoever was coming would see her plain before she got away.

By the time she had thought all these things, Archie Hastings's yellow car had come in view, topping the little rise between the gate and the house.

He braked the car. She felt her face flame.

"Isabel!" he called. "You look wonderful—like Maud Muller, or somebody."

"Don't you dare look at me, Archie Hastings," she shouted. "You go right on to the house, and don't look back."

He gave her his rare, boyish grin (and somehow she cared less, already, about the way she looked). "All right," he said, "I'll wait on the porch till you come."

She watched till he passed the row of lilac bushes that cut off the view of the front porch and part of the driveway. Then she snatched up her bucket of vegetables and ran, circling widely around to the back of the house and in at the kitchen door.

Sophie was in there, doubled up with silent laughter, which broke out into high gleeful giggles when she saw Isabel.

"He caught you!" she cried. "Your highfalutin Yankee feller caught you barefooted in the mud."

"Hush, he'll hear you," Isabel begged, but Sophie wouldn't stop giggling.

Isabel realized then that actually she didn't mind as much as she had thought she did with that first wave of embarrassment. Archie's grin helped—and the way he compared her to Maud Muller. That, in a way, was another link between them: she had always liked the poem by Whittier, the boys (Jack and Ray) always made fun of it, and maybe Archie would, too, she didn't know; but it was at least something they had in common. It showed she had a little education; she wasn't completely ignorant of Archie's world.

The water in the reservoir on the stove was still warm. She dipped it up into a wash pan, which she carried, with soap and a towel and washrag, into the shedroom where Sophie slept. Isabel still kept all her better clothes in there, having no very good place to put them in the dugout.

"Would you get my blue plaid dress out of the trunk for me," she said to Sophie, "and find my black button shoes? I've got to look decent for him."

"I think he liked you the way you was," Sophie said, "to judge by the look on his face when he drove up."

"Oh, do hush," said Isabel.

She washed as fast as she could, and combed out and pinned up her hair, while Sophie found clothes for her to put on.

It seemed hours, but could scarcely have been fifteen minutes, between the time she stood up in the garden and saw Archie Hastings smiling at her and the time she walked out onto the front porch and found him chatting with her mother, who had gone out to greet him.

"I'm sorry to have come without letting you know," Archie said. "Uncle Will unexpectedly gave me the day off, because I've had to work at night several times this week, and it seemed like the perfect day for you to show me your farm and the Greenfields community."

"Yes, I did promise to do that," said Isabel uncertainly.

"It sure is a pretty day," said Lizzie, "after all this nice rain we've been having. It'll be nice driving around or walking down on the creek, I guess."

"Come with us, Mrs. Doane," said Archie. Isabel almost believed he would have been pleased if she had.

But Lizzie, smiling, said no, it would take her too long to get ready. "Sophie might go with you," she said.

Suddenly Isabel realized someone ought to go. It would have been a good idea to take Leonard, perhaps, if the boys had been at home—or Burnie, though he might not have been willing to go. She did not much like the knowing little remarks she could imagine Sophie making as they drove, but she remembered what Mrs. Waters always said: a child makes the best chaperone. At first the prospect of a drive with Archie Hastings had seemed so natural and pleasant that she hadn't even thought to wonder what Mrs. Waters or Mrs. Goolsby would think if they saw the two drive by.

"Yes, do come, Sophie," she said.

"Well, I'm not gonna go all over the country with you," Sophie said. "But you can take me by Bessie Akers's, 'cause I've been aiming to go and stay all day with her."

But then, of course, Lizzie would be left by herself. "Are you sure you want us to leave you here, Mama?" Isabel asked.

"Why, sure, I'll have Blackie," Lizzie said, laughing as the dog came to her at the sound of his name. "You run on, both of you, it's such a pretty day."

Sophie decided to have them let her out at Greenfields. Ray had given her a nickel, and on hearing that news, Archie obligingly gave her another. She meant to buy a sack of candy to take to Bessie's house, which was just across the railroad from the store. As Archie pulled up in front of the porch, they saw a face framed in one of the dirty panes of the post office window.

"Looks like you're fixing to get talked about, Sister," Sophie said. She jumped from the car and hopped up on the porch, where she turned back to them, laughing, before she opened the screen door and went in.

Archie drove on. "Across the railroad?" he said. "I haven't been that way yet."

She nodded, still thinking of the face at the window.

"Who was that looking out?" he asked. "And who will talk?"

"Mrs. Waters," she said. "And everyone will talk."

"Will you mind?"

"Oh yes, I'll mind," said Isabel. "Mrs. Waters will scold me, and make sure I do. But I won't give up a day's pleasure because of it." She almost said "innocent pleasure"; it was the phrase that came to her mind, as an unprecedented feeling of rebellion against Greenfields rose in her breast.

"Your mother didn't seem to disapprove," he said, "so why should Mrs. Waters say anything at all?"

Why should she? Isabel realized she had never asked herself that question before.

"Mama's had such troubles," Isabel said, "that I guess Mrs. Waters thinks she scarcely notices what we do. And Joanna and I have been so close—I've felt like her mama was somebody to go to when mine wouldn't even talk to me."

"Even so," said Archie, "she's not your mother, and if she sees anything wrong with the two of us driving around the community together on a bright summer morning, I have to say I'm kind of glad she's not."

It seemed to Isabel then that she was, too, and always had been. But what she said was, "We have a strange family. I'll tell you all about us sometime."

"But not now?"

"Oh, not now! Drive on, and let's have a good time."

She sat quite properly apart from him, yet utterly aware of his presence. He was more casually dressed than she had seen him before, except at the rabbit drive. He had on his usual summer suit, but had left off the coat and rolled up his shirt sleeves. A cool, provocative scent hovered round him; she guessed it came from his shaving soap. She wrenched her gaze from his bare forearm, brown and hairy, where it lay along the steering wheel, and turned to the level landscape moving by.

"Nearly all this land south of the railroad is in cultivation," she said, "or soon will be. It's the best cotton land."

"And who lives there?" he asked, gesturing toward a neat, white-painted frame house, not large, but clearly new and well built.

"Oh, that's our doctor," Isabel said. "Dr. Venable. I don't know whether he's very good or not—or really why he's here, instead of practicing in some town. People wonder, but they send for him if they need a doctor in a hurry."

"Is he the one that came when your father died?"

"Oh yes. But of course there wasn't anything any doctor could have done for him."

"No," he said, "I realized that."

"You could turn at that next road coming in," she said. "It follows what you might call the boundary of the community. On the other side of it is the Walnut Grove school district."

She directed him to turn again, and then again, and they crossed back over the railroad about a mile and a half from the center of Greenfields. "Now," she said, "you've seen pretty well all of the nice, flat farmland—I guess the part that gives the community its name. Here's the cemetery—it really stands between the two kinds of country."

"Yes. I drove here once before," he said, "and noticed then that it's what you might call on the brink. Shall we stop?"

"We might as well," she said. "I suppose it's really our main point of interest."

The cemetery was isolated on a high brow of land. Below it, toward the railroad, they could see the handful of buildings that was Greenfields. Beyond it, in the opposite direction, lay ranch country, with no house visible. Up and down the road, on either side, farmhouses stood, but the thick mesquite and chaparral of pastures cut off the view of them.

As they walked toward the graves he took her hand. "Surely no one can see us here—no one to talk."

"No, the people here won't talk," she said, "or those cows over there across the fence." She left her hand in his.

"It's rather a pleasant place," he said.

She had always thought so. There were a few trees there—arborvitae, which people by some superstitious custom always planted in graveyards, and a blooming willow with a scattering of ragged, fading flowers. It had a dove nest in it—the bird flew off in distress, leaving two pure white eggs.

"Life goes on here," she said. "I like that."

"May we see where your father is buried?" he asked.

She nodded, and led the way toward the east side, the longest-used part, to a new grave near a crimson-flowering crape myrtle bush.

"We haven't got a tombstone yet," she said. "Mr. Waters is going to see about getting one through the lodge—Woodmen of the World, you know. It will be like that stone over there that looks like a tree trunk."

"Who planted the shrub?" he asked.

"Mama," she said. "This is not our first grave, you see."

She turned to a low white marble stone, with a lamb recumbent upon it. It marked the grave of Baby Boy Doane, who died the day he was born, some seven years ago. No doctor ever attended Lizzie Doane, so no one could ever know whether he died because his father kicked his mother in the stomach while the baby still lived in the womb. The incident was always spoken of as a fall, but inevitably the women of the community had known what really happened. And Isabel. Isabel had known, for she was there.

She realized tears were falling down her face, and groped for a pocket handkerchief.

Archie handed her his. "I'm sorry," he said. "I shouldn't have suggested that we stop."

"It's all right," she said. "I wanted to. I don't know why I cried."

They drove on, and she showed him where the Vartons lived, whom he had met on his first Sunday at Greenfields, and on down the road, the Goolsbys' house, set in its grove of chinaberry trees.

"Mr. Goolsby is the justice of the peace," Isabel said. "He was the first man to break sod anywhere around here, so they say. Those are the oldest trees planted in this community."

"Is he the man who ruled on your father's death?" Archie asked.

"Yes," she said. "Ray went after him."

As they drove by, a woman in a floor-sweeping, Mother Hubbard dress stepped out onto the porch. Isabel waved to her.

"I might as well wave," she said. "That's Mrs. Goolsby."

They drove on, deeper into the breaks, where no houses stood along the roadside.

"Stop here," she presently said. "We'll get out, and I'll show you something."

He stopped on a hilltop. She led him to stand looking southward across uneven, unplowed land.

"This is our place," she said, "but to get to our house in the car we'd have to go all the way back to Greenfields crossroads, or two miles farther down this way and across to the main road on a track through rough pasture."

"You like this side of it, don't you?"

"Of our land?"

"Yes—and Greenfields. I knew it that evening we stood on the hilltop looking east, away from the sunset."

"The dark side, you mean."

"I wasn't thinking of the dark. I guess I mean the uncultivated side—where nature has been least interfered with."

"Well—yes—I've always liked the pastures and our creek. Sometimes it seems good to get away from anything people have made—or land they've changed."

"I wish you could go with me to the river I told you about— far up toward the source of it, where the Sunday walkers and boaters don't go. There's something about water."

"I guess you think this is a desert," she said.

"No," he said. "I might have once. I think I see what you see now."

She did not ask him what that was. They stood together and looked across the rugged brown prairie, marked with a line of green where the creek cut through the Doane land, to the far horizon swimming in the waves of intensifying heat. Suddenly she hated the thought of turning back, driving again along that road with the houses where people looked out at windows, back by Greenfields, even back home.

"You know," she said, "that place I told you about—our pool, where the hackberries grow—is not very far from us here."

"We could go there now," he said, "explore this side of your land, before I take you home."

"We might get hungry though. I was thinking I'd cook us some dinner at home."

He laughed heartily then, and turned back to the car. "Well, if that's all," he said, "then I'm prepared to meet that objection." He lifted a blanket that lay on the backseat of the car, and revealed a large wicker basket. "I've brought lunch," he said, "with the very healthy plan of eating it whenever we get hungry."

If there were any other objections to going on to the pool, Isabel didn't think of them. "It's like a fairy story," she said. "Like the table that appeared by magic under the tree, laid with a feast for the poor little girl."

"This day is a fairy story," he said. "I designed it that way."

Down by that round pool of shadowy brown water, surrounded by rocks and one grassy bank, protected by hackberry and chittam from the sun, Archie spread the blanket and then laid out their lunch on a white cloth. Isabel had never seen a picnic lunch like it—dainty white sandwiches filled with delicately flavored meat ("Veal, not chicken," he said, "chicken spoils sooner"); lettuce, small pear-shaped tomatoes, peaches, grapes, and fancy iced cakes.

"It really is magic," Isabel said.

"Not really. It came from Mrs. Blossom at the New York Hotel."

"Fixed at the hotel!" she exclaimed. "Oh, Archie!" She realized it was the first time she had called him by that name (instead of Mr. Hastings), and she blushed, but if he noticed he gave no sign.

She had sat back on the grass to marvel at the sight, and he kissed her on the cheek. Though only lightly, and he said at once: "But we must eat—no time for dalliance."

Although she had tasted a sandwich, she was too excited to eat, and she told him so. Then he fed her tidbits until he had her laughing, and she told him she was able to feed herself. In the end she ate like a country girl, she thought, like a girl who had stood barefooted in the garden mud in the cool of the dewy morning.

But he liked such a girl. So he said. He lay back on the grass ("You'll stain your shirt," she said, but probably the heat of noon had burned away all dampness)—he lay and talked, lazily, of how she had appeared to him that morning in the garden.

"Not like the young women in town, or the girls I knew where I came from. Not even like your friend Joanna and her mama—always concerned with proper dress, and proper language, and proper behavior."

"But Archie, I am proper," Isabel said. "At least I try to be. I want to be like the girls in town, the girls you used to know. I guess that's one reason I want to go to college. I want to learn things out of books, but I want to learn to *behave* like an educated woman."

"You will," he said. "No doubt you will. And I'll be sorry, in a way. But as Emerson said, for everything you lose, you gain something."

(Emerson, she thought. Emerson—Trust thyself: every heart vibrates to that iron string. She couldn't remember what he said about gains and losses.)

"Have you decided?" Archie asked her. "Have you thought about Miss Lona's letter anymore?"

"Yes," she said, "I've thought. I can't go this year. At least I can't decide now. We're too uncertain about how Mama's going to be. The children might not be able to go to school this year if I couldn't be here to help when the time comes. I have made up my mind what to write her." Actually, she had written two or three letters already, the first on the day Mrs. Goolsby talked to her, but she had torn them all up. Perhaps she wasn't as certain as she sounded even now.

"Well, I'm not so sorry," he said. "Unless you are. I think you have wanted to go."

"I do, and may yet," she said. "But not this year."

"If you never happen to go," he said, "you mustn't mind too much. You can learn from books, and from friends. And there's something you have that couldn't be learned, more important than anything a college could teach you."

"And what could that be?"

"Two things, really. One every woman would like to have, and not many do: that's natural grace. And the other few women ever think to seek: that's a regard for truth. I've seen both in you, from the first day I met you."

She did not answer that. That last word, the way he said it, had taken her back to the Sunday Jack Waters had guyed Mr. Birdsong and disturbed the Sunday school class, then later talked with her of truth as they walked along the railroad. She could not have imagined then such a falsification as she had now submitted to—as her family had connived at, and the whole community of Greenfields acquiesced in. As the very embodiment of falsehood, she did not see how she could sit modestly smiling and pretend to be all that Archie Hastings praised in her. Yet for Ray's sake—for her whole family's sake—she could not tell the truth.

"Have I said something to offend you?" he asked at last.

"No," she said. "I was thinking about a talk I had with Jack Waters on that subject—truth."

"Is Jack your special friend?"

"No," she said, "he never has been. I like him though. He talks about ways of thinking—he wonders about things."

"Yes, I've noticed he does. He has a keener mind than Winnie, although I suppose Winnie is the one who will go on and be something or other that will make Greenfields sit up and take notice."

"He really had the Sunday school class going that day—he practically made everyone admit that there was something or someone they would lie for. And then later—when we talked—he said he didn't think such lies as the class had thought about had anything to do with the basic concept of truth."

"And you—did you agree?"

"Well, in a way. But I believe in the truth—I don't like lies of any kind." She paused, frowning thoughtfully. "That doesn't mean I'd never lie. But I go against myself—what I really believe—if I do."

"I like what you say. It's my business, you know—truth. Some newspapermen would not agree with me—they print deliberate lies to gain power, or bring about some particular thing they want to have happen. But as I see it my whole profession is to find out truth and let it be known."

She could not think of anything to say to that. It seemed to her that anything she would say, without telling all she knew about the death of Harvey Doane, would be a lie. And also—obversely—that she must keep away from him, that Ray was right, and Mrs. Goolsby was right, and sooner or later she would tell him what happened, and because he was for truth he would make that truth known.

"We ought to go," she said.

"Why should we go?" he said. "Lie back on the grass beside me."

The image of Mrs. Waters came to her; ludicrous it seemed, and she could almost have laughed at it. No, Mrs. Waters, you're wrong, she said to the image. Archie Hastings wouldn't touch me, and if there were truth between us I would lie down on the grass.

She stood up. "It's really time to go," she said.

"I suppose it is," he said. "Could we go on, the long way, and take the pasture road?"

"It's a bad road—and might be muddy today. I guess we'd better go back by Greenfields crossroads."

They didn't talk much on the way back to Isabel's house. Mrs. Goolsby came out on the porch again, but this time Isabel didn't wave. She wonders where we've been so long, was her inward observation, but she did not mention it to Archie.

As they approached the crossroads, he said, "Are we to pick up your sister on our way home?"

"No," said Isabel, "she'll really stay all day. Bessie will walk halfway home with her, and they'll tell each other all their secrets on the way."

As she said it, she wondered why she had mentioned telling secrets. Thinking of herself and Joanna, of course, when they were Sophie's age: their secrets had to do with boys they liked, parties they knew about, or even a pet cat about to kitten. Such secrets as Sophie knew could never be revealed in girlish chatter.

Or they might. Such darkness enshrouded her family—she dared not say what anyone might do.

"What's the matter?" Archie said. "You can't be cold."

"What is it they say? A goose walking over my grave?"

The boys were still not home from fishing, and Lizzie had fallen asleep in her rocking chair.

"If you still want me to," Isabel said, "I'll take you around our place."

"Then you're not angry with me?"

"Oh no," she said, in real surprise.

"I wouldn't have touched you."

"I knew that, " she said.

She took him down the path that led by the barn and across the fence at the spot where, he already knew, her father had lain dead. He did not mention that fact, but accepted, laughing, her instructions on how to help a girl through a barbed wire fence.

"I think I could write an essay on that subject," he said, once they were through. "With the right touch, it could be amusing."

"Did I look funny?" she said.

"Oh no, Isabel, not you. You're graceful even climbing through a barbed wire fence."

"Stick to the truth," she said. They laughed together.

They walked across the grassy south pasture, which sloped northward and dropped into a depression that she pointed out as the head of the creek. She showed him the fields, where cotton was blooming and the feed crops grew thick and green.

"We've got good crops," she said.

"I should make a note of that," he said, "for the *Western Message.*"

As they walked along the edge of the maize field, leading them back to the barn, she began to feel free and good again. After all, she thought, I have not lied to him; and there seemed now no reason why he would ever ask the question that would compel her to lie.

They came back into the pasture, and again crossed the fence near the barn.

"This is not much like the barns on farms back home," he said.

"They're bigger, I guess."

"Bigger—with enormous haylofts, you know. I suppose it's because you don't need so much protection for animals, or storage for their feed, in this climate."

"We don't even raise hay," she said. "But we've got a loft. We store some bundle feed in it, in the winter, but I don't think there's anything there now, except maybe a few scraps of fodder."

"Well, let's look at it," he said. "I always loved the barn loft, when I was a boy visiting my grandfather's farm."

She unfastened the lot gate, and led him to the cowshed, and through it to the ladder to the loft.

He knew he must go first, and didn't make a joke about it, the way boys sometimes would, who found it funny to think of looking up a girl's skirts as she climbed the ladder.

The loft was not large, and probably seemed cramped to Archie. It covered about half the space of the entire barn, and had a tall window opening to the east.

They instinctively went there to look out—could see most of the farm from there, along the fence south, past the well-worn path, to the dugout, and on to the main road; and eastward to the rugged land of the ranches.

But Archie did not, as Isabel expected, stand looking out over the country. He bent to pick up something from the floor.

"Curious," he said.

"What is it?" she said.

"An empty rifle shell. Who shoots from the barn loft?"

"Why no one. I can't think why anyone would."

He put it in his pocket. "Some child playing, maybe."

"Yes," she said doubtfully. "Leonard might carry empty shells around, I guess."

Archie looked around the loft, without much apparent interest.

"It isn't very nice, I guess," Isabel said. "I've seen pictures of those big barns with haylofts. They must be fun."

"To a child they are," he said. "But so must this one be, I suppose."

They climbed down, and he wanted to walk along the path again, to the place where they crossed the fence.

"Where was your father lying?" he asked.

"Just there." She gestured.

He stood looking down as though studying the ground.

She wished him away from there, not quite certain why. "Come on, and I'll show you the dugout," she said.

He came back over to her, shaking his head. "It must be hard to believe," he said. "Was he very unhappy?"

"I didn't think so," she said. "No one suggested suicide."

They walked back up to the hackberry tree, where the path to the dugout forked off.

"This is really interesting to me," he said. "I've never seen a dugout, as I told you." He took a notebook and began to write down a description of it, as it looked from where they stood. "I want to look at it from all sides," he said, "and then see what the interior is like."

It was almost too dim down there, after the harsh glaring sunlight, for them even to see each other. They stood a little while getting used to the dark.

"It feels wonderful," he said, "after that heat. I don't know why everybody in this country doesn't live in a dugout, at least in the summertime."

"They're pretty nice in the winter too," Isabel said. "Most of our houses have such cracks in them, but the cold winds can't get into a good dugout."

He began to observe the details of construction and furnishing, and was surprised to see the walls were lined with pine plank reaching about halfway to the roof. "I guess I expected earth all around me," he said. "And I had no idea it would seem so spacious down here."

"Our whole family lived here till after Burnie was born," she said.

He looked around searchingly. "Yes, a family could live here," he said. "But it makes a really spacious apartment for a young woman."

"I don't really live down here," she said. "I just brought a few things."

"But it's yours," he said. "Of course it is. The books—the pictures on the walls—that pleasant counterpane. It tells me so much about you—I feel you've let me into your secret heart at last."

"Don't say such things, or we'll have to go."

"Let's stay a little. I like it here."

"Well, you may sit in my one chair," she said. She herself sat on the edge of the bed—a suggestive movement, Mrs. Waters would have thought, but Archie did not seem to.

"It's so absolutely right," he said, "that you should live down here. I should have guessed. You're so apart, so close to the land here, so—"

"But I really don't," she repeated protestingly. "I've just been sleeping down here since—well, this summer."

"Wasn't it used, before that? It seems well kept."

"It had been used. For a little while." She thought of Alma Creeping then, vividly, for the first time in many weeks. Now the whole idea of Alma came back, so repulsive that she wondered how she could ever have borne to come down here and sleep, on the very bed where her father had lain with his whore. She let the word form in her mind, perhaps for the first time; it seemed to taint the dugout, and thus, herself. And her resolution, which had wavered all day, became strong in this self-disgust. He thought her so modest, so pure: she could no longer deceive him, it was time he knew what kind of people she and her family were.

She sat up very straight, and looked at him. It seemed to her that he had a puzzled, studying look, as if he might be anticipating what she would say.

"I am going to tell you about my family now," she said. "I have promised I would, but I never could. I think this is the place we had to be, for me to tell you."

"Isabel, you need not," he said.

"Yes," she said, "I will." She began then with Alma, and told of her sojourn there where they sat. "You will marvel that I could bear to sleep here," she said.

He shook his head, began to protest, but she went on.

"It is strange," she said, "but Alma seemed to everyone the worst. He used to beat us all, and mistreat my mother in ways I don't dare to think of. I believe he was responsible for the death of the little baby, and I know the women believe Burnie would have been all right if he had let them have a doctor." She stopped, resting her chin in her hand.

"You need not tell me more," he said. "I understand."

"But there is more, so much more, more than you'd believe."

"I don't need to know it. I understand now. That's all that matters—I understand."

She knew then that she could not say anything more. The main thing—the terrible dread secret—would remain unspoken.

"Our unhappy family," she said. "I wonder if you really do understand us. Are we different, do you think, from any other unhappy family in the world?"

"I don't know about that. Don't think of it. Surely it's over now."

"Maybe. And yet I think it—whatever it was—is still here. The wickedness—the darkness—I don't know if it ends. And maybe Tolstoy was wrong. Maybe it stretches out like a net to take in all the unhappy families in the world. Different things may happen inside the net, but the thing it's made of—the dark thing—it's always the same."

"I forbid you to talk this way," he said sternly. He came and sat beside her on the bed. He put an arm around her. "Darling Isabel," he said, "you must not feel this way. You're all right, you're my wonderful, true girl. You've been miserable, but that's over. You'll be all right now, because I promise you I'll see to that."

She turned to him with widened, startled eyes.

"Don't you know what I'm telling you?" he said harshly. "I love you, and I am not going to let you be caught in any net."

For the briefest moment, she closed her eyes and leaned against him, while his long-fingered hand clasped her waist.

Then "No, no," she said, moving away from him, "you cannot love me."

"You can't prevent it," he said. "Nothing can. Because I do."

"But I told you about my family. And there's more—I told you there's more."

"I don't want to hear more. And I don't care about your family. As far as I can tell, your family and I will get along just fine, when we get to know each other. But what if we don't? It's you I love."

She knew he believed what he was saying, and she believed in his truth. But what further truth he must learn she feared to contemplate. And he would learn it. If they loved each other (if she let herself love him), if they continued to meet and talk together in the sort of intimacy that had begun today, she could not doubt he would learn it. And then when his love for her came in conflict with his dedication to truth (to learning and disseminating truth, as he had carefully explained), she could not tell what he would do. He might not know himself. She wanted him never to be required to know.

"It can't be," she said.

"It must be," he said. "Unless you don't love me."

She did not respond.

"Tell me," he said. "Tell me you don't love me, and I will know you are right, it can't be."

"You're not kind," she said.

"You love me," he insisted. "I will prove to you that you love me."

Once more he moved near her, put an arm around her, then another arm around her, enfolded her in his arms, drew her close, and kissed her long and gently on the lips. And Isabel (as Joanna had done not long before, up on the high road in the sunlight) returned the kiss of a man for the first time in her life.

At last they drew apart. She was weeping.

"Now wash your face," he said. His voice seemed weak, but there was still a rough sternness in it that made her smile even while the tears fell.

She went to her makeshift washstand and poured a little water out of her cracked pitcher. She willed the tears to stop—thought of Mrs. Waters and Mrs. Goolsby, and forced herself to try another smile. She washed her face, then went to stand before the mirror, took up a comb, and smoothed her hair in place.

"Do I look all right?" she asked, facing him.

"You look all right," he said.

"We'd better go," she said. "I don't know how long we've been down here."

"Yes," he said, "we'd better go. And of course I must apologize to you. I've wanted to do—what we did—since the first time I saw you, but I never meant to force you."

"You know you didn't," she said. She wanted to say she wasn't sorry, but she felt he would not expect a modest woman to say that. She could not imagine what would come of it—nothing must come of it—but no matter what happened she could never be sorry.

"We must go," she said again.

He rose from his seat on the bed, and they went up into the light.

Ray was coming along on the path from the hackberry tree.

"By God, you'd *better* be coming out of there," he shouted. "I'd just about figured out that was where you'd have to be."

"Hush, Ray," Isabel said.

The three younger boys sat on the porch edge, watching. "Hit 'im, Ray!" Leonard shouted.

"I don't aim to hit nobody," Ray said, addressing Archie. "I just want you to get off of this place and stay gone. That's all. I don't know what was going on down there—I'll ask my sister about that later. You may hear from me. But just don't show your face around here no more."

"Go, Archie," said Isabel.

"You want me to go?" he asked her.

"Yes," she said. "Please do."

"Walk with me to my car," he said.

"Yes," she said. She did not look at Ray, or speak to him.

"I'll be back," Archie said to her as they walked away, close together.

"Better not," she said.

"Never?" he said.

"I think—never," she said. "I told you it just couldn't be."

"You must think about it all again," he said, "in a day or two, when Ray is no longer so angry, and you're not unhappy with him. I want to give you time, but you remember what I told you. I mean to see that you're all right."

"It couldn't be," she repeated.

They were standing by his car, his hand on the door handle. "Go," she begged.

"Promise me you'll think some more, in a day or two. And then write to me. I won't come back, if it makes you too unhappy. But you must let me know."

"Well—I'll write you, but I know what I'll have to say."

"Wait, though—wait a few days—but promise you'll write."

"I promise," she said. "And if I can, I'll say come back to me. But Archie, you must not count on it, because I just don't think I can."

"I love you," he said.

"Good-bye," she said.

She waited while he backed his car, turned around, and drove out of sight. Finally, she walked back slowly toward the porch, where now Ray and their mother had joined the younger boys.

"Why didn't he fight Ray, Sis?" Burnie asked her. "If he's so fine, why did he let Ray run him off?"

"Because he's a gentleman," Isabel said.

"You may call him that," Ray said, pale with rage, stepping

down to stand facing her in the red-dirt yard. "I call him a nosy bastard. And if he comes prying around here again, or tries to lay a hand on you—"

Isabel stood looking up at him, pale as he.

"You needn't finish, Ray," she said, and couldn't believe what she was saying. "I guess I have reason enough to know what you'll do."

"What the hell do you mean?" he said.

"What you've done before," she said.

He turned on his heel and walked off toward the barn. Isabel went back to the dugout.

CHAPTER FIFTEEN

"We have got to talk," Ray said to Joanna. "I mean where there can't nobody hear us."

"Why don't we just walk around a little?" Joanna said.

This was Saturday night, as they called it—time for Ray's regular visit—but the sun had not set. Houses were hot, everyone wanted outside. Martha Waters made no objection to "the children" going for a stroll, but they noticed she sat on the front porch where she could watch them as they went along the road to the store and then followed the path that led by the schoolhouse. They were not especially aware of the lengthening, cool-looking shadows, or the birds of evening wheeling through the sky.

"I guess it's about Isabel," Joanna said.

"What do you know about it?" Ray asked.

"She was all over the country with Archie Hastings yesterday. Everybody knows that."

"Yeah? What have you heard?"

"Well, Sophie told Bessie Akers—but I think Sophie lies, don't you, Ray?"

"Oh, I expect she does," he said.

"Forget that," she said. "Of course Mama saw them to start with, when they let Sophie out at the store. She said she felt like she ought to have gone out right then and stopped Isabel."

"If she could."

"Yes. Then Mrs. Goolsby saw her. She saw them drive by her house, and said they stayed down in the breaks about three hours."

Ray growled.

"Of course we all know Isabel wouldn't do anything she shouldn't, but she ought to consider the looks of the thing."

"She's gone crazy over that feller," Ray said. "I told him not to come back."

"Why did you do that, Ray?"

"You think I'm wrong?"

"No—except you might just make Isabel stubborn." Joanna frowned. "No, what I meant—I just didn't think you could know all I know."

"I know enough."

"Ray, he's been asking questions."

"I knew that. That's one reason I told her to keep him away from us."

"If you haven't heard anything today, then he's gone farther than you know. I'm not talking about those things he asked Papa about the killings on Block Ninety-seven—that sort of thing."

"I guess I haven't heard," he said.

"Yesterday before he went back to town he went to see Mr. Goolsby. Mrs. Goolsby didn't know all they said, but he was asking about your papa."

"Mr. Goolsby wouldn't tell him anything."

"No. Then we heard he went by Dr. Venable's."

"Dr. Venable don't even know anything."

"And I may be the only one that knows this, so far, but he talked to Isaiah Birdsong."

"That blooming idiot might say anything."

"Isaiah stopped by and talked to me at the store yesterday evening. He said he thought I might like to know that Mr. Hastings of the *Western Message* had come to talk to him because he was the moral leader of the community."

"Agh! I can't believe even Hastings would say a thing like that."

"Well, he might. To soften him up, you know, try to pump him."

"Did he? Pump him?"

"I don't know. What he told Isaiah was that he wondered if a rural community like this—still really part of the western frontier, as he said—had its own special moral code. Sounded like he thought we didn't have the Ten Commandments, or something."

"What did that fool Isaiah say to him?"

"Oh, I think he just did a lot of preaching, like he likes to do. I think he really believed Archie might write him up for the paper."

"You don't think he asked him anything about me?"

"Well, he didn't say so. And I kind of think he would have. And I don't much think Isaiah would tell about anybody in the community—not to an outsider."

"You don't know what Isaiah would do. He's plumb crazy sometimes. He might get it in his head that if I was out of the way he'd have some luck with you."

"He couldn't think that, Ray. I wouldn't ever give him any cause to think that."

They were coming across the schoolground then, where some swings for the little kids had been erected. Joanna sat in one, and Ray on a broken slab of sandstone, left over from the schoolhouse foundation.

"You don't think he might really want to write about Isaiah Birdsong?" Ray asked.

"I can't imagine why."

"Well, I don't know as I quite see what he meant about them moral codes."

"He also asked Isaiah if he thought the community would band together to protect somebody that broke the law, if Greenfields thought he was justified."

Ray picked up a stick and drew lines in the loose dirt.

"I really don't think Isaiah took the hint even then—at least I couldn't see any sign of it."

"Well, that's just the trouble. He's so dumb he might tell stuff without even knowing he was telling anything."

"But you see what Archie Hastings was driving at, don't you, Ray?"

"I'm not a damn fool!"

"Ray!"

"I'm sorry, Jo," he muttered. "I guess I'm pretty cut up about all this."

"Well, anyway, you do see what I mean. Isabel ought to know about what Archie's been doing. I don't think she would see him anymore if she did."

He looked up at her. "She won't anyway, I don't think—not

after what I told her. I caught him and her in the dugout yesterday evening, when me and the boys come in from fishing."

"Just Archie and Isabel?"

"Just them two. Mama was asleep and didn't even know they'd got back—from wherever they'd been."

"Oh, Ray."

"Well, she said she was showing him the dugout because he never had seen one."

"That's probably true, Ray. You mustn't think she'd do anything wrong. I don't, for a minute."

"Oh of course. I know he's interested in stuff like that."

"But still—"

"Yeah."

He looked down again, began to draw a figure like a wagon wheel on the ground.

"She asked me a funny thing today," he said. "She asked me where I was when I shot Papa."

Joanna didn't answer him.

"Don't you think that's peculiar?" he said.

"You never talk about it, Ray."

"Maybe I'll tell you something else about it someday. But I don't especially like to talk about it, you know."

"Nobody would."

"I don't see why she'd ask it, unless it's something that feller said. She never has wanted to talk about it either, up to now."

"Did you answer her question?"

"Nah, I just asked her another'n—why did she want to know? She didn't answer me, and so we just sort of come to a standstill."

"Well, there's no use talking about it, really."

"Not a bit."

She sat swinging back and forth, with her feet on the ground. There was no use talking about it, she never wanted to. All that trouble was over.

"Your mama's better, isn't she, Ray?" she asked him.

"Sure, she's better—as long as Isabel don't start something to set her back."

"She won't do that. Everything's going to be all right now." Neither spoke for a little bit. She was waiting to see how she would say what she had made up her mind to say to Ray.

"Ray—"

He looked up.

"Ray, can't we start making plans again?"

"We never stopped, that I know of."

"Ray, when *will* you go to school?"

"When I can."

"The crops look good, don't they?"

"They do now. You can't tell about cotton, from one day to the next."

"You could go, when the crops are in."

He waited a little while to speak. "I don't know," he finally said. "I've been thinking—maybe if there was to be any money—maybe it's Isabel that ought to go to school."

"You could both go. Miss Lona would loan her the money, she said so."

"And leave the little kids to take care of Mama?"

"They're not as little as you think. You've been doing a man's work since you were younger than Travis, and Isabel was already taking your mama's place when she was the age of Sophie."

"Sophie's not like Isabel."

"Maybe she could be, if she had to."

"I don't know, Jo, we'll just have to wait and see."

She stopped swinging; her hands clinched the rope. Sometimes it was hard to be patient with Ray. He was everything she could ever imagine wanting in a man, only sometimes he seemed to move so slowly.

"But, Ray," she said. "You've waited and waited. And what did you—I mean, what's it all *for,* if we can't go on with our plans and get married?"

He spoke to her very quietly. "It wasn't—just for that," he said.

She hadn't meant what he seemed to think she had. Or maybe he didn't think that. She decided not to deny what had probably never entered his head, anyway. It had never been in her own mind, she was sure, till Jack put it there with his accusations, that Ray or anyone else could believe she thought he killed for her sake.

She got up from the swing. "Let's go to the house and make some lemonade," she said.

As they walked on toward the house, trees now dark against the pale sky, a mockingbird began singing. Ray took Joanna's hand for a little while and they went along in silence.

"Do you blame me for anything, Ray?" she asked.

"How could I, Jo?" he answered.

After a minute or two, she said, "I'll talk to Isabel. I know she thinks a lot of Archie Hastings, or imagines she does, but I think I can make her see how much damage she might do encouraging him to come around Greenfields. People might tell him things whether they aimed to or not."

The next morning, Lizzie surprised her children with the announcement that she would go to preaching that day.

"It's old Brother Donner, Mama," Isabel said. "You never did like him, and he preaches longer than anybody."

"Well, that's all right," Lizzie said. "I never do pay much attention to him anyway. I just thought maybe I'd like to see folks."

"Don't try to talk her out of it, Sis," Ray said.

Isabel didn't answer. It seemed to her that ever since Friday Ray had deliberately kept trying to put her in the wrong.

"I wouldn't want to go home with anybody for dinner, though," Lizzie said.

"I don't think anybody would ask us," Sophie said. "They'll all be wanting to talk about Isabel."

"Why would they talk about Sister?" Lizzie asked.

"Oh, she's just being silly, Mama," Isabel said. "Let's think about what you want to wear to preaching."

She did well on her outing, the first of its kind in so many years. No one in the family could remember (or really cared to try) how long it had been since she had been to church or Sunday school. She looked nice in the ten-year-old dress Isabel freshened and pressed for her, and she did without her snuff. After preaching, several women asked her to go home with them, but she only smiled and said she did not feel quite well enough yet.

"Well, that's all right this time," Mrs. Waters said, "but I won't take no another time."

All the children were invited home with someone, but Ray and Isabel and Burnie chose to go home with their mother.

"I may come to see you this evening," Joanna said, apart, to Isabel.

"Do," said Isabel. "I'll be lonesome."

At home, Isabel and her mother worked together to cook a good dinner—fried chicken and vegetables from the garden—but when it was over Lizzie seemed exhausted and Isabel got her to take a nap. Burnie came to help Isabel with the dishes. Ray said he was going to saddle Whitestar and ride around to look at the crops. He looked lonesome and glum—Isabel wondered why he hadn't gone to the Waterses', but she didn't say anything.

"You don't need to help me, Burnie," she said as Burnie picked up the cup towel.

"I want to," he said.

He did not seem to want to talk, though. They worked in silence for a while.

"Sister, don't let that man come back again," he finally said.

"Do you mean Archie Hastings?"

He nodded. "He won't do us no good," he said.

"But what if I love him, Burnie?"

He reddened, frowned, and turned away from her. When he was a little boy, that was the way he would always start to cry, but she thought now that maybe he was embarrassed because she spoke of love.

"But, Burnie, you'll want me to marry someday," she said.

"Not him," he said. "Because if you marry him, you'll go against the family." Again he said, "He won't do us no good."

"I don't think you know what you're talking about," Isabel said with unusual sharpness for her.

Burnie looked at her hard. "I know," he said. "He's a nosy bastard."

"I don't want you to use words like that," Isabel said.

"Ray did, and it's the truth."

"Burnie, we've always been such friends, you and me. I can't believe you wouldn't like any man I could love."

"I don't want to talk about love," Burnie said. "I don't know nothing about love and never will." He threw down the cup towel and went stumping out of the house.

Isabel wanted to go after him, embrace him, soothe him—"let Sister kiss it and make it well." But this was a new hurt, one she did not know how to heal. She really did not know what was the matter with Burnie. It could be, she supposed, that he was simply jealous, thinking he might lose some of the attention she had always lavished on him.

When she finished her work, she took some embroidery and went out on the front porch. She did not know when Joanna would

come, but she might as well watch for her. She had no idea where
Burnie was, or Ray.

Meanwhile, at Greenfields, Joanna was not easily getting her
way. Jack wanted to use the car.

"Just take me by Isabel's then, and either she or Ray can bring
me home."

"You know I don't much like the idy of you going over there to
visit," Martha said. "Folks might think you're going to see Ray, especially if he brings you home. It just don't look right."

"Mama, I have got to talk to Isabel. There's things being
said . . ."

"Yes, I know that," Martha said.

(Joanna knew she knew; she waited while her mama accepted
the talk as a strong enough reason.)

"Well," Martha went on, "you go ahead this time, but let's try
not to make too much of a habit of it."

After the brother and sister had started down the road, Jack
said, "This must be pretty important to you. You don't usually go
against Mama."

"I can't afford to very often," Joanna said. "But I keep things
so I can, sometimes."

Jack laughed. "Yes, you do, Jo," he said.

"I save for emergencies," she said, "and this is one right now."

"So you think you'll help by going and telling Isabel everything folks are saying about her and Archie Hastings."

"Well, something's got to be done."

"You always think something can be done about anything."

It would be a pretty hopeless world if you couldn't, she
thought, but only said, "I haven't had much chance to visit with
Isabel lately, anyway."

Isabel waved happily from the porch when they drove up. It
was good to see Jack; she wished he would stay.

"Y'all get out," she called.

"I can't, Isabel," he called back. "I've got to go see some old
gal at Walnut Grove."

She laughed, and waved good-bye to him, as Joanna came
around the car and across the yard.

"Where's everybody?" Joanna asked.

"Gone off somewhere," Isabel said, "or the boys have. Mama's
asleep, I reckon."

"It's hot," Joanna said. "Let's go to the dugout."

Actually, the weather was cooler than it had been for a while. There was a southeast breeze blowing that had some moisture in it.

Isabel looked up questioningly, and saw that this was one of the times Joanna meant something she wasn't saying.

"Well," she said. She gathered up her embroidery work and led the way.

In the dugout, she sat on the chair and tried to keep embroidering, but the light was almost too poor down there. Joanna lay across the bed, propped on an elbow.

"I heard Archie Hastings was here Friday," she said.

"Yes, he had the day off," Isabel said. After that question she knew what Joanna was up to. Or almost, anyway; there might be some surprises coming.

"My goodness, did you spend the whole day with him?" Joanna said. That was more like an accusation than a question.

"Not all of it," said Isabel calmly. "I saw your mama when we stopped by the store."

"Sophie said you'd stopped to hug and kiss on the way there from home."

"Good Lord, did you believe her?"

"No, there's a better time for hugging and kissing than when you've got your little sister in the car. That's what I told Mama and Mrs. Goolsby."

"What was it, a meeting of the sewing circle?"

Joanna sat up, facing Isabel. "Well, the word is out, just the same as if it had been. Everybody around Greenfields saw you driving all over the country with him Friday, in broad daylight."

"Would it have been better to go in the middle of the night?"

"You know what I mean. It's just what Mama always says about the looks of the thing. You gave everybody good reason to believe anything they want to, even what Sophie said."

"Well, if they want to I can't help it, can I?"

"I don't know why you have to be like this, Isabel. Just when everything ought to be going so well for us."

"Listen, Jo, we had such a wonderful time. I was wanting to tell you all about it, but maybe we'd better just talk about something else."

"I didn't come for anything else."

"You mean you came here just to—scold me?"

"Not that. I just thought you'd want to know—I thought you'd realize, when you stopped to think, that we just don't do things like that at Greenfields."

"Well, maybe we ought to then, because I sure had fun." At that moment, Isabel didn't care what Joanna and Mrs. Waters thought. She jabbed her needle into the linen dresser scarf and crumpled the cloth in her hands.

"Especially down here in the dugout, I guess," Joanna said drily.

"I suppose Ray was the one that told you to come and talk to me."

"He didn't tell me to. I said I would."

"Don't, Jo." Now Isabel wished she had accepted Joanna's criticism without resentment, as all through the years of their friendship she had sometimes had to do. "Don't, Jo, we've never quarreled. Even when we were little tiny girls, we never got mad at each other. Remember how we always shared our candy or our tea cakes. How we worked to see that neither one had more than the other."

"It's not candy and tea cakes now, Isabel. It's my man."

"I thought it was mine you were so worked up about." As soon as Isabel had said that she wondered why. She didn't want to make Joanna mad, and certainly Archie Hastings wasn't her man. But Joanna didn't seem to notice. She planted her feet on the floor; she leaned toward Isabel.

"Now look here," she said. "You'd just as well know something right now. You've been my best friend a long time, and I'd hate to see you ruin your reputation, but I wouldn't lift a little finger to stop you. But when I see you setting out to ruin Ray I'll do more than lift a finger. I'll fight you any way I can."

Isabel got up and put her embroidery work in a dresser drawer. (When she wanted it again, she looked for it a long time, not remembering she had put it in that place where she never had kept it before.) She walked around the room, perplexed and very nearly frightened.

"You know what I mean," Joanna said.

"Jo, I don't know. I don't have any idea in the world how I could ruin Ray, or why you would think I could want to."

"Then simmer down and stop acting like an idiot, and I'll tell you."

Isabel sat on the edge of her chair.

"Don't say anything till I get through," Joanna said.

The girls sat and looked at each other a long moment. Even before Joanna spoke, Isabel, having calmed herself, began to realize what she would say. It was something she had put completely out of her own mind, only now it came back to her with a reasonless recollection of an empty rifle shell.

She listened while Joanna told her what she had already told Ray: of Archie's visits to Mr. Goolsby, Dr. Venable, and Isaiah Birdsong. She said Ray already knew something was up, because of Isabel's question about where he was when he shot his father.

"Now I'd just like to know what made you ask that," Joanna said.

"Joanna, we never have talked about what Ray did, and I don't want to now. I've tried not to even think about it—just leave it to him, because he made it his affair."

"But you talked to Archie Hastings about it, didn't you?"

"No!" Isabel began to walk about the room again. "No, Joanna, no! I swear I never have, to anyone. If Ray thinks I have, he misjudges me, and I don't believe he does."

"All right, let's say you haven't. Simmer down. The fact remains that Archie's asking questions. And you know what that means. If he pries long enough, he might find out something. And he is a newspaperman."

"He wouldn't—"

"He's said from the first he'd like to write articles about the things he finds out about us. And Papa thought that was just fine at first, but I can tell you for sure he has changed his mind now."

"I still don't think he would."

"Well, help him find out the whole story then, and when it comes out on the front page of the *Western Message*, and they come and take Ray to jail, we'll see how you feel."

Isabel sank to her chair once more, her face in her hands. She tried to reason clearly about what Joanna had said, but now when she thought of Archie Hastings (especially down here in the cool dimness where the certainty of love had suddenly blazed with light and warmth), all her mind seemed capable of was the overwhelming conviction that Joanna couldn't be right. It was simply not fair, not possible even, that what had happened here to her and Archie could have anything to do with the thing Ray had done and what the consequences of his act might ever be.

She looked up. "Joanna, it's not right for you to do this to me," she said dully.

Joanna looked coldly into her face. "It's not me," she said, "that's made a fool of herself and betrayed her brother."

Then anger stirred in Isabel, displaced the heaviness, and she stood up against the friend of well-nigh all her days and said: "Joanna, this dugout is the only place in all the world I dare to call my own. I suppose Ray could take it away from me if he wanted to, but right now it belongs to me. And I want you to get out of it this minute and never come back again."

"Well, I'll go hunt Ray so he can take me home," Joanna said, her voice harsh with some repressed emotion. She thought later it might have been grief.

Isabel stood still till she heard Joanna's steps reach the top of the stairs. Then she fell across the bed and cried till the cotton-filled quilt beneath her face was soaked clear through.

She went to sleep, and hours later came awake struggling through thick layers of heavy darkness that covered her like black fleece. Someone was calling her name, as though from far back in half-remembered time.

When at last she opened her eyes, she saw in the deepened dimness a figure at her bedside.

"Mama!" she cried, and sat up, astonished, even in her sleep-drugged state.

Lizzie sat down beside her then, and drew her close. "Supper's ready, honey," she said; and Isabel's tears flowed anew, from a different source: it had been so many years since she had heard those soft words.

"Mama, I'm so miserable," she said.

"It's all right, honey, it's all right."

"You don't know, Mama, you can't know."

"He's a fine young man, that Archie Hastings is, and I told Ray to leave you alone about him."

Isabel could not remember when she had heard such strength and certainty in her mother's voice. Through her tears, she smiled at this simplification of the troubles Joanna had heaped upon her. It didn't matter that her mother didn't know, couldn't guess, mustn't be told the extent of them.

"Oh, Mama, I love you," Isabel said.

"Come to supper," Mama said.

Isabel got up and rinsed her face, and they went to the house, to the kitchen, where supper was set out and the rest of the family gathered already. They looked up and saw their mother and Isabel coming in together, and nobody said anything.

"Did you fix supper, Mama?" Isabel asked.

"Why sure," Lizzie said. "I saw you didn't feel like it."

Isabel tried to eat. She tried to talk. It was a quiet meal, though, and nobody talked to her.

But when it was over, Lizzie said, "You run on, Sister, I know you don't feel so good. Me and Sophie will wash the dishes."

Isabel looked at Sophie, who appeared about to protest but after all closed her mouth without speaking.

Isabel kissed her mother and said good-night. No other good-nights were said as she left the house, to return to her place in the dugout.

There, she took out her diary and after recording briefly the events of the day, wrote down a series of statements derived from her consideration of them. She did not write in her usual somewhat spiky schoolgirl style of penmanship, but printed the words carefully and neatly, as though she wanted to read them over like words in a book, as though she could pretend they did not concern her at all but would be the basis for a decision affecting some stranger or some person in a story.

She loved him, that was first.

But it seemed no one else in the family, or even the whole community, even liked him—except Mama.

Mama liked him, and for Isabel's sake would love him.

But Mama did not understand everything. She did not know he might probe where even she dared not look, and reveal a truth the whole world (as Mama knew it) conspired to keep hidden.

The dissemination of truth meant more than anything else to Archie Hastings; he had said so.

But the truth would hurt Ray, the Doane family, Joanna, her family, and the entire community of Greenfields, for they had all involved themselves with the troubles of the Doanes.

Archie Hastings would not want to hurt anybody, but because he was naturally curious he might find out something he would prefer not to know.

Once he knew the truth, he would have to make it known, or go against his deepest convictions.

Isabel could never ask any man she loved to do that.

Isabel loved Archie Hastings.

She loved him enough to leave her family behind, but not to ruin them.

If she begged him to take her away to some far-off country, he might go and never learn their secret.

But her mother was becoming more like her old self; if Isabel should leave just now, the sudden loss might set her back to where she had been when Harvey died.

She would always love Archie Hastings.

She would stay at Greenfields forever, and he must not come back anymore.

She closed her diary then and wrote two letters, one to Archie saying he must not come back because no good could possibly come of their continuing to see each other, and one to Miss Lona saying it would be impossible for her to leave her family now or any time in the foreseeable future.

The next morning she drove to Greenfields and dropped both letters through the slot marked U.S. Mail. She did not see Joanna.

CHAPTER SIXTEEN

In the days after Isabel wrote the letter that cut her off from Archie Hastings, one hopeful development kept her going through the motions of her usual way of life. Her mother was decidedly better. She got up in the mornings and had a fire going in the cookstove before Isabel was out of the dugout. She would pick up a broom without any suggestion from Isabel, and she knew how to use it. She found less time for her crochet, but when she sat down with it, she never left it idle in her lap.

And so Isabel tried to conceal her misery, in the fear that her mother's awareness of it would intensify the darkness now dispersing in her soul. Even doing the best she could, Isabel aroused her mother's concern, and more than once had to reassure her about the absence of "the nice young man."

"I told him not to come back, Mama," she said. "I did like him a lot, but I could see Ray was right. He's too different from our kind of people for us ever to be happy together."

Sometimes Isabel was able to believe that what she told her mother was the truth. Though she did not doubt that Archie loved her and knew that she loved him, there was a vast gap between the kinds of lives they had lived. "Perhaps unbridgeable," Isabel wrote in her diary.

With Ray she never spoke of Archie, and for all Ray said he might have imagined she had forgotten the stranger already. Ray and Isabel talked together sometimes, and yet she thought they both felt awkward and self-conscious when they did. It was as though they had lost track of all they ever had to say to each other.

Wednesday evening, before he left for Joanna's, he came to the kitchen, where Isabel was helping clean up after supper. Lizzie was clearly in charge, having put Sophie to washing dishes while she herself had decided to dry and put them away. Isabel had been scraping leftover food out of plates and bowls, into the slop bucket.

"Mama, if you can spare Sis a little bit, I'd sure like to talk to her," Ray said.

"Sure, go on, Sister," Lizzie said, and Isabel put the last scraped plate in the dishpan and followed him outside.

"Let's set in the car a little bit," he said.

He already had it out of the shed, and parked in front of the house. It was a good place to go for a private talk—there were not so many spots around there where you could be sure no one was listening.

He sat at the wheel, and she not very near him, her arm resting along the top of the door.

"Sis," he said, "wouldn't you like to send some word to Joanna tonight?"

"I don't know what it would be," she said. She was still so angry with Joanna that only now and then, thinking of her, did she experience a desolation similar to the feeling that came with thoughts of Archie Hastings. And she seemed to think almost constantly of him. Now, with the realization that she had nothing to say to Joanna, she sensed anew the bleakness life would hold for her without her friend. Even so, she failed to think of any message. She shook her head.

"Things could be pretty good for us, Sis, if you'd get that feller out of your head and act like yourself again. I kind of thought you'as feeling better about that."

"I can't help how I feel, Ray. I've sent him away. I thought that was what you and Joanna wanted."

"I didn't think he'd do any of us any good," Ray said, "and Jo agreed with me."

"She seemed to think I had told him all about—Papa."

"I think you misunderstood her. I didn't think that, and I don't believe she did either."

"She was awful hard on me, Ray."

"Maybe she didn't realize that. Jo's kind of—well, one-track-minded, sometimes. She's wanting me to go on to mechanics school, so we can get married. I guess maybe she's thinking mostly about that."

"And she blames me, that you can't go?"

"I guess she thinks everything would get back to normal quicker, if there wasn't any strangers messing around Greenfields."

"Would you go to school now, if things seemed normal to you?"

"Depends on what you mean by normal. I have to wait till I've got more money, too, of course, but I ain't leaving till I'm satisfied everybody can get along without me. Till I know Mama's well, and I'm certain the boys can manage the place. I reckon I feel the same way you do about going off to college."

"Well, as for that," she said, "I guess it would be easier for you to go than me. Travis can farm all right, but who can take care of the house and children if Mama can't?"

"I reckon you'd leave us to marry."

"Not now, I couldn't, Ray. I'd do nearly anything to bring peace and happiness to our family—and that includes you, whether you think so or not. But I've done more than I ever thought I could already. And I just don't think I can ever feel the same about Joanna again."

"Or me neither, I reckon."

"It hurt me the way you acted about me being with Archie in the dugout, and went and told Joanna, like you'd caught me committing some horrible sin."

"You wouldn't do nothing you oughtn't to, Sis, I know that. But right then it looked so bad—and I just don't want that man around here."

"Well—he's not, Ray. Like I told you, I'm doing the best I can."

"And so am I, Sis. It'll all come right someday."

Sighing, she released the latch on the door. "I hope so, Ray," she said.

"I'll tell Joanna—" he said tentatively, as she stepped out onto the running board.

"Don't tell her anything for me," she said, and went on into the house, leaving him to drive away without a message.

Two or three times, as the week went by, she almost wrote to Archie and begged him to come back to her. But then she would think of her mother, and the younger children, and the chance of a happy family at last.

They seemed still a very long way from being a happy family, and surely no one had really believed an execution (no matter how just) could effect such a transformation. Release from miserable bondage had undoubtedly been all Ray hoped for when he called the conference at which everyone but Isabel agreed on death. She alone had held out, reluctant to acquiesce in a plan to extinguish any human life and fearful of what price might be exacted. Now she began to feel that she would be the one to pay the biggest price. And if only she could pay and forget, go back to what she was before Archie Hastings became more than a fantasy figure for girlish games, there might be a way the Doanes could live contentedly together.

One night when she admitted in her diary the temptation of sending another letter, she conjectured again about what lay ahead for them all. Ray, it seemed possible, might get what he had wanted for so long: automobile mechanics school and marriage to Joanna, with a life in town away—but not too far away—from Greenfields. And then for the first time a strange doubt came to her: Is that what he really wants, or what Joanna has dreamed up for him? Isabel had never heard Ray express dissatisfaction with farm life, though it was true he liked cars and had what seemed a natural-born understanding of their engines. And without doubt he wanted Joanna. But, equally without doubt, he felt strong bonds to his own family and a deep sense of responsibility for them. He would not willingly leave them until he was certain they would be financially able and well cared for. Suddenly, Isabel saw a possibility of trouble for Ray and Joanna that she had never guessed at before. For Joanna was not a very patient girl.

If their mother continued to recover, so that she could look after the younger children, both Isabel and Ray might feel different about leaving home. And yet Isabel wondered whether Ray ever would be willing to turn the farming over to Travis, no matter how capable the younger brother might prove to be.

She might leave—Ray might leave—but if there were money to send anyone to school, she still thought it should be Burnie. She hadn't talked to Ray about this plan of hers, and now that she realized what demands Joanna must be making, felt doubtful about his response. But more than any of the Doanes, Burnie needed the help in his life that extra schooling could give.

What Sophie and Leonard needed was hard to determine. For Sophie, the guidance of a mother like Mrs. Waters might afford the greatest help. Once Isabel might have believed she could provide such guidance, but now for the first time in her life she felt confused and doubtful about the scale of values that determined Greenfields morality. Sophie needed strong guidance and control— but where draw the magic line that would contain her, even supposing one possessed the magic to succeed? That night, Isabel asked herself many such questions.

Leonard, too, needed firm parents to watch over him. He was a good boy, really—somewhat inclined to mischief recently, but when Ray commanded or forbade, Leonard always obeyed. He looked up to Ray, without needing to cower in fear before him as he once had done before his father. Neither Travis nor Lizzie was likely to replace Ray in that respect, but no one could expect a man to give up his dreams and ambitions for a younger brother who (since he was an intelligent boy) might reasonably be expected to turn out just as well, left to himself.

How much she herself owed the family—how much she was even capable of doing for them—Isabel in her present state was more uncertain than she had ever been before. She felt she had changed—or moved decidedly in the direction of being herself; yet exactly what that self was like she could not yet be sure. Since her break with Joanna, she had seen more clearly the profound difference between herself and this young woman who had been her almost inseparable friend. Joanna was never uncertain: for years, her clearly delineated plans had shown precisely where she wanted to be at any given time for the rest of her life. And though Isabel had with part of her mind envied this certainty, and had seen it as a sign of Joanna's superiority to her, she always knew, too, that such a limited view of her future would have stifled something inside her that needed to be untrammeled and free. What she had told Archie was true: she had no clearly defined goals; she did not much care where she lived, in country or town, in Texas or Missouri. What she had really always wanted (so she seemed now to believe and for the first time, confiding in her diary, articulated) was simply to be set free.

And wasn't love the ultimate freedom? She thought so then. "With him," she wrote, "I could go anywhere or nowhere. I could think as I pleased, read as I pleased; he would never dictate to me, but with him to show the way I would find my world opening out to greater and greater pleasures. And if love is what I think it is, even an ignorant country girl like me could open worlds for him."

She stopped; perhaps she prayed; and then, with a newly dipped pen, wrote heavily, and underlined the words:

"Oh God, please send my lover back to me."

They turned the calendar to August, and in the long afternoons while the locusts sang and heat shimmered in the air, Isabel and Lizzie often sat on the front porch with sewing or mending or sometimes, if everything else was done, embroidery and crochet. Sophie worked with them once or twice, hemming flour sacks her mother had given her to make cup towels for her hope chest, but usually she would say she had something else to do. On a Friday afternoon, when they picked up their work after dinner, Sophie announced that she was going to Greenfields.

"You fixing to walk over there in this heat?" Lizzie asked.

"I could drive the car if Ray would let me have it," Sophie said.

"Ray's right," Lizzie said. "It takes gasoline to run a car, and gasoline takes money. We can't be running around all over the country just whenever we happen to feel like it."

"So I'll walk," said Sophie, with evident unconcern. "It's not any hotter walking than it is setting."

"I don't know as you've got any business traipsing around anyway," Lizzie said. "What are you going for?"

Sophie stood and looked at her mother for about half a minute before she answered. "Me and Bessie's gonna meet there and drink a sody pop together."

"Where'd you get the money?" Lizzie said.

"I've just got two cents, that I found," Sophie said. "She's got some."

"Well—" Lizzie said with a sigh. Then, as Sophie turned away, she thought to add, "Be sure and put on your bonnet."

Sophie picked up her bonnet from the porch floor, where she had dropped it sometime in the last day or two, and put it on. "I'll be back in time for supper," she said, and started around the house, to cut through the pasture.

"Be sure and ask about our mail," Isabel called to her.

Sophie stopped and looked back, a long look. "Sure, Sister," she said.

After a little while Lizzie said, "I ought to have kept her from going, oughtn't I?"

"Oh, Mama, I don't know," said Isabel. She had been tempted to suggest that Sophie ought to sit down and hem a cup towel (thinking, This is what Mrs. Waters would have done); but without advice from anyone, she had already made up her mind not to interfere anytime her mother dealt with Sophie.

"I hate to be hard on her," Lizzie said. "She had such a bad time before."

Isabel looked at her mother keenly. "Do you think it was worse, for Sophie?" she asked.

"You had Joanna," Lizzie said. "You come along before he got so bad, and so you had a chance. Sophie never did, till now."

If Lizzie meant any more than what she said, Isabel would never ask her. There were some truths that could not bear to be spoken.

"I expect you're right to let her run and play," Isabel said.

"But you mustn't have to pay too big a price," Lizzie said.

With recurring astonishment, Isabel was learning that her mother had begun to see much farther into her children's lives than anyone had believed her capable of.

"Don't worry, Mama, I'll be all right," she said.

"Oh yes," Lizzie said, "I expect he'll write in a day or two."

Isabel knew the whole family suspected she was hoping for a letter, but she told herself they were wrong. After what she had told Archie, she could not expect him to write. She wished he would, she prayed he would; but no mail came for her and she was not surprised.

"No mail for us today," Sophie announced gleefully when she came home.

Isabel and Lizzie were in the kitchen putting supper on the table, and Sophie came up close to Isabel, to add: "If he cared anything about you, he would write whether you do or not."

And so the week ended—the second week of wondering if he might write after all. Ray went on his Saturday night visit to Joanna, and Isabel waited up for him. He brought no mail for her, but something else: a problem that Joanna had presented.

"Are you giving Sophie money?" he asked.

"Why no, I haven't got money to give," said Isabel.

"She's spending money at the store," he said. "Joanna said she come in with Bessie Akers yesterday and bought candy and sody pop."

"She said she had two cents, that she had found."

"Talk to her," Ray said.

"She has more respect for you than she does for me, Ray," Isabel said.

"I don't know what to say."

"Neither do I. Do you count your change?"

"Sure I do." He pulled some coins from his pocket, looked at them in the palm of his hand. "I haven't got so much but what I'd know it if I lost any—even if it wasn't no more than two cents."

"Well, I'll try to think of something," she said.

Sophie's unexplained money was only one of several subjects moving through Isabel's mind that night, after she had gone to the dugout and lay sleepless on her bed; but she came to no decision about that problem. She did make up her mind not to go to Sunday school the next day. She had gone the week before, submitting to the pain of not speaking to Joanna, and trying to ignore the speculative glances, the little smiles and frowns, the quickly hushed whispers. These were not new to her—they had reminded her of what Mrs. Waters said once before, that she'd just as well go on and hold up her head and face out the talk. But Isabel decided she didn't care whether Greenfields talked or not this time. Without Archie Hastings, it was all the same to her.

There was only one reason she feared she might regret her decision: her mother might feel she had to stay at home too. But Lizzie said she would go, only she still wasn't ready to go home with anybody. The rest could all do as they pleased, but she would get Ray to bring her back when Sunday school was over.

"You're not helping Mama very much," Ray said to Isabel after breakfast, as the two met briefly on the side porch.

"I told you, Ray," she said to him, "I'm doing the best I can."

When Lizzie came back she told Isabel that Ray had gone to

join the rest of the children at the Vartons'. The Waters children had gone there for dinner too.

"And Mrs. Goolsby sent you some word," she said. "She told me to tell you God missed you this morning."

"Oh, was He there?" Isabel said.

(She was recalling a time when she was a little girl and had stayed home sick one Sunday. Mrs. Goolsby—her teacher then—had written that message on a Sunday school card and sent it home to her, and Isabel had cried and cried because she had disappointed God.)

"Sister, I'd be ashamed," Lizzie said, but Isabel thought she suppressed a giggle.

"I am, Mama," Isabel said. "But just the same, it's hard to think the only place to find God this morning is there at the Greenfields schoolhouse, in the middle of all that gossip and suspicion and—and—hate."

They were eating what Lizzie called their little dab of dinner. Isabel started to stack their dishes, but Lizzie said, "You go and do what you want to, Sister. You don't have to help me all the time—there ain't much to do."

"Mama, I won't leave you by yourself," Isabel said.

"I don't have to be entertained all the time," Lizzie said. "I remember how it is to be young and want to get off somewheres away from folks and think about a feller."

"It would be better," Isabel said, "if I could keep from thinking about Archie Hastings."

"Yes," said Lizzie simply, "but you can't."

"Then, Mama, what can I do?" begged Isabel.

"Write and tell him come back, that you made a mistake," Lizzie said.

"But you don't know, Mama, you don't know why I sent him away from here."

"I ain't such a fool as folks thinks I am," said Lizzie. "And that young man's all right."

Alone in the dugout, Isabel thought a long time about what her mother said. She couldn't believe Lizzie really understood what had happened, but it was not hard to accept her judgment of Archie.

I know he wouldn't do anything to hurt us, she said to herself, as she had often done before. I was wrong to listen to Greenfields talk. I will write him.

Then she tried to dissuade herself: he could have written to her—couldn't he?—if he had really wanted her. (Sophie had said that; she was right.) Yet he had promised to respect her wishes, to do what she said. In the end, of course, she wrote to him—page after page, scratched out, discarded, and at last a sheet that bore a single line: "Come back. I miss you." It was that sheet she sealed in an envelope and took to Greenfields the next morning.

She told Ray she wanted to go get a few groceries—and that was true, she did. She said the children could go if they wanted to, but only Leonard did. She gave him a penny, after the rice didn't come to as much as she thought it would, and he spent a long time in front of the candy showcase. She wondered then a little about Sophie's money, but thought, Joanna is always looking for something that needs correcting. Probably it was Bessie that had the money, and Sophie had two cents just as she had said.

One thing she was thankful for, Joanna wasn't working at the store this morning. Mr. Waters and Winnie were gone somewhere, and only Jack was there.

"They missed you at Sunday school yesterday," Jack said.

"Yes, I thought they would," Isabel said.

"Are you feeling better today?" he asked.

"I don't know, Jack, but I think I will soon," she said.

"Good for you," he said. "Don't let the little female puppies get you down."

"What did Jack mean about the puppies?" Leonard asked her on the way home.

"Oh, I don't know, I guess he thought Blackie was a girl dog," she said.

"A bitch," Leonard said, looking up at her, pleased with himself.

He wanted her to scold him, but she thought, After all, why shouldn't they call a bitch a bitch.

"Yes," she said.

CHAPTER SEVENTEEN

Joanna saw the Doane car drive up in front of the store that morning, and stopped what she was doing (hanging out clothes on the
line north of the house) to watch and see if it was Ray who had
come to Greenfields. He had told her he had to head maize that
day, and she wondered if something might have happened at the
Doanes'. Then when she saw Isabel get out and go in the store, she
has several conflicting thoughts. In the first instant, habit asserted
itself; and she thought, I'll go in and put on a clean dress and run
up to see her. Isabel might have come after something that was
needed at home in a hurry; she might not have time to come to the
house to see Joanna. Actually, such a thought was never even completed before the full remembrance of their quarrel came surging
through her, and Isabel's deliberate absence from Sunday school on
the previous day. If she wants to see me, she'll come, I reckon,
Joanna said to herself then, and picked up a handful of socks from
her tub of wrung-out clothes.

Still, she kept her eye on the car in front of the store, and
when she saw it drive away, she said to herself, All right, if that's
the way she wants it. Even so, she felt herself close to tears, until
the proper feeling of anger at Isabel's unfeeling stubbornness reas-
serted itself. "She don't care nothing about her family or her
friends anymore," she said aloud, not bothering to be careful about
her grammar.

"What's the matter?" Martha called from the wash pot where
she stood punching clothes with a broomstick.

"Nothing," Joanna answered. She finished pinning up a skirt
and walked across the yard to her mother. "Isabel was at the store
a few minutes, but she's gone home now."

"I'd a thought she'd come down here a little bit," Martha said.

"I guess she meant what she said to me at her house that day."

"Oh, she'll get over that. You ought to have just gone on up
there and talked to her, whether she wanted to talk or not."

"No," said Joanna thoughtfully, "I think she'll have to apologize to me and ask me to come back again. I think I'll have to wait for that."

"Well, I've told you before, and it's no use telling you again, but if you'd asked my advice, I would have told you it wouldn't do no good for you to go and try to tell Isabel what to do. If you'd talked to me about it, I would have said wait. And I would have found a way to make her see what she was doing, without having to put herself in the position of being chastised by a girlhood friend."

"And as I've told you, Mama, if it wasn't for Ray I could have done that. But she won't have any regard for him or his plans, and so why should I have regard for her?"

"I don't know why," Martha said. "Except that you've done no good this way, that I can see. And she used to be your friend."

"Oh, Mama," Joanna said, "I do still want her for my friend. I can't imagine doing without her. And especially when I marry Ray —and she's my sister-in-law—"

"Oh well, you both will come around," Martha said, "but it will take a little time. You could go to her now if you wanted to, but I guess you're as stubborn as she is."

"If Ray asked me to, I guess I would," Joanna said. "And if he wanted us to go on with our plans as much as I do, I think he'd talk harder to Isabel than he has."

"And ask her to give up any notion she might have of going off to school?"

"Oh, I don't think she wants to go anyway. But if she does, why shouldn't she be the one to wait instead of Ray? He's older—I think she should be the one."

Martha resumed her punching with a sigh. "Give it time," she said. "Give it time."

But Joanna was always conscious of time passing; there was never enough time. "I'm going up to the store, anyway," she said, "just as soon as I finish hanging out these clothes, and ask Jack what she came for."

"Why to buy groceries, of course," Jack said when the question was put to him.

"What would she be out of, that couldn't wait, on a Monday morning, when they ought to be putting out a wash?"

"Well, I don't know," Jack said. "I believe she did buy some blueing."

"Hmph," said Joanna.

"And, dear Sister," Jack said, "if I may ask, what business is it of yours if Isabel comes to the store?"

"Did she mail a letter?" Joanna asked.

"I wasn't watching her all the time," Jack said.

Joanna went into the post office, and the letter lay there, fallen into the space where half a dozen letters lay, with uncanceled stamps. The envelope addressed to Archie Hastings was on top.

"I knew she'd do that," Joanna said.

"Do what?"

"Write and beg Archie Hastings to come back to her."

"Oh, I thought she had got some letters from him just in the last few days," Jack said.

"No," Joanna said, "you're mistaken about that."

She might have known then that he would guess what was happening—that their papa had taken the responsibility of a father to Isabel, as he had done before.

"Don't touch it, Jo," he said.

"Oh no," she said. "I won't."

Isabel did feel better, as she had told Jack she expected to. The moment she had dropped her letter through the slot, she had felt a weight lift from her heart, but day by day it settled back again.

She had decided Wednesday was the first day she could possibly hear from Archie. He should get her letter on Tuesday. If he got it early enough, he might mail one back to her that day, and she could get it Wednesday. Thursday would be more likely, and if there was any delay in the mail it might be Friday before a letter came. She did not go to the store until Wednesday, but after that she went each day without making any excuse. She never saw Joanna. She never saw Jack again either. Mr. Waters would say "Howdy, Isabel," and she would say, "Good morning, Mr. Waters," and she would take the mail if there was any and go home without another word to anyone.

Toward the end of the week she knew she was looking ill. She could look in the glass and see how strangely round and dark her eyes looked and how hollow her pale cheeks.

Thursday morning Ray said to her, "Had we better send for the doctor?"

"You know better than that," Isabel said.

That same day, after she had been to get the mail and found no letter, Burnie talked to her. She had gone out to the garden, which was drying up in the summer heat but still might yield a few cucumbers and tomatoes. She stood forgetting what she was there for, remembering a day after rains had come when she stood there with her feet cool in the mud and a soft breeze on her face—and the sound of an automobile on the road. But there was only the summer silence now (the stillness that contained insect song so monotonous it was more like part of the heat than any sound). Then the silence was broken: it was Burnie stumping along the hard-beaten path from the house.

She turned to look at him.

"Let me help you," he said.

"You can't help me, Burnie," she answered dismally.

"I meant with the cucumbers," he said.

She tried to laugh. She knew it sounded more like crying.

"You really do love him more than us, don't you?" Burnie said.

"When a woman loves a man it's different from the way she loves her family," Isabel said. "Not more, but different. And she loves him enough to leave the home she's always had. It says that in the Bible."

"I guess you're sick of love. It says that in the Bible too."

"Well, I have to admit I'm unhappy. Do you think that's what that means?"

"No, I think it means sick, just like it says. You sure look sick, anyway. Your face looks like your bones are just about to come through."

"I'm not sleeping very well right now," she said. "But I'll soon get things figured out. I'll be all right."

"Even if you don't hear from him?"

"Sure," she said, with an effort that felt as if it broke something in her throat.

"Well, then, I'm sorry," he said, "but I hope that's the way it turns out."

She turned away from him, bent to pick a tomato, and added it to the few in the bottom of her bucket.

"Sister," he said—he spoke pleadingly, his voice seemed full of tears.

"It's all right, Burnie," she said. "I don't blame you. I know you're worried about Ray."

"Sister, tell me," he said then. "If they found out about it—I mean away from Greenfields—if the sheriff knew—would they take Ray to jail?"

"I just don't know, Burnie," she said. "I've thought about it a lot, and sometimes I can't believe they would. Or if they did, seems like they'd let him go when they found out how bad things have been for us. But then I guess the law's the law—and it says in the Bible it's wrong to kill."

Burnie, while she was speaking, had let himself down to sit in the dirt, which he was carefully rubbing smooth with the flat of his hand. Not looking up at her, he said, "They wouldn't hang him, would they, Sister?"

"No," she said, "they wouldn't. Or I don't think they would. And besides, no one will ever know, outside of Greenfields. Why should anyone ever know more than they do now?"

"Stay away from the newspaperman, Sister," he pleaded, and again he seemed near tears. "If he never had come to Greenfields, everything would have been all right for us."

"Things will be all right, Burnie," she said. "Things will be fine, whatever happens. Trust me."

He shook his head. "I can't, Sister, because you just don't know. Things ain't like you think they are—you just don't know."

He struggled up from his seat on the ground and went off toward the barn. He had forgotten to pick any vegetables.

The next morning Isabel said to herself this would be the last day. If he hadn't written by now, there was no reason to think he ever would. Then for that very reason she began to build once more her daily expectation. That day she asked no one to go with her to Greenfields, nor did she even speak to Ray about taking the car. In her anxiety, she left too soon, and though she drove slowly, the mail wasn't up when she got there and several postal patrons were waiting around in the store. They all spoke to Isabel and she answered their greetings, but stood apart from them all, in a spot where she could keep her eye on the row of boxes. Each box had a small rectangle of glass, through which—though it was grimy and smeared—one could discern faint outlines of pieces of mail if any were there. Isabel saw something in the Doane box, but in accordance with custom waited patiently. Mr. Waters would have been understandably upset if anyone had opened a box to take out mail before he called out "Mail's all up!"

Isabel stood big-eyed, silent, and still, half aware that the

women in the store were all taking quick glances at her and then
turning to comment on her appearance to someone nearby. She noticed Mrs. Akers, who had Bessie with her but was not paying
much attention to the child. Neither was Isabel—she was not paying attention to anyone—but then Bessie came up to her with an
air of boldness and said, "Isabel, why didn't you bring Sophie with
you?"

"I guess she was busy," Isabel said.

"Well, tell her to come this evening," Bessie said, "and meet
me at the store."

Isabel did not answer, and presently Bessie tossed her head
and walked away. Then Isabel thought, Oh, I didn't answer her,
and feeling somewhat ashamed of that watched her idly as she
slipped behind the candy showcase, bent quickly down, and then
stood up again and sidled away along the main counter and out the
front door.

At that moment her mind opened up suddenly to an understanding of what was going on. Mr. Waters kept a bucket of pennies under the candy showcase; most children who bought candy
had pennies to spend, or if someone had given them a nickel or a
dime they wanted change in pennies. This arrangement was a con-
venience to him, and it would never have occurred to him that any
Greenfields child would think of going behind the counter to steal.
Probably he never even knew how much money he had there.

So that's it, Isabel thought. I'll have to tell Ray.

Then Mr. Waters called out, and the problem of Bessie and
Sophie went out of her mind. She waited for all the rest to check
their boxes first, not altogether out of courtesy. She wanted to
know and yet she could not bear to know what manner of letter
waited there behind the little door.

But when at last she went and with shaking hands turned the
knob to the different numbers of the combination that unlocked the
box, and pulled back the door, there was nothing in it at all. She
stood a moment swallowing hard. She cleared her throat. "Mr.
Waters!" she managed at last to call out. He was still in the post
office, opening some sort of mail.

"What is it?" he said, in a gruff voice that had no particular
significance—he always talked that way when he was preoccupied.

Still, familiar with his habits though she was, Isabel felt
rebuffed and only with great effort spoke again. "Mr. Waters, I
thought I saw some mail in our box when I came in," she said.

"No," he said, without any evident interest. "No, you must have been mistaken, Isabel. There's nothing in your box."

"No, sir," she said, and went back to the car. She stood a moment leaning against the door, in the hot sun, feeling an enormous emptiness as though the wellspring of all hope had been drained dry.

The road seemed to swim before her as she drove home; the frantic heat waves around the horizon closed in around her, and bright lights danced in her eyes. I may run off in the ditch, she thought, not caring much. She did not know then that the first of the migraine headaches she would suffer from all her life was about to strike her. She didn't really wonder much what was the matter, but felt almost grateful for the headache when it came. It was like a block of pain that mercifully kept back coherent thought, so that Archie Hastings moved through the dark part of her mind among a hundred other shadows and the ache that came from losing him was indistinguishable in the throbbing darkness.

Her mother ministered to her—gave her white powders, a wet rag, led her to the dugout, where she lay all the rest of that day in the dim coolness and finally, late at night, fell asleep. She awoke the next morning, in her gown (of her mother helping her change she had only the faintest recollection), feeling weak—spent and drained. Gradually she recalled what had happened on the morning before, the disappearance of the letter she had seen so clearly in her mind, the strange onslaught of light and daze. Now all that remained was this emptiness—every last scrap of meaning subtracted from her life, every last shred of hope. She had no doubt that what had happened yesterday was the physical manifestation of the ultimate loss of hope. The wrenching of Archie Hastings from her dreams could be no simple thing. She lay wondering if it had left her with the strength to climb the dugout steps.

While she lay so, her mother came bringing the coffeepot and one of the big thick china cups.

"Coffee helps," said Lizzie matter-of-factly. "I brought it in the pot, to keep it hot." She set the cup on the washstand and poured out strong, steaming coffee, made (as theirs always was then) from freshly ground coffee beans.

Isabel sat up. "That smells so good," she said.

It seemed to bring some life back, to send blood through her whole listless body.

"Your papa used to have these spells. He always said coffee helped."

"I never knew he had headaches," Isabel said.

"He got over them somehow," Lizzie said. "Or else he kept me from knowing. In the last years, you know, he didn't want anything from me."

"Except suffering," Isabel said.

"Well, yes—he wanted me to suffer."

"Men do, maybe, whether they know it or not. I mean want women to suffer."

"No, child, you mustn't think so. I think now there was something wrong with your papa, and he couldn't help hisself."

"Oh, Mama," Isabel said. "Will I ever be as good and forgiving as you?"

This embarrassed Lizzie, and she didn't answer. "Come on to the house when you feel like it," she said, "and I'll fix you some breakfast."

But Isabel didn't feel like eating, even at dinner, though she dressed and went to join the family at the table.

"Gosh, Sis, that must have been a booger," Ray said.

"You look like a witch," Sophie said.

"Hush, children," Lizzie said. "Isabel's all right now."

She made Sophie help with the dishes after dinner, and sent Isabel off to rest.

"I'll sit on the porch awhile," Isabel said. "Have you got any patching, Mama, or buttons to sew on?"

"No, you do what you want to," Mama said. "You're nearly through with your dresser scarf—you finish that."

"For your hope chest," Sophie said, with her little dry laugh.

Later, Sophie said she was going to the store to spend some pennies and added she'd be sure to look for the mail.

"Don't bother," Isabel said. "But if you really want to do something for me, find Ray, and tell him I'd like to talk to him."

She thought he was in his room. They were through heading maize, and he had meant to rest a little and shine his shoes, getting ready for his Saturday night visit.

Sophie never agreed to anything without that long look—sizing them up, Travis called it. But she went and told Ray what Isabel wanted, and presently he brought his shoes and shoe polishing kit to the porch and sat down on the floor near Isabel.

"There goes Sophie, to the store again," Isabel said.

"Yeah," he said. "Did you talk to her?"

"No, but I think I've got an idea where her money's coming from. I guess I nearly forgot about it, but she's got pennies again. That reminded me."

She told him about Mr. Waters's box of pennies, and Bessie's maneuvers behind the showcase. "I expect they're both up to something," she said.

"Yeah, you're right," Ray said. "I haven't got the slightest doubt but what you're right."

"What will you do?"

"Me?"

"Ray, it's up to you. Really it is. Unless you think we ought to tell Mama."

"No," he said. "Mama's better, but I don't aim to put nothing like that on her. Not yet."

"Well, I can't do anything. I told you she's got no respect for me. I expect she'd laugh at me."

"Is it because of that feller—the way she is to you?"

"I don't know, Ray. I haven't even tried to find out. I thought maybe she was jealous of me—just because I was older, and maybe had a better chance."

"Or didn't have to put up with what she did from Papa."

"I don't know, Ray. Do you think that's really true, what she said?"

"She's a little liar," he said. "I don't know why she'd make up a thing like that, but I can't tell. I believe she'll give us more trouble, in the long run, than any of the rest of the kids."

Isabel laughed. "Ray," she said, "you make it sound like we're their papa and mama."

"Well, I've nearly thought we was," he said. "But maybe things will turn out better than that."

Isabel remembered what Burnie had said, but she only said to Ray, "Oh yes, I think they will. Somehow they will."

They didn't decide what to do about Sophie. Maybe Ray would talk to Joanna about it tonight. Joanna might know what to do.

Soon after Ray finished shining his shoes, Lizzie came and sat by Isabel, still and seemingly content. Isabel worked on the French knots that formed the centers of the last of the daisies on her scarf. She did not know what she would do with the scarf when she had finished it, but whatever happened to her, she didn't think she would ever use it, anywhere. She looked upon it as Joanna once, when she thought she had lost Ray, had looked upon her quilt. The design didn't even look like daisies to her, and never would: it looked like the pain of this terrible summer pricked into the thick white linen as it pricked into her heart.

"For your hope chest," Sophie had said.

Isabel and her mother sat in silence—in the vast, shimmering silence of the baking earth under a brassy sky. No birds sang; no insects even were audible or visible anywhere. No wind turned the wheel of the windmill; its creaky music was stilled. Then a sound began to form itself, almost at first like something in the mind, but as it came closer, its character was clear. A car was coming down the road.

At first Isabel's heart raced, and her mother said, "Maybe it's him." But Isabel knew the sounds of the different automobiles in her life, and after listening a moment shook her head.

"I think it's Mr. Waters's Maxwell," she said. "Maybe it's Joanna, coming to bless me out again."

"Oh, I don't think she'll do that again," Lizzie said. "I think she's already sorry she done that."

"Why should you think so?" Isabel said.

"I don't know. I thought at Sunday school last Sunday that she looked like she missed you."

Isabel didn't answer. She couldn't imagine who would come today in the Waters car, but lacked the strength to wonder very much. She was watching as it came past the lilac hedge, and the one in the car was Jack.

Ray stepped out on the porch then—for he of course had heard the car and watched for it. "Hey, Jack, get out," he called.

Jack got out and came up to the porch, spoke to Isabel and Lizzie.

"It's hot to be out on the road, ain't it?" Lizzie said to him.

"Not as hot as you might think, Mrs. Doane," he said. "I've got the top up, to keep off the sun, and driving down the road makes a little bit of a breeze. It's really pretty good, and I was wondering if Isabel would come and drive around with me."

"Well, I don't know why not," Lizzie said. "That seems like a plumb good idy to me, don't it you, Sis?"

Isabel looked at Jack, trying to fathom the reason for this unprecedented invitation. She couldn't, but she knew there was one, from the look in his smoldering eyes.

"Yes," she said, "I think I'd like to go."

Ray said, "Well, if y'all haven't got anything better to do." She could tell he wasn't quite pleased—was wishing for Joanna, maybe, to give them a lecture about the looks of the thing. But he couldn't go against his mother, after all.

"I'd better get my bonnet," Isabel said.

Jack drove on down in the breaks, among the ranches. The road petered out to nearly nothing and narrowed as it rounded little steep-sided hills; but he knew it well, he was a good driver. They came out after twenty minutes or so upon another level road, one that eventually intersected the main county road that ran north of the Doanes'.

"We'll turn back along this road now," Jack said. "It don't take much concentration, so I can tell you what I've come for."

They hadn't talked much up to then. "Well, I've been waiting to hear," Isabel said.

"There's something you've got to know," Jack said. "And seems like I ought to build up to it, but I don't know how."

"Don't try, Jack. Just tell me. I know it's something about Archie." Nothing in the world but Archie could be as important to her as Jack was making this sound.

"You haven't heard from him, have you?" Jack said.

"I show it, don't I?"

"Do you? I don't know. You look beautiful to me, as always, Bel."

"Thank you, Jack—but if I don't show it I feel it," she said. "I've waited so long. It's been hard."

"You couldn't believe he wouldn't write to you."

"What have you heard?" she said. "Is he sick?"

"He wrote," Jack said. "He wrote to you at least three times, and the letters came to Greenfields."

"Why, Jack—what do you mean?"

"Have you forgot that kid from Walnut Grove—what was his name?"

"Norman Nix." She said it absently, tonelessly. What Jack meant was coming clear to her, taking shape slowly, moving up through the mist, as though it had been in her mind unrecognized all the time.

"There was a letter in the box yesterday," she said. "It disappeared."

"Yes," he said. "There's been letters. Some from him, and one from you—the second one you wrote. The first one was all right. I began suspecting a few days ago that Papa had interfered in this, and I saw Joanna knew all about it. I finally got the truth out of her."

"The other time, she told me." Isabel felt dull, as though she still were not understanding the picture that had emerged for her. "Why wouldn't she tell me now? Why would she do this to me?"

"She thinks it's best for you. And Ray."

"She's the one that got us together in the first place. She didn't think Archie was bad for me then."

"All right. I guess it's Ray. Her and Ray."

"It's Ray with everybody."

"Damn it, Bel, you've had too hard a time about all this."

"If it wasn't for me, everything would be all right now. Mama's lots better. The kids are doing well—except maybe Sophie. But I think if I hadn't got my own life so messed up I could have helped her more."

"You know about the pennies?"

"I guessed. Does Mr. Waters?"

"I don't think so, yet. But they're getting pretty bold—he'll soon get on to it."

"I've told Ray—he'll have to handle it."

"Ray's all right. He thinks he's responsible for the family now, and that's as it should be."

"I don't believe Joanna thinks so."

"She don't want to think so."

Isabel looked at Jack. He was frowning; his lips were full and trembling, a look he got when he was half angry and half thoughtful about something. A new thought struck her: there might be someone on her side.

"Jack," she said, "I've never talked to anybody about all this. I can't talk to Ray—I was against what he did. He's a good man—somehow in spite of everything I know he's a good man, and in my heart I still don't really believe he did what I know he did. But I can't forget it, and he knows that. Sometimes we can barely talk to each other about anything."

"And there's not anybody else."

"No one else. Of course I can't talk to Mama. And I would have given anything to tell Archie, but no matter what anyone may say I never did. I never gave him any inkling of what happened."

Jack didn't answer what she said. "I'm gonna stop up here on this rise," he said. "There won't be nobody coming but we could see 'em a long ways off if there was."

Isabel didn't say anything else till they were stopped—in the middle of the road, on the high land, with the community of Greenfields spread out before them. Clumps of trees rose darkly here and there, marking where farmsteads stood along the land that sloped down ahead of them and then up again to the far horizon. Fields of cotton (with bolls on the point of opening, but still green) and dry pasture dotted with scrubby mesquite, all likewise seemed distant—swam blue-tinted by the waves of heat, seemed blued by distance. The whole world (which was Greenfields) seemed blue and far away that day.

"Jack, I love Greenfields," Isabel said. "I haven't been anywhere much in my life or known anybody much but Greenfields people. But I don't think I could ever find any place I loved more. Or any people."

"I know it," he said, encouraging her.

"And everybody always seemed to like me. Not that I was ever popular like Joanna. It didn't come natural to me to be as friendly as she is with everyone, or maybe my family—the way things were with us—made me feel different and shy. But I never, till this summer—since Papa died—had the feeling that everyone around me was hating me. It's like they were—" she thought of a phrase she had read somewhere, it seemed the right one—"it's like they were ill-wishing me." She paused, looking out the window in the direction away from Greenfields. "And I haven't done anything!"

"And what if you had?" Jack said. "I mean what if you had done whatever it is the old gossips are afraid you might do with Archie Hastings?"

She didn't see what he was driving at. "But I wouldn't," she said. "I know what you mean, and I wouldn't."

"I know that, Bel. But for the sake of argument, what if you did? Would it be worse than taking a life—more terrible than a man picking up a gun and shooting his own father dead?"

She bowed her head. She did not want to face what he had said to her, yet she thought: What a strange comparison. One act, creating a child. The other, destroying a father. But she didn't think of anything else to say.

"Bel, do you remember that day we talked about truth?" Jack said. "That Sunday evening on the railroad?"

"I've thought about it a lot," she said.

"Did you ever think what Greenfields does to truth?" he asked.

"No," she said, "I don't believe I ever thought about it that way." She had no idea what he meant.

"Well, I'll tell you what they do," he said. "They turn it wrong-side out. They think Ray done right—and I don't know, I won't say, maybe he did. They knew something ought to be done, and then Ray done it. They felt relieved, and maybe they felt guilty, so they wanted to protect Ray. You know he told Mr. Goolsby and Papa the truth. It was them that said make it look like a accidint."

"Yes, I did know that," she said. "I knew Ray was prepared to take the consequences."

"But Greenfields didn't want it that way. They fixed up how they wanted it to be, and that was their truth."

"The looks of the thing," she murmured.

"Exactly," he said. "And as soon as they got afraid somebody might be making it look some other way—might let out what really happened—they turned on that somebody like it was a crime that had been committed."

She had thought of that before. "Yes," she said, "they made me out worse than Ray because they thought I'd told the truth."

"And not only that," he went on. "Think about what else they accuse you of. They know perfectly well you wouldn't go to bed with Archie Hastings. But they've got their damn looks-of-the-thing so mixed up with the truth that they think it's worse for you to get out of sight somewhere with him than it was for Ray to kill his daddy." He cleared his throat. She guessed he was embarrassed because he had talked so earnestly, perhaps had gone too far. "Now figure that out if you can," he said.

She didn't say anything. It seemed to her that what he said made sense, was "true"—it seemed to turn everything upside down, but in the end nothing had changed. Life would still be lived by Greenfields truth.

"Would it be different somewhere else?" she asked.

"I don't know, Isabel," he said. "But by God I aim to find out —and I kind of think you will too."

He got out and cranked the car, and they drove on.

"I didn't aim to say all that," he said then. "Some of it I hadn't even thought about before. I hope it's not gonna bother you much."

"I don't believe it will, Jack," she said. "It's something to think about, and I'll think about it. But do you know what was on my mind the whole time?"

"Archie Hastings."

"I've got to get him back somehow."

"Well, if I can help, Bel, let me know."

"You have already, Jack, by bringing me the truth."

"About Greenfields?"

"About my letters."

CHAPTER EIGHTEEN

Isabel could not decide on the best way of letting Archie know what had happened to their letters. If she wrote, she would of course not be able to mail the letter at Greenfields, but it would be easy enough to drive to Walnut Grove. She would have trouble explaining everything in a letter, though. She thought if she could see him face to face and talk to him she might make him understand why Mr. Waters would think it was his right and duty to intercept their letters and interfere in their lives.

She could take the car and go to Walnut Grove Monday morning, but once she had gone that far no one could keep her from driving on to town. She wondered if she would have the nerve to go the newspaper office and ask for Archie Hastings. She wouldn't know how to find the house where Archie lived, and in any case would never have thought of looking for it, because she knew no decent young woman would go to visit a man at his place of residence. (As long as she lived, she would not cease to be affected by Mrs. Waters's dicta.)

On Saturday night, she still did not know what she would do, but she had fully determined that she would take some action no later than Monday morning.

Meanwhile, she decided, she would go to preaching and Sunday school the next day. Sometimes she had wondered (and had talked to Jack about this) whether there was anything very spiritual about Sunday mornings at Greenfields schoolhouse. Isaiah Birdsong was ridiculous, and the preachers not often inspired. All the same, this was the religious service Greenfields offered, and

Isabel had always gone. That night she made up her mind not to let herself be kept away again by judgments built on any truth but God's.

By ten o'clock, the sun bore down so hard on the unshaded schoolyard that hardly anyone cared to stand outside visiting, in the usual way. A few children, who would have preferred almost any degree of heat to imprisonment in the gloomy chalk-scented schoolhouse, ran about in apparent aimlessness, kicking up little clouds of dust. It seemed to Isabel (as she arrived with her family a minute or two before ten) that she had never really looked before at this place where Greenfields educated its young and came for spiritual sustenance. The big square box of a schoolhouse, built of pine boards never painted and now weathered a desolate gray, stood in the center of a beaten, reddish brown patch of earth, where no one had ever thought to plant a tree or flower and only a few straggling weeds tried to grow. Isabel seemed to feel her soul fill up with choking dust as she contemplated the scene, and she wondered why she had wanted to come today. Why she had ever come.

"Everybody's done gone in," said her mother cheerfully. "No wonder, in this heat." She began walking, in crisp little eager steps, with scarcely a trace of the limp left by the winter's injury, toward the schoolhouse door, glancing back to offer a shy smile to her children following after her.

Really, Isabel thought, the whole change is in me. To Mama this looks just the way it did years ago, when the boards of the schoolhouse were yellow and her hair was bright brown and her husband walked by her side.

Isabel watched with a lump in her throat as Lizzie hopped up the steps and entered the big, bare room, greeting friends among the congregation that was milling about and chatting, just as though they were out on the grounds. Somehow, she thought, things must be made to go right for her mother. It seemed too much to try to think how her own problems could be solved—how there might be a restitution of her old feelings about Greenfields and its people, so that life might be nearly the same for her mother, for them all. Instead she thought: She has got to have a new dress. Maybe I can get her to go to town with me tomorrow. I could even tell Ray, because he would understand the importance of a dress for Mama.

This was old Brother Crenshaw's day to preach, and he turned away from a conversation with Mr. Waters and Mr. Goolsby to greet the new arrivals.

"Mrs. Doane, I sure am proud to see you back in the Lord's house," he said. (This was the first time Lizzie had been back, on his preaching day.)

Now Mrs. Waters and Mrs. Goolsby came, the leaders, and after them, the rest. What they were wanting, Isabel would scarcely have tried to say. They spoke lovingly to Lizzie, but Isabel was their target. (She knew that: that very word occurred to her as she watched their approach.)

"Well, Isabel," Mrs. Waters said. "Everything's gonna be all right now, ain't it?"

"Isabel's come back to us," Mrs. Goolsby said, moving in close to hug her.

"Why, Mrs. Goolsby," Isabel said, "I haven't been away."

"You know what I mean," said the old woman slyly. "Now the next thing we've all got to do is hunt you up a man."

Across the wide room, Joanna was moving toward the organ, through a group of younger girls who liked to hang around her. The organ stood revealed and ready, but because so many had come inside early today, wanting to talk, she had not sat down to play as soon as she usually did. Isaiah had opened the box for her, and stood a full five minutes waiting to adjust the stool for her to sit down. She caught herself wanting to whisper to Isabel: "He looks like something that just crawled out of the box, himself." Then remembering she might never whisper anything to Isabel again, she felt bleak and lonely (at the moment not even thinking of Ray) and went on without looking around her to sit on the organ stool and play the song with the mournfullest tune she could think of, the one ending "Sinner, come home."

Isabel thought Joanna was playing to her. But this is not my home, Joanna, she said inwardly, nor have I sinned a whole lot more than anyone else at Greenfields.

In the Sunday school class, after the congregation had divided and gone to their separate places, she felt much as she had done when she first arrived at the schoolhouse. She sat bemused, not noticing (after the first few introductory words) what Isaiah Birdsong said. For what *could* Isaiah Birdsong say? What could he know? Neither he nor any of his pupils knew what she knew, for what had ever happened in their lives to part the gray gauzy curtain formed by Sunday school clichés and reveal the hard jagged truth? Nothing at all, or so she believed. Even Jack, though he saw more clearly through the gauze than most, had never felt the hard bruising force of what he at best dimly perceived. Even Joanna, though she had bravely clung to the man she loved, willing to share whatever troubles he might face, had not seen because she refused to see. Even murder, even patricide, seen through the veil, seemed smoothed and shaped by Greenfields Sunday school.

So at least Isabel said to herself, while around her various pupils (mostly girls) recited texts from the Sunday school book in answer to Mr. Birdsong's not very searching questions. She was not paying much mind to what they said, or to anything else except her thoughts. Toward the end of the class time, she heard someone come in, someone that wanted to hear the preaching but didn't belong to a Sunday school class or hadn't got off in time. There were often one or two, usually old people, who came in at this time. Isabel did not bother to look around, nor did she notice the face of Joanna, who had looked and was evidently surprised or shocked at what she saw.

Most did not look back, for such a latecomer would only be some old Greenfields person of little interest to these lively members of the young people's class. Most of them were paying attention to the subject under discussion, and several of the girls seemed utterly absorbed in it.

Isaiah Birdsong stood before them with his eyes bugging out and his face blotched with red. What on earth, Isabel wondered, was he finding in today's lesson to get that excited about? Without real interest, she began to listen.

"Sacrifice," he said. "That is asked of us, for the sake of God and our fellow man. We have read about blood sacrifice, and how Christ took on that burden for us all. God no longer wants men to kill goats and sheep on His altars. But in His service we may sometimes see that we have to give up something that seems as dear to us as our own lifeblood.

"Some make sacrifices gladly. We all know mothers who work their fingers to the bone and do without things they need so their children can have clothes to wear to school and something in their stockings at Christmas. There is many a person sad and empty-hearted—many that have sacrificed everything that could have brought them happiness in this world. That sacrifice might be for a family, or a whole community—so that the people could live together happy and secure in their Christian lives."

Isabel looked at Isaiah, who stood before the class, looking not only at them, but also turning his head so as apparently to address the other classes, which all met in different parts of the room at a level below the stage, where the young people's class was. Isabel thought he sometimes imagined he was preaching to the entire congregation, and in fact she had heard persons in other classes say that when Isaiah commenced preaching they couldn't keep their attention from wandering to him.

She briefly met his eyes, in which tears shone. He's thinking of Joanna, she said to herself. She wondered whether he had ever been tempted to speak—to Archie Hastings, perhaps, who was said to have visited him—and bring trouble down on Greenfields and Ray Doane. Impossible as it seemed, he might have imagined that if Ray had to go to prison Joanna would give him up and accept Isaiah's proposal after all. When he spoke of sacrifice for love, she guessed he meant himself.

But he spoke her name. "Isabel is one who understands the meaning of this kind of sacrifice," he said. "Is this not so, Isabel?" He spoke with a warmth, almost an intimacy, as though those two had shared an experience few others in the class could understand. It went through her mind that having sacrificed Joanna, he was preparing to offer Isabel the chance to console him and be consoled —perhaps even (oh Lord forbid) a chance of marriage to him based on martyrdom instead of love.

A sudden and unprecedented anger flashed in her breast. Isaiah's shallow soul might feed on such inane martyrdom, but he had no right to pretend to any knowledge of her own soul's condition.

She looked him in the face again, and saw he really waited for an answer.

"No, Mr. Birdsong," she said then, without considering what she would answer, or consciously choosing her words. "If what you mean is the sacrifice of truth, I'm afraid I have to say I do not understand it."

He stood still with his mouth open, as though he had been prepared to speak but suddenly found the words inappropriate.

She vaguely knew that every member of the class was staring at her, but she paid them no heed. Jack spoke under his breath from somewhere behind her. "Tell 'em, Bel," he said.

She got to her feet, perhaps because she wanted to stand face to face with Isaiah Birdsong. Yet perhaps not, for still she was not giving conscious thought to what she said or did.

"How long has it been, Mr. Birdsong," she said, "since we had our lesson on devotion to truth as—what was it we called it?—a cornerstone to Christianity?"

He still stood as though befuddled. She gave him the answer. "It was May the sixteenth," she said. "I remember the day well. And today is the thirteenth of August. Three months. Or thirteen weeks, I suppose—it must be thirteen weeks.

"I remember because it was then I began to learn what people really believe about devotion to truth. You might be surprised at what I've learned in these thirteen weeks, Mr. Birdsong."

She glanced around her. Most of the members of the class avoided her eye; they looked down, no doubt embarrassed. And so they well might be, she thought.

She went on: "On that day, my father came home bringing a woman that lived with him in the dugout not a hundred feet from my mother's front door. All Greenfields knew this—just as everyone had always known how Papa treated Mama and us kids. And they felt sorry for us, and they wished there was something to be done. But as everybody always said—the men said it, and the women believed it—a man is the head of his family, and no other man has any right to interfere. Only when there was a woman—then one time they did. But even then they never spoke a word to Harvey Doane, but went to her and drove her out of the community. And then when he brought her back the women talked and the men said something had to be done. They knew what it was, and I know what they said: Harvey Doane needed killing.

"Was there anything they could have done to help us through the years? I don't know."

She stopped and thought—she tried to remember. The house was quieter than it ever was during a sermon, but so far Isabel had failed to realize that everyone was listening to her.

She didn't wonder then why she was standing up before the Greenfields Sunday school going over the history of the Doane family troubles. It was something she evidently had to do, for she was doing it. That was all.

Was there anything that Greenfields could have done? Oh yes. There was. There was Mrs. Waters, giving advice on how to help her mother live the life she had to live. Put up with it. That was what they said—Mrs. Waters, Mrs. Goolsby, the other women who followed their lead.

"For years you told us we had to put up with it," Isabel said, "as if a man like my father was some terrible affliction sent by God —a cross we had to bear."

She did not notice she had begun to use the second person pronoun in her speech, nor that (as she made the change) she turned to face what had become her true audience. The people of Greenfields.

"You felt sorry for us, but you did not feel yourselves affected until my father began to flaunt his mistress before you, so that it was no longer possible for you to close your eyes to his adultery."

Throughout the room little gasps rose up like offerings. She paused then, realizing for the first time that she was actually speaking to those people, whom she knew, who were individually sitting out there, aghast at her daring, scandalized by this strange, unheard-of manner of speaking forth the truth.

Mrs. Waters's face was tight, pale, unrevealing. Mrs. Goolsby's angry and red. Across the room, in the men's class, Mr. Waters frowned and cleared his throat, as though he might consider speaking. But there was someone else—someone out of place, someone who had come in. She turned her head, turned her gaze back on the seat near the door. Oh yes, she had known, had seen, who sat there; only something that was paralyzed inside her had kept the name from forming in her brain.

Archie Hastings sat there, looking at her with large, solemn eyes. They softened as they met hers. He loved her, and was there. She thought she might sink down then, cease this strange harangue she had begun without design and continued as though led by some force outside her. Yet as she looked at him he gave a little nod, like an answer, and she knew he meant: Go on, what you're doing is right.

"Go on, Bel," Jack whispered from behind her.

"Oh yes, then something had to be done," she said, continuing as though without pause in the vein she had been speaking in. "But even then you could not do it. You left it to his children, and when it was done you refused to know it. My brother told the truth." (And suddenly she realized that she had never said outright that her brother killed their father; she had not said it because although she knew it was the truth, she still could not wholly believe that Ray was capable of that act. But she forced herself now, for she had let herself be led into this position where the truth must be spoken.) "My brother—and whether he was driven by you who claim to be his friends I cannot say—did all he could see to do. He killed his own father, and when he told you, when you knew, you still refused the truth."

Now Mr. Waters did rise, and Brother Crenshaw too; but she prevented them from stopping her.

"No," she cried. "I will speak. I will say it. I will say what I have in the last two days completely realized. You condoned murder, but you refused the truth. And when there came to me a friend, who cared for me, who might help me, you feared him as an outsider. You were afraid he'd learn the truth from me."

The congregation was still again. They would let her have her say. Perhaps they thought she had gone as far as she could go. She did not in fact know whether there was anything else she wanted to say, or could say. She looked out over her audience again. At her mother (and for the first time a pang of doubt struck her), who sat looking serene, with her hands in her lap. She even looked beautiful, it seemed to Isabel—not shocked and scandalized like the rest, but somehow fulfilled, as though Isabel had said what she had been waiting to hear. And in the intermediate class, Sophie sat with sparkling, gleeful eyes; and Burnie, his face flushed and his eyes smoldering, looked back at Isabel with an intensity she could not interpret. Was he angry, frightened, or gloriously pleased? She could not tell.

"You may say, when I am finished, that I stood before you and confessed to fornication. Or maybe you think it doesn't matter whether I do or not, since everyone knows that I drove down into the breaks in a car alone with a man that is my friend. The appearance of evil to you is the same as the evil itself, and so I might as well plead guilty before you. Whatever you may think, though, I am not confessing. That sin is not mine to confess. All I want now is to ask you one question, and then I promise I'll be silent. Even if I had done all you seem to be accusing me of, why shouldn't you protect me, shield me, as you have done my brother, and for my sake—as for his—refuse the truth?"

Exhausted, she sank down.

Scattered whispers and murmurs began to break the utter silence. Someone needed to assume control before they grew into a wave of something frightening. But Isaiah Birdsong stood as though transfixed, looking not at Isabel but at Joanna. (He thinks

if truth is to break loose, he might still hope for her, Isabel observed inwardly.) Brother Crenshaw, with an expression both stern
and sad, stepped up onto the stage then and took his place behind
the lectern.

"Brothers and sisters," he said, "we have heard strange words
here this morning, a testimony that may trouble us. It may be that
we ought to be troubled—that we ought to ponder these words of
our unhappy sister. We must pray for her, surely, but we must also
pray for ourselves, that we may discover whether God has guided
her to speak some truth that we must heed. That we may give our
hearts and minds to this troubling proposition, I am not going to
preach the sermon I have prepared for you this morning. It may be
God meant these words of our poor sister as the sermon for this
day. I would like to lead you in prayer, and dismiss you. And may
God help us all."

He bowed his head and prayed, a short prayer and a humble
one. Then the congregation went out of the house into the scorched
schoolyard, under the bearing-down sun.

Isabel, alone, as if groping in darkness, made her way to the
door, where she felt a strong hand take her arm as she walked out
into the dazzle of the sun. She knew whose hand it was; the
strength from it poured through her, and she lifted her head.

It was an unfamiliar scene before her, for no one lingered, no
one laughed or called out to friends. People moved slowly, as if
hampered by the heavy, shimmering blanket of heat, and each one
seemed somehow separate and alone.

Yet with that hand upon her arm, Isabel herself no longer felt
abandoned. She turned and looked, smiling and pale, up into
Archie Hastings's face.

"Let me take you home," he said, "or wherever you want to
go."

"All right," she said. "I don't even know if they'll let me come
home, but if they won't have me you can take me away."

"We'll go the long way round," he said. "I need to talk to you."

"I must tell Mama."

"Yes," he said. "I'll wait for you in the car."

Lizzie was already sitting in the Doane car, though none of
the children were there yet. Isabel went to her and kissed her
cheek.

"Can you forgive me, Mama?" she asked.

"I don't blame you, Isabel," Lizzie answered. "You've got more nerve than I ever had, and I thank the Lord for that."

"Archie's going to drive me home," Isabel said. "And we're going around by the ranch road."

"You both come for dinner," Lizzie said.

"Thank you, Mama," Isabel said. It seemed to her unlikely that she would ever eat again.

She turned and saw Burnie coming stumping along, kicking up the red dust.

"If you go with him you'll be sorry," Burnie said.

"Burnie, you don't understand," she said. "He loves me—he won't do anything to hurt us."

"You'll be sorry," he repeated, making his slow halting way on past her to the car.

She didn't speak to anyone else.

Archie opened the door for her and helped her into his car. "By the cemetery," he asked, "and down the ranch road?"

"I think so," she said.

They sat close together, but not touching, as they drove away. She didn't think she could bear to touch him. At first she could not even bear to speak.

"I don't know what I've done," she finally said. "I scarcely know what I said. Did you hear it all? Was it very bad?"

"You were splendid," he said. "I was proud of you. And I understood at last why you sent me away."

"I was wrong," she said. "I would have come to you tomorrow if you hadn't come today."

"Why didn't you write to me?"

She gave him the account she had had from Jack about what happened to their letters.

"Yes," he said. "I can understand what Mr. Waters must have done. The first letter telling me not to come back was the only one I got."

"And you wrote to me?"

"Three times," he said. "I never imagined the mail might not be delivered. Doesn't the man know he has violated federal law?"

"We seem to be above the law at Greenfields," Isabel said. "Above the truth, and above the law."

"I want us to talk about that," he said. "But before we do, I want to tell you a truth I haven't spoken yet." He took his right hand from the wheel and reached out and clasped hers. "This may not be the best time—and I don't want you to take what I say as a question. Don't answer me, don't say anything at all unless you want to. But there's something I have to say to you, and I have to say it now. I want you for my wife, Isabel Doane."

Even if he had begged her to speak, she could not have uttered a word.

"I love you," he said. "You do believe I love you?"

"I know it, Archie, but I'm ashamed of what I said today."

"That you spoke of me to Greenfields, and said I was your friend?"

"They knew I meant I loved you."

"But Isabel, our love is not a shameful thing."

"No," she said.

"We'll talk about this some better time," he said. "But I want you to think about it."

"I will," she said.

At that time they were passing Mr. Goolsby's house, and she thought, Though I love him, there are things I must know.

"You went to see Mr. Goolsby, didn't you?" she said. "They said you suspected what happened to Papa, and would put it in the paper."

Archie laughed. "Well, if that had been what I had in mind, that old man would sure have foiled me. He didn't tell me anything, except to mind my own business."

"But what did you want, Archie, when you went around asking people questions?"

"The truth, Isabel. I thought I could find out the truth."

"Well, I told you that today. You won't have to investigate anymore."

They were driving past the place where they had stopped when they followed the path to the hackberry pool. "We had a good time there," he said. He didn't answer what she had said to him.

"In these last weeks," she said, "when I have thought I had lost you forever, I have often imagined I was happier there that hour with you than I will ever be again."

"There are better times than that to come," he said.

But she was not ready yet to think of times to come. Her mind went back to what he said about the truth. He had found out about Ray, even before he heard her speak today. In her joy at having him beside her again, she had not even thought what he might do with his knowledge. He said he didn't mean to put it in the paper, but if not, then what? She knew what Ray—what all Greenfields—thought he would do. But she could not believe he would do anything to hurt Ray. If he loved her, he couldn't hurt Ray. He was so smart. He would know some way that the truth could be freely known and still Ray would not suffer.

"Have you really known a long time?" she asked. "About Ray?"

"I suspected the first time I came here after your father's funeral that people believed Ray had done it. And yet I doubted that was so," he said. "I doubt it still."

"It's the hardest thing I've ever had to believe," she said. "But Archie, it's true. He called us all together, when everything got so bad, and he asked us what we thought. I was the only one that held out against the killing, and he said he would have to go ahead."

"Even your mother didn't speak against it?"

She shook her head. "Archie, you just can't know—there's no way a man like you could know—how mean my papa was to her."

"No," he said. "Perhaps not. I can see it was bad."

"Right up there is where you turn across the country," she said.

He slowed and made the sharp turn onto the narrow track that wound across the ranchland.

"And there was never any talk of anyone but Ray to be the executioner?" he said.

"I don't think so," she said.

"Try to think," he said, "whether anyone made any other suggestion."

She looked at him sharply. He was watching the narrow, winding road. He was frowning. She asked him no question, but cast her mind back to that day Ray stood before them and told them he had made up his mind to kill their father. Her mother had sat silent and withdrawn; the white crochet cascaded to the floor. Sophie said nothing, but there was the look of glee in her eyes that Isabel since had learned to know so well. Travis had simply agreed, in his taciturn way. Burnie had said something—had not easily accepted Ray's plan. Oh yes, he had wanted to draw straws. Leonard, she thought, had looked frightened but said he agreed with Ray.

"Burnie," she said, "was the only one that protested. He said it wasn't Ray's place more than anybody else's. He said we ought to draw straws to see who got to do it. I think he said it that way."

"But could he have done it, if he had been chosen?"

"Oh, I guess he could have. He's a good shot. All the boys are good shots."

"But with his crippled arm? And moving so slowly?"

"Well, he can't hunt the way the other boys do. He needs to rest the gun on something. He has to set up a blind, and wait for game to come to him. Mostly, he shoots at a target. He hardly ever misses, with a stationary target."

Archie reached inside his coat and drew out of his pocket something that he handed to her. "Do you remember this?" he said.

She opened her hand, and he dropped a rifle shell in it. She could not think what he meant but she knew when he had found it.

"Yes," she said.

"How did you think it came to be in the barn loft?" he asked.

"I don't believe I thought," she said. "I was thinking about you."

"Could Burnie shoot from there?"

"Yes—from that window. I didn't think before, but I know he used to do that."

"That place where you're accustomed to crossing the fence— where your father was found—you can see it clearly from the window, can't you?"

"Of course. It's just east of the barn a little way." She was beginning to guess what he was saying—but resisting it, not letting her mind work.

"And now something else." He reached into the pocket on the other side of his coat and drew out an envelope. "Look at that letter," he said.

The envelope was addressed to Archie Hastings, at the *Western Message*. It was printed in block capitals, and there was no return address. (Whatever Mr. Waters might have thought when he saw that, he would have known it wasn't from Isabel.) She drew out a sheet of cheap tablet paper, such as the children used in the lower grades at school. In the same block letters was printed: "YOU HAD BETTER KEEP AWAY FROM GREENFIELDS IF YOU VALUE YOUR LIFE. FROM SOMEONE WHO KNOWS."

"When did you get this?" she said.

"A few days ago. I believe it helped me make up my mind to come on back to you as soon as I could."

"But surely you don't take this seriously."

"Maybe I do. To write such a thing as that, anyone has to be seriously disturbed. Who can tell what he or she might do?"

"Then you should not have come," she said.

"If the person is really dangerous, there is danger for everyone. There is danger for you."

"No," she said. "That cannot be. I don't believe it."

"You know who wrote it, don't you?"

"I might guess." (That cramped, tight lettering, slanted just slightly backward, though the intent had clearly been to make square letters that would reveal no handwriting secrets.)

"Burnie wrote it, didn't he?"

"Oh, I think so, Archie. But that doesn't mean—Archie, what *does* it mean?"

"I think I know," he said. "I want to tell you all that I think has happened in your family this summer. Could we stop here in the road awhile? Is anyone likely to come along?"

She shook her head. She was not thinking much about his question.

"I suppose I could pull out of the track, though, if anyone did." He gestured to the roadside grown up in tall dry weeds. "Those don't conceal a gully, or sharp rocks, or anything like that?"

"No," she said, "people pull off the road when they meet."

He stopped at the top of a low rise. "We can see from here, and be seen," he said.

She scarcely heard him, was waiting for him to tell her what she was literally trembling to hear. She seemed to know it would be something she had sensed—that it wouldn't surprise her. She did not think it would be a happier thing.

"I can't tell how to begin," he said. "How to prepare you. I don't know how you will take it. You won't be glad. I don't know if you'll be more or less sorry. I don't know if you'll believe me."

"I'm prepared to believe you," she said. "But I don't want to think what it is."

"I will start at the first, then," he said. "As I told you, I knew almost at once that Ray had shot his father—or that Greenfields believed he had. You couldn't help overhearing little things—he had to do it—his daddy needed killing—how sorry Mrs. So-and-So felt for Ray."

"Oh yes, everyone said it," she said. "And yet, somehow, I never could. I don't think I ever said the words till this morning—

that Ray had killed our father. And when I said them I still couldn't believe they were true. Ray wouldn't kill anyone."

"No, I don't think he would," Archie said. "I felt that way myself, when I first realized what Greenfields believed about the killing. For Ray's a gentle man, a good and honest man, and basically a truthful man."

"Oh yes," she said.

"Yet he lied about this."

"But why?"

"I asked myself that. I began to wonder what other possibilities there were, and so I asked questions." He shook his head. "I didn't get very good answers. At Greenfields they mostly told me to mind my own business. The Sunday school superintendent is a fairly stupid man, I think. I didn't ask him anything about Ray at all—only said it seemed a strange accident—and he began telling me what a good man Ray was. It seemed to me, as Shakespeare said, he did protest too much."

"He might not be as stupid as he seems. He might have wanted you to think of Ray, and suspect him. I've wondered if he hoped Ray might be found out and sent to prison."

"Yes, that occurred to me. He wants Joanna, doesn't he?"

"But that's a joke. Joanna has never done anything but laugh at Isaiah Birdsong."

"Well, whatever his motive, he confirmed me in my twofold belief. Ray was the reputed killer, but he was a very unlikely one. After we found the rifle shell, I went to both the doctor and the undertaker. I wanted to know if they had any idea about which direction the bullet had come from, or how far."

Isabel had gradually let the understanding of Archie's theory grow to completeness in her mind.

"And did they?" she said.

He shook his head. "It's incredible how unobservant people are. Dr. Venable said since I mentioned it, he did seem to remember wondering if Mr. Doane was really shot at close range. Not that there was anything he could swear to now, he said."

Cold crept into her veins again. The old doubt revived: what he might do, what he might be justified in doing, for the truth's sake.

"But it wouldn't come to that, Archie?" she begged. "There never will be any swearing?"

"I'm sure there never will," he said. "But tell me this: wouldn't it be better for Ray—for Joanna—for you—for Burnie—if the truth were to be known?"

Better? Surely the truth must always be better? But why had Ray concealed it?

"Ray must know," she said. "Of course if he didn't do it, he must know who did. And he would protect Burnie. We've always protected Burnie."

"Burnie may not need as much protecting as you think."

"But if this comes out?"

"You know, Isabel, I think it should come out. It truly would be better for you all. Especially Burnie. With all the testimony Greenfields could give about the kind of man your father was, I don't believe any judge would be very hard on him. I don't believe he would ever even have to leave his family. But Burnie would learn that criminal acts against society have to be judged by society. With the best intentions in the world, Ray may be teaching him that killing is an easy solution to any problems he might have. And he's always going to have problems."

"Oh, I know Ray hasn't thought of it like that," she said. "Archie, please don't say anything to anyone until I talk to Ray."

"I won't say anything at all," he said. "I'll leave it up to you and your family to decide what must be done."

"Thank you," she said. She reached out and touched his hand. "And take me home now?"

"Yes," he said. "I'd hoped we might talk of other things. The future . . ."

"I can't think of any future now."

He leaned and kissed her cheek. "Could you think of love?"

She shook her head. "Not even that. It seems like every feeling I ever had inside me is dead."

"It will be all right now," he said. "Everything will be all right."

She sighed. "How often we've said that," she said. "I remember when Papa went off and brought back Alma Greeping. We didn't know where he was gone, or when he would come back. We began to think he might not. To hope he never would. And Ray and I talked. Everything would be all right then, we said, if Papa was gone forever. And then—"

Remembering, she began to cry. "It never will," she sobbed.

He gave her his handkerchief. "Yes, things will be all right," he said. "I promise that. You'll see."

He got out and cranked the car. When he got back in and began to drive again along the narrow track, she had gained control of herself.

"The pastures are so dry," she said. "We really need rain."

He talked of the kinds of grasses spread in shades of brown and gray on either side of them, of the pale blue cloudless sky, the far hills swimming in haze.

His voice soothed her. Everything really will be better now, she inwardly said, for it must always be better for the truth to be known.

"I see the gate is down," he said.

"Yes," she said. "Ray's still got the cows in the other pasture."

He slowed and turned in.

As they passed the lilac hedge, she noticed that all the boys except Burnie were sitting on the porch. Her mama and Sophie were probably putting dinner on the table. Burnie—well, Burnie might be anywhere; he liked to be alone.

"Why don't you drive on and stop in the shade of that hackberry tree?" she said to Archie. "Then the car won't be so hot when you get ready to go."

He smiled. "I may not stay long," he said. "I may not be welcome."

But he drove on, as she suggested, and pulled off the driveway under the tree. She started to open the door.

"I'll come around and help you," he said.

He got out to walk around the back of the car—to where she sat on the side away from the house. She sat still and waited, hope freshening in the deadness of her heart, only to vanish once more when the sound of a sharp explosion came and a startled cry of astonishment or pain.

At once she knew everything that had happened, and before she had ever completed a clear thought about it, was out of the car, kneeling beside Archie Hastings, who lay on his side in the hot brick red dirt. A stream of bright red stained the shoulder of his gray seersucker coat and ran down to darken the dust.

She laid her face against his, and tried to embrace him. Her hands were bloody, and her white dress stained with blood, when Ray came and pulled her away from him.

CHAPTER NINETEEN

Archie was wounded in the shoulder, not as seriously as Isabel had feared. Ray laid him down on a quilt on the front porch, cut his coat and shirt off him, and managed to stop the blood. Isabel brought strips of an old sheet to bandage him, and one of Ray's shirts that Archie partly put on and partly wrapped around himself.

"Give me just a little while to rest," he said, "and I'll be fit as a fiddle. I expect I can drive myself home."

He tried to sound so gay—it broke her heart to hear him. She brought a pillow from the front room for his head, and then finally went and washed herself and changed her dress. Sophie went to the dugout to get her something to put on, and then kept hovering near her, frightened or excited, but not gleeful—she seemed more understandable today than Isabel had found her in a long time.

Lizzie, her freckles splattered gold across her lily-pale face, came into the bedroom where Isabel was washing.

"Who done it, Sister?" she asked anxiously. "It was some stranger, wasn't it? Some tramp come up from the railroad?"

"Hush, Mama," Isabel said. "We don't know."

Dinner stood untouched on the table. "Maybe he ought to eat," Lizzie said, as the three came into the kitchen.

Isabel took Archie a little slice out of the middle of a fried chicken breast, sandwiched in a biscuit, but he said he didn't think he could eat. Ray said it might be just as well if he didn't.

"You're not sick at your stomach, are you?" Isabel asked.

"No, I'm not sick. I'm all right."

All the Doanes but one were waiting on the front porch, watching him anxiously.

"I'll go in just a little while," he said. "But I sure would like to talk to Burnie before I go."

"Where is Burnie?" Sophie asked.

"Travis, go call him," Ray said.

Travis walked around calling him. They could all hear his

calls, which must have reached a great distance, but there was no response. Ray sent Sophie and Leonard to look for him too.

But there weren't many places to look. They were soon back. "He's gone off somewhere," Leonard said, "but it must not be very far, 'cause Sancho's in the pen."

"Look everywhere," Ray said. "The hen house—the dugout—"

"Look in the barn loft," Isabel said. (But the shot that wounded Archie could not have been fired from there.)

No one found Burnie.

"Don't worry about it," Archie said. "I guess he's just wandered off somewhere. I'll talk to him another time."

(But he knew—oh, how very well he must know, why Burnie was not to be found.)

"You ought to get to the doctor," Ray said, "if you feel like it. And I ain't fixing to let you drive anywhere. Me and Travis will go with you, and he can take our car. We'll stop by Dr. Venable's, and if he says you can go on home we'll take you."

"I expect I could drive," Archie said, but he didn't argue with Ray.

"You boys had better eat something then, before you go," Lizzie said.

Everyone but Isabel and Archie went in to eat. She sat on the floor next to him and put her hand on his uninjured arm.

"You mustn't worry," he told her. "That looked like a lot of blood, I guess, but there's no way the bullet could have done very much damage."

"But Burnie—"

"Don't worry. I'll have a talk with him, when I can. I want him to understand what he's done, but I won't bring charges against him."

As always, she believed Archie Hastings. He could help Burnie maybe, could help them all. Everything might still be all right.

Soon the three brothers were back, ready to go. Travis was taking Leonard, to have someone to ride with him.

"If that kid shows up, don't let him out of your sight," Ray said to Isabel.

Isabel followed Ray and Archie to the car and kissed Archie good-bye, on the lips.

"I love him, I don't care," she said to her mother and Sophie when she went back to the porch, where they sat watching.

"I don't care either, Sister," Lizzie said. "You love him while you can."

Finally they went back in the kitchen, and Isabel ate a piece of chicken, and they washed the dishes and put the food away.

There was still no sign of Burnie.

Lizzie and Isabel went to the porch to watch for him. Sophie said she wanted to go see Bessie Akers. "I was aiming to go home with her anyhow," she said, "till Sister pulled that crazy stunt at Sunday school and messed everybody up."

"No," said Lizzie quietly. "There won't none of us go nowhere till we've got our family all together again and everyone's all right."

Sophie gave her mother a long look and went and got her flour sack to hem. Isabel entertained a hopeful thought: If we ever do get through all this, I believe Mama will be able to handle Sophie.

She had known all along what she was going to have to do, where she must go, and presently she said, "I'm just going to look around a little. I might find Burnie—he might have just gone off and gone to sleep somewhere."

The shot had come from somewhere behind Archie's car, which they had been sitting in. Somewhere Burnie had hidden and waited for them to drive up in front of the house—somewhere in range of that space he had waited, resting the barrel of his gun. He might have expected them to be closer to wherever he waited, not thinking Archie would drive on to the shade of the hackberry tree. If they had been where he expected them to be—but no use thinking of that.

There was one shelter in the direction the shot had come from: the small abandoned chicken house where in spring they used to keep the brooder hens and their chickens. Isabel went there. She saw where he had dragged his foot across the loose dirt of the little wire pen. Inside, she would find further traces. She dreaded to see. She went and opened the chicken-wire door. The shed was so low she had to stoop to go in.

She never went in. She saw his gun where he had dropped it on the dirt floor.

For a little distance she was able to follow the track of his dragging foot. But he had left the path, evidently gone off over the grass-grown ground along the creek bank. There was no way to tell which direction he had taken.

She came back to the path and followed it as she would on

any day, going to the dugout. In the bare loose dirt in front of the door she saw the sign that he had been there—but Leonard had looked in the dugout and found no one. She descended the steps, even so. She wanted her own place, relief from the dry dusty heat, and if only for a few minutes her pillow beneath her cheek. She was so tired. She had dropped across the bed before she noticed the pale blue envelope from her own box of stationery, propped against her dresser mirror. It must have been there when Leonard was looking for Burnie, but he would not have paid any attention to an envelope. Isabel might leave an envelope lying about anytime. Wearily, blocking her mind as she had learned so well to do, she rose from the bed, crossed the small room, and picked up the letter.

Her name was written in the tall, cramped, back-slanted letters she recognized at once. She tore the envelope open.

"Dear Sister," she read. "I have killed him. I sent him a nonnymous letter to say I would. And I warned you to keep him away. I killed Papa too. I listened to what you said about the truth this morning, and I wish that I had told it all the time. But Ray wouldn't let me. I'm sorry I done this today. It wasn't the same as when I killed Papa, because I don't think Archie needed killing. I thought I could make things like we always wanted them to be. Like we thought they would be when Papa was gone. But that was wrong. I saw that when you run to him and got down in his blood. But then it was too late. We won't ever be happy, after all. I guess they will hang me if they catch me. But I don't reckon they will. I love you all. Tell Mama. Tell them all. Your loving brother, Burnet Loyal Doane."

The last two lines were such a hasty scrawl that she could scarcely make them out. He must have grown steadily more frightened, as he wrote. But he took the time to tell her what he wanted her to know. Dear God, how she loved Burnie. No matter what he had done.

She stood with the letter in her hand a minute or two, then sank back down onto the bed. She tried to think, tried to guess what Burnie could have had in mind to do. What plan he could possibly make to get away without being tracked down and overtaken. She could think of no direction he could go, no safe destination he could hope to reach.

She wished Ray were there. It might be hours before she could begin to look for his return. Someone—she or Sophie—might go to Mr. Waters, she supposed. What he would do she couldn't tell. Probably say just wait, he'll come home. Or he might decide to organize a search party. Knowing Archie had no intention of pressing charges, he might want to call the sheriff for help. And then Burnie might find out he was being chased. And imagining Archie was dead, what would he do then?

At last she went back to the porch.

"Was there any sign of him?" Lizzie asked.

Isabel didn't answer that. "I'll look for him in the pasture," she said. "You-all stay here, and if he comes send Sophie to call me."

She went the whole length of the pasture, keeping mostly by the creek, going up sometimes onto little hills to call and look around for him. As she walked, slowly, ploddingly, she went over the events of the strange, unbelievable day. Her own loss of control —her wildness, for so she now thought of her outburst in Sunday school—might have been to blame for all the rest that happened: her deliberate public acceptance of Archie, letting him take her home—the wounding of Archie—the loss of Burnie. Even while she searched she thought of him as lost; against all reason (so she told herself) there had come the deep certain feeling that they would never find him again.

If she had accepted the role Greenfields designed for her— made of herself a willing sacrifice, such as Isaiah Birdsong so much admired—none of these things might have happened. But even now, she could not admit to herself that she was altogether wrong. If Ray hadn't killed Papa—but no, that was Burnie: the strange revelation of that truth was part of the nightmarish day. But if Ray hadn't proposed the killing, Burnie might never have thought of it at all. And if Papa hadn't needed killing—oh, but he did, he did. And why he did—what was the root of his terrible cruelty—who could ever know? The devil in him. Mrs. Goolsby once said that. But why in him, and not in Mr. Goolsby or Mr. Waters? She remembered her father telling the children once, long ago, about his own father. About beatings with a stick before he was four years old. About so many sad things: the one she remembered best was her papa finding corncobs in his stocking that he had hung up for Santa Claus at Christmastime. She had cried about that; almost, she still could shed tears for that long-lost little boy. For the first time in her life she wondered if there could be an answer to her question. Where does evil come from, and once it establishes itself in a family, can there ever be an end to it?

She was coming back up toward the house from the barn, sweating and tired, and she saw her mother sitting on the porch, her white crochet lying still in her lap, her eyes fastened on the far distance. I may not marry, she thought. I may never marry anyone at all.

"How long as it been?" Lizzie asked abruptly, after Isabel had been sitting near her on the edge of the porch awhile.

"What, Mama?" Isabel said.

"How long has he been gone?"

"Oh, I don't know, Mama. I haven't been thinking about the time."

"Well, I know what time it was when Archie got shot, because when you-all drove up I said, now we can put dinner on the table, and just as I said it the clock struck one. I know it wasn't the half hour, because I looked up to see and it was one o'clock."

"But we don't know when Burnie left," Isabel said.

"Or why," said Lizzie.

"Oh, Mama, I'm afraid we do know why," Isabel said. She hadn't told about anything she had found, neither the gun nor the letter, but the reason had been clear though unspoken among them from the time they realized Burnie had disappeared.

Sophie got up and went to look at the clock. "Well, it's nearly five now. I bet he's been gone three hours anyway."

"How far could he go in three hours?" Lizzie said. "Dragging his poor foot—had far could he go?"

"I bet he hasn't really gone anywhere," Sophie said. "He's just down in the pasture, hiding somewhere. He's scared he hurt Archie worse than he did. He'll be back when he gets good and hungry."

"We don't know it was him that shot that gun," Lizzie said.

Isabel wondered if she ought to go ahead and show her mother the letter. No—wait for Ray, she told herself.

The five o'clock passenger train whistled in the hollow south of their house. That was sooner than it usually whistled for the Greenfields station. It was a long whistle, uncommonly long. It came again, strangely long; then a short blast, and then long again, a moaning cry like a lost soul in hell. (But perhaps that comparison only came to Isabel later, when she was writing in her diary—when everything was over.)

"Cow on the track," Sophie said smugly. The children were used to interpreting the train signals, showing off their knowledge to each other.

But the signal wasn't complete. The long, shrieking cries kept coming up out of the hollow; it seemed they would never stop. But they couldn't have gone on very long, really; they ended, and the silence seemed deeper than before. Even the sound of the locomotive had died.

"Train's stopped," Sophie said.

Later, Isabel could not remember whether she had any inkling then of what had happened. Even Sophie did not offer conjectures about the awful whistling of that train. It seemed to Isabel that her own mind was blank—stayed blank, as the three on the porch stayed silent, until they heard the Waters car and watched it come past the lilac hedge and stop in front of the house. The whole family had come: someone ought to have shouted, "Get out and come in!"

But seeing the faces of the family in the car, none of the three on the porch felt able to say anything at all. They sat and waited; they knew the wait was nearly over then.

Mr. Waters came first across the yard, with Mrs. Waters following a step or two behind him. Jack, Winnie, and Joanna all got out of the car; the two older ones came on slowly, but Winnie stood back near the car, a long time, looking down, dragging the toe of his shoe in the dust.

Mr. Waters came and stood by Lizzie's chair. She looked up at him, her eyes wide and dark—terrible, anticipating, knowing eyes.

"It's Burnie," he said. "He's hurt—there's been a acci*dint*—the train—"

Lizzie calmly picked up her snuff can and spat, then stood and faced him. "We had better have the truth, Mr. Waters," she said. "We have done without the truth too long, and it's done us no good. If Burnie was hit by a train, he's not hurt—he is dead. And if he was on the railroad track in front of the train, that was no acci*dint*."

That was the last time Isabel ever heard her mother speak more than three clear words together. Having faced that one last truth, Lizzie Doane collapsed. Mr. Waters caught her before she hit the floor, and carried her to her bed, where Mrs. Waters undressed her and put a nightgown on her and sat with her through the night.

The whole story, which Lizzie perhaps never comprehended, though in time it was told to her, was this:

Winnie had gone, in spite of protests from his mother about getting out in the hot sun, to look for some certain kind of insect so he could test some theory he had about how it reacted to extreme heat. No one else was out that afternoon—no one strolled Kodaking along the railroad. But as Winnie followed the track down into the hollow, he noticed a figure far ahead of him, moving along the track, and he knew by the limp it was Burnie. He called, but Burnie must have been too far away to hear him. About that time, Winnie realized the train was coming, and he shouted as loudly as he could and began to run. He was still unable to get Burnie's attention—no doubt the noise of the train now drowned out his voice —and he could see the engine coming up the rise. It began to whistle then, as the Doanes on their front porch had heard it; and although the time seemed so long to Isabel when she was listening to the fearful sounds, Winnie said it could not have been more than a minute. He saw Burnie standing straight in the middle of the track, he saw the train come close to him, and then he threw himself on the ground and hid his face.

"Somebody's got to come and see him," Mr. Waters said, when the story had been briefly told. "Somebody in the family."

"But there isn't anybody," Isabel said. "Ray's gone—I don't know when he'll be back."

"I know about that," Mr. Waters said.

Isabel didn't ask how. Of course he would know.

"You'll have to go," he said. "The engineer says somebody in the family has got to identify him before he can move the train. And he can't hold the train up much longer."

"I can't—" she said.

Jack came then and put an arm around her. "I'll go with you," he said.

And Joanna then. She came and, drawing Isabel away from Jack, embraced her, kissed her, and weeping said she would go too. "I'll go with you all the way," she said. "If you can bear it I can bear it. We will look at him together."

Thus it was that late in the afternoon, beside the shining steel tracks that ran through Greenfields like a river, Isabel and Joanna stood clasping each other and looked upon something destroyed that must onetime have been a human child.

CHAPTER TWENTY

Archie was not in any danger, but it would be several days before he could go back to work or drive his car. Ray brought back that report when he returned, but it was no time then for asking questions. Only after the funeral—after Greenfields had come with their offerings of food and gone away again—after the sealed casket had been buried between the graves of Harvey Doane and his unnamed infant son—after Lizzie, who never spoke Burnie's name but wandered searchingly through the house, had been given the pills from Dr. Venable and put to bed by Mrs. Goolsby—and the younger children had all gone off quietly apart—did Isabel ask Ray to sit and talk with her.

They sat on the front porch, where a faint breeze reached them, and watched the rising moon through the branches of the hackberry tree.

"You want to know more about Archie, I reckon," Ray said.

"Yes, that," she said. "Other things, but that first."

"He's all right, I told you that. The doctor had to cut the bullet out. He don't want Archie to do anything very strenuous for a few days, but he's all right."

"He might get blood poisoning or something."

"He said he'd get the woman there—the housekeeper at his uncle's house—to send you a line or two every day. But if you want to go to see him, I will take you."

"No, I can wait. I guess I think I'd rather wait. Till I get over everything a little—and he does."

"You think things won't be the same between you?"

"No—not that. We'll be the same. He will and I will. But now —there's Burnie."

"You-all haven't got anything to blame each other for," he said.

"No," she said slowly. "I don't think we ever would feel that way. It's got to fade a little, that's all." She covered her face in her hands.

Ray put his arm around her. "I'm sorry," he said. "I'll be sorry the rest of my life I wasn't here."

She leaned against him. "It wouldn't have been any easier for you, Ray."

They sat awhile in silence.

Then Ray said, "He told me he didn't aim to press charges. I know he wouldn't have."

"He said it would have been better for Burnie if the truth had been known. He said no judge that knew anything about Papa would have sent Burnie off anywhere—but he needed to understand that people have to abide by the law."

"He's probably right, Sis. I know I was wrong—from the very start of things I was wrong."

"But, Ray, I believe I always did know you couldn't have been the one. I never did really think you could have shot Papa."

"No use in talking about that," Ray said. "I was aiming to, and it would have been a whole lot better if I had. But then when it happened like it did—I come on him already dead, and Burnie getting down from the loft—I ought to have took Burnie and gone to the law right then."

"I wouldn't have. None of us would have."

"No, we always wanted to protect him. I told him it would be better for me to take the blame. And so I drove him to—" His voice broke.

"We don't know, Ray. We never will know that. He might have stumbled—might have caught his foot."

He shook his head. "Never talk about it, Sister. Never try to know."

There was silence again for a while, and then she said, "It was my fault, I guess, as much as anyone's. I ought to have kept away from Archie, just like all of Greenfields kept saying."

"No, Sis. Archie's all right. I told you that."

"Even so, it was him Burnie was afraid of. And then I had to do all that crazy talking in Sunday school. I reckon that set him off."

"No. You was right in what you said, and you done the best you could."

"We both did, Ray. We all did. Let's always try to think that.

We might have done wrong, but we meant it for the best. I don't think we ought to be afraid to say to ourselves where the blame belongs. It was Papa."

"And who was to blame for him?"

It surprised her that he asked that. "I don't guess there can be any answer," she said. "Once it starts, you can't go back to the source of it; you can only try to stop it, but I don't know whether you can do that either."

"Stop what? What is it, do you think?"

"Oh, I don't know. Meanness."

"Evil."

"Oh yes. Yes it is. It's a hard word to say."

"And some folks says it comes from the devil, and the only way to stop it is to pray," Ray said.

"Deliver us from evil. But I don't know what that means."

"Me neither. But I don't think you can just set back and wait for the Lord to do everything."

"But killing—surely that's not the way."

"Anyway it don't seem to work very good."

"There ought to be some better way," said Isabel. "There ought to be ways the law could help—before something bad happens, I mean. There ought to have been a way to stop Papa."

"Lock him up, you mean?"

"I don't know. But that would have been better than what we did."

"I guess there's not no way. No way to stop it—no way to know how it starts."

"But Ray, do you think it runs in families? I know when I saw Burnie dead, and thought of all that led up to that, I said to myself it might have come to an end there. But I'm afraid. I'm afraid it hasn't—I'm afraid it never will. Not in our family."

"If I thought that, I couldn't marry. I can't afford to think that, and neither can you."

"I can't help it. I'm afraid. I don't think I ever will marry."

"I know somebody that thinks you will."

"He may not want me now. I don't know. Lying up there with his wound, thinking about all he's found out about us. Why would he want to marry me?"

"If he cares enough about you, all that won't make no difference."

"I guess I think he does. But I need to think a long time about all this before I give him any answer. I really mean it, Ray, I may not marry."

"Well, I may not either. I don't think I can be all Joanna wants me to. If things don't change a lot for us Doanes, I don't see how I ever could go off to school. But Joanna will go—she's got her head set on it. And once she goes—she may never want to come back to somebody like me."

"Maybe we'll be old maid and old bachelor together. You'll farm and we'll take care of Mama, and I'll keep house for us all. And we'll be a story for Greenfields to tell, even when we're dead and gone."

Ray didn't say anything for a long time. Finally he said, "We could do that, Sis, couldn't we? I mean there ain't no hard feelings between us. If that's what it comes to, we could."

She got up and kissed him. She knew now that was what she had waited for him to say. "Yes, we could do it, Ray," she said. "If it comes to that."

Within a day or two, Greenfields was putting all the events of the summer in place, fitting what had happened to the Doanes into the pattern of Greenfields life. They could not deny what had happened, at which they lifted their hands in horror, but they preferred to see the future as they had seen the past: never so bad but that living by Greenfields ways could make everything come right.

"What else could happen to them, I'd like to know," Mrs. Waters often said—thinking perhaps, as Isabel had, that there must be an end at last. And then, like Isabel, she would correct herself. "Oh, I know there's no end to the bad things that can happen, but surely the good Lord has sent enough on that poor family."

"If it's the Lord that done it," Mrs. Goolsby said. That was on the Wednesday afternoon after the funeral on Monday.

Joanna, at work on her quilt again, listened to their talk but said very little.

They were right, she thought, in their assessment of Mrs. Doane. "Lizzie won't never be no 'count anymore." This seemed true. Joanna had seen her only that morning, and she appeared to have gone back to what she was in the time of Harvey Doane's worst treatment of her. She sat with her crochet and her snuff, and for hours at a time (so Isabel said) would forget to ply her crochet hook or even to spit.

"Isabel can't never leave home now," was the conclusion of the women around the quilt. "She'll have to stay there and raise them kids."

"What about that newspaper feller she's struck on?"

"What about going off to college with Joanna?"

She would have to give up both these plans, the women agreed, and it was too bad because she was a good girl and deserved better. Course she didn't mean a thing she said that day in Sunday school. She was overwrought, as anyone well might be, with the troubles she'd had. Greenfields would do well to forget all that, and welcome her back among them, as if she had been off on a journey to foreign lands.

Someone raised the question of whether Ray could afford to leave either—whether there was any way the Doanes could get along without him—but of course they didn't say much about that.

Joanna listened, and spoke when she was spoken to, and sometimes smiled down at a diamond-shaped piece of yellow cloth that seemed to glimmer at her like a sliver of a star. Sometimes this summer she had wondered if the Lone Star ever really would be finished; but now she knew it would, in no more than a couple of days. And she would sleep under it with Ray (later she would put it away with the best quilts, but she wanted them to use it for a little while). She would sleep under it sooner than anyone thought, too, if she had her way.

She put on a Sunday dress that night—a Nile green dotted swiss with a ruffled bertha. It looked cool. It wasn't, very. She sat on the porch swing with Ray and fanned them with a cardboard fan that had a picture on it of pine-covered mountains and a bright blue lake. She had never seen such a place and didn't suppose there was one, really. One thing sure—she didn't care. Greenfields was good enough for her.

"Ray," she said, "let's get married." With her parents on the front porch and the boys off playing dominoes with Sam, she didn't think she would be overheard, but she didn't much care if she was.

"I thought that was understood a long time ago," he said.

"Too long," she said. "We've waited too long. I mean now."

"*Right* now?" he exclaimed.

She laughed at him. "Well, not tonight," she said. "But I wondered about Saturday."

He turned to her. He took her hand and gripped it. "Oh God, Joanna," he said, half under his breath. "If only we could."

"We can, Ray," she said, "for what's to stop us?"

"You—our plans," he answered. "College. Mechanics school. Teaching."

"Ray, you'll never go to school," she said.

"It gets harder and harder," he admitted, "to think I ever could. I'm sorry, Jo."

"Don't be," she said. "I have been to your house, and I have sense enough to recognize the inevitable when I see it."

"But what will we do?" he asked.

"You'll be a farmer," she said, "and I'll be a farmer's wife. And I'll be a mother to Sophie and Leonard, and I'll take care of your mother. And I'll be to Travis—just a sister, I suppose, as I am to Winnie and Jack."

"You'd move in there—and take on all that?"

"Yes," she said. "It's what I mean to do."

"But it's too much. You couldn't. I couldn't ask it of you."

"Everybody thinks Isabel can do it. They don't seem to think anything else. And I reckon I can do as much as she can. Maybe more, because I'll have you. And I have figured out something today, Ray. Of all the plans I've ever made, there's just that one I can't give up—just having you to love me."

He didn't say anything. He bowed his head, and his fists were clenched in his lap.

"What's the matter, Ray?" she cried. "You do want to, don't you? We can, can't we? Is anything wrong—that will stop us?"

Suddenly he lifted his head and turned to her with his arms outstretched. Then he held her, he kissed her, and tears from his eyes wet her cheeks.

Martha Waters stood clearing her throat in the doorway.

They parted and looked up at her.

"We're getting married, Mama," Joanna said, laughing. "It's all right, we're getting married."

"There's many a slip—" Martha began ominously.

Joanna jumped up and interrupted her with a kiss. "Not very many, Mama," she said. "We're getting married Saturday."

Joanna had expected opposition from her mother and father, but after talking with her and Ray for several hours that night both parents gave their approval. They had their reservations, but Joanna suspected that after all they liked this plan better than anything else she might have done.

"I hate to see you marrying into such a job," Martha said, "but then I'll have you here close to me and I never counted on that."

"You'll take care of her, Ray," Tom Waters said to his prospective son-in-law. "If I had any doubt whatsoever about that, I couldn't consent to this marriage."

Winnie, Joanna had supposed, would not care very much what she did, but she thought Jack might tell her she was making a mistake.

But "No," he told her, "this is right for you, Jo. You're gonna have to work hard, but I don't think you'll ever be sorry that you didn't go to college."

On Thursday morning, Joanna drove over to the Doanes' and she and Ray revealed their plans to his family.

"Come in the kitchen," Ray told them. "Me and Joanna's got something to tell you."

Isabel hoped she was the only one reminded of a day in June when Ray called them in there and proposed a different sort of plan.

Just as she had done on that day, Lizzie Doane sat in her rocking chair, with crochet in her lap and snuff dribbling down her chin. "We-e-e-l," she said when Ray and Joanna had made their announcement. They thought she was pleased, but they couldn't even be sure she understood, and that was the only word she ever said about it.

The children didn't say much either. This was not a thing they knew how to respond to, and they seemed somewhat embarrassed.

Then Ray put the question to them bluntly: "Is it all right with you-all if Joanna moves in?"

"But who will do the cooking," Leonard asked then, "Isabel or Joanna?"

All but Leonard and Lizzie laughed at that.

"I guess we'll have to work that out," said Isabel, but she knew Joanna didn't expect her to stay there.

The children seemed to take the laughter as a sign of dismissal: they went about their own affairs, and Joanna said to Ray that she and Isabel needed a chance to talk, just the two of them together.

"Sure," he said. "Why don't you-all go to the dugout and I'll just stay around the house and see for sure Mama's all right."

As they walked down to the dugout, Joanna said, "Do you have to watch her all the time?"

"No," Isabel said. "Or at least I guess we sort of feel like we ought to be with her right now. But I don't think she's going to be much different from what she was before, when she was at her worst. She won't give anybody any trouble."

"I wasn't thinking about that," Joanna said.

"Well, you have to know what you're getting into. You will have to help her along a little about cleaning herself up, being sure she eats her meals, things like that. And she won't be much help to you. Dr. Venable says it's not a condition he knows how to treat, but he doubts that she'll get any better. I guess she'll just draw back into herself until there's not anything left of her."

That was how it really would be. Isabel hadn't thought about it that way before, but she could see now how the years would go. Tears came in her eyes and fell; she couldn't stop them. And I won't be here, she thought. She had no idea where she would be, but her mother would sink slowly down to her end and Isabel would not be there. Somehow she knew that.

"I always feel like I'll get claustrophobia down here," Joanna said as they came into the dugout.

"I know you never liked it much—but it's my place."

"I like it because it's like you—but I'd never want to live under the ground. I need sun and air, and windows to look out of."

"And I'm like some little animal burrowing into the ground to escape my enemies."

"Isabel, you don't have enemies. All Greenfields has forgiven you."

"But have I forgiven them?"

"It doesn't matter—you'll never live here."

"What will I do then, when you come?"

"Surely you don't think I'm driving you away."

"No, Joanna, I don't think that. But still, you know, if you weren't coming, I don't think I'd ever leave this house."

"You know you can stay as long as you want to—always, if you want to."

"Two women in the same house never do get along, Jo. You know that. I've been the woman of the house too long now; I doubt if I could ever change."

"We'd get along, just like we used to do."

"No matter. I have to go. I want to go. I thank the Lord you're coming to take care of Mama and the children."

"I'll do that, Isabel. You know I will."

"If it's what you've made up your mind to do you will, Jo. I know that."

"And what will you make up your mind to do?"

"I'm not like you, Jo. You control your destiny. I wait and see."

"If I controlled my destiny, I'd be getting ready to go to college, wouldn't I?"

"Maybe. I don't know. But the thing you always wanted most is Ray. And you'll have him."

"But won't you have Archie?"

"I don't know. I can't think I'll marry. But even so, how could he want to marry me? It's pure accident that he's not in his grave, shot and killed by my own brother."

"Well, if he lets that stop him he don't love you, that's all. I know more about the Doanes than he does, and nothing could keep me from marrying Ray."

"Well, it's like you say, Jo. You know us all so well. You're prepared for what might happen."

"What might, Isabel?"

She wanted to say, We're an evil family. Evil might happen. But there was no point in talking that way to Joanna; she wouldn't understand it or accept it. Jo would cope with each thing as it happened, without looking for the original cause of it all. And she would be better off that way.

"I don't know," Isabel said. "But even you might have trouble, Jo. Sophie's not going to be an easy girl to raise."

"I've thought about Sophie. I think I've thought about everything. I believe I can handle her."

"You know that she's been stealing at the store?"

"Oh yes, I know that."

"You may not know—I don't believe Ray would ever tell you. There's something else—it goes way back. She said that Papa—that he made her—oh, Jo, do you know what I mean?"

It was clear that Joanna didn't. In her world of sunshine and open windows, she perhaps had never believed that such things happened.

"I don't think I do," she said.

Isabel spoke the word. "Incest."

Joanna paled. "No," she said, a soft incredulous protest.

"She told me this summer," Isabel said. "But she's such a little liar, sometimes I've thought she might have made it up. Either way, it's bad."

Joanna was quickly restoring herself. "Yes," she said. "I understand what you mean. Even if she made it up, it shows how different her thoughts must be from yours and mine."

"She's warped, I guess. Maybe forever. And I could never help her. I could never think what to say. I don't think I could really understand—"

Joanna interrupted. "Don't worry, Isabel," she said firmly. "I can handle her as well as you, and if I need help I can go to Mama."

Isabel shook her head sadly. "Our own mother has never been much of a guide for us—and never will be now, I'm afraid. The Doane children could do worse than be raised by Joanna and Mrs. Waters."

"You see, it really will be all right. Ray and I will be all right. But will you?"

"Oh yes. One way or another—I will."

"You may not want me to say this. I know I always make plans for everybody's life. But I've got something in mind, Isabel."

"All right, Jo."

"I've got to write to Miss Lona and tell her I won't be going to college. Could I tell her you'll take my place and work for her, and go to school this year? Papa will give you the money to get started —what he aimed to use for me. I know he will, I've talked to him. I told him he owed you something, on account of those letters. And he agreed—he's sorry about that."

"Oh, I don't hold that against him," Isabel said. "He was just using the ways of Greenfields, to do what he thought was right."

"But will you do it?" Joanna said. "Isn't it the best thing to do —unless you're fixing to marry Archie?"

"It may be," said Isabel. "I'll think about it."

"But I do need to let her know soon."

"Yes, I'll decide by Monday." (After I've seen Archie one more time, she thought, but she didn't say that to Joanna. The time had passed when they told each other everything.)

Joanna rose from her seat. "I've got to go," she said. "I've got to finish that quilt this week."

"I wish I could come and help you," Isabel said. "But it's hard to get away."

"I wish you could too," Joanna said. "I wish we could finish it together, but I won't have any trouble getting through now. Did I tell you I aim to really use it? On our bed?"

That quilt! Joanna had started piecing it years ago. They must have been about fourteen; she had been thinking of Ray then, but not of going away to school. She wanted Isabel to make a Lone Star too, but Isabel wouldn't even start one. Not that intricate, difficult pattern. If she ever sewed all those tiny pieces of material together, they wouldn't come out a star. But Joanna had finished it, the big beautiful, mechanically perfect star, and the women of Greenfields had helped her with the quilting of it. And now it would be ready in time to cover the marriage bed. Picturing that quilt spread over Ray and Jo, Isabel seemed to look down through the years at them always together.

"Oh, Jo, you're actually going to marry him!" she exclaimed.

Then, laughing and crying together, Isabel and Joanna came together embracing. They might have thought of this rare embrace as a sign of their reconciliation, but each one knew her thoughts had flown elsewhere while they still stood close to each other. They would never be girls together again.

When they drew apart, Joanna picked up her bonnet preparing to go.

Then "Oh," she said, "I meant to ask you something. We aim to go to town to marry. Just find a preacher or a justice of the peace, then spend the night in the hotel before we come back home. All I really want—except just to marry—is to have you and Archie go with us."

"Do you really want Archie?" Isabel had to ask.

"I've always liked Archie," Joanna said. "You know that. Let's don't remember all the misunderstandings."

"If he's well enough, I think he would go."

"You have heard from him, I think."

"Yes. Or at least the woman that keeps house for him and his uncle wrote a note for him. He's nearly all right, just can't use his right arm. He wanted to come out here Saturday, and I wrote him that he could." She smiled ruefully. "And I guess Mr. Waters let the letter go through."

"Oh, Isabel, of course he did. But you won't have time to write and hear from him now, so if you don't care I'll call him on the telephone from the store."

Isabel pictured herself and Archie standing up with Joanna and Ray, as the marriage lines were said. Whatever else happened, she thought she would like that.

CHAPTER TWENTY-ONE

(From the diary of Miss Isabel Doane)

The time has come now to tell of Ray and Joanna's wedding day. When I first came up out of the dugout my heart sank, for it was a gray, cold day—cold for August, cold in contrast to the heat of the last few weeks. A norther had come up in the night, bringing a mizzling rain, but the change had not reached me down in my burrow.

Ray was cheerful anyhow. He said something about this weather not being any good for the cotton (which is just now beginning to open), but I could tell he wasn't thinking much about crops.

Then I said to myself that weather wouldn't make any difference to this day, as long as it didn't keep us from getting to town. And I knew there wasn't enough moisture to make the road muddy. Joanna likes sunshine, but she is always capable of making her own. I knew she would, on this wedding day.

In a way I could be glad of the cool spell, because I could wear the Oxford gray coat suit that Mrs. Waters made me out of an old suit of hers. It's the best-looking garment I have, and a lot more appropriate for wearing in town than my best cotton summer dress. I thought Joanna would probably wear her tan suit, that her mama made about the same time she did mine.

She did, and she looked wonderful. I don't think I ever realized before that she is so much all one color. Her skin and hair were a kind of a honey beige, just like her soft wool suit.

They had decided not to go till after dinner, because they wanted to stay all night in the hotel and didn't know what they would do all day in town. Ray and I left home in time to eat dinner at the Waterses'. I guess it was the first time in Joanna's life that she didn't have to help wash dishes. We went on right after we finished eating. As we started down the front walk to the car, Jack and Winnie threw rice at us. It was just like them to think of something like that. Of course they were really throwing it at Ray and Joanna, but quite a lot got on me. Joanna laughed and said that might be a sign of something that was fixing to happen to me as well as to her.

I tried not to think much about what she meant. But I couldn't help thinking, almost constantly, about Archie. We all tried to talk about such subjects as the change in the weather, but we traveled much of the way in silence, because of course Ray and Joanna had their minds on something else too.

Archie had told Joanna on the telephone how to find his house, and Ray drove to it easily. It was about a block off the square, a large two-story stucco house, impressive, but to my mind not very pretty. Ray went up on the porch and rang the doorbell, which was so shrill we could hear it on the street. Archie must have been waiting just inside, because he came out immediately and the two men came down the steps together.

Archie looked pale. He was wearing a dark suit, which made him look even paler than he was, and he carried his arm in a sling. Ray, beside him, looked red-skinned and coarse, and his brown suit seemed ill-fitting and (though I had pressed it myself) not nearly as smooth and sharply creased as Archie's. I love my brother, but he's not especially handsome and he is a country boy. Archie—oh, Archie simply looked beautiful. I know you're not supposed to say that about a man. But that's the way Archie Hastings looks to me. He's manly, but he's beautiful.

We drove at once to the house of the Methodist preacher, who with his wife was waiting in their front room. Ray had telephoned them on Friday, and they were ready for us. She had put two or three vases of flowers around the room, and it looked very nice for a wedding.

It is amazing what a little span of time it takes to say the words that link you forever to a person in a way that will change your life more than any other one thing ever could. Soon the four of us were back in the car again, and Joanna and Ray were married. It was about three o'clock.

Joanna said she wanted a strawberry phosphate, so we went to the drugstore for that. I had that too, and the men drank Coca-

Cola. Then Archie said that if the newlyweds were not in any hurry to get to their hotel, he would show us where he worked. We met his uncle, who seems like a nice old man, and we looked at the presses and the Linotype machine.

Then we drove around town a little and saw some of the new brick houses being built. I wondered if there would ever be a time when farmers could build themselves homes like that in the country. We guessed not.

As we were coming back along a residential street toward the square, where the hotel is located, Archie asked if Ray and Joanna would let him provide the wedding supper. They said yes, and we had a wonderful meal in the hotel dining room, with chicken fried steak as the main course and pie a la mode for dessert.

Then at last Archie and I stood in the lobby and watched Ray and Joanna mount the wide, carpeted staircase. I couldn't follow them even in my imagination. I had never been upstairs at the New York Hotel—I had never seen a hotel room anywhere.

I stood in a strange sort of trance, my ears ringing, my heart pounding, as though the thing that was about to happen to Joanna would happen to me too.

Archie touched my arm. "Shall we go?" he said. We planned to walk the short distance to his house, and then he would take me home in his car.

At his touch I felt I might faint, like a girl in an old-fashioned novel. At my first attempt I couldn't even move a foot forward. But I recovered, and we walked down the street.

"I wish there were some wonderful place I could take you tonight," he said. "Some ball—some play—some concert."

"Just drive slowly home," I said. "Just let me be beside you."

I cranked the car for him, and we started out on the road that leads to Greenfields.

In the car, he slipped his arm out of the sling.

"Should you do that?" I said.

"Oh yes," he said. "It comes off Monday anyhow, and I won't be using the arm for anything very strenuous."

He put it around me, gently, but then removed it again until we were out of town. The mist had stopped falling sometime in the afternoon, but as night came on the air grew chillier. I snuggled against Archie.

But I had passed the worst of my torment. My head seemed fairly clear.

"Someday I won't be heading down the road to Greenfields anymore," I said.

"What have you decided to do?" he asked.

"Oh, I haven't decided," I said. "Now Joanna wants me to go in place of her to work for our old teacher and go to college."

"But you do mean to go—somewhere?"

"Oh yes. I won't be needed at home now. I want to get away."

He asked me a strange question then. "Is it too cold, do you think, to pull off into that lane down there, so we can stop and talk a little while?"

"I'm warm," I said.

He turned off the main road, stopped under a tree, and took what he called a rug out of the backseat of the car. Actually, it was that blanket we sat on at our picnic. We sat close together and drew it around us.

"I want you to stay with me," he finally said.

I actually couldn't think what he meant. "I don't understand," I said.

"Marry me, you precious little idiot," he muttered against my hair.

I struggled with the thoughts—the convictions—that had come to me during our troubles.

"You couldn't want to marry me," I said. "We never could forget poor Burnie. And you see, I love him yet."

"Of course you do. I know you won't soon forget these bad times, but someday you may remember this as the summer you met Archie Hastings."

"But Archie, even if it wasn't for that," I said, "I still don't see how we could marry. Because when I had first met you, and never guessed at all the troubles we would have, I knew we really couldn't marry each other. Even then I thought you loved me, and I knew I loved you, but I was just an ignorant country girl. And there's still that, besides the—the darkness in my family."

"I like what you are," he said. "And as I told you once before, it's you I want, not your family. The question is, could you want to marry me?"

"You know I want you," I said. "I want you so much I was almost hating Ray and Joanna in the hotel a little while ago, because it wasn't you and me climbing those stairs."

"Then you would marry me?"

"Of course. Right now. This minute if I could."

He didn't say anything for a good little bit. Then he sat up straight, pulling the blanket from around me. "We couldn't, this minute," he said, "but I believe we could tonight."

"Oh no," I said. "The license—"

"The county clerk is a good friend of mine," he said. "I think he would open his office for me, and make us out a license. Then we might go to that same preacher Ray and Joanna did, or find a justice of the peace." He caught me in his arms again. "We can do it, if you say so, Isabel."

"Oh, Archie," I said, "let's do."

We held each other close then—closer than we'd ever been before, but not very long.

"We'll do it," he said.

And we did. In less than two hours (after a visit to the courthouse and the preacher, who was at home and willing), we were climbing those hotel stairs.

The thing I'd never guessed at till I met Archie Hastings was better than I ever dreamed it would be. In his arms I did indeed forget everything—all anguish, all regret, all consciousness of evil.

I hope that in the room down the hall Joanna was forgetting too. But she, it may be, had nothing that she needed to forget.

I have written all that because it is, in one way, true. It truly is what might have been. I remember when he called me Maud Muller that day in the garden, and I thought then that poem came too near the way things really had to be for us. And it seemed to me those last lines were a prophecy:

> *Of all sad words of tongue or pen,*
> *The saddest are these: It might have been.*

And when I think of them I think of Jack and Ray when they were young, and had those silly pieces making fun of "Maud Muller." One ended:

> *Of all sad words of tongue or pen,*
> *The saddest are these: an old wet hen.*

I don't know what the rest of it was about. It was so long ago. But thinking about the boys in those days with all their silliness can almost make me laugh now. I'd like to laugh again at things like that.

It really might have been. He said he could get the license. What I wrote is true that far. We were parked alongside the railroad track and a train went by, whistling for a crossing. He felt me go stiff in his arms.

"We can't, can we?" he said.

"Not yet, Archie," I said. "I want to but I can't. I can't forget." I began to cry.

He held me close again and kissed my face, but he didn't say anything else for a long time.

After I had hushed, and wiped my face on his handkerchief, he said, "It will be good for you to go to college for a year."

"A year?" I said.

"We'll write. I'll come to see you. A year won't be so long. And you'll read lots of books and learn all kinds of things. You won't be able to call yourself an ignorant country girl anymore."

"I guess things might be different then," I said weakly.

"They will," he said.

"But I can't promise anything," I said.

"No," he said, "I don't want you to. But you see, I know you love me, so I'll wait until you can."

We didn't say much more than that. All the way home we didn't talk very much, but we sat close together.

I didn't let him come in.

We stood in the moonlight and kissed good-night, and then I cranked the car for him.

Even before I took out my diary to tell about this day, I wrote to Miss Lona. I will go to her just as soon as I can. I can't get very much education in a year, but I'll work hard, so he'll be proud of me.

It might turn out that somehow, sometime, everything will be all right.

EPILOGUE

I really wish I could have known my great-aunt Isabel. I would like to know whether, in the end, she thought everything had turned out all right. I am almost sure she did, but I would have liked to hear her say so, because my grandmother was not so clear about that.

Joanna thought that Isabel had had an empty life because she never married. "She wanted him so much," Joanna said to me, "I don't see how she ever could have been happy without him." She told how Isabel would talk to her, those last days when both of them were living at the Doane house, about her hopes and fears. She really worried about some recurring evil in the Doane family, and doubted, on account of that, if she ever ought to marry. Joanna herself never gave any thought to it, she said, because she had known all her life what a good person Ray was. (And as far as I know to this day, she was right about my grandfather.)

Isabel would have forgotten all that, too, if things had turned out different. So Joanna believed. But an evil neither young woman had given much thought to caught up with Isabel and Archie. Before the end of Isabel's first year in college, the United States entered World War I. Archie joined the army (a flying unit) and was killed in France the following winter.

Isabel, as Joanna always said, just kept on going to college. She said it as though that fate were the saddest she could imagine, and I always thought that was funny, because she had often told me that as a girl she had wanted above everything else to go to college and become a teacher. But she said her life had been just what she always wanted it to be, and I don't think she saw any contradiction in what she said. She taught in Sunday school, organized the first P.T.A. at Greenfields, and often acted as a substitute teacher in the days when substitutes didn't need any qualifications except natural ability. People said she did more for the school than any teacher they ever had there.

And she raised the Doane children, as well as five of her own. She never learned to manage Sophie, who left home early and perhaps became a prostitute. (At least I guess from things the family used to say that they believed she did.) She died in her fifties, of cancer.

A strange thing happened. The family received a large sum of money from the railroad on account of Burnie's being killed by the train, and they bought back all the land that Harvey Doane had lost and eventually, as they prospered, even more. The three Doane men became partners in the largest stock-farm operation in that part of the county. Leonard, the last Doane of his generation, is still active in the work. Travis, who died two or three years ago, never married. (Nobody ever seemed to know much about Travis, and I have often wondered if he felt the way Isabel did about the dark strain in the family.)

Joanna's brothers never lived away from Greenfields after all. Tom Waters died of pneumonia a few years after Harvey Doane died. Jack came back and ran the store and married Mary Varton. He gained some fame as a cracker-barrel philosopher, and the county newspaper used to run articles about him from time to time. The Associated Press picked up one of these, and he got letters from people all over the country.

Winnie married a farmer's daughter and eventually took over the farm. I remember he used to talk about the insects that attacked the cotton; he was quite an expert on exterminating bugs.

I really don't think anyone at Greenfields knew exactly what Isabel did. She rarely came back, but I remember she was at my grandparents' house one summer when my family came for our visit. "She's some kind of a doctor," the kinfolk said. "Not a real doctor. Not a medical doctor. She teaches in some college up north."

I think that was really all my grandmother knew then, although in the last years of her life the two old women began exchanging letters, so she might have learned more. "We used to write," Grandmother told me once, "when Isabel first went off to school. But through the years we got out of the way of it."

When Isabel died last year, at the age of eighty-four, she left instructions that her body be buried at Greenfields, in the Doane family lot. It happened that there was a space beside Joanna, who had lain there five years then, and thus the two childhood friends are reunited.

For whatever reason, I never really knew what Isabel's profession was until she died and they sent me her diaries, scrapbooks, and other miscellaneous papers. I imagine Grandmother told Isabel about me, that I was the only one of her grandchildren to go to college, and that is why she had the papers sent to me. Or she might have known I was interested in the story of Harvey Doane. I know she had more valuable papers, that she left to the university where she taught, but she must have wanted these personal remains to come to someone in the family.

From these I learned more about the summer of 1916 than Joanna had been able to tell me, and found out what Isabel had actually done with her life. She was a sociologist, a professor as well as the author of books and articles that were considered pioneer works on the place of women and children in the family relationship. I think her work must have been almost altogether academic, but it was often translated into practical results by people who worked actively for the rights of women and children in the family.

One of the most unexpected finds among these papers was a large box labeled "Unhappy Families." It contained newspaper clippings, saved for the last twenty-five or thirty years, all concerning the deaths of men at the hands of wives or children whom they had cruelly mistreated. One of the most recent articles reported a trial in a town near Greenfields, in which the wife and daughter of a man killed by a hired gunman had been convicted of plotting his death. A marginal note said: "What would verdict have been if they had done killing?" In another case of recent years, a grand jury had failed to indict a woman who shot and killed her husband because he beat her and their thirteen children. In that instance the family had concealed the death for four years.

Not long ago I sent the clippings to a woman who wrote me that she had been a student and then a colleague of Dr. Doane, and would like to have the collection in order to complete a manuscript Dr. Doane had begun writing. I surely would like to read that book when it comes out.